The Devil's Necktie

The
Devil's Necktie

JOHN LANSING

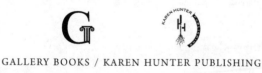

GALLERY BOOKS / KAREN HUNTER PUBLISHING

New York   London   Toronto   Sydney   New Delhi

G

Gallery Books
An Imprint of
Simon & Schuster, Inc.
1230 Avenue of the Americas
New York, NY 10020

Karen Hunter Publishing,
A Division of
Suitt-Hunter Enterprises, LLC
598 Broadway, 3rd Floor
New York, NY 10012

First Karen Hunter Publishing/Gallery Books print edition June 2015

GALLERY BOOKS and colophon are registered trademarks of Simon & Schuster, Inc.

For information about special discounts for bulk purchases, please contact Simon & Schuster Special Sales at 1-866-506-1949 or business@simonandschuster.com.

The Simon & Schuster Speakers Bureau can bring authors to your live event. For more information or to book an event, contact the Simon & Schuster Speakers Bureau at 1-866-248-3049 or visit our website at www.simonspeakers.com.

Design by Jill Putorti

Manufactured in the United States of America

10   9   8   7   6   5   4   3   2   1

Library of Congress Cataloging-in-Publication Data is available.

ISBN 978-1-5011-1029-0
ISBN 978-1-4516-9834-3 (ebook)

The Devil's Necktie

1

Jack Bertolino stood on the balcony of his loft in Marina del Rey, tending a dry-aged New York steak on his prized possession, a top-of-the-line Weber gas grill. He didn't miss winter, not one little bit. Here he was manning the barbecue in his new uniform, a black T-shirt and jeans, while his cousins were chasing heart attacks shoveling snow off their Staten Island driveways. That image never ceased to put a smile on his face. That and the salty ocean breeze that floated in over the marina.

Jack nursed a glass of cabernet and watched the long line of bright white FedEx trucks return home from their final deliveries and park in neat rows in the lot next to his building. It sure beat the sight of patrol cars jammed onto the sidewalk in front of a precinct house.

Early evening was Jack's favorite time of day. The sun was just starting to paint the clouds a muted orange. From his fourth-floor vantage point, Jack could see a string of jumbo jets in the distance, silently making their final approach to LAX. Stacked eight planes deep, their slim silver bodies glinted in the setting sun.

For the first time in Jack Bertolino's life, he felt at ease.

His cell phone chirped, snapping him out of his reverie. He tossed some Japanese eggplant onto the grill, closed the lid, and checked his cell phone screen for the name of the caller.

"Hello."

"How's my Italian stallion?"

"Mia . . . ," he said instantly, his tone neutral, giving away nothing.

"All the planets are aligned, Jack. It's time for you to man up and make an honest woman out of me."

Jack couldn't help but smile. Mia's throaty voice and light Colombian accent had the power to make a grown man weep. More important, it could make a bad man give up his secrets.

He hadn't really been surprised when he received her text. He knew it was only a matter of time. Payback's a bitch.

"What can I do for you, Mia?"

"It's what I can do for you, *papi*. My lips . . . they're still magic."

"I love it when you talk dirty."

"Only for love or money."

Although Jack was enjoying the back and forth, he was no longer in the business. "Why are you calling, Mia?"

Mia dropped her act as well. "We need to talk."

"It's not a good time," Jack said as he opened the lid of the grill and pressed his fork against the steak, checking for doneness.

"Face-to-face, Jack."

"I'm not in New York."

"That's why I'm in Los Angeles."

Jack didn't reply right away. He did a quick analysis of how Mia could know he was living in L.A., what kind of trouble she might be in, what kind of blowback he was going to suffer just from having this conversation. He came to the instantaneous conclusion that however this new wrinkle in his life played out, it would definitely have an impact on his newly found state of bliss.

Mia answered some of his unspoken questions. "I'm still connected, Jack, and you're still on the radar screen. There are certain people—who will remain nameless, because I'm not on your payroll anymore—who are not convinced you're out of the game."

"I'm happily retired," Jack fired back, wondering if his response sounded forced, wondering why he cared.

"And happily divorced?"

Jack didn't respond. His private life was none of Mia's business. He had strict rules when dealing with confidential informants, a line in the sand he never crossed.

But Mia had the kind of beauty that could make a man contemplate leaving his wife, his job, and his kids. Jack had never taken the bait, but had to admit he'd been tempted.

Mia was one of the best CIs in the business, and she and Jack had done groundbreaking work together. With the help of Mia and DEA agent Kenny Ortega, Jack and the team of NYPD narco-rangers he headed up had put away a heavy hitter in the cocaine trade.

Manuel Alvarez was the head of a Colombian drug cell that had been importing a thousand keys of coke into Florida on a weekly basis, and the poison was dripping into New York City. Jack and his group had put away a major cartel scumbag, and Mia had gotten rich.

The feds had a financial equation in place when dealing with CIs. The greater the quantity of drugs an informant was responsible for delivering, the more money it was worth to the United States government. They were happy to give to get. Mia did very well for herself at great personal risk. Informants had a short shelf life. Once a major domo got busted, the cartels worked very hard to discover where the "sickness" had come from. If your name ended up on the short list, you turned up dead.

Jack had made a promise to Mia that if things ever got too hot to handle, he would do whatever he could to help her out of the jam.

Mia was turning in her chit.

"Meet with me in an hour, after I get settled in."

"I'm about to have dinner, Mia."

"Vista Haven Road, 3468. You owe me, Jack."

"It was a two-way street," he reminded her.

"And I don't want it turning into a dead end."

Jack was about to protest, but she clicked off. He turned back to his grill, but now he was unsettled. Mia had always been a cool customer, but there was an edge of panic in her voice. Jack let out an irritated groan. He shut off the grill with a hard snap. He wouldn't be able to eat anyway until he found out what the hell was wrong.

The San Diego Freeway was a more direct route to the house where Mia was staying, but Jack liked the way Beverly Glen snaked up the hillside to Mulholland Drive. Eclectic homes lined the tight canyon and his sterling gray Mustang GT convertible held fast to the winding road. Out here he felt as if he was in the country in the middle of the city.

Jack hung a right onto Longbow and felt a touch of vertigo as he made the sharp winding descent, leaning on his brakes most of the way. Two blocks down, he made a left onto Vista Haven. The street was thick with Beemers, Lexuses, and Mercedes. Someone must be having a party. Jack discovered it was the house next door to Mia's when the Mustang's British GPS voice informed him that he had arrived at his destination on the right.

The single-story midcentury modern home had an Asian feel. It was set back from the street, allowing Jack to pull onto the paver-lined driveway. He swung a one-eighty, so that his car was facing the street. Old habits, he thought.

Jack knocked on the large black-lacquered door and waited. He knocked again and waited, wondering if the GPS could have gotten it wrong, and he was now standing foolishly in front of the wrong house. He could hear screams from next door as the partiers dove into their pool, followed by splashes, laughter, and the loud barking of the family's dogs. The music was rowdy, and even though a thick hedge separated the two properties, it did little to dampen the sound.

Jack was about to use his cell phone when the door opened and slender arms pulled him inside.

In the shadowed hallway Jack stared at Mia, taking in the changes she'd made to her physical appearance since the last time he had seen her. He was at a loss for words. Breathtaking would have worked. Her striking blue eyes, offset by her now darkened hair, were stunning. Her skin was perfect, her scent intoxicating.

Mia was saying words of welcome to Jack in Spanish, but he wasn't listening. He stood there mesmerized by Mia's pearl pendant earrings, which swayed gracefully as she tilted her head to look up at him with those killer eyes that crinkled slightly as she smiled. She was self-possessed, and aging well. Jack didn't know if it was her scent or the sway of her pendant earrings, but he was falling under her spell.

Mia kept talking as Jack's eyes moved from her eyes to her earrings, back and forth, guided by the hypnotic lilt of her voice and the tilt of her head. Jack could almost hear himself saying "No fucking way" as she stepped in closer, but he chose silence. Twenty-five years of discipline and resolve and lines in the sand disappeared as if they were an afterthought.

Mia folded into Jack's arms, and he lifted her easily off the polished hardwood floor. As he held her close, he could feel her heart beating wildly. It reminded him of an injured sparrow he had cupped in his hands as a young boy. He realized that his heart now matched hers, beat for beat, as if an electric current was passing from Mia's body into his, then from Mia's lips to his.

Jack carried her down the hallway and into the bedroom. The duvet cover had been pulled back, as if Mia had foreseen the outcome of his visit. Jack didn't care. He felt good, damn good.

They never broke eye contact as they undressed each other. The sound of laughter filtered through the screen door, but Jack didn't hear.

He unclasped Mia's sheer lace bra, and his lips found the pink swell of her breast. The slight friction of his teeth played over her taut skin, eliciting a ragged exhale of breath.

Jack gently laid Mia's head on the silk pillow, kissed the side of her neck, lingering to take in her scent, and then moved slowly down the valley between her perfect breasts. Mia grabbed his hair and guided him lower.

Her stomach quivered, and her hips rose slightly as Jack traced her sex with his lips. Their eyes locked as he parted her with his tongue. Her moan was deep, haunted, and then hungry.

She rolled Jack onto his back and mounted him, rhythmically tightening and rocking.

He closed his eyes and calmed his breathing, wanting to prolong the feeling, prolong the perfect moment. He sat up, wrapped his arms around her smooth back, and pulled her tighter against him, slipping deeper inside. Then the lovers dissolved into a fury of flesh and lips.

They were wet inside and out as Mia buried her head in Jack's chest. He looked over the perfect curve of her shoulder and realized that the bedroom had an unobstructed view over the garden and pool to the valley below. The entire scene took on a dreamlike quality, as if they were perched on the edge of the earth.

Mia reached up and touched Jack's flushed cheek with her warm hand. He was a handsome, big-boned man with a thick shock of dark hair. Mia traced the thin strands of gray that feathered his temples with her perfectly manicured fingernails. She ran the back of her hand along the creases on his chiseled face, a road map of the years spent doing undercover work in New York City. She kissed the bump on the bridge of his otherwise straight Roman nose, a gift from a crack dealer named Trey he had traded punches with outside the Red Hook projects.

Mia stared into Jack's intense brown eyes, took a deep breath, and then spoke. It was almost a whisper, almost a prayer. "The huntress is being hunted, Jack. I'm so tired. I'm going to need some help disappearing. Will you help me, *mi amor?*"

"Count on it," Jack said without a pause.

And then his cop muscle flexed, and Jack hoped he hadn't spoken too soon.

2

After their breathing returned to normal, Mia seemed comforted by Jack's assurance. "I need to sleep," she whispered in his ear. Like a light switch being thrown, Mia was out.

At least one of them could sleep, Jack thought. He was in full cop mode now. He couldn't turn it off. It was pure reflex.

Who was Mia running from? What kind of game was she into? Had someone discovered her secret? Had Alvarez tumbled to the fact that Mia was the reason he was eating jail chow?

If her problem was serious enough, he'd reach out to Kenny Ortega in Miami. The feds might be able to put her back in the system and arrange for witness protection.

Jack sat up and swung his feet over the edge of the bed. He gazed at the slight rise and fall of her breasts and then traveled down to where her hair was still blond. What a woman. He carefully covered her with the sheet.

Jack decided to let Mia sleep. He'd get his answers in the morning.

He slipped on his clothes and looked out through the sliding screen door to the view beyond the garden and the aqua green pool. A single old-growth olive tree off to the left of the yard was silhouetted by a spotlight flooding the backyard. The lights in the distance seemed to undulate from the heat escaping the valley floor.

Jack left a note, with the rest of his contact numbers and plans to get together in the A.M., on the long, black-granite countertop in the kitchen, next to an iPad clad in black leather. He gave the modern living room a quick once-over and slipped out of the house, locking the heavy door behind him.

The neighbors were still in full party mode. The sound of mockingbirds fought for airtime with the thrumming music. Once in his Mustang, Jack hit a button and watched his convertible top fold down into the back compartment, revealing a star-spiked sky. He could see Orion's belt, and then Orion proper, with his arms outstretched, gripping a war club.

Jack decided to take the San Diego Freeway south to the 90 Marina Freeway and home. He picked an old Diana Krall CD and hit Play. The orchestrations were as lush as her voice and a perfect match for the night and his postcoital mood. He could still smell the lingering scent of sex on his hands, and it almost made him dizzy. His back didn't hurt for the first time in weeks. Jack felt like a teenager who had just experienced his first sexual encounter, and he was just going to roll with it. He vowed not to second-guess himself as he made a left off Mulholland, down a slight incline, toward the freeway entrance.

An LAPD police car hurtling up the road in his direction drifted dangerously into his lane. Jack shouted an expletive as he jerked the wheel hard to the right, barely averting a collision. He looked in his rearview mirror, heart pounding, expecting the black-and-white to execute a U-turn and pull him over even though the fault definitely lay with the cop.

But no light bars flashed on, blasting red and blue and blinding spotlights. No controlled voice over the car's public-address speaker demanded that Jack pull over to the side of the road. The LAPD cop car continued up and over the rise, made a sliding right onto Mulholland, and disappeared into the night.

"Sons of bitches!" Jack shouted to no one in particular. In a sour mood, he made the left onto the ramp that merged with the 405. The highway was a crawling parking lot, even at this hour. As he edged forward, accelerator to brake, a bad feeling came over him.

He replayed the scene of the near accident in his mind. He realized that when he had started down the incline and first seen the police unit, what was conspicuously absent were any numbers painted in black on the white roof behind the car's light bar. The young cop was wearing mirrored sunglasses at night. He never even glanced his way when Jack shouted that the cop should go fuck himself.

Jack felt a sudden constriction in his chest. His heart started thudding, and his throat went bone dry. Jack had once arrested a group of predatory drug thieves in NYC who used decoy cop cars and uniforms. They would torture rival dealers, find out where their cash and stash were hidden, and then kill their victims.

Jack stayed in the far-right lane. He decided to take the next off-ramp and drive back to Vista Haven. He was probably overreacting, but alarm bells were going off, and his instincts told him something was very wrong.

He cursed the traffic as he dialed Mia's number on his cell with one hand. No answer. He turned the wheel hard to the right with his free hand and started illegally speeding down the shoulder of the freeway. Car horns blared as he raced dangerously fast past the bumper-to-bumper traffic, oblivious to the flying gravel that was wreaking havoc with his car's metallic finish. Mia's phone went to voice mail. Jack asked her to call him back, snapped it shut, and slipped it into his breast pocket. He used both hands now to grip the steering wheel. He could only pray she was taking a shower.

He flew off the freeway at the next exit, executed a tire-squealing right turn, fishtailing before gaining control of his Mustang as he rocketed back up Sepulveda Boulevard. His speedometer inched toward seventy-five as he screamed past MountainGate, toward the top of the ridge.

Jack thundered by the American Jewish University and swung a hard left onto Longbow. His Mustang kicked up a spray of sand on the uneven surface as he tore down the steep road. Blowing through two stop signs, he slammed the wheel into a hard left, skidding onto Vista Haven. The party next door was still in progress, and Jack forced himself to take a deep breath.

He saw no sign of the police car as he pulled into Mia's driveway and set the parking brake. Maybe he was losing it. Then Jack's eye caught the reflection of a large pool of oil on the driveway. He was sure that hadn't been there when he left the house.

He jumped out of his car and banged on the black-lacquered door while ringing the bell insistently. No answer.

Maybe Mia was in the pool. Be in the pool, he thought.

Jack felt a tightness behind his eyes and his head was pounding as he heard the glad screams from the pool party and that damn loud music and the fucking barking dogs. He ran around the side of the house, saw that the rear lights were on, and jumped over the low side gate.

The pool was empty, but Jack could see that the sliding screen door had been kicked off its runners at the far end of the house and lay bent in on the bedroom rug.

Jack dialed 911 and shouted out his location as he ran into the empty bedroom. The smell of blood flooded his senses even before he stepped into the bathroom.

Mia's naked, brutalized body was hanging in the sunken shower stall. The white tiles were stained dark red with her flowing blood.

Jack never cried, but he felt a roar erupt from his throat and blinding tears obscure his vision as he struggled to unbuckle Mia's belted wrists from the chrome showerhead.

Her blood soaked his clothes as he stubbornly checked for signs of life. He knew it was hopeless. Her neck was entirely still.

Jack used to say that ice water ran through her veins. But it was hot and red and mortal now.

Jack's arms grew leaden from trying to calm Mia's spasming

naked body as she bled out in his arms. He squatted in a growing pool of her blood, cradling her broken and mutilated body. Too little, too late, he thought, waiting for a response to his 911 call.

The drug kingpins called it a Colombian Necktie. Some called it the Devil's Necktie. The murderers had slit Mia's throat and pulled her tongue out through the opening, leaving it hanging and swollen and bloody.

Jack Bertolino forced himself to look at the inhuman, tortured expression on her once beautiful face. He didn't want to forget. He'd never forget her crystal blue eyes, cloudy and sightless in death. They would spur him on—until he took down the animal who had killed her.

3

Jack's frozen shock was shattered by a vortex of sound, fury, and blinding light as a massive LAPD police helicopter, like a breaching whale, rose from below the edge of the property line. Its thousand-candle spotlight arced across the house and blasted through the bedroom, into the bathroom, where it lasered onto Jack holding Mia's broken body.

The light shifted briefly, revealing the ominous black-and-silver helicopter that blocked out the night sky and reflected light from the valley floor below. The thundering downwash created by the flying machine's blades created choppy waves in the pool and a swirling cloud of garden detritus and olive leaves. Jack thought it looked like something out of an action movie, as if Matt Damon would suddenly leap out of the flying monster, AK-47s in both hands, guns blazing.

The backyard filled with LAPD swat team members, rifles trained on Jack. Their shouted orders were muted by the thrumming, rotating blades.

Jack tenderly laid Mia's lifeless body down on the bloody tiles. He had already placed a towel over her horrific wounds, knowing full well he had altered a crime scene. It had been the right thing to do.

Ten men brandishing weapons with hairpin triggers rushed the house and surrounded the bedroom. Orders were shouted. It was all white noise to Jack.

Finally the loudspeaker on the chopper came to life, cutting through the deafening roar, and a disembodied voice intoned, "Move away from the body and get down on the floor! Move away from the body, get down on the floor, and place your hands behind your head!"

Jack knew he had to force himself to move or things would go from ugly to deadly. He'd been in his share of these high-intensity situations and understood that with one false move he'd never see his son graduate from Stanford.

Jack's back was spasming, and all he could muster was the strength to crawl out of the bathroom and collapse on the brown Berber carpet in the bedroom with his arms and legs spread-eagled. He'd wait until the energy in the room settled down a bit before trying to communicate who he was and how he came to be there. Jack knew supplication was the better part of valor.

"Sit down, Jack. Jack, we can't continue the interview until you take a seat." Lieutenant Gallina was trying to sound collegial but was losing patience.

Jack remained standing, refusing to acknowledge the stabbing pain running up his leg and shooting into his lower back. He wouldn't allow these detectives to look down on him and put him on the defensive.

When Jack was a rookie, the precinct cops used to sandpaper the front legs of the chairs in the interrogation room, forcing the suspects to lean forward, keeping them off balance. They'd turn up the heat in the summer and turn off the heat in the winter. Feed the perps dry baked goods but no liquids. Fill the bad guys with carbonated soda, but not allow them to use the john, anything to control their environment. Keep the bad guys on edge and facilitate them spilling their guts. Jack knew all the tricks.

"Fuckin' Serpico," Lieutenant Gallina muttered under his breath to his partner.

"What did you say?" Jack snapped.

"Nothing, let's get down to it."

"No, spit it out."

"It's always the cops with you, huh, Bertolino?"

"Respectfully, go fuck yourself."

Jack had taken down more than his share of dirty cops in his career. Anyone who was an active player was constantly being tested. It went with the territory, and his history was all in his files. Gallina, clearly, wasn't a fan.

But to Jack's mind, if you were a drug dealer, you couldn't hide behind a three-thousand-dollar suit, and if you were a dirty cop, you sure as hell couldn't hide behind a badge. He hadn't spent a career in narcotics to make friends.

Lieutenant Gallina's jaw tensed, and his left eye reflexively twitched. He was in his midthirties, prematurely balding, struggling to keep control of his weight. He kept glancing up to his left. It was a tell, and Jack was now sure his interrogation was being secretly taped.

He had been driven from Sherman Oaks to the Parker Center downtown. The brand-new police administration building was located at 100 West First Street. The building was a vast expanse of glass; geometric angled walls; and tall, solid columns decorated with mosaic tiles.

"Sit down, Bertolino. It's not a request."

When Jack was just a boy, his grandfather had taught him never to poke a snake with a stick. The old man's wisdom made absolute sense to Jack, but sometimes his response was just street.

"Turn off the camera, take off your badge, and send Frick out for a doughnut so it's just the two of us. I'll beat the shit out of you."

Gallina all but jumped out of his loose skin before he recovered himself.

"Oh, the man's funny. He spends twenty-five years on the force, and I think he missed his calling. I'm thinking he should take his act on the road."

"I'm Frick to your Frack," Gallina's African-American partner deadpanned.

"How'd you get your shield? Time in?" Jack couldn't help himself.

"You see, that was a good delivery. Leno would be all over a talent like that."

Jack was dressed in a black rock 'n' roll T-shirt with CBGB emblazoned on its front, and sweatpants provided by Terry Molloy, the on-scene medical examiner. Jack had dropped his blood-soaked clothing into a green evidence bag for forensics and was more than happy to squeeze into dry, clean clothes, even though the proffered T-shirt and sweats were a size too small and made Jack feel exposed and vulnerable. Jack made a mental note to return the clothes the following day.

He took control of the interrogation room. "You need to get a list of everyone who was at the party next door. The music was loud enough to cover the attack, but someone may have been getting a blow job out in a parked car or smoking a joint, whatever. And the neighbors across the street had a direct view into the victim's driveway. If there was a squad car parked there, someone must have seen something."

"I never thought of that, did you, Tompkins?" The lieutenant's eyes drilled into Jack, his expression as acerbic as his tone.

Jack went on as if Gallina and Tompkins weren't in the room. He had already laid out the call and text he'd received from Mia, their professional history, and his theory as to what he thought had gone down. He failed to mention their sexual encounter, though he was sure the ME would do a rape kit, and they'd find his DNA. He was hoping for a few days of grace to find some answers. He couldn't accomplish much sitting in a jail cell.

Jack started talking to the men behind the camera. "You need to take a sample of the oil spill in the driveway. It wasn't there when I left the house the first time or I would have stepped in it."

"He still doesn't get the concept of pecking order," Gallina said to his partner and then turned back to Jack.

"You no longer wear a badge. You are no longer an inspector," he said sharply. "Therefore, you do not get to ask the questions. You admit to altering a crime scene. You were drenched in the victim's blood, and you're not being forthcoming about your personal relationship. The vic was naked at the time of her death. By your own admission you'd only been gone twenty minutes."

Gallina was working up a full head of steam now, enjoying the sound of his own voice, playing to the suits on the other end of the camera.

"You developed a close working relationship with a confidential informant, and now here you are, retired, and trust me, I understand the temptation. A little quid pro quo doesn't seem out of line. She was a beautiful woman, after all. She flies into town, rings you up—your own words—and you think she's yours for the taking. Mia maybe doesn't see it that way. Maybe she tries to brace you for some unpaid debt. Who knows? One thing turns into another and things get out of control."

Tompkins, who was six feet tall, without an ounce of body fat on him, was about to add something to the dialogue, but Jack cut him off.

"The cop driving was a young Hispanic male, about twenty-eight years old. Had the look of a player. The passenger was a blur but filled the seat, thick shouldered, around one-eighty. I didn't pass them on my way back to the house, so it's likely they took another route away from the residence. They had a ten-minute lead, but they couldn't have been inside the house for more than five. In and out, professionals. Could be a cartel hit. It was their MO."

Jack was keeping it analytical, one step removed from the guilt and pain, objectifying the images swirling around in his head. He'd deal with his own emotions at a later date.

"It looked like there was blunt-force trauma to Mia's face. They must have startled her in bed, knocked her out, dragged her into the bathroom, belted her to the showerhead, and slit her throat. There should be blood spatters on the bed from the initial assault. If she wasn't startled and knocked out, she would have put up a fight, so I'd check under her fingernails. There would be trace DNA on the bedding.

"I'd check all male Colombian nationals, twenty to forty-five, traveling in and out of LAX, Burbank, Long Beach, and John Wayne airports in the past seventy-two hours, and cross-reference them with ViCAP.

"Someone rented those men a police car. I'd check with all the film rental companies in the area but I'd start in the valley. Now, if you don't have anything else, stop wasting my time and yours and start the investigation. I'm out of here. You know where to find me."

Jack walked over to the door without looking up at the camera.

"Any objection to leaving a DNA sample?" Gallina added.

"None. And my fingerprints are a matter of record."

Gallina's nod to the camera was almost imperceptible. The door to the interrogation room was pulled open by a uniformed officer who had been standing guard. A med tech who was positioned next to the young cop looked to Jack for permission to collect the DNA sample. Jack answered the unspoken question by opening his mouth, allowing the man to insert a mouth swab and rub it gently around the inside of his mouth, gathering cells. The tech then waved the cotton swab to air-dry it, like an old-school family doctor preparing a mercury thermometer, before placing it in a small brown envelope to preserve the sample. Jack nodded to the two men as he stepped past. Hell, he thought, they were only doing their job.

Gallina followed, hard in his wake. He stopped Jack in his tracks.

"Hey, that was a good show you put on for the suits."

Jack, who was bone weary, summoned all of his strength to keep from knocking this ego with a badge on his ass.

"Just find the pricks who did this."

Even as the words spilled out of his mouth, he knew the odds were close to none. The killers, if they were cartel hires, had probably crossed into Mexico or Arizona and were chasing shots of tequila with lines of coke on a charter plane to Mexico City and then home to Colombia. Jack knew he'd have to discover who ordered the hit, and then do a regression analysis. If they were local, he'd hunt them down.

Gallina stared at Jack for a beat. His eyes narrowed, creasing into a smile with no warmth.

"Between you and me, Bertolino, I think I'm looking at him."

4

The blackout shades were drawn in the modest apartment in Ontario, California. It could have been two in the morning or high noon. A young woman was handcuffed to the metal bed frame. Naked, gang tattoos across her chest and small, firm breasts. A dreamy look on her hard face. Her pupils tweaked, her dark eyes framed by eyebrows that had been plucked into nonexistence, replaced by a thin, harsh pencil line.

The light green wall paint was peeling in patches where rainwater had seeped through. A movie poster was thumbtacked to the wall behind the bed. Al Pacino seemed to be looking down on the naked woman over a huge pile of cocaine, SCARFACE printed in bold red letters at the top.

A twenty-something Hispanic man was sitting at a computer. He was also naked, his wiry body lit only by the green glow of the empty computer screen. He was in the process of downloading a silent video image from his cell phone to his laptop. He hit Enter and his partner Hector's jerky image filled the screen and quickly moved off.

The video screen pixelated and then refocused as Mia, startled, disoriented, sat up in bed and the large bull of a man—wearing latex surgical gloves—punched her squarely in the face, breaking her nose and knocking her head back against the wall unconscious.

Blood spattered the pillow, the white sheets, and arced across the wall behind her. He dragged her across the bed, ripping out one of her earrings, and muscled her into the white-tiled bathroom like a child's doll, her bare feet scarcely touching the floor.

The camera jerked wildly and then found the action as the broad man with thick ham hands whipped a leather belt from his pants, cinched it around Mia's wrists, and fastened her to the overhead shower fixture. He was all business.

Hector's father had been a butcher and had taught his son the trade. Beaten the knowledge into him. Hector's job as a boy had been to prepare the *carnitas* for the Easter feast. Failure was not an option. The suckling pig would squeal and scream like a human baby when Hector cut its throat. It bothered him at first and then not at all. He was a natural.

Cutting Mia was child's play compared to the thick skin of a pig. He had been told this woman was not only a pig but also a whore.

"Come back to bed, Johnny," the woman purred seductively.

Johnny didn't respond, concentrating on the task at hand. Anyway, he thought, Angelina wasn't going anywhere. The cuffs had been her idea.

Johnny Rodriguez, with black hair that fell over his ears, dark smoky eyes with thick lashes, and a youthful face that was almost too pretty, averted his eyes from the screen and stared at his handcuffed girlfriend as Hector pulled out his carving knife and went to work. Hector used the shower curtain as a butcher's apron to keep the blood spray off his rented police uniform and methodically drew the knife across Mia's neck, slitting her open from ear to ear. The one earring that remained on her head swayed as the blood pulsed out of the gaping mortal wound.

Johnny, the man who had videotaped the murder with his new cell phone, knew what had come next. He'd have nightmares reliving the horrible scene until the day he died. He'd killed men before, but that was gang-related business, cut and dried. A man had to build street cred to get ahead in his world. But this murder was bad, it was a woman. He thought guiltily about his own mother and two sisters.

With the download completed, he typed in an e-mail address, banged the Send key with more force than was needed, and in a matter of seconds, after the proof of the kill was transmitted to Arturo Delgado, thankfully hit Delete. The now empty green screen gave him some relief. No reason to keep evidence that could put him away for life. The phone would be disposed of, the cost of doing business.

Johnny stood up and walked over to the bed. He pulled a vial of cocaine from the top of his simple pine nightstand, next to his pair of mirrored aviator sunglasses, and poured a fat line on his girlfriend's body, onto the cleft between her smooth rounded thigh and her meticulously shaved pubic area. She arched her back, beckoning him forward. He started getting aroused again as he snorted half the line and then nestled his member into the remaining cocaine. Johnny straddled Angelina, who emitted a guttural moan as he slowly moved up her body, rubbing himself against her small, dark, pierced nipple before placing his drug-laden phallus into her mouth.

Johnny's back straightened as the young woman went to town, making sure none of the cocaine was wasted. Then his back twisted and bucked and quivered. In the dim light, 18TH STREET ANGELS, the name of Johnny's gang, tattooed in florid script on the small of his back, seemed to glow in the dark.

5

The violent wall of sound was an assault to the senses. Throughout the federal penitentiary roared the unrelenting din of metal doors clanging, men screaming, pipes banging, orders shouted, music blaring.

Manuel Alvarez sat on his bunk. On the surface, total serenity—just below, volcanic rage. He had a book propped open on his lap and wore a Bose noise-reduction headset he had ordered online. He was never without it.

Alvarez was reading the latest mystery by Robert Crais. Alvarez thought Crais was quick-witted and told a compelling story. Reading was one of his few pleasures.

His mind was wandering today, though. He slammed the book shut when he realized that he hadn't retained a thing he'd read in the past ten minutes. He thought he would have gotten news by now. Then he opened the book to where he'd started and tried again.

Alvarez stood five foot seven, one hundred and forty pounds. His eyes were coffee bean brown, his gaunt face the color of rice paper, with clear, flawless skin.

He hadn't seen an exercise pen in over a year. He paid men for protection. He still had hard, ropy muscles under his jailhouse grays, just in case, but he wasn't one to do any heavy lifting. That was what cocaine afforded him, even locked down in an eight-by-ten cell. He was only five years into a twenty-five-year prison sentence, and he had to get by somehow.

He could have talked—turned on the men who supplied him—and made a deal with the prosecution for a reduced sentence. But he didn't, and the cartel was grateful. They allowed him to work and introduced him to Arturo Delgado, who provided the cocaine that made life bearable, even behind bars. Now Delgado was supposed to give word that he'd performed another favor.

Manuel looked up from his book, carefully placed a bookmark in the last page read, laid the book on his meticulously made bed, and walked over to the heavy metal cell door. One of the trustees on Delgado's payroll had pushed a book cart in front of Alvarez's cell and was waiting to be acknowledged before going about his business.

Alvarez checked up and down the cellblock before nodding to trustee 776325, who took one novel from the stack of books and magazines on top of the cart, and then, like a sleight-of-hand magician, slid another from a hidden compartment underneath the top shelf.

"Mr. Delgado said you should enjoy the read, and then he would appreciate a review," the trustee said, all business, as he handed the books through the opening of the cell door.

Without warning Alvarez grabbed the trustee's hand and yanked him forward with such force that the man's face, wedged against the bars, turned an off shade of purple.

"Is that everything?"

Alvarez let go of his grip and the trustee jumped back, putting the cart between himself and the bars.

"Ask Delgado," he croaked, glancing up and down the cellblock to see if anyone had caught the attack. Nobody had.

Alvarez walked the few steps back to his bed, slid the new Michael Connelly into a small shelf of hardcover books in the corner of his cell, and then opened the Ian Rankin. A rectangular slot had been cut into the center pages of the book, creating a space large enough to hold a cell phone that Alvarez pulled out and secreted beneath his pillow. He slid the doctored book onto the shelf with the rest of his collection. The next time his trustee made a delivery, Manuel would return the Ian Rankin with the clean phone—memory purged, minus the 8GB microSD card—and five crisp hundred-dollar bills.

Alvarez picked up the Crais novel but hadn't read more than a paragraph before a guard walked up to his cell. He stopped and stared at Alvarez for an instant. Satisfied it was business as usual, he continued down cellblock C into the bowels of the penitentiary.

Alvarez ripped off his headphones and listened to the echo of the guard's leather boot heels recede down the cellblock before pulling out the cell phone Delgado had provided. He punched in his secret code, keyed into an e-mail account, waited for the download, and hit Play. His features hardened, his coffee brown eyes black as pitch.

Manuel Alvarez watched Mia, the woman he had entrusted his fortune to—and foolishly opened his heart to—get butchered to death.

6

Cultivating a proper hatred for someone doesn't happen overnight, Arturo Delgado mused. He was watching a blue wave crest, the rolling curl edged in silver. It gained momentum and then dropped, turning to white foam as it spilled onto the expansive beach of Playa del Rey.

No, hatred had to be developed over time, meditated on and nurtured. Arturo's ruined leg was a constant reminder.

Delgado had harbored a grudging respect for Jack Bertolino after the bust all those years ago. Seven, to be exact. He had been one-upped mano a mano. As brilliant a tactician as Arturo Delgado had been, Bertolino had remained dogged. And in the end, he had won.

The cops had named the case Operation Green Door. Delgado had smuggled huge quantities of coke into the United States in crates of fruit. He read everything he could find, on the Internet, in the news, and on court transcripts to find out where it had all gone wrong.

Green Door was Arturo's play from the inception, and if successful, would have cemented his reputation forever. He would have earned more money than God, and back in Colombia he would have been treated like one.

Delgado was forward thinking and had forged a relationship

with the Betos, a Mexican group that was responsible for the transportation of major quantities of cocaine throughout the Southwest. Delgado would provide the Colombian cartel's cocaine, and the Betos would provide the distribution. This new alliance brought the Colombians together with the Mexicans in the northeast sector for the first time in history and would have changed the drug game in the States forever.

But it was not to be.

The Betos got sloppy, Bertolino dropped the hammer, and Arturo Delgado paid the price.

The eighteenth-floor, three-bedroom furnished apartment in the Azzurra del Rey cost Arturo Delgado ten grand a month. Chump change and worth the investment, he thought as he walked past the granite and stainless steel kitchen over to the bank of back windows. The 180-degree view ran from downtown L.A. to the Hollywood Hills. He bent down over the telescope he'd recently purchased at Brookstone on the Third Street Promenade. The viewing lens was focused on a five-story building a few blocks away. Within its silvery circle was displayed an orange metal balcony with a wooden bench, a barbecue grill, and a single tomato plant in need of water.

As if on cue, Jack Bertolino pulled open the sliding glass doors. He walked stiffly with a glass coffeepot and carefully watered around the edges of the tomato plant. Satisfied with his work, he walked back inside and closed the sliding door behind him.

Delgado tilted the telescope from the balcony down to the parking level, where he could just make out the nose of Jack's gray Mustang. He was about to give up the surveillance, when he caught a glimpse of Jack walking toward a line of retail shops a half block away.

Arturo picked up his phone and quickly texted two words: FIFTEEN MINUTES. He couldn't see his man, but knew he was in place. The professional would make short work of installing a GPS bug on the undercarriage of Jack's Mustang.

Jack tried to stretch his back as he walked down the sidewalk. It didn't help. After his fall at Ground Zero doing cleanup post 9/11, shooting pains ran down his six-foot-three frame on a daily basis and had forced him into an early retirement. He had to occasionally stand while eating, and pop pain meds like vitamins. He worried sometimes about the side effects. The pills might dull his brain and slow him down a bit, but after three unsuccessful operations he'd vowed never to go under the knife again. He'd read somewhere that Homo sapiens used only one-tenth of their brains. He could live with those odds.

Jack walked up Glencoe toward a Coffee Bean & Tea Leaf behind the Barnes & Noble bookstore. Once inside, Jack decided on a pound of Italian roast.

"You a cop?" the shaggy-haired barista asked as if he was in the know.

Jack didn't want to go there and ignored him.

"That's ground for a cone," Jack said, handing off the bag of whole beans.

"So, you're a cop." It was a statement.

"I used to be," Jack admitted.

"Once a cop, always a cop," the barista said with the maddening wisdom of youth as he walked away to grind Jack's beans.

Ever since he woke up, Jack had been sorting through his priorities. His first order of business was to call his old friend in Miami, DEA agent Kenny Ortega. They'd worked Mia as a team during the Alvarez case, and he might still have a line on her. At least Jack could get the lay of the land.

The next call would be to Tommy Aronsohn. He had been a baby DA back when Jack was an up and comer. Fiercely loyal, an impartial jurist, and a pit bull in a court of law. He had a high-end private practice now with an office on Park Avenue after a successful career as a Manhattan district attorney. The two men had made their bones together and remained steadfast friends. Jack was hoping he would stay out of the fray—more specifically, out of jail—but he'd give Tommy a heads-up just in case. He knew Tommy would have his back.

Jack was crossing Maxella on the way home when he heard, "Car wash . . . donations . . . car wash."

The high-pitched voices of twenty-something Hispanic women and children pierced the industrial sounds on Glencoe. "Car wash . . . caaaar . . . waaaash." Jack knew what was up before he was close enough to read the hand-painted cardboard signs. Someone was dead.

Lean, tattooed men in cutoff tees were working in the parking lot directly behind their women and children. The men manned wet rags, buckets filled with soapy water, and leaking hoses for the final rinse. There was no joy in their work. One of their own had died of a bullet wound to the abdomen. He needed to be buried. It was as simple as that.

Jack understood the culture of violence. It had been part of his catechism growing up in a Mafia infested neighborhood. But the wanton disregard for human life that allowed one man to slaughter another like so much chattel—those were the lives he wanted retribution for. But even higher on Jack's food chain were the men, removed from the violence, who gave the orders to kill. The men protected by their wealth, politics, and religion. Protected by their soldiers and bankers and lawyers and true believers. That's who he wanted to track down in avenging Mia's death.

Jack folded a twenty as he crossed the street. He stood for a moment before a makeshift shrine to the recently departed and slid the bill into the uneven slit cut into the top of a red shoe box. He thought about Mia and got deadly angry.

––––––––––

Delgado studied his reflected image in the full-length mirror hanging in his walk-in closet. The closet was about the same size as the house where he'd been born and raised with his three sisters, drunken father, and beloved mother, just ten kilometers outside Bogotá. His long silver mane of hair framed his chiseled, weathered features. The thick lines that accentuated his clear gray eyes and cut across his wide forehead lent him an air of gravitas, a life filled with battles won.

Delgado worked to minimize his limp as he crossed the expansive living room. He wore a metal brace that was undetectable under the tailored, navy linen slacks he was wearing. Unseen was a rage that could erupt at any moment. He could still kill a man with his bare hands. Success was all about control.

The sound of his cell phone brought Delgado back to now. He didn't give Manuel Alvarez a chance to speak. "I'm being told there was no iPad. They delivered her phone, but there were no financials, no information I didn't already have."

"The cunt always used an iPad," Alvarez stated. "All of her notes, all of my accounts, so that she could manage my affairs when she traveled."

"Mia's gone, don't worry about a loss. We'll make it up in six months."

"I want what's mine," Alvarez hissed, unable to control his emotion.

Delgado didn't respond at first, wondering why the hell Alvarez was worried about something stupid like this. Then his voice became stern. "I delivered on a promise made. You don't sound grateful. You should rethink your tone."

"You don't understand."

"Sure I do. Send me everything you've got," Delgado said. "Banks, offshore accounts, passwords, the entire portfolio. I'll get my people on it."

The other end of the line was silent for several beats. Then Alvarez admitted, "She had it all. I had nothing on paper."

Now the situation became clear. The anger, the wet work. Delgado understood what it took for Alvarez to admit weakness. He himself had never traveled that road, but he understood the emotion in lesser men. He became conciliatory, the benevolent leader.

"What are we talking about, Manuel? How much did she take?"

Alvarez all but whispered, "Twenty-four million."

The six zeros were enough to give Delgado pause. That was a formidable amount. It could, he realized instantly, comfortably round off his own bank accounts.

"Then I'll find another way. But don't waste my time, Manuel," he said softly, with a trace of menace. "We're on the eve of greatness. Trust is an issue."

"It won't buy me any time," Alvarez said bitterly.

"But they will remember you on the outside when you're released. You'll be older but revered. Money alone can't buy what I offer."

And Delgado clicked off with something to add to his personal mission statement. Find the Colombian *puta's* iPad.

7

The Miami sky was gunmetal gray. Billowing cumulus clouds threaded with black created the illusion of a mountain range towering over the Everglades. The humidity was as thick as the cloud cover, and the still air smelled of ozone. Rain wouldn't be too far behind.

Kenny Ortega had taken his usual long, cold morning shower after his daily five-mile run and regimen of push-ups and sit-ups. The shower had gone south on him in the amount of time it took to walk from his government-issue gray Ford Taurus through the automatic doors of the Federal Building.

He draped his gray sports jacket over the worn upholstered chair in front of his desk and pulled his blue pin-striped dress shirt away from his back, hoping it would dry before lunch. Was he thinking about lunch already?

Kenny didn't know when work had changed for him, but lately he spent more time thinking about fishing for grouper. Not that retirement was without its own perils. His father had retired after thirty years of teaching high school math and dropped dead of a massive coronary two weeks later.

But the DEA wasn't an agency where you could sleepwalk. It was a dangerous business. Lives were at stake, and Kenny knew he had to man up or get out.

His secretary, Claire, buzzed his intercom and announced that a Jack Bertolino was on line two. That elicited Ortega's first smile of the day. He picked up his phone, cradled it between his neck and his shoulder, and punched 2.

"Mi hermano!" Kenny all but shouted. Ortega and Bertolino had worked well together. A fed and a cop. Worked hard, had some laughs, put some major drugs on the table, and sidelined some seriously bad dudes.

"How the fuck are you? I heard you moved to la-la land. You forget your old buddies?"

"Mia . . ." was all Jack could get out.

"Did you finally knock off that piece?"

But Kenny Ortega knew something was off. He clutched his phone and leaned forward to wait out the silence on the other end of the line.

"Someone did . . . Mia's dead."

"In Miami? Why didn't I hear about it?"

"No, she flew into L.A. two nights ago. I saw her yesterday. She was alive when I left her, dead a half hour later. Looks good for a cartel hit, but the LAPD thinks I look good for it."

"How's that?" Kenny asked.

"We spent some time."

That didn't surprise Kenny. "What'd she want?"

"Protection."

"How can I help?"

"Get a line on Alvarez. See if he's been running anything out of the pen, who's been on his guest list, who he's hanging with on the inside, the whole nine yards. And, Kenny, whatever you can dig up on Mia."

Mia had been one of Ortega's best confidential informants. He had introduced her to Jack when they were working a case that overlapped. Manuel Alvarez had been importing cocaine into Miami from the Dominican Republic and then shipping the drugs to New

York City. The DEA had Alvarez in their crosshairs and Bertolino had him on his hit list. Alvarez was one slick operator, and the only way to get close to the man and infiltrate his cell had been through Mia, the beautiful woman with ice water in her veins.

"It's been a few years, but she's gotta be somewhere in the system. How did they do her?"

"Devil's Necktie."

"Shit."

"Is right."

"I'm on it, Jack. I'll buzz you back when I know anything. Oh, Jack?"

"Yeah, Kenny?"

Kenny Ortega chose his words very carefully.

"Don't beat yourself up. You were off the clock. You punched out two years ago."

"Thanks, Kenny. That means a lot."

"Later."

———————

Jack was on the run. He took a last swig of coffee, slid the ME's cleaned sweats and T-shirt into a brown grocery bag, snugged his Glock into his shoulder holster, and threw on a lightweight sports jacket to hide the nine millimeter. He was picking up his keys and heading out the door when he heard his land line ringing.

"Christ."

He hurried across the concrete floor and grabbed for the phone before voice mail picked up.

"What?"

"Turn on your computer."

And the line went dead.

It was his son. Jack immediately walked into the smaller of the two bedrooms that he used as an office and opened his MacBook Pro, which had been left on sleep mode. The screen was black for an instant and then light, a jerky image filling the Skype screen and then settling on his son's very serious face.

"Hey, Dad. Holy shit, you look like hell."

"Thanks, Son. Just what I needed," he said, trying to downplay it. "Listen, I'd love to talk, but can we do this later?"

"I really need to talk."

His son was the most important person in his life, and he'd already let him down too many times in the past when police work had taken precedence. Life experiences he could never get back. First steps, ball games, choir recitals, and just plain time in. Since his retirement, he'd vowed never to let that happen again, and he'd been trying very hard not to backpedal.

Jack settled into his chair. He could see his son was worried and instantly shared his concern. "What is it, Chris?"

"I'm thinking about quitting the team."

Wow, Jack thought. Out of all the possible turmoil his son might have been facing in his first semester at Stanford University, quitting baseball would not even have made it onto Jack's long list.

His son had played ball since the time he was tall enough to hit one off a tee. He was the captain of his high school team and had been scouted by a few organizations. But his son still wanted an education; he was one smart kid.

Young Chris's dream had always been to play hard, win a scholarship, and then if all things were equal, take a shot at the big leagues. Jack had never pushed, or tried not to, but had always been supportive. And now he'd try, damn hard, to think before opening his mouth and saying the wrong thing.

"Really?" was the best he could come up with.

"I'm just not happy."

"Who is?"

"Dad . . ."

"Right. It's just that, well, you've only been practicing for two months now. Don't you think it might be a little early to make such a drastic decision?"

His son's image jerked around in disconnected blurs on the computer screen. They had decided that Skype would allow them to keep in closer contact. Jack had been all for it.

"I haven't totally made up my mind yet. I just wanted to run it by you." His son's mouth had taken on a petulant stamp Jack knew very well. "I'm not really getting along with Coach Fredricks. It doesn't look like I'm going to be in the starting lineup, and I know that I've got the skills. I think it's personal."

Jack's heart swelled with pride. How had he gotten so lucky? Even with the contentious divorce, his son had weathered the storm. The boy was so intelligent and thoughtful. Maybe he had gotten it from his mother, because he didn't think it came from his gene pool.

"You know what, Chris? Wear him down. Don't take no for an answer. You never have before. And you've never given up before. It's not in your DNA."

"But I've been working my ass off."

"Christopher." Jack only called his son Christopher when he was being very serious.

"Dad," Chris returned with mock sarcasm.

"Love you, Son. I'll stand by you whatever you finally decide, but let's give this a little more time, huh?"

Chris stared at his father for what seemed like an eternity and then said, "Later."

He clicked off—just like that—leaving Jack Bertolino staring at an empty screen. Teenagers, that wonderful age.

———

Jack pulled his Mustang left onto Vista Haven, and when 3468 was just a few houses farther up, he made a hard right turn onto Lisa Place. The ME's wagon was still out front, and a single black-and-white was snugged up behind it, guarding the crime scene. Both vehicles sat empty. The parade of reporters and vans had disappeared earlier in the day, eager to find the next tragedy to feed the voracious news beast.

Jack unlimbered his gun and locked it in the trunk of his car in case he had a run-in with the uniformed cop. He walked back up the street and made a right toward the murder scene. As he turned the corner, he could now see the neighbor who lived across the street. He was standing on his front patio, holding a hose and watering his azaleas. The man's lot was uphill from the crime scene, affording him a bird's-eye view of 3468 and the yellow police tape strung across the entrance to the driveway.

"Afternoon," Jack said.

"What?" the man shouted.

Jack could see the man had buds in his ear and a thin set of wires leading into his lime green iPod. The man turned down whatever he was listening to and pulled out one of the buds.

"Sorry, what?"

Jack repeated, "Afternoon."

"You here for the murder?" he asked, still too loud.

"Beg your pardon?"

"Name's Mayor." Better, Jack thought.

The slight man walked down his flagstone steps toward Jack and reached out a hand. It was a firm, dry handshake. The man was small, couldn't have been more than five foot four. Thinning close-cropped brown hair and intelligent, lively eyes.

"They call me the Mayor because I'm always around, retired, but my first name really is Mayor," he shared with pride.

"Good to know." Jack smiled. "Jack Bertolino. Listen, I wonder if I might ask you a few questions?"

"Wouldn't be the first of the day," Mayor said as he turned the spray of water onto the ivy that covered the front hillside. "You're not a reporter, are you? You don't look like one. You look more like a cop."

"I was a cop, retired now."

Mayor nodded his head. "Go ahead, shoot."

"Did you see a police car parked in that driveway around five forty-five yesterday evening?"

"Police asked me the same question."

"And?"

"I saw twenty if I saw one, and then the helicopters and the emergency vehicles. I couldn't get out of my driveway to get to the movie theater. We had six-thirty reserved seats for *Another Earth*."

Jack had a hard time empathizing with the loss of movie tickets when a woman had been brutally butchered a hundred yards away, and his emotion wasn't lost on Mayor.

"Oh, I must sound terrible. The poor woman. I apologize. I'm just not used to the . . . to the violence. It's got me and Marilyn shaken up."

That was more than Jack expected.

"Understood. Did Marilyn see or hear anything?"

"She was playing bridge with the girls, and the plan was to meet at the theater."

"And nothing before that? A single car? A sound? Anything out of the ordinary?"

"I saw a gray Mustang in the driveway, and then the noise from that damn party forced me into the house. Had to close the windows. College kids. Their family owns five cars, and they never park in front of their own house, so we have the joy of looking at their kids' vehicles."

Jack shifted his weight from one foot to the other, and Mayor finally understood that he was going on for too long about something off the point.

"What's your interest here?"

Jack leveled his gaze and stared straight into Mayor's eyes. "The cops think I did it."

Mayor reflexively took a step back before recovering. "Oh,

you're the one they led out in handcuffs. I can see it now. It was dark, and I was looking down, I couldn't see your face." He scrutinized Jack's face. "You don't look like a killer."

"Good to know," Jack said.

"I'm a good judge of character, and I don't think you'd be standing here asking these questions if you'd done it. Doesn't track."

Jack nodded his head in agreement, trying to develop a rapport.

"So what are your plans?" Mayor asked.

"I'd like to take a look around the property when the police finish up. See if they missed anything."

Mayor shot a furtive glance toward the county vehicles and gave the request some serious thought. He turned the sprinkler nozzle to stop the flow and set the hose down on the walkway.

Jack prayed he hadn't made a mistake confiding in him. The last thing Jack needed was for Mayor to call the police if he detected movement in the house without knowing who it was.

"I won't stop you," Mayor said, adding, "I'm supposed to lock up after they leave. No hurry now. The owner won't be back for two weeks. He's in Greece, on a cruise." Mayor lowered his voice conspiratorially, and Jack stepped in closer. "Michael, the owner of the house, is a real estate agent. Very nice man, good neighbor. I called him on his cell. Anyway, they had a mutual friend in Miami, the dead woman and Michael did. It's how they met."

Mayor tilted his head in the direction of 3468. "I guess they got along because when he heard the woman was headed to L.A., he offered her the use of his house until she got on her feet. He's got an extra room set up for guests and loves company. Big heart, that Michael. Didn't work out very well for the woman. Michael was devastated. I think he said her name was Mia."

"It was," Jack said. Using the past tense made him angry. "Did Michael mention the name of his friend in Miami?"

"Just a first name, Greg. He's with Michael on the ship and I think they work for the same real estate organization."

Jack was about to ask a question, when Mayor all but read his mind.

"If you wait a second, I'll jot down Michael's cell number. I don't think he'll mind one bit. Just keep the number to yourself."

"Did you give the police this number?"

"They already had it," Mayor said as he walked into his carport and opened the door to his white Lexus. He pulled out a pen and pad and in seconds handed Jack his first real lead.

"Thank you, Mayor."

"You're very welcome. And watch yourself. It's still a city."

"Excuse me?"

"Look around," Mayor said as he extended one arm expansively. "It only looks like suburbia. Don't let it fool you."

8

Jack stepped under the yellow police tape that was stretched across the driveway entrance and retraced his steps to the rear of the house. He walked past the sliding glass door that led into the bedroom. The screen door the perpetrators had kicked in to gain entry was bent and leaning at a strange angle, propped up against the side of the house.

Jack peered around the corner and saw that a narrow concrete path ran alongside the house and the detached garage, through to the street beyond. Spindly oleander bushes obscured the path from the road.

The sliding door had been pulled shut but not latched. Mayor would be locking the house down later that evening when the police had finished their work.

Jack knew he was flying blind, trying to clear his name and find the killers. This was the first time since he had retired that not being in uniform was a profound negative. His access to information would be limited, and working alone was not the most expedient way to cover a sprawling city like Los Angeles.

Terry Molloy, the ME, walked into the bedroom and was startled when he saw Jack standing outside the door holding a brown paper bag. He blocked Jack's entrance into the house, and the two men stepped out near the pool, where he thanked Jack for the quick turnaround on the sweats. He was tight-lipped about the case in general and whatever physical evidence he had turned up. Jack did get him to admit that Mia's wallet, with her ID and cash, and her iPad, were found at the scene, but not her passport or cell phone. Molloy had no trouble sharing that the district attorney's office was still weighing its options on filing charges against Jack.

The uniformed LAPD officer came striding out of the rear of the house, interrupted their discussion, and told Jack that he was illegally trespassing on an active crime scene, and to beat it. Jack didn't have to be told twice.

He looped his car around the corner and up onto the ridge of Vista Haven and parked under an old-growth canyon oak with a narrow, protected view of the ME's truck and the police car. He sat there for three and a half hours, until Molloy and the uniform ducked under the yellow tape, mounted up, and drove out. Jack knew he had to make short work of this expedition. It was too late to poison the crime scene. The technical work had been done, videos and digital pictures taken. Blood samples, hair and fiber samples. The bedroom and bathroom had been vacuumed for trace everything, the drains cleaned. But it was still the scene of the crime, and as far as Jack knew, he was the only suspect. Not comforting, he thought as he pulled on white disposable rubber gloves and blue paper booties.

He had lucked out, keeping his face and name out of the media. Tommy being an ex-district attorney hadn't hurt. Tommy still had some juice and had immediately gotten on the horn and raised such a stink, the Los Angeles DA's office thought it might not be prudent to drag a decorated ex-NYPD inspector through the mud just yet. They would hold up on that until the DNA came back.

Jack pulled the sliding door open, and the coppery, acrid smell of dried blood overwhelmed him. That third cup of coffee, which he had drunk sitting in the car, made him edgy. He pushed the door the rest of the way open to air the place out and make it almost bearable. He sucked in a deep breath, walked into the bedroom, and took in the bed where he had spent time less than twenty-four hours ago.

The ME had bagged the duvet cover, the sheets, and the pillowcases. Jack knew his trace elements would be all over them. The mattress had bloodstains, and the blood on the wall behind the bed fanned out like a Rorschach test. The brown carpet in front of the bathroom was stained a dark purple where Jack had lain facedown, waiting to be cuffed.

The blood had pooled in his lap while Jack cradled Mia's body. Jack prayed that some of the blood would be the killers'. He walked the few steps to the bathroom and turned on the light. Even if a police car did a drive-by, the light wouldn't read from the front of the house. If the cop came around the back, he'd be fucked.

The white shower tiles and floor tiles were stained a thick dull brown, a crazy amount of blood. Jack held on to the doorjamb for support. His pulse started racing, his breath staggered, his stomach soured. If any prints had been found on the showerhead, they'd be his.

Jack didn't expect to find anything of substance in the bathroom. The technical team was skilled and thorough. He just had to see where she was killed. One last time. Get a feel for the kind of men who could snuff out a life with such cruelty and so much precision.

Jack knew if he didn't keep moving forward, he'd shut down. Luckily, something Mayor had said brought him out of his stupor. Mia had been invited to stay at Vista Haven, and the guest room would be hers until she got on her feet.

He hadn't taken particular notice of any guest rooms yesterday. He walked out of the bedroom past a second bathroom on the right. It was empty. No toiletries or anything of Mia's on the soapstone counter. Just striped guest towels and a dish of small multicolored soaps shaped like seashells that had never been used and probably never would be.

He stood still for a second to listen for any unwelcome sounds, but the only noise was the traffic bleed coming over the ridge from the San Diego Freeway.

The small bedroom directly in front of him appeared to have been turned into an office. There were a few framed real estate platinum awards on the wall behind a modern glass-and-steel desk, a phone, a printer, a computer. Jack walked in and pocketed one of Michael's business cards from a holder on the desk. He took a silver-framed picture down from the white bookshelves built against the side wall. The man with the big smile in the center of the photo was clearly Michael. He wondered if the man sitting next to him, obviously lit, drinking a large margarita, was Greg. Attractive, happy people. It pissed him off. He would have Kenny Ortega meet the cruise ship when it docked in the Port of Miami in two weeks and interview them both.

Jack continued up the hallway toward the kitchen and living room and discovered the second bedroom on the right. It was a small, nicely appointed room with three orange pastel walls and a full wall of glass that opened onto a private garden protected from prying eyes by the detached garage and a six-foot wooden fence. The room was far enough away from the master suite for privacy.

The queen-size bed had been dressed in high-end Calvin Klein linens and pillowcases that were stripped back, exposing the mattress. They now lay in a heap at the bottom of the bed. This was to have been Mia's room. She might have enjoyed it with the garden and all.

A large Louis Vuitton suitcase was laid open on the carpet in front of the closet, along with a smaller carry-on. Mia had been traveling light. The closet itself was an architectural detail, raised off the floor, creating the illusion of a floating box with sliding white panels to gain entry.

Jack rifled through the suitcase. The handle and locks had black fingerprint dust on them, as did the sliding glass door handle. The tech had already worked it over and was obviously satisfied that there was nothing more of interest, just a few nightgowns and delicate undergarments.

The keys to the suitcase sat in the webbed key compartment. Nothing appeared to have been secreted in the silk lining. No hidden compartments that might hold a passport, a phone, plane tickets or stubs, anything to give Jack a hint as to what Mia's plans were or who she was running from.

The carry-on had been emptied. It had probably held her makeup and toiletries and would be gone over at the lab to see if anything was hidden there.

As Jack stood up, something nagged at him. He couldn't put his finger on it. He wasn't thinking clearly. He opened the closet and audibly sighed as he saw hanger after hanger of Mia's dresses, skirts, blouses, and a jacket, some hanging by one shoulder, some bunched and roughly shoved back onto the hangers in total disarray. A colorful pile of silk and cotton blouses and balled-up nylons had been searched and discarded on the closet floor.

"Evening, Officer. I'm Mayor, a friend of the owner, and I was just coming over to lock up," Mayor said a bit too loudly, sending Jack a verbal smoke signal.

Jack moved quickly, his pulse quickening. He slid the closet door shut and tiptoed out of the room, cursing himself for not working faster and getting into the kitchen. He could hear Mayor and what sounded like the same uniformed cop he had talked to earlier walking up the driveway, heading for the front door. Jack was halfway down the hallway when he turned abruptly and headed back into the guest bedroom.

"Terrible thing," Mayor said.

Jack approached the Louis Vuitton suitcase, pulled the keys out of the webbed compartment, and slipped them into one of his socks. He hurried down the hallway, through the master bedroom, and out the sliding door, pulling it closed behind him just as he heard the front door swing open. He stepped past the broken screen door on the side of the house, stood stock-still, and controlled his breathing as he heard the front door slam shut. He pulled off his disposable gloves and booties, slid them into his back pocket, and stayed in the shadow as he made his way along the back of the garage, through the bushes, and out onto the street. He walked uphill away from the black-and-white, whose engine block was still ticking.

The two keys that appeared to fit the suitcase were, on second thought, a size too large. Maybe they were nothing, but maybe something Mia had hidden in plain sight.

Jack keyed the ignition. His growling stomach demanded to be fed. He pulled away from the curb and got the hell out of Dodge.

9

A thick layer of yellow-brown smog was enveloping the hazy winter sun as it slipped behind the electrical towers in the distance. Hector Lopez viewed the sunset dispassionately, smoking a joint. He was reclined in the tuck-and-rolled black leather interior of his 1960 hardtop Impala sports sedan, blue, with a white roof and a white band that ran along the rear fender. A classic, Hector's prized possession and his favorite location for getting high and perusing his own little piece of the American dream.

His car was parked behind his mother's house, and he sat there doing a mental accounting of all he possessed. He clicked the remote, and the warped garage door yawned open. Track lights that had been attached to an exposed wooden beam were turned on, throwing pin spots onto his unmade bed, couch, and semifinished living quarters in the tired one-car garage. He had a hot plate, a toaster oven, an avocado green refrigerator, a top-of-the-line sound system, and a newly purchased Vizio LCD flat-screen television mounted on the wall. On the opposite wall was a window so dirty, no one could see in or out. He had a swiveling Barcalounger that he loved, with cup holders set into the padded, black-upholstered arms. The recliner sat on a large burgundy area rug that nearly covered the entire stained concrete floor.

Hector's mother cooked all of his meals, did his laundry, and never set foot in his living quarters. He knew she was afraid of him, but would never say as much to his face or say no to his paying the bills.

Eight years ago his father, in a drunken rage, had made the fatal mistake of beating the shit out of young Hector in front of his newly acquired friends in the Lil' 18th Street Angels—a subset of the local gang, the 18th Street Angels, which had laid claim to Ontario for the past fifty years. Hector had been recruited in high school but still had to prove himself.

No one questioned his father's disappearance. But everyone knew the truth.

Hector killed his father with the old man's own carving knives. He stabbed him in the chest, the abdomen, the neck, until the bloody holes were too numerous to count. Then he drank a six-pack of his father's Dos Equis while he systematically dismembered the body with the skill of a master butcher.

Hector carefully wrapped the desecrated body parts in pieces of plastic drop cloth, bound the parcels with duct tape, and buried them next to an orange tree situated near the rusted chain-link fence that ran along the rear of the property.

Someone from the Pro's Ranch Market over on Desoto Street, where his father worked as a butcher, came around a few days later making inquiries, but fifteen-year-old Hector sent him on his way with, "My father got homesick. He is back in Guadalajara visiting family."

Hector moved into the garage and up through the ranks, becoming a full member of the 18th Street Angels, where a kill was needed to prove your worth. He had built a reputation for being a go-to guy. At five-ten and weighing in at two-twenty, he was all muscle and no fear. Thick brown hair, heavy brows, and black eyes that made other men blink first. He was being groomed by Armando "Mando" Barajas, who was a member of the Mexican Mafia and who also controlled all of the 18th Street Angels' activities.

He didn't have any trusted friends besides Johnny, but that was okay. Life was good. Money, dope, sex were all for the taking. Yet Hector had discovered years ago a rush that was more intense than shooting crystal meth. A better high than heroin. More satisfying than a sexual orgasm.

The kill.

But more important, the cutting. His sharp knives gliding through flesh.

Hector had to hide his arousal from Johnny after slashing the woman's throat up on the hill. But that was easy because Johnny wasn't really looking at him. He took the video but seemed distracted.

It had been Hector's idea to go old school on the whore and stage it like a cartel kill. He was smarter than he looked and took pride in his God-given talent. Change the play, save the day. He was taking his skill set to a new level, thinking on his feet.

He took another deep hit of his joint and realized that, in a very strange way, he owed it all to his father.

10

It was close to eight o'clock before Jack found a parking space on Abbot Kinney, in Venice, and walked the two and a half blocks to Hal's. Abbot Kinney reminded Jack of the East Village. Art galleries, furniture stores, coffee shops, restaurants, overpriced designer clothing, multimillion-dollar loft buildings, '60s-era junk shops, and a fancy medical marijuana establishment. Bicycles begrudgingly shared the road with cars, and aging hippies with guitars shared sidewalk space with west-side professionals being tugged along by their designer dogs.

Hal's Bar and Grill had a New York feel, with huge eclectic canvases on the walls, oversize metal sculptures acting as room dividers, American cuisine, and a great bar scene. Rebecca, one of the revolving maitre d's, read the distress on Jack's face as soon as he walked through the door. She pushed through the crowd waiting for tables, grabbed him by the arm, and immediately ushered him to a private table in the back of the large, open dining room where he'd have plenty of privacy. If Jack wasn't grilling, he ate at Hal's, and Rebecca, an aspiring actress who had auditioned for *Law and Order SVU*, *Blue Bloods*, and *CSI*, understood an ex-cop's reticence about sitting with his back facing the door.

Jack wasn't much of a drinker, but he ordered a double Stoli on the rocks. His stomach was still off, but he knew if he didn't eat something, he'd pay for it later. He ordered a dinner salad with blue cheese and a medium-rare flank steak with fries, and settled into his drink.

The vodka was spreading a welcome warmth when he noticed a woman slide into a rare empty space at the bar, pull off her hat, and glance in Jack's direction, looking very pleased with herself for having scored a stool. Whatever relief Jack was feeling from the drink was immediately lost as the woman shook her blond hair loose. With her long hair draped sensually over her shoulders, she looked like a younger version of Mia.

Over the years he had learned most of Mia's story. At the beginning he listened to gain her trust and establish a good rapport. As time passed, however, he became genuinely interested in all she'd been through.

Confidential informants came in all shapes and sizes, but their motivations fell into two main categories. Some CIs did it for money, and some had been busted and wanted to work off their prison time. From Jack's experience, one wasn't any better or more reliable than the other. They were both necessary evils if a New York City cop wanted to infiltrate major drug cells.

Mia had been a beauty pageant winner in her late teens. Voted Miss Colombia, she was a real head turner. She'd had plenty of suitors, but one young man stood out like a thunderbolt, and Mia fell hard, in true love, her soul mate.

The one wrinkle in their storybook love affair was that the young man's father was Jose Ordinola, a notorious drug kingpin. Well, two wrinkles: he didn't approve of their relationship. That was a problem. This was a man who got what he wanted. He controlled a multibillion-dollar cocaine empire. A nod of his head could end a life. A whispered order could destroy an entire village. Ordinola loved his son more than life itself, but refused to be disobeyed. It set a bad precedent.

The young lovers were impetuous, willful, and naïve, having the arrogance of youth. They continued to see each other behind closed doors, in out-of-the-way bistros, at friends' flats, hidden from prying eyes, in nearby cities. But as careful as they were in planning their assignations, they fell short on birth control and Mia got knocked up.

She was overjoyed, as was her young suitor, thinking that their love child would eventually heal all wounds. After all, Jose Ordinola was a devout Catholic who donated vast amounts of money to the church. The Colombian archbishop was a frequent dinner guest.

When Ordinola's operatives informed him of the pregnancy, he was furious but controlled his rage and tried to reason with the young couple.

He asked Mia to have an abortion. He promised to send her to America, pay for an education at the university of her choice, set her up in business after she graduated, and take care of her and her mother for the rest of their lives. She respectfully said no, as did his son. They planned on getting married with or without his father's approval.

Jose Ordinola threw down the gauntlet. He *ordered* Mia to have an abortion.

He sent men to her home to have a "discussion" with her mother. The harsh message was disturbingly clear, and her mother, severely chastised and hysterical now, tried to intercede on Ordinola's behalf. But Mia refused. It was a mortal sin. It went against everything she believed in, would break her heart and send her to hell. The lovers accelerated their plans to elope before the week's end.

When Mia had first recounted her story, she had started to shake uncontrollably. Her eyes looked haunted, her skin visibly paled, but she'd struggled to go on. She needed to be understood—wanted Jack Bertolino to understand why she did what she did. She forced herself to continue.

Mia had received a handwritten letter inviting her to a weekend retreat at the Ordinola country estate just days before the secret marriage was to have taken place. A car would pick her up, she could spend time with her boyfriend and his extended family, and all would be forgiven. It was time to bless their union.

Her boyfriend was overjoyed when he heard. He was doing some work on one of his father's stud farms but promised to meet her there. Mia felt that her prayers had finally been answered.

Saturday afternoon, at the appointed time, a long silver limousine pulled to a stop in front of her home. Her mother was understandably anxious, but also hopeful, knowing the wealth and position in Colombian society that would follow the wedding. Neighbors lined up two deep on the sidewalk in front of their modest home to see the finely waxed car sweep their most famous daughter away.

Mia had chosen to wear a proper white cotton summer dress with a light blue collar that accentuated her blue eyes and blond hair. It had impressed the judges at her last pageant, and she hoped her father-in-law-to-be would approve. Just give her some time, and she'd win him over.

Mia, feeling pampered, leaned back against the thick leather seats of the grand car. Her freshly manicured hands cupped her budding pregnancy, and she wondered what it would feel like when the baby finally kicked. She laughed inwardly at the horror stories she'd heard about morning sickness, because she had never felt as strong or as happy in her entire life.

Mia remembered catching brief glimpses of the imposing Spanish-style mansion through passing tree branches. Her palms had uncharacteristically started sweating. She pulled out her compact, powdered her nose, and then sat back ready to experience whatever miracles life had in store.

The limo pulled into the wide, sweeping, pavered driveway and eased to a stop in front of massive oak doors. The only movement she could detect was the thick spray of water shooting up from the ornate carved stone fountain in the center of the impressive courtyard. The driver opened her door and helped her out. He lifted her bag out of the trunk and assured her that they were the first to arrive, but the rest of the party would follow shortly.

The driver lagged a few steps behind, and then reached around her and rang the doorbell. Mia understood that her sudden nervousness wasn't unfounded as soon as the thick wooden doors were pulled open and she saw the thin man with the black eyes and the tight smile extend a hand. She reflexively took a step backward but was violently shoved into the foyer by her driver. The man standing at the entrance to the grand house was one of Jose Ordinola's enforcers.

He grabbed Mia by her long blond hair and stopped her scream by driving home a gut punch, knocking the wind out of her. She fell to her knees, gulping, choking and fighting to catch her breath, unable to speak or call out. The thin man dragged her along the polished marble floor into the large kitchen. She was heaved on top of the table and gagged. Her white summer dress was pulled up over her head, her panty hose and panties were ripped off, and her wrists and ankles were bound to the legs of the wooden prep table.

Her young heart raced, pounding out of her chest. It felt like a heart attack. Then someone she couldn't see entered the kitchen from behind. A soft, compassionate male voice told her not to worry. And then he tore into her vagina with a bent metal coat hanger.

Blackness turned to blinding light as Mia slowly regained consciousness. She was disoriented, and she felt excruciating pain.

Mia was lying in a pool of her own blood. Her white dress stained a violent red.

She rolled onto her side and puked, trying not to soil herself. When her vision finally cleared, she realized that she'd been dumped in a muddy gutter on the side of a dirt road, like yesterday's refuse, somewhere in the Colombian countryside. The contents of her weekend bag were strewn about the field behind her. She rolled onto her back and let out a primal cry.

Mia became an informant for revenge.

Jack didn't remember finishing his drink or ordering another, but he polished that one off too. He threw down enough money to cover the bill, added a good tip, and left his plate of food untouched on the table behind him.

A layer of marina fog had descended on Venice like a harsh warning. He carefully drove his car through the thick, wet clouds that roiled with the fast-moving ocean breeze. The streetlamps he passed created halos of diffused light that pooled on the uneven sidewalk below. As he sat idling at a red light, the murky night was so surreal that two men walking up Washington Boulevard reminded him of Bogey and a uniformed Claude Rains on the tarmac at the Casablanca airport as they disappeared into the billowing white mist. The light turned green, and when Jack rolled up alongside the men, "Bogart" and "Rains" turned out to be two homeless guys he recognized from the neighborhood, sharing a joint.

Jack took the elevator in his building, and as he stepped off, he was treated to the shadowy figures of Lieutenant Gallina and Detective Tompkins hovering in front of his door. Fuck, Jack thought.

"Where've you been?" Gallina demanded with an attitude that definitely needed adjustment.

"What's it to you? How'd you get into my building?" So much for security systems, Jack thought.

"You been drinking?"

"Wish I hadn't stopped."

But Jack forced himself to stand a bit taller, pleased he'd left his nine-millimeter Glock in the trunk of his car.

"What were you doing up at Vista Haven?" a smug Gallina asked.

"So many questions, Lieutenant. I was returning Molloy's sweats. If that's all you needed, I'm dead tired."

Gallina and Tompkins made no attempt to move away from his door.

"No, after that?" Tompkins added.

"I went to Hal's. Tossed back a few. Now, if you don't mind . . ."

"What's wrong with the Cozy Inn?" As if Gallina cared, Jack thought.

The Cozy Inn was a seedy bar frequented by off-duty cops, cops on shift—a little hair of the dog, a quick liquid lunch—and the women who loved cops.

"I'm not a cop anymore."

"My point exactly," Gallina stated. "Now, what were you doing up there *after* you dropped off Molloy's rags? You see, if you were illegally trespassing on an active murder scene where you're a suspect, that would be a crime and enough cause to lock you up. Now, the word we got was, you showed up at around two, finished your conversation with Molloy by two fifteen. But your car wasn't reported to have left the scene until after dark. What the fuck?"

Jack's stomach churned and audibly growled. He hoped the cops hadn't heard and started talking to cover his discomfort, realizing that he should've eaten his steak.

"I left right after talking to Molloy, who you'll be glad to know is a company man. I don't know where you're getting your information, but your time line's bogus."

Jack flexed his back, feeling an angry knot. If Mayor hadn't talked, which he thought highly unlikely, then who was watching his movements? And why didn't he know he was being watched? Jack worried that he was losing his edge.

"We got a list of everyone at the party next door, and the girl who threw it, and her parents who were home at the time, and no one— are we on the same page here?—no one saw a police car parked in front of the house. Nada. I talked to that guy named Mayor. What a mouth on him, same thing. No cop car.

"Everybody in the neighborhood. Only car anyone ID'd was a gray Mustang. Yours. Parked in the driveway, all afternoon, and oh, by the way, at the time of the murder. So, you tell me."

Jack realized they were only fishing. They really just wanted to tell him that he'd been sighted at the house. "Any luck with the movie rental companies?" he countered, thinking fancy footwork, keep 'em moving.

"Not that I'm disposed to answer your questions, but we wasted a shitload of shoe leather today that the county will not fully reimburse. Are you taking this down, Inspector? Squat. That's what we got."

"If you give me a list of places you hit, I can narrow my search," Jack said, knowing the detectives would give up nothing.

"Jack," Tompkins said, "stay out of our investigation. Stay out of our way."

With that, the two men moved past Jack and toward the elevator. Bertolino waited until he heard the ding of the elevator arriving, and the whoosh of the stainless steel doors closing, before he opened the gray metal fire door to his loft and locked it securely behind him.

Jack kicked off his shoes, pulled off one sock, and grabbed the keys he had taken from Mia's suitcase. He'd been right. They looked too small to be a safe-deposit-box key, but he didn't think they'd open her bag either. Maybe a P.O. box? he wondered. He wasn't sure what they'd open, but just having something of hers in his possession made him feel strangely better. He made a mental note to call the locksmith who had relocked his loft door and check with him.

Jack walked across the concrete floor, one sock on, one foot bare, grabbed the jar of Skippy super chunky peanut butter off the pantry shelf, rifled through the silverware drawer for a spoon, and dug in.

11

Sleep was becoming a rare commodity. Ever since that fatal night, Jack's mind had been spinning on hyperdrive. The only thing he was sure of was that Mia's murder wasn't random. It was an ordered execution. Mia had set up, stolen from, or disrespected the wrong man or organization. Her death was payback, pure and simple.

Could he have done anything to prevent Mia's death? If he had stayed while she slept, things would definitely have turned out differently. This weighed heavily.

And if he wasn't a suspect, could he now just walk away? He had made a promise years ago, but wasn't that verbal contract null and void, the void being Mia's death?

Jack realized he had to pull it back a notch. Whenever he was having a crisis of conscience, he'd look at the issue through the purity of his grandparents' eyes. They both lived by a simple immigrant logic formed from life experience and heart.

His grandfather wouldn't even recognize the man who could turn away. He had been young Jack's mentor and role model, his only safe haven during a violent youth. For her part, Jack was sure his grandmother would give him a tough Italian squeeze to the cheek until he saw the truth, and did the right thing. And that was seeing this case to the end.

The comforting memories of the two of them allowed him finally to drift off into a deep sleep at five o'clock in the morning.

Four Panasonic wireless telephones were set up in different parts of the fifteen-hundred-square-foot loft, with one in the master bathroom. At seven A.M., the main phone rang. The clones followed suit, creating a vortex of electronic bells that startled Jack awake and made him seriously question the need for land lines.

Jack fumbled for the receiver next to his platform bed, and hit three wrong buttons before jabbing the one that actually stopped the ringing and answered the phone. He kept his eyes closed, hoping to make short work of the call and drift back to sleep again. He knew it was shy of eight thirty because the FedEx trucks hadn't left for their daily routes.

"Yeah," came out dry and raspy, like Janis Joplin on a bad day.

"Your son is going to quit college."

It was Jeannine, Jack's ex. He seriously thought about hanging up but knew he'd eventually have to pay for that. "What, no hello?" he all but croaked.

"Jack, did you hear what I said?"

"Do you know what time it is?" Jack asked, matching her tone.

Jeannine never liked to be questioned and responded as if she was standing in front of a class of third-graders. "I worked very hard to get Chris into one of the finest schools in the country, and now he wants to quit." The "quit" came off as a question.

"He's thinking about quitting the baseball team."

"That's not what I got from our conversation."

"Were you talking or listening?" Jack regretted the words before they left his mouth.

"Now you listen to me, Jack Bertolino, I've had just about enough of your bullying to last me a lifetime."

Jack rubbed his eyes, contemplated gouging them out, and then sat up on the edge of the bed. The sleep train had left the station. He wondered almost out loud how he'd ever married this woman. Then he reminded himself that Jeannine was the mother of his only son. Jeannine was the vessel that had helped create everything that held meaning in his life.

But it didn't really help.

"I need you to step up to the plate and be a man," she said.

Jack appreciated the baseball metaphor, and it almost made him smile. "I talked to Chris yesterday, and he said he'd give it some more time."

"When did you talk?" Jeannine asked. The question sounded like an accusation.

"Yesterday morning about ten thirty. I was on my way out the door."

"Well, I talked to him late last night, and he didn't sound all that convinced. I was going to phone, but I didn't want to wake you."

Jack tried to explain in measured tones. It wasn't the first time they'd had the conversation, and it probably wouldn't be the last. "The three-hour time difference works the other way."

"Don't talk down to me . . . oh, that's right. Stay on this, will you, Jack? Please." All of the defensiveness drained out of her voice, replaced by her genuine concern for their son.

"I will. I'll call you if I hear anything."

"Thank you. Oh . . . where's the pilot light on the water heater?"

Jack used to enjoy her non sequiturs, thought they were cute. "On the water heater."

"Yes, that's what I said. The water heater. I'm only getting cold."

"It's *on* the water heater," Jack said, the edge firmly back in his voice. He wasn't at his best on two hours' sleep. "Can't Jeremy figure it out? I thought he was the smartest man you ever met."

"Jack!"

She was right. He was headed straight for Niagara without a barrel. He changed course.

"The pilot light is on the bottom of the water heater. If you can't find it, call the gas company and they'll be happy to come out and relight it for you."

"Okay. Are you all right, Jack? You sound a little . . ."

"I'm fine."

"Jeremy! Okay, Jack, call your son." And she hung up.

Jack reached for the green bottle of Excedrin he kept within reach of his bed. While he tucked the phone into its cradle he popped the top with his free hand, tilted the bottle back, and dry-chewed the first two bitter pills that fell into his mouth.

The phone rang again.

"What!"

"Did my ex-wife just call you?" It was Kenny Ortega, laughing on the other end of the line.

"Un . . . fucking . . . canny," Jack said, a little embarrassed he'd gotten caught on the short end of his emotions. "You kill me, Ortega."

"I can read you like a book, Bertolino. Anyway, your tone was male, primal, and all lawyers' guns and money. Speaking of which, are you hooked up with an attorney?"

"Tommy's on the case. He offered to fly here, but I told him to keep his powder dry until I sorted a few things out."

"Okay, here's what I got. Alvarez started bawling when I told him about Mia. Jabbering in Spanish, carrying on. I couldn't understand a word he was saying and I *habla*."

"Did you believe him?" Jack asked.

"It was Oscar worthy."

"Judas cried too. What does that prove?"

"I'm just saying." But Jack knew Kenny wasn't convinced.

"Has he been getting many visitors?"

"Mia was a regular up until a month ago. Did you know she hung in with him after we closed down the case?"

That made Jack think. "Didn't have a clue."

"Strange, and no one else has asked him to the prom yet, but someone claiming to be part of his legal defense team visited twice in the past three weeks. Name didn't match any of the partners or associates. I've got a blurry image we're trying to match with a name. The man was aware of the cameras and tried to obscure his face.

"And it looks like Mia was planning a permanent move, Jack. She shut down her penthouse and all of her bank accounts. We're trying to follow the money, but the banks aren't being forthcoming. Speaking of which, I had a conversation with the owner of the house on Vista Haven and his buddy Greg Stavos. Didn't have much of value. Greg was the connection. Said Mia wasn't hurting for cash. Picked up a three-hundred-dollar lunch at Escopazzo and offered to write a check for the guest room. He said Michael turned down the offer. Must be nice."

"Do we think Alvarez is still running his game from the inside?"

"That's affirmative . . . word is, Alvarez's developed a relationship of convenience with the Mexican Mafia. Protection and whatever. Drugs are probably running in both directions. Can't keep a good entrepreneur down.

"Hey, have you rung up Gene McLennan? He's retiring at the end of the year but still firmly in the game out on the West Coast. He's a good resource. I remember you two got along on that task force deal."

"He's on my list," Jack said. "Can you e-mail me that picture of Alvarez's visitor? Maybe I can ID him."

"I'll scan and forward it. I should have more on Mia posthaste. FYI, a lot of the men here feel terrible you're jammed up and are willing to work off the clock to do whatever they can."

"Thanks, brother."

"*Hasta* la bye-bye. Fight the good fight, Bertolino." And Ortega clicked off.

12

Gene McLennan had just gotten off the phone with Kenny Ortega from the Miami field division. Ortega gave him a heads-up regarding Bertolino's issues, and he agreed to meet Jack at Phillipe's on Alameda Street in Chinatown. He'd let him pick his brain while he got to eat one of the best French dip sandwiches known to man. One of the few things he was going to miss about L.A.

Gene wasn't sure if he was just asking for trouble getting involved, but he remembered Bertolino as being a stand-up guy. He didn't buy his involvement with the murder, but it was still a dirty business and blowback was a bitch. With two months left to his full retirement, Gene didn't need any bumps in the road. But he'd agreed, and Jack was on his way. He really had to learn how to say no.

He glanced out of his twentieth-floor window, admiring the view that ran across the L.A. skyline to the Hollywood Hills. Damn beautiful, he thought. But hell, the view from the lake house he had just purchased in Michigan a half hour outside of Detroit was nothing to sneeze at. It was a long-standing dream of his, and with the state of the economy, he'd gotten it for a song. Gene glanced at his watch and cranked it up a gear. If he didn't get a move on, he'd be late, and Gene McLennan prided himself on punctuality.

Four years had passed since the last time he'd seen Bertolino, who had headed up the New York Drug Enforcement Task Force. A heroin case called Liquid Death overlapped with the L.A. office, and they'd hit it out of the park.

The Mexican cartels had been hiring mules in California and sending them on eight-day, all-expense-paid cruises to the Mexican Riviera. When the *Princess* cruise ship docked in Cabo San Lucas for an afternoon of duty-free shopping, the women were met at the open-air market by cartel operatives who handed each woman a bag of dresses to transport back to San Pedro with their own personal belongings.

The dresses had all been dipped in liquid heroin.

The women were paid a modest sum, and the dresses were boxed and shipped to New York City, where the cartel's chemists would leach out the drugs.

Bertolino had built the case in New York from a single phone number and shared the glory with the feds in L.A. They brought cruise ships to the forefront as a viable means of smuggling drugs and forced the cruise ship industry to tighten its security policies. Gene knew Jack was looking for a little payback, and if he could accommodate, he would. Up to a point.

The two men made small talk while they moved slowly in one of four lines toward the glass-and-stainless-steel food cases. The women who carved the meat behind the counter had been working there since forever and still managed to smile. Jack got the lamb, and Gene the pork. Both ordered theirs double dipped, with macaroni salad, and pickles on the side.

Phillipe's was a California icon that'd been in business since 1908 and in Chinatown since the fifties. They were said to have created the French dip sandwich, and no one who had ever eaten there would argue the point. Gene steered Jack toward the rear of the restaurant, past the timeworn, scarred communal tables, and was lucky enough to grab one of the booths for a little privacy.

He glanced across the table. "You look like shit."

"And that's just on the fucking outside," Jack said as he took a bite of his sandwich and audibly sighed. "This is damn good. So how about you?"

"Well, I don't think about sex every fourteen seconds anymore. That opens up a few things."

"Is that where wisdom comes in?" Jack asked.

"We'll see . . . so talk."

Jack quickly switched gears, getting down to business. "My feeling is, if it was a cartel hit, there would have been some kind of chatter. We've still got people set up in the office, but Ortega said it's been business as usual. If it was local, I need help."

The "office" was the central clearinghouse the cartels used to set up and coordinate drug and money-laundering cells throughout the United States. If the cartels discovered a "sickness" in any one of the cells—if the cops or feds were on to them—the office was responsible for moving the players to a cell in another state, or if the cell was totally compromised, back to Colombia.

"This is under the auspices of professional courtesy," Gene warned. "I could get hung out to dry if this goes public."

Jack was fighting for his life and Gene was worried about being politically correct. Jack kept his face blank and let the man talk.

"In April of this year the Organized Crime Drug Enforcement Task Force pulled a RICO on a Latino gang down in Ontario. We had fifty indicted and picked up twenty-seven. I wasn't happy with the numbers. Anyway, what I thought was interesting was the gang. They call themselves the 18th Street Angels. Cute, huh? They specialize in meth and heroin smuggled up from Mexico. They've been in business and controlling Ontario for fifty years now."

"Fifty years? Doesn't seem right," Jack said, pissed off.

"They're ingrained, like the IRA. It's multigenerational. They start recruiting kids in middle and high school. Nice guys who'd steal your skin before you knew you were standing there bleeding out.

"Needless to say, a lot of their brothers are enjoying life on the state's tab. So these scumbags provide the drugs to their incarcerated members."

"Right," Jack said, hoping he'd get to his point.

"So, when we rounded up the gangbangers, we not only got meth, weapons, vests, marijuana, and heroin—you know, the usual—we picked up four keys of Dominican cocaine."

That bit of information got Jack's full attention.

"Now, the Mexican cartels are creating a bloodbath south of the border," Gene went on. "Los Zetas are fighting the Sinaloa cartel for control of the smuggling routes into the Southwest, creating a lot of heat and leaving a trail of bodies. These are violent pricks. The Zetas are ex-Mexican Special Forces—deserters—who used to provide security for the Gulf cartel and now want a bigger piece of the pie. No, let me amend that. They want the whole pie."

"So, someone on the East Coast could be trying to fill the vacuum, circumnavigating Mexico's reach and providing the drugs," Jack said.

"Dangerous proposition," Gene added.

Jack thought about Alvarez doing business behind bars and wondered about a possible connection.

"And then, I don't know if it's pertinent," Gene went on, "but the guy who runs the 18th Street Angels is also a member of the Mexican Mafia. They have three or four crossover members."

That piqued Jack's interest. "Alvarez is paying protection money to the Mexican Mafia. I don't know. It could be something. Worth looking at."

Gene looked pleased.

"I could eat another sandwich," Jack said, picking at the macaroni salad.

"Let's give my Lipitor a run for its money. Same?" Jack nodded and Gene rose from the booth.

Jack watched Gene make his way past patrons holding trays

filled with food, looking for seating, busmen cleaning tables, moving with ease across the long wooden floor. The sound of clanking glasses, dishes, silverware, and loud voices enjoying the old-world ambience and comfort food filled the busy room.

Gene had always been a natty dresser, and the navy pin-striped suit he wore must have set him back a few. He was starting to look his age, Jack thought. Good, but older. His fine brown hair was thinning on the top and dusted with gray on the sides. His blue eyes were still lively but never without his wire-rimmed bifocals. His six-foot frame was still lean, but a slight stoop was creeping in, as if he was carrying a weight and the weight was winning.

But Gene might be on to something, and Jack was grateful for the help—for any help he could get. He knew how office politics played out. Gene was putting himself on the line.

Jack's own career had been cut short, or at least detoured, because the NYPD thought he'd been federalized. His boss at the time thought if there was a choice on a case between supporting the feds or the NYPD, Jack Bertolino would go federal, which couldn't have been further from the truth. Jack just believed you had to give to get in building a case, and so he traded intelligence with the DEA and the FBI when needed, and it came back to him threefold. His arrest record had been second to none. But when Jack was up for a well-deserved promotion, instead of retaining him in narcotics, where he had more than proved his worth, the powers that be transferred him to the Housing Authority.

A Housing assignment could have been a career ender, and Jack seriously considered quitting the force. But because of what he had endured as a kid, nothing was going to stop him. And no Italian-hating drunken boss was going to keep him from succeeding.

Jack eventually rose to the top of his profession. In a dazzling display of poetic justice, he was assigned to run a crew of 220 men and women comprised of DEA, NYPD, and state police.

Jack always felt that what didn't kill you made you stronger, but the circumstance he now found himself in was one daunting challenge.

Mia had been dead for a little over forty-eight hours, and Jack was feeling anxious again—feeling the pressure of the ticking clock. He was well aware that the odds of finding the killers diminished with every hour that passed. He'd make short work of his second French dip and hit the road before he got stuck in the afternoon commute on the 10.

Jack had to check on those keys. Discovering where they fit was his next stop.

13

It was like winning the lottery, Jack thought as he pulled into 1573 Franklin Street and the home of his locksmith, Bundy Lock and Key. The trip took a mere twenty-five minutes.

He'd developed a relationship with Cruz Feinberg, who had tried to talk Jack into investing in a high-tech security system for his loft, but in the end settled on installing a Primus cylinder into his Schlage front door lock. The young man was dark, quick witted and good-looking. His mother was Guatemalan and his father, who'd founded the business, was Jewish.

The lock had started sticking a few months after installation, and when Jack called for a repair, he was told by whoever was on duty at the time that it would cost close to $240 for the service call and the repair. Before Jack could let loose with a series of expletives, Cruz picked up an extension line and put Jack at ease with, "Put a little WD-40 on your key, work it in and out of the lock a few times, and you'll be good to go."

It had worked and Jack was a fan.

He had never been to Cruz's shop, and he wasn't disappointed. Every safe on the market, from a small, file-size portable to a three-ton built-in solid steel job that could protect a small fortune, was on display on the tight showroom floor. The full back wall was a thick sea of keys, every make, model, color, and size. There were four machines to cut the keys, and an older gentleman in a plaid shirt was in the process of doing just that. The sound was shrill and sparks were flying like a Fourth of July sparkler as the man made short work of cutting a key. He turned as Jack opened the front door, setting off a buzzer.

"Afternoon. Is Cruz in?" Jack asked.

"Cruz," the man yelled and started grinding another key.

Jack could live without small talk, and so he wasn't put out by the brusque response. He spun the dial on the big safe a few times as Cruz walked in from the back room.

"Can I help you?"

"Cruz, I'm Jack Bertolino . . . ," he shouted over the noise.

"Oh yeah, I remember, the New York cop."

"Ex-cop," Jack reminded him.

"Right. How are you? What can I do for you? How's the lock? Still sticking?"

"No, and I appreciated the help. I was hoping you might be able to help out again."

At last the older man finished cutting the key.

"My father always said knowledge equals dollars," Cruz said.

"I thought it was knowledge equals power," Jack countered.

"Dad thought money and power were the same thing. I chose not to argue the point."

"Smart man."

Jack pulled out the keys from Mia's suitcase and laid them on the wooden counter.

"I found them in a suitcase and was wondering . . ."

"Why they didn't open the suitcase?"

"Yeah," Jack said, wanting him to go on.

"They look pretty much the same, but these are P.O. box keys. I can't make copies of them if that's what you want. I could lose my license."

"No, that's all right. I need to know if there's any way to trace the location of the post office box?"

Cruz's eyes widened with interest. "You working a case?"

"I could use some help."

"Wish I could, but there are hundreds of locations. We've installed more than our share, but I'd need something to go on. If you could give me a general area? But even then."

Jack flagged the Brentwood, Sherman Oaks area and Cruz promised to do a little research. It was worth a try. Jack left his card.

———————

The Mustang's Bluetooth device rang, and Jack punched the Answer button as he made the left turn off Washington onto Glencoe and hit the gas.

"Jack . . ."

"Tommy, I hope you have some good news."

But before he got an answer, Jack could see three black-and-whites and two unmarked black detective rides parked in front of his building, lights flashing. A small crowd had gathered, and another small crew was standing across the street in front of Bruffy's Tow and Police Impound.

"An arrest warrant has been issued in your name, and a Judge Yamashira approved a search of your premises."

"I can see that. Should I keep driving?"

Tommy didn't even dignify the question with a response.

"I'm on my way to the airport. I'll be in L.A. before you're processed."

Jack didn't know what to say. He couldn't hear himself speak over the pounding of his heart, in any case. He could see the first news van slide to a stop across the street and felt the vibration of a news helicopter flying overhead. He drove the last half block in silence.

Tommy continued. "The preliminary DNA report came in, and there were no surprises there. We were expecting to take a hit."

"I could have used a few more days," Jack said as he made a right turn into the building's driveway, hit the remote, and as the gates swung open, drove past two uniforms, who immediately got on the phone.

"Do not say word one, Jack. To anybody about anything. Now, is there anything else I should be aware of?"

"No, let them look. Could you please put in a call to Jeannine and Chris? I don't want them to hear this secondhand."

"Done."

"I'm gonna lose you, Tommy. I'm going into a dead zone."

Jack hit the Off button and parked in his space. He had barely slid out of the car when he was met by the two patrol officers he'd passed on his way in. Bertolino locked the car with his remote key and walked into the lobby while one of the uniforms called for the elevator.

Jack was seriously pissed off by the time the elevator got to his floor and he saw that the cops were already crawling all over his loft. As he crossed the threshold he noticed that the jamb hadn't been broken, and the safety lock and handle were still intact. He charged into the room.

"How the hell did you get in?" he said through clenched teeth, moving threateningly toward Gallina. The lieutenant jumped off the stool he was sitting on, prepared for battle. Tompkins ran up from behind and threw a bear hug around Jack, who was knocked off balance, but still managed to pull the detective down onto the concrete floor as he fell.

Two uniforms jumped into the fray and cuffed Jack as he pulled back a fist to slam Tompkins while his partner recited the Miranda, his voice rising in pitch with his adrenaline. Tompkins jumped up, dusted off his suit, and looked like he wanted to punch Jack in the chops while he was in restraints.

"You happy, Bertolino?" Gallina shouted. "We're trying to do this by the fucking book and you're going all rabid on us. Now calm the fuck down."

"How did you get in?"

"The fucking door was cracked open," Gallina said, waving the search warrant in Jack's face. "It was all by the numbers."

"My door was locked."

"Well, I have nine other officers who would beg to differ. Sit down while we complete the search, or we can take you in *now*. Your call."

Jack sat on the edge of his couch so that his cuffed hands wouldn't push against the back of the sofa and work against him. He did a quick visual check of the loft. All of the drawers and cabinets in the kitchen were standing open. Some of the drawers had been pulled out and were sitting haphazardly on top of the counter. A detective wearing latex gloves was examining and tagging the kitchen knives and placing them in a box for transport.

A detective popped his head out of the bathroom. "You gotta see this, Lieutenant. He's got a damn pharmacy in here."

He could hear another pair of cops going through his office, but they were out of Jack's field of vision.

Tompkins glared at Jack as he walked past him, over to the built-in bedroom closet. He did a cursory examination of the hanging dress shirts, which he grabbed in a compressed pile and threw on Jack's bed, which had been stripped. He rifled through the shoe rack, checking the inside of each shoe, and came up empty. Then he stooped down and slid out two heavy plastic containers from the bottom shelf, which held Jack's tools. He pried off the white plastic tops and tossed them onto the bed next to the shirts. The small opaque plastic boxes contained an assortment of screwdrivers, hammers, pliers, rasps, vise grips, saws, blades, nuts, and bolts, the usual stuff.

Tompkins started inspecting the second container and got very quiet. He lifted the container, stood up straight and tall, and did a slow turn. The entire room picked up on his energy, stopped whatever they were doing, and stood watching in anticipation.

———

Arturo Delgado was enjoying himself from his eighteenth-floor vantage point as he watched the quick response his phone call to the LAPD's anonymous tip line had generated. He was the architect of the scene that was unfolding before his eyes. He stood with his eye to the telescope, watching one of the detectives pick apart the barbecue grill on Bertolino's balcony. Then he watched the detective dig his hands into the soft soil of the tomato plant—being thorough but wrong. Frustrated at not finding anything, he ripped the plant out of the pot and flung it on the metal balcony floor.

And then the detective made an exacting turn toward the inside of the loft, a hunter downwind of his prey.

"There," Delgado whispered as he saw a flurry of movement behind the reflective sliding glass door of the loft.

Detective Tompkins set the plastic storage container on the prep island in the kitchen area. He carefully reached in with a latex-gloved hand and pulled out a retractable utility knife. The exposed razor blade was clearly covered in dried blood, which had also dripped onto the handle.

He held it up for the entire room to witness and then carefully placed the weapon back into the container. Another cop started snapping digital photos of the utility knife, the toolbox, and then the closet where the container had been secreted.

Jack strained against the cuffs. His back began to spasm, and he was having difficulty breathing. Every eye in the room was trained on him with the intensity of a red laser on the end of a silenced automatic pistol.

Delgado watched Jack Bertolino being led out of his building in handcuffs. He reveled in Bertolino's reflexive head twitch away from the pulsating strobe lights of the reporters' cameras.

But this was just the beginning. Arturo wouldn't stop until Bertolino had lost the will to live. Until the people who once loved Jack and called him a friend would shake their heads in disgust. Delgado wouldn't sleep through the night until the Bertolino name left nothing but a stench.

14

It started as a light sprinkle but quickly turned into a downpour. The homeless man tried to batten down the hatches as he tightened one edge of the blue tarp that served as his lean-to's roof. The rain pounded the waterproofed tarp like the hail balls he remembered from his youth growing up in rural Texas.

The small, sandy island in the middle of the Los Angeles River had served as his home for the past three months, and it suited his solitary nature. He'd had enough of folks to last him a lifetime.

The last man, who had called this little island home, had died in his sleep. Jerry wasn't sure how. He had been walking by with his shopping cart when he noticed the commotion. When all the emergency trucks left, he moved in. He'd needed a few weeks of scavenging to furnish the plot, but it was well worth the effort, he thought.

His small fire was extinguished as the torrent of water blew the tarp's overhang into the small pit and the can of Sterno where he prepared his food. Jerry went with the flow and wrapped a blanket tighter around his stiff body and watched God's miracle. The amber security lamps that ran along the concrete river channel provided the only illumination. The reflected light seemed to dance as the river grew from a trickle to a rapidly moving force of nature.

The rhythmic sound of the rain and a pint of Thunderbird lulled Jerry to sleep. For how long, he had no idea. But when he woke, the black night was turning into a dark gray sunrise as the rain continued to pour down.

After he got his bearings and rinsed the sleep from his eyes with rainwater, he assessed his situation. The island had seriously eroded during the night, and that could create some problems. Jerry couldn't swim. He'd heard stories of people being stranded like this and ending up drowned, but he hadn't paid them any mind until now.

A man still had to eat, and as he was reaching for a can of tuna, packed in oil the way he liked it, he saw something protruding out of the sand about fifteen yards to his left between two scrub bushes and the fast-moving current. A thick object meticulously wrapped in a plastic drop cloth and bound with duct tape. Someone had taken care, and the package looked to be the size of the leg of lamb his great-aunt used to make after Easter Sunday mass.

Jerry, exposed to the rain, ran the few yards, his feet sinking into the wet sand, and grabbed up the heavy, fat package. He was drenched before he stooped into the precarious safety of his lean-to shelter. He sat on a small wooden stool he had picked up from the remnants of a garage sale, and went to work on the package with the pocketknife that had been his friend going on twenty years.

He made one long slash down the side, but when he pulled back the plastic, he instantly dropped the parcel. He fought to keep a wave of vomit down that was threatening to erupt. Jerry sprang up from the stool, ripping the tarp off its tether, and stood with the rain pouring down his head and face.

He didn't want to look again but couldn't stop himself. The open flap of the plastic drop cloth revealed what was once a man's thigh. The desiccated flesh was covered in gang tattoos. The exposed bone, cut clean, was the color of ivory.

15

He clearly had nothing to smile about, but Bertolino couldn't fight the urge. In his experience, the only men who could sleep in holding cells were guilty as sin.

Jack had busted one cop who was making trips down to Washington, D.C., every two weeks with six or seven keys of coke. He was making eight grand a month in cash on top of his salary as a police officer, a healthy living. Jack busted the cop's ass doing a wiretap that overlapped another case. Although the cop was caught with the drugs in his car, he claimed his innocence. The dirty cop was in the holding tank for a grand total of twenty minutes before Jack was called down to check out the scumbag. The man was snoring like a chain saw.

In Jack's case, sleep deprivation and the rhythmic pounding of the storm did the trick. Jack got a good five hours before he woke up with a splitting headache. He reached for the Excedrin bottle and then remembered the nightmare that had overtaken his life.

The first thing he saw when he opened his eyes was I SUCK BIG DICKS and a phone number scratched into the smudged beige wall of his jail cell. For a man who had spent twenty-five years of his life working for the NYPD, the injustice of being isolated in this cage was almost more than he could comprehend.

The only thing Jack was sure of was that someone kept setting him up.

Someone had alerted the police to the fact that he had spent more time than reported up on Vista Haven, and now someone had planted evidence, and alerted the cops that the bogus murder weapon was hidden in his loft. Jack would have to find out who was taking such an active interest in his life.

The list of possibilities was extensive. If you were active on the job, you made enemies, on both sides of the thin blue line.

He knew that whoever had picked the lock on his front door was good. The lock was high tech and would have been difficult for anyone but a professional to breach. He wanted the techs to check it for fresh scratch marks.

But if they were professionals, why would they leave the door open other than to expedite the search? The bust would have been more powerful if the door had been locked up tight.

Plus, the door was exposed to the entire loft building across the way, so someone might have witnessed the break-in. He made a mental note to have Tommy check with the HOA at his building. Security cameras that might have picked something up had recently been installed in the parking structure and the lobby. Jack had been too scattered to mention it during his arrest and processing.

Jack's body was screaming for a strong cup of coffee to kick-start his brain, but he dismissed that thought. He wasn't going to be catered to. He'd have to wait for the breakfast tray like any other inmate. Then he'd be able to experience, firsthand, what his tax dollars were paying for.

As Jack sat on the hard jail bench, he had a gut feeling that he should discover the source of the cocaine found in the raid in Ontario. Cutting into the Mexican cartel's turf was a risky business. The Sinaloa cartel operating out of Baja was in a pitched battle with Los Zetas for control of Mexico's Gulf Coast and the Tijuana smuggling routes into the border city of San Diego. Twenty-eight men had recently been gunned down along Highway 15. The dead bodies of the Zetas had been dressed like military commandos, and they'd been armed to the teeth.

To throw your hat into that ring sounded like Colombian hubris to Jack. The only name that floated to the surface was an old nemesis, Arturo Delgado. But Delgado had been in the wind for a long time. It might just have been some cocky independent contractor. He'd have to get Ortega on it—if his arrest didn't stick.

Could Mia have been killed to set up Jack, or had he unwittingly stepped into her plot and become embroiled out of convenience? An opportunistic crime. That was the question gnawing at his gut.

Alvarez, after all, had the motive to go after both Mia and Jack. Mia had set him up, and Jack had knocked him down. But Bertolino wasn't sure after five years behind bars that Alvarez alone still had enough juice to pull it off. Jack needed to see the picture of the man who had visited Alvarez on two separate occasions, using a false identity. Maybe some puppet master was orchestrating the entire affair. The police had confiscated Jack's cell phone, so even if Kenny had forwarded the picture it was a moot point until he got out. Or make that if he got out.

His scalp started tingling, and Jack ran his fingers roughly through his hair as he relived being led out of the loft building in handcuffs, past neighbors, past print and television reporters who were peppering him with questions, lights, and cameras.

He was more worried about his son than himself. It's not as if the boy needed any more pressure. Boy, Jack thought . . . he was a man. Jack remembered his own first year of college. Away from the neighborhood and his family, he'd felt like a fish out of water and didn't last long. He dropped out in his second semester and floated for a few months before he enrolled in the police academy. He hoped Chris would have better luck.

Jack needed to get back out on the street ASAP, but he knew the wheels of justice never moved fast enough when you were on the wrong side of the steel bars.

Tommy Aronsohn's flight had been delayed because of the storm, and after circling the airport for three hours, he'd been forced to land in San Francisco. Tommy had rented a car and was probably blasting down I-5, pedal to the metal. He should be arriving in the Los Angeles area sometime in the afternoon.

The only message Tommy had been able to pass along to Jack was, "Zip it."

"You've gotta be kidding me. This is bullshit. The blood work came back positive," a red-faced Lieutenant Gallina said with a mixture of outrage and defensiveness.

Gallina was standing in front of a long, burnished table in the conference room at the district attorney's offices. Tommy Aronsohn was sitting at the far end next to Leslie Sager, the deputy district attorney, who occupied the power seat at the head of the table. Jack was seated on a bench outside the room but could be seen through a glass window.

Jack enjoyed watching his friend work. He didn't think it was an accident that the security blinds had been left open.

Aronsohn was in his midforties, with a ruddy complexion, broad shoulders, and short curly brown hair. He had expressive eyes and an easy youthful smile that could turn dark on a defendant's lie. And when they did, you didn't want to be sitting on his witness stand. His slight New York accent was accompanied by a full-blown New York attitude. But this was the DDA's show, and Tommy, ever the gentleman, deferred to Leslie Sager.

"But it wasn't the murder weapon," Leslie said firmly. She was in her early thirties, with shoulder-length blond hair. Her wide-set hazel-brown eyes drilled the lieutenant, and her manicured nails tapped the tabletop to accentuate her point.

"When did *you* become a CSI?" Gallina fired back.

"Watch your tone with me," she said with enough attitude to

make the detective pause. "Molloy said that a four-inch blade was used to make the deep, clean cuts to the victim's neck. The woman was almost decapitated, for chrissakes. Plus, there was a nick on the victim's sternum unique to the murder weapon, caused by an anomaly on the blade. The utility knife found in Bertolino's loft had a razor blade with a quarter-inch throw. Molloy said you'd be hard-pressed to cut a chicken wing with it."

"So he tossed the four-inch blade," Gallina said, grabbing for straws.

Aronsohn couldn't hold back any longer.

"All technicalities aside, Lieutenant, you didn't have any questions at all about a decorated ex-NYPD inspector storing the alleged murder weapon in his toolbox? A toolbox that was clearly marked blades and small tools. For what? So he wouldn't forget where he put it? Sentimental value? In case he ever needed it again? Does it make any sense at all that he would have walked away from the damning evidence and left his door unlocked for the police to . . . what?"

"Crisis of conscience," Gallina offered impotently. "Some people want to get caught."

Tommy looked incredulous. "And how did you know to look for the planted weapon in Inspector Bertolino's loft?"

"It was a tip."

"What?"

"A tip." The word barely made it past his lips.

"Anonymous?"

Gallina could only nod.

The deputy district attorney instantly picked up Tommy's train of thought. "Can you trace the tipster?"

"The call came from a clean phone into our anonymous tip line. That, with the DNA from the rape kit, was enough for a warrant approved by DDA Becker and Judge Adison. And please, let's not forget, Bertolino lied about having sex with the victim."

"He did not lie. He refused to answer the question," Tommy said, restraining himself and letting Leslie continue her assault.

"So, what do you think now?" she demanded.

"It could have been a setup. Jury's still out," Gallina said.

"It stinks and you know it."

Leslie Sager let that hang in the air. Then she dropped the bomb.

"Try this on for size, Lieutenant. This came across my desk this morning. If you hadn't been so busy patting yourself on the back, you might have seen it."

The DDA opened a manila envelope and pulled out a nine-by-twelve photo of a ghoulish severed thigh. "This body part was found on an island in the middle of the L.A. River." She pushed the photo across the table to Lieutenant Gallina.

The severed tattooed thigh had been photographed on a stainless steel examination table under a harsh light.

"A homeless man had the joy of discovering this and almost drowned because of it. When the local cops pulled him out of the drink, the man was hysterical. He'd run off the island and almost got swept away during the storm." She glanced down at the photo. "It's a human thigh. Gang markings. Clean cut. Same depth of blade as at Vista Haven. There's a nick on the femur identical to the one left on our female victim." Her lips pinched together hard as she delivered the final blow to Gallina's "case."

"Molloy's crew did a preliminary dating that put the body part in the ground before Bertolino moved to Los Angeles."

There was an extended silence in the room. Gallina glanced over his shoulder through the glass window at an unshaven Bertolino, sitting expectantly on the bench in the hallway. Gallina, resigned, broke the silence.

"Who's gonna handle the press?"

"That would be you, Lieutenant. You're going out in front of the cameras with hat in hand. It's an ongoing investigation. We'll get to the bottom of it. You're sure Mr. Bertolino understands the gravity of the crime and that he had to be eliminated from the process because he was the last person to see the victim alive . . . et cetera." Her voice remained icy as she listed the other consequences.

"Apologies to Mr. Bertolino and his family for any inconvenience that might have occurred because of the overzealous press coverage. Plus, if he sues, Gallina, you can stand before the city council and explain why they shouldn't pay him damages because of your rush to judgment."

Gallina didn't have anything to say, and the DDA finally let him off the hook.

"Thank you, Lieutenant. Please send in Mr. Bertolino on your way out."

Gallina stood frozen, assimilating all the new information before he accepted his fate. He nodded to the lawyers, then turned on his heel and left the room.

The lieutenant was now back to square one and not happy about it. He stopped next to Jack. "Ninety percent of the time it would have been you. You probably don't want to hear it, but I'm kind of glad it's not. Gives us all a bad name. But let us do our job, huh?"

Gallina tilted his head toward the conference room. "They're ready for you now."

That was the apology.

Jack stood, stretched his back a few cricks, and then entered the conference room. Tommy was smiling and the district attorney stood up to greet him.

"Jack, I'm Deputy District Attorney Leslie Sager, and I want to personally apologize for the terrible mistakes made." She extended her hand, and Tommy witnessed her demeanor and tone subtly change.

Jack walked the length of the conference table and took the proffered handshake. Her grip was firm.

"Accepted."

Tommy took over. "Now, first, Jack, I want to make it clear that you are free to go."

Tommy turned to Leslie and continued.

"Jack Bertolino is not litigious by nature. I, on the other hand—quoting your lead detective—well, my jury is still out. I'm sure you vetted me as I you on my erratic flight to the West Coast, so we're both up to speed as to our bona fides. But I just want you to understand the man you're dealing with.

"Whenever I found myself under the gun running the New York DA's office, really struggling with a complex issue, life and death, right or wrong, I'd ask myself a simple question: What would Jack Bertolino do?"

He paused to gauge the effect his words were having, and Leslie looked impressed.

"Now, whoever set Jack up for this horrible fall—we've got some serious issues that don't disappear when Jack walks out these doors. That party has a shitstorm coming. And I would hope that your office would help facilitate Jack in clearing his good name, and doing everything in your power to help him take these killers down."

Jack was feeling better than he had all morning as Tommy finished with:

"It's your call."

16

Jack keyed his door open and stopped in his tracks. The loft was a mess. Cops were great at deconstruction, but that was the extent of their expertise. Tommy continued into the kitchen area unfazed, as if he had just walked into a suite at the Plaza Hotel. He stowed a six-pack of Pacifico beer in the fridge.

"It's what half of New York and L.A. are going to look like when they turn sixty. It's not going to be pretty. They'll probably scare their grandkids clean."

Tommy was referring to the gnarly state of the tattoos on the severed thigh's wrinkled skin. He was enjoying himself after their victory.

"So, how about DDA Sager? Not too harsh on the eyes. They build them sweet out here on the left coast."

Jack was walking around the kitchen, closing drawers and assessing the damage. He walked into the office and laid down his laptop, which Gallina and crew had confiscated the day before. Jack was able to retrieve that, his phone, and his nine-millimeter Glock upon his release.

"Sager said they were going through the gang books," Tommy continued. "Maybe find a match on the ink. It's a place to start."

"Right," Jack said, preoccupied.

Tommy picked up on Jack's state of distress and tried to lighten his mood.

"Funny story. Very L.A., by way of Long Island. My brother-in-law was having trouble at work with a female manager. So, my sister tells him he needs to cleanse the energy in his office by burning sage. Well, my brother-in-law, ever dutiful, listened to his wife and first thing in the morning went into his office, closed the door, and burned a bundle of that crap." Jack had stopped to see where all this was going, and Tommy delivered the punch line. "Well, he came home from work that night looking like his puppy had just died. Turned out he almost got fired. The manager thought he was smoking pot in his office, and he had to do a dog-and-pony show to keep from getting shit-canned."

"That's funny," Jack said, but the smile never reached his eyes. "You saying I should burn some sage in here?"

"No, I'm saying you need a cleaning crew, and you need to relax."

"Tommy . . ."

"I know, I know, but they're not going to be happy if they catch you running your own investigation."

Jack had known Tommy would get to this sooner or later. "What would you do?"

"The same thing you're going to do," Tommy said lightly. "Look, I'll let you get settled, make a few calls. I booked a room around the corner at the Marina Ritz-Carlton. I'll check in, and we can grab some dinner later on if you're up for it."

"Sounds good. Thanks, Tommy."

"Later."

Jack walked him to the door and took the opportunity to crouch down and examine the lock. He could see minor scratches but nothing to indicate with the naked eye that the lock had been picked. That level of professionalism gave him no comfort.

Jack returned to his desk, booted up his computer, and tried to Skype his son, but got no answer. Jack hoped he was at practice and would try again later. He left an e-mail that he knew Chris would pick up on his cell, letting him know everything was fine, and checked a message from Kenny Ortega.

He had sent the info Jack wanted. He hit Play on the download and watched in black and white what appeared to be a well-dressed elderly gentleman, from the way he was walking, move through the reception area at the prison, well aware of the camera. The man tilted his head away, and the wide brim of his hat obscured most of his face. He had a prominent chin, and when Jack replayed the download, he realized that the man had a slight limp. That didn't ring any immediate bells.

Then he played the second download. This time the man exposed a little more of his face, but the blurry image was still not enough for a positive ID. The man's limp was less pronounced on this visit but still there, if you were looking for it.

He banged out a thank-you to Ortega, told him he wasn't able to ID Alvarez's visitor, and requested any information he could gather on the task force bust of the gang in Ontario. He also asked him to look into who was peddling Dominican coke on the West Coast. He was looking for any connection he could find to Alvarez.

Jack's land line rang, and when he checked the caller ID saw that it was from his ex-wife. He just couldn't handle her now and let the call go to voice mail. He dry-chewed a couple of Excedrin on his way to the bathroom, leaving a trail of the clothes he had slept in the night before. What he needed now was a long, hot shower.

Then he'd restore order to his home, and go after the men who were trying to destroy him.

17

Arturo Delgado sat on a wooden bench perched on a promontory with an expansive view of the white sandy beach and the dark blue Pacific Ocean. The sky had a smattering of wispy cirrus clouds, and there was a chill in the winter air. Venice Beach was normally too hectic for Arturo's taste, but late in the day, it was desolate in sections. The breeze blowing across the crisp blue water created small whitecaps and buffered whatever sounds were bleeding off the walkway, eclectic shops, and restaurants behind him.

Arturo was dressed to impress in a two-thousand-dollar black linen suit with a Panama hat worn low to obscure his face.

The long afternoon shadow of a man announced his presence. Arturo turned his head slightly and looked into the lifeless eyes of death.

Armando "Mando" Barajas stood as tall as his five-foot-three frame would allow. Two teardrops tattooed under his left eye spoke of murders committed, and his neck was awash in blue jailhouse tats that must have made his mother proud, Delgado mused. But he was unimpressed.

"That's how easy it can happen, *ese*. And then you become a ghost," Mando whispered with all the warmth of a lizard. "You're an old man in a young man's business," he continued. "Maybe your time has passed."

Mando hiked up his oversize white T-shirt from his baggy jeans, pulled a cloth handkerchief out of his back pocket, and used it to wipe off the section of the green wooden bench that he now claimed as his own. A learned behavior, bred in the exercise pens of the state prison system. He scanned the horizon, carefully folded the handkerchief, and slid it back into his pocket.

"Understand one thing, Mando, this is a relationship bred out of mutual need and mistrust. We both move forward at great personal risk," Delgado stated.

Mando's body tightened to the point of snapping as Delgado reached into his jacket pocket. He pulled out a flask of Macallan instead of a gun, unscrewed the metal cap, and took a sip. His first of the day, and more for effect than desire. He didn't offer the flask to Mando, who tried to cover his instinctive first reaction.

Delgado enjoyed Mando's discomfort almost as much as the eighteen-year-old scotch. In another life, he would never have met in person with a fucking punk like Mando. But the business had changed, and one had to stay agile in order to succeed these days. The 18th Street Angels controlled a valuable piece of Southern California real estate, and Mando, who was also a member of the Mexican Mafia, controlled the Angels. Arturo needed them both to make his plans come to fruition.

"I offer you one opportunity to make the Angels great," Delgado said as his attention was drawn to the billowing red, white, and blue spinnaker of a sailboat a quarter mile offshore.

"I'm . . . what does Obama call it?" Arturo asked, not expecting an answer. "Empire building."

"We can get product on the other side of the border," Mando said in a voice so low that if the man weren't so deadly, Arturo would have laughed out loud. The affectation of the emotionally stunted, he thought.

"But you'll always be under the thumb of Los Zetas. I offer you autonomy. Power. Control," he went on, in case Mando didn't know what "autonomy" meant. "But you only get more of my product, and your name in the history books, once you've proved yourself."

Delgado could feel the heat radiating off Mando, but he knew the small man was motivated by greed. That was good, because Delgado was about to get a lot harsher.

"Did it ever occur to your men to get Alvarez's financial statements from their target? Her iPad with his records, her passwords, any of that before they killed her?"

"The situation was handled as instructed."

"Not to my satisfaction and not to Alvarez's. Your people were inept," Arturo snapped, gloves off. "And Bertolino spends only one night in prison? Why? Because your men chose not to plant the bloody murder weapon, as ordered."

Mando winced at this remark, showing that he agreed. "Hector is an effective killer. He will be brought to heel, though."

"Get control of your men or I will find new partners."

Arturo waited until a family of four pedaled their bicycles down the concrete path that curved in front of them. He turned, and his own dead eyes bored into Mando's.

"Are we clear?"

The anger in the young man's face was quivering as he weighed his options. Delgado could see his hand reach toward the cloth handkerchief in his back pocket. That must be some signal to the assassins Mando had planted nearby. Instead, Mando decided to bide his time. Another skill developed behind bars.

A simple nod of his head was his reply.

"There are people close to you on the payroll of the DEA."

"Talk's cheap. Give me a name and it will be handled," Mando said, voice tight.

Delgado reached into his pocket again and pulled out a single Post-it with the name Ricky Hernandez and an address written on it. "No mistakes this time."

Mando pocketed the information without looking at it or Delgado.

"Afterward, if there are no fuckups, and your people are ready to move forward, the first shipment will be in transit. The second shipment is of a magnitude that will change your lives," Delgado said without the slightest trace of bravado.

"When?"

"When you have proved to me that the first batch of shirts made it to the cleaners without incident."

Delgado turned back to face the ocean.

The meeting was over.

As Mando stood up, seething at the insult, he could see his two armed gang members in flanking positions, ready to give up their own lives protecting his. And then his gaze moved beyond his men to a second-story rooftop.

A sniper.

Dressed entirely in cammo gear, holding a high-powered rifle with a telescopic sight trained directly on Mando.

"With age comes wisdom," Delgado said, sounding bored, not looking up as Mando walked heavily toward the safety of his men.

18

The drive from Ontario to Hollywood Boulevard took an hour on I-10 East, but Hector had a rare date, and Johnny wanted to show Angelina a good time. So they cruised the boulevard until they got bored, stopped in front of Grauman's Chinese and checked out the hand and footprints of famous movie actors, grabbed some slices of pizza and Cokes, and headed up Laurel Canyon Boulevard.

Hector loved the throaty sound his Chevy Impala's exhaust system made as it echoed off the canyon walls. Izel, his date for the night, was duly impressed with the car, but she hadn't made up her mind about Hector. He seemed angry, tight, distant, and although he had a reputation in the Angels for being a badass, Izel wasn't convinced theirs was a match made in heaven.

She applied another layer of thick black liner to her perfect almond-shaped brown eyes, which was no mean feat on the winding canyon roads. Izel angled the vanity mirror and could now see Johnny and Angelina making out in the backseat, his hand moving under her blouse. She could almost feel their heat.

Izel could have done Johnny. It was a mistake not to have made a move on the pretty boy, but she was a pragmatist and didn't dwell on the past. She knew a decision concerning Hector would have to be made before the end of the night, but if she was totally honest with herself, the decision had already been made. She wasn't feeling him.

Hector made a left onto Mulholland and, after a tight hairpin turn that threw Johnny across the backseat of the car, out of Angelina's embrace and into a fit of laughter, pulled off the road at a scenic overlook. A low wood fence kept tourists from falling off the edge, and a small dirt hillock afforded a spectacular view of the twinkling lights on the valley floor, spreading all the way to the San Bernardino Mountains.

Angelina pulled a chubby joint from her leather bag, took a huge hit, and blew the sweet smoke into Johnny's mouth. Then she passed it up to Izel, who took a hit and did a quick handoff to Hector.

Hector sucked in a lungful and seemed to let go a bit on the exhale, filling the car with pot smoke. He gave his date a look that left no question as to what he'd like her to do for him.

"How did you find this place?" Izel asked, hoping Hector didn't expect her to put out in the car.

"Doin' some business. Speaking of . . ." Hector opened his door and signaled Johnny out of the car. The two gangbangers walked up the hill and shared another hit of the pungent weed. Hector hiked up his baggy shorts and glanced over at the car to make sure they were out of earshot before getting down to business.

"You think I was going to leave *my* tools behind because some *pendejo* ordered me to? He don't own me. Hector don't take no orders. Hector's got the power."

Johnny knew better than to interrupt when his partner was on a rant. They were in some deep shit with powerful men who could order them killed. Johnny had received the call from Mando. Mexican Mafia Mando—no one to fuck with—used his low-talk voice, which was as deadly as a rattlesnake. Scared the shit out of him. Johnny had reassured the OG that no more mistakes would be made, and the Original Gangsta had fired back that no other mistakes would be tolerated.

Message received and delivered.

Johnny would let Hector vent now, but later, make sure orders were carried out.

"You know where the power comes from, homeboy?" Hector continued. "No fear. I been to hell and back. You just held the devil's cape," he added in a scornful aside. "So we'll do his business when it suits us, with respect on both sides, and kill him if it goes wrong, strike first." Hector's glare left no doubt that he would. "Now, Johnny, I got a call from Mando this afternoon. He wasn't happy, kept throwing that Delgado dude all up in my face, *ese,* but I talked him down."

This bit of news didn't make Johnny feel anything but dread and a stabbing pain in his gut.

"They found out who's the rat. It was no Angel—it was a contract player. Mando wants him done so every brother, all twenty-seven, know that we've got their backs, and everyone else knows not to fuck the Angels."

"Johnny," Angelina called out the back window.

"What?" Johnny snapped back in a tone that shocked them both.

"Hey, don't get crazy on my ass!"

Johnny looked at Hector, whose eyes were dark and vacant now, and nodded his head in assent. It was so ordered. There would be another body to haunt his dreams, destroy his sleep, and guarantee him a place in hell.

Hector took a last monster hit of the killer Mexican weed and then flicked the burning roach, sending it pinwheeling into the bone-dry brush below.

19

Jack was already seated at his favorite rear booth, which afforded him a view of the entire dining and bar area. He felt a smile form as Tommy walked through the door, spotted Jack, and tried to maneuver through the gauntlet of west siders waiting for a table. America might be suffering the greatest economic downturn since the Great Depression, but he was hard-pressed to tell from the eager crowd in Hal's.

Tommy reached the booth at the same time Arsinio, their waiter—who was a Hal's institution—arrived to take drink orders. Tommy was all over a twelve-year-old Dewar's on the rocks and Jack ordered the house cabernet. Tommy, still standing, made a sweeping, grand gesture as he pulled a manila envelope from under his arm like a broadsword from a scabbard. He slid it across the table, where it spun and came to rest directly in front of Jack. The two men bumped fists as Tommy settled into the booth across from his friend.

"Nice joint. Very Tribeca," Tommy said as he took in the art on the walls and the uptown women standing at the bar.

"I thought it would make you feel all warm and fuzzy."

Jack picked up the manila envelope and tapped it on the table, preoccupied.

"Are you going to play with it or look at it?"

Jack folded back the metal tabs and opened the envelope, sliding the contents onto the table. Out spilled a stack of official-looking documents with notarized seals. Jack picked up one particular laminated card and studied it carefully before laying it back down on the table.

A private investigator's license.

Jack's picture, his thumbprint, and his name, typed on the front, sealed in plastic, and sanctioned by the state of California.

"You've been busy," Jack said.

Tommy was pleased with himself and couldn't hold back. "Mayor approved, chief expedited. And hand-delivered by DDA Leslie Sager, who, by the way, inquired about your marital status."

"Why?"

"I asked myself the same question. Why you and not me?"

Jack stared Tommy down, amused, waiting.

"Because there's a recession and Los Angeles doesn't need any more bad news or, more to the point, major lawsuits. The mayor is trying to push through a billion-dollar subway system running underneath Wilshire Boulevard, and 90210 dilettantes are blocking him. The new police chief spoke very highly of you, and your record, and was ready to do anything it took to help out a retired inspector. I actually believed him."

"What am I going to do with it?"

"Stay out of trouble? It could help. A civilian doesn't stand a chance in your situation."

"Who's my client?"

"You're buying him dinner."

Jack wasn't fond of private investigators, but thought they were a necessary evil. A few of his cop friends had hung out shingles—international security work, missing persons, hostage negotiations, industrial espionage—but it was certainly nothing he aspired to. Still, he knew the license would lend him a measure of legitimacy as he moved forward with his investigation.

He could always shred the card the minute he was finished.

"Thank you, Tommy. This couldn't have been easy to pull off."

"Happy to cash in a few chits. You'd do the same and not think twice."

One of Tommy's specialties as a white-collar criminal defense attorney was representing targets, subjects, and witnesses in criminal investigations. As usual, he had exceeded expectations.

Arsinio arrived at their table doing a precarious balancing act with a tray full of cocktails.

Jack sat back in the booth and looked at the colorful Saturday-night crowd walking in tight knots on the sidewalk in front of the restaurant. Arsinio expertly moved a martini on the tray for balance and placed the dark amber scotch in front of Tommy.

As he reached for the red wine, Jack suddenly spied an older gentleman wearing a stylish large-brimmed hat. He walked past the front window, out of sight for a beat as he was obstructed by the wooden doorway, and then exposed again in the picture window on the right.

Jack's pulse quickened. He was certain the man had a slight limp, and for a split second the man glanced in Jack's direction and they locked eyes.

Jack launched himself up and out of the booth, knocking over the full glass of cabernet Arsinio had just set down.

Jack muttered, "Sorry," as he raced up the length of the room, fighting his way through the thick throng of patrons blocking his exit as the man disappeared from view. He finally cleared the door, pushed his way through the crowd of pedestrians in his path, and took off running down Abbot Kinney. Yet he had already lost his quarry.

Jack scanned the area in all directions as he sped past pedestrians window-shopping. He ran up one block, and then another, ducked in and out of retail shops. He checked both sides of the street and then spun, looking behind him in case the man with the hat had doubled back. Nothing.

Jack juked dangerously across the street, thick with traffic. Horns blared and expletives were yelled, but he was oblivious to the vehicles as he tried to visualize exactly what the man he had seen looked like and what he was wearing. An expensive, well-tailored black suit and a black wide-brimmed hat—the style of the man who had been videotaped visiting Alvarez. Jack couldn't be sure of the limp, but something about the man's gait had hinted at forced control. And then the eyes. Those eyes, too familiar, filled with pure hatred. Jack couldn't be sure, but he wouldn't rule it out.

No, Jack Bertolino was ready to bet the farm it was someone from his past.

Arturo Delgado.

———————

Tommy Aronsohn was standing by the curb in front of Hal's when Jack crossed the street. Jack filled him in on Delgado disappearing like smoke as they returned to their booth. Jack apologized profusely to Arsinio, who wasn't in the least bit fazed. He already had a fresh tablecloth laid for them. Tommy ordered a turkey burger with a Caesar salad, and Jack ordered the flank steak he hadn't eaten two nights before. Arsinio left them to work on their drinks.

"Delgado wanted me to know he was here. That I was in his crosshairs," Jack said angrily. "He's got a huge fucking ego. It's always been a game with him. One big chessboard." He shook his head, thinking about the scumbag. "Man never touched the product, never got his hands dirty. He was one hell of a tactician, but he lost and he wants payback. Simple as that."

"How long has it been?" Tommy asked.

"Six, seven years. I'm telling you, I've seen presidents age, first term in office—but if I'm right, Green Door cost him big-time. I mean this was one vital dude when I was hunting him. He was the best. He got away, but it looks like he paid for the loss." As Jack was talking, he was thinking through the implications. "My first impulse about Mia is that it wasn't a cartel hit. At least not directly. It was a personal vendetta. And somehow it was farmed out locally."

Something about that link didn't quite sit right. "Alvarez to Delgado—the puppet master? Maybe it was Delgado who hit paydirt and not Alvarez looking for a twofer. Mia might be dead because she contacted me. But if she was running, why? Did she rip off Alvarez? Makes sense. Did she rip off Delgado? Maybe. Someone's supplying Alvarez in prison. Delgado looks good for it. The Mexican Mafia might be protection and the delivery organization, but someone else is supplying the cocaine."

He was looking at too many questions, without enough answers. "I've gotta get my car checked out. I'm being followed and I drive with one eye on the rearview. He knows where I live; he may have been in my loft. Someone planted the utility knife. I've gotta get my loft, my computer, my phone swept for bugs and new locks put on the door."

Tommy saw something in Jack's eyes he hadn't seen in a while, the look he saw when they were first starting out in law enforcement, Tommy as an ADA and Jack as a rookie narcotics detective. When Jack had the "disease." When work, the rush, the pump transcended family, friends, and personal well-being.

"Gene McLennan was talking about a RICO bust down in Ontario," Jack continued. "Entrenched street gang called the 18th Street Angels with a few crossover members in the Mexican Mafia. They picked up a litter of the scumbags and were surprised to find four keys of Dominican cocaine."

He nodded as he expressed his thought process aloud. "Alvarez is starting to look good for the product. Could be payment for the contract on Mia. Anyway, I'm thinking another look at Vista Haven, then Ontario's a place of interest. Check out their turf so I know what I'm dealing with."

"My rental car's clean," Tommy offered. "Road trip?"

"How are you time-frame wise?"

"I've got a forty-eight-hour window."

Jack nodded in approval, swirled his cabernet around in his glass, and took a deep drink, happy to have a friend like Tommy. He felt good about that, but something else was barging in on him.

It was too close to the death of Mia. He wouldn't admit it even to himself. But it was there, right below the surface.

He was back in the game.

20

Johnny wasn't going to get any sleep. The blackout shades weren't going to help. The problem wasn't the pot or the coke or the booze. And he'd definitely fucked his brains out. That usually did the job.

Angelina, wearing his mirrored aviator sunglasses and nothing else, innocently asked him where he got the handcuffs, and Johnny's head started spinning. He jumped out of bed with a fading hard-on, said he had to take a piss, and threw cold water on his face, but it didn't help.

Not getting rid of the cuffs when he smashed the cell phone and threw the pieces into the reservoir was a bone-headed move. Maybe his father was correct. Maybe he wasn't worth an ounce of shit.

The truth was, Johnny was afraid. Not for the first time in his life, but maybe the most intense fear he'd ever experienced. The most of the most. He was caught in a full-blown panic attack.

Hector was scaring the living daylights out of him. Johnny hadn't signed up for any serial-killer shit. And Johnny realized there was no other reasonable way to look at the path his life had taken. And when it went south, which was where these things always went—end of the day—he wasn't even Richard Ramirez, Ted Bundy, or Juan fucking Corona. He was just the soldier who took orders from the general and killed the fuckin' kids and grandparents in their sleep.

At least his old buddies, who had made it out of the hood and landed their asses in Iraq or Afghanistan, they were at least sanctioned by the government to kill. Johnny knew that they weren't sleeping any better than he was. They came back more fucked up than when they left. They were all Johnny's clients now, buying his coke and meth and weed.

Angelina murmured, rolled over in bed, and her pale tattooed arm dropped lightly onto his chest. Johnny knew he couldn't stop his heart from pounding but tried to get control of his breathing, not wanting to awaken her. He didn't want to have to explain why he was still awake. Why he wore the mirrored sunglasses 24/7. Why his hazel eyes looked the way they looked when he didn't wear them.

Hell, he couldn't even face the truth himself.

After the third line of coke, the marijuana, and the beer, Izel had lost all inhibitions. She was numb, but she tingled. It was all sensual, all the time, and Hector's dick was just an extension of her high.

She was wet, hot, horny, and then, bang!

What?

The fat fuck had just hauled off and smacked her on the side of the head.

Hard.

She saw light clusters behind her eyes.

"Too much teeth, you fucking whore," Hector admonished.

Izel sobered on the hit and got her bearings for a second before she got smacked again. Harder.

She fought not to gag as he held her head with his meaty hands, tight, like a vise grip. And she fought not to cry. And then she fought to keep it down and swallow when he shot his load.

Hector made a few guttural grunts and moans before rolling over onto his side, exhaling, and falling into a deep drug-induced sleep.

Izel was afraid to breathe as she wiped her mouth and tears on the sleeve of her opened blouse. She left her panties on his side of the bed, afraid to make a sound as she silently slid into her jeans, grabbed her boots, and took off barefoot out of the garage, gaining speed as she rounded the corner of the house.

Izel ran for her life.

———————

Jack could read the tension and confusion on his son's face, and he felt like someone had driven a spike through his heart. He wanted to reach through the computer, wrap his big arms around the young man, and ease his pain.

"It's just human nature, and cops aren't immune to it. Taking the path of least resistance," Jack said, trying to be the voice of reason even though he was harboring evil thoughts about Gallina and Tompkins. "My grandpa used to say, anything that came too easily in life wasn't worth having. These detectives thought I looked good for the crime. Well, the setup was too easy and now they're probably feeling bad about their decision. It was bad law enforcement. That approach, and the glory hounds, used to really piss me off a lot. Now I just want to find the killer before he does it again."

"You think he will?" his son asked, trying to make sense of a crazy situation.

"You get away with it once, the second time comes easier. And in all honesty, this doesn't have the feel of a first."

"Why do you have to get involved?"

"What would you do if you were in my shoes?"

Chris paused for a moment, and then his intense young eyes blazed through the computer screen. "Find the killer, find out who set you up, and take 'im down."

That sudden burst of ferocity left Jack unable to speak for a moment.

"Mom's upset."

"I'll take care of your mother. Now shut down your computer, and don't worry about your mother or me. You've got enough on your plate. How was practice?"

"I'm working on it, Dad," he said, as if to say don't go there.

"That's all I ask. You know what I thought about, sitting in that jail cell?"

Jack watched his son shake his head no and marveled at the new technology and how full his heart felt.

"I thought about how lucky I was to have a son like you. My only fear was that I wouldn't be there for you."

Father and son stared through the computer screens and let that sink in. They enjoyed a comfortable silence.

"Love ya," Jack tossed out, like a fastball across the plate.

Chris laughed for the first time that night. "Ya got me."

"I'm just that good." And he clicked off of Skype and sat still for a moment, gathering his thoughts and his emotions.

Then he grabbed a yellow pad and pen and got to work.

Having Delgado in the hunt changed the equation. Jack knew he now had to watch his front, his back, and his reflection.

21

Jack stared at the open face of the handsome priest sitting in one corner of the Vatican, hearing confessions, and he questioned his motives for standing in the slow-moving line. He was caught up in the moment, he decided, intoxicated by Rome, awed by the majesty and opulence of the basilica, as simple as that.

The young man of God wore an unadorned black robe and sat facing a long line of supplicants. Not hiding behind a veiled burgundy curtain—acting as the conduit of heaven and earth—like the great Wizard of Oz.

When it was Jack's turn to be absolved of his sins, he knelt stiffly in front of the priest, feeling very exposed, and in a hushed tone stammered, "Bless me, Father, for I have sinned. It's been twenty years since my last confession."

"Two years, son?" the priest said, leaning forward, not sure if he had heard correctly.

"No, Father, twenty years," he said a little too loud this time.

The priest's brow furrowed for a fleeting moment. Then his laughter, like a set of tuned bells, pealed and echoed off the marble floor, the stone walls, and the exquisite objects of religious art in the cavernous room. In a thick Italian accent he forgave Jack and welcomed him back into the fold.

Jack woke up from his dream feeling surprisingly warm and comfortable.

Then he got his bearings and remembered that his own Catholic experience hadn't been as warm and fuzzy.

Jack had known too many Mafia chiefs and drug kingpins and dirty politicians who paid for stained-glass windows and pipe organs and Thanksgiving turkeys to gain a place at the head table—sitting shoulder to shoulder with cardinals and bishops and priests for holiday feasts. Drug money and the death it delivered was casually traded for the forgiveness of mortal sins and entrance to heaven's gates.

Jack sat up unsteadily, ran his fingers through hair that was sweat-plastered to his forehead, and reached for the ever present Excedrin bottle. He stumbled into the bathroom, and drank hungrily from the sink before tossing a few aspirin into the mix. He cocked his head back and swallowed, looking for the relief that he knew would be short lived if it came at all.

He scrubbed his face with a fury of hot soapy water and, knowing what the day entailed, decided against shaving. Jack was pulling a clean black T-shirt over his head when he was startled by a loud pounding on his front door. He clumsily stepped into a pair of jeans and fought to keep his balance as he shouted, "I'll be right there," knowing full well that whoever was banging on the thick metal door couldn't hear a damn thing he was saying.

That knowledge didn't stop Jack from yelling out a few more times as he crossed the concrete floor, in his bare feet, with a bad attitude, and yanked the door open, startling Cruz Feinberg, who stood there holding two cups of hot coffee. One cup was jostled as the door flew open, burning his hand.

"Dude, my hands are my meal ticket," he said, scowling. "Chill, you called me."

"How'd you get in?" Jack said, by way of apology.

Cruz's father was no joy to work with, so attitude didn't faze him. He walked past Jack into the loft.

"I'd tell you, but then you'd have to arrest me. Oh yeah, you're not a cop anymore," he deadpanned.

Jack grabbed a dish towel and traded it for one of the coffees.

Cruz flipped the dish towel back onto the counter and wiped his hand on his pants.

Jack had left an early morning message on Bundy Lock and Key's voice mail while he was yellow-padding in the wee hours, and it had totally slipped his mind. He wanted Cruz to secure the loft and check for bugs.

Cruz went downstairs into the garage to inspect the Mustang while Jack finished dressing and his haphazard grooming.

The kid already had the front door lock broken into pieces by the time Jack stepped out of the bedroom area, dressed and ready to face the day.

"Here's the deal," Cruz said. "First of all, nice ride."

Jack nodded. Cruz continued. "There's a bug secreted under the front-right panel of the car and another device attached to the left-rear wheel well that even Stevie Wonder could have found. That being the point, I think. They're generic devices, untraceable. Anyone could pull this equipment off the Internet. I can disengage them, you can go at them with a hammer, or you might be better off knowing that they know where you are. Might give you more control."

Smart kid, Jack thought. "I like the notion. Delgado wants to play chess . . . but then he'd be able to keep tabs on everyone I visited. I wouldn't want to endanger anyone and pull them unwittingly into his game. I'll still need a clean car he can't ID."

Chess was the way Jack had approached his career as a narcotics detective and a philosophy he had shared with his men—to always play chess and not checkers when building a case, always be thinking three moves ahead.

"Can't help you there, but I'll kill the bugs," Cruz said while inspecting the lock's cylinder.

"How long would it have taken for *you* to breach the door?"

"Three minutes max. But I'm special."

"Is that what your mother told you?" Jack asked, not happy with the number. If these men were specialists, nobody in the building across the way would have noticed anything out of the ordinary. With people moving in and out of the building, workmen were coming and going on a regular basis. He'd still canvas the building across from his on the off chance that someone had seen something meaningful.

"I was born with the knowledge. It's a Guatemalan thing," Cruz said without the slightest trace of irony. "I'm adding a second dead bolt that should slow down a professional."

"Slow them down?"

"If they're good, and they want to get in . . ."

"I'll need a few extra sets of keys. I want my son to have a set." Jack made a mental note to stick a key in an envelope for the afternoon mail.

"Done."

Cruz handed Jack the old lock cylinder and a jeweler's loupe. "Almost invisible unless you know what you're looking for."

Jack could see microscopic scratches near the tumblers. He felt his blood pressure rising. He made a mental note to copy Lieutenant Gallina on the evidence.

"I'll set you up with a camera," Cruz added. "If they break in again, at least you'll know who you're dealing with. You'll be able to access the loft from your computer when you're off-site. Speaking of which, I have a friend who works on the Geek Squad. He'll stop by in about an hour to check out your computer. And I called the security company that monitors the surveillance cameras in the lobby and garage area. They did the installation a month ago, but the HOA dragged its feet with the paperwork and it won't be activated until next week."

At least Jack knew where he stood on the home front. He also knew why Delgado had made his cameo appearance. Now he just had to find more pieces of the puzzle.

Jack pulled Tommy's rental car—a silver Lexus GS 460—to a stop in the front of the Vista Haven house just as two Hispanic men were off-loading a king-size mattress from a Sit 'n Sleep delivery truck. "I hope they didn't take the old one!" Jack said, jumping out of the car before Tommy and striding through the open doorway and into the house. He raced down the hall—and relaxed a bit when he saw that the bloodstained mattress was still propped up against the wall.

Mayor led Tommy into the room as Jack wheeled around, about to nail him for not giving him a heads-up for altering the crime scene. Mayor stopped him with, "I called you on your cell phone. I didn't get an answer. I left you a message."

Jack glanced down at his cell and saw that there was a message pending. Mayor continued. "The police released the crime scene, and I promised Michael I'd oversee the cleanup. It's a depressed real estate market in L.A., and Michael does a lot of staging. He contacted his regular crew from the ship, and luckily another job had just fallen out, so here they are, happy to have the work." He pointed in various places. "The rug is coming up after the wall is painted and the bed is removed. Then the cleaning company will work their way through the master suite and bathroom, and then the new rug will be installed."

Jack could see a crew of four men sitting on lawn chairs next to the pool and eating an early lunch.

"I told them to wait until we had a chance to talk."

Jack nodded his thanks.

"Michael arrives the end of next week. Things will be back to normal. No reason he should have to suffer through any of this. He was just doing that poor woman a nice turn."

"Back to normal," Jack said, leaving an uncomfortable silence hanging in the room. The stained rug and the blood-spattered wall were all that was left of the violence, all that was left of Mia. Now they were inconveniences.

"Thanks for the call," Jack managed. "You didn't have to do that."

"It was the right thing to do."

"Have Lieutenant Gallina or Tompkins been around?"

"First thing this morning. I tagged along as they did a cursory walk-through of the house. They didn't seem to find anything of interest and gave me the go-ahead."

Jack picked over the mattress, checking the seams for any cuts or openings. He knew the LAPD techs had already been over every square inch of the bedroom, but this was his last shot.

Jack said to Tommy, "Let's start in the kitchen and work our way back. Mayor, will you let me know when the men are about to pull up the rug?"

Mayor nodded.

The delivery guys had propped the new mattress against the wall in the hallway, and as Jack and Tommy searched the kitchen, they moved the bloodstained mattress out the front door and up the ramp into the truck, away from prying eyes.

Jack could hear Mayor directing the cleaning crew as he started searching the freezer while Tommy combed the silverware drawer. He knew from years in the narcotics business that the freezer was a drug dealer's go-to place to hide their stash. But there was nothing.

"What exactly are we looking for?" Tommy asked.

"Mia knew she was being hunted. I don't know what's in the P.O. box, but there's no way she wouldn't have her passport close at hand in case she had to bolt."

Tommy watched Jack work for a beat, then, "My wife wanted me to buy her a Sub-Zero fridge."

"Yeah? Did you?"

"Oh yeah. I spent ten grand on a refrigerator to keep a two-dollar head of lettuce from wilting. And I'm not a big salad guy."

"But Elizabeth was happy?"

"She likes her lettuce."

Jack came up empty in the fridge and started on the upper cabinets while Tommy rifled through catalogs, warranties, and instruction manuals he found for kitchen appliances that were gathering dust on the lower shelves.

The two men were careful to put things back where they found them, and after going through every drawer, cabinet, and nook, they started in the living room. Again, nothing. Jack worked to control his frustration as they made their way back into the guest bedroom.

The room sat empty now. The bed had been stripped; Mia's belongings had been taken into police custody for storage until family members could be found and notified.

Jack eyed the private garden just beyond the sliding glass door and tried to visualize it from Mia's point of view. It was Zenlike and well manicured, with a nice combination of annuals for color and perennials to keep order. A two-foot-tall, fat metal Buddha with a green patina sat serenely on a stone pedestal in the center of the garden. It probably made her happy, he thought. It made his heart ache.

Tommy searched inside the closet while Jack felt underneath the closet's overhang, and on the top, finding nothing of interest. Jack got on his hands and knees and moved slowly around the perimeter of the rug, looking to see if it had been tampered with in any way, creating a space to hide Mia's papers.

All of a sudden Mayor called out from the bedroom.

The workers had finished putting a fresh coat of paint on the bloodstained wall—another piece of Mia gone—and had started to rip back the brown Berber carpet, exposing the foam-rubber padding underneath. They pulled it back in sections, cutting the rug into smaller pieces as they went.

The men moved expertly from the sliding glass door over to the custom-built closet, and when they pulled back the piece of rug, from under the overhang, Jack felt his pulse quicken. A small blue plastic packet had been hidden from view under that corner section of rug. Jack grabbed up the packet and carefully pulled back the Scotch-taped edge. He pulled out the enclosed papers.

Cleaning instructions.

The instructions for the care and maintenance of the Berber carpet, which had probably been left behind by the installer. Jack, Tommy, and Mayor exhaled in disappointment. Unfazed, the workers used their utility knives to cut the remaining carpet.

Tommy saw something in Jack's expression that gave him pause. "What?" he asked.

But Jack was in a zone. He turned on his heel and walked out of the bedroom, followed by Tommy and then Mayor. But instead of walking to the front door, he made a right turn into the guest bedroom, pulled the sliding glass door open, and stepped out into the private garden.

Jack, being careful not to damage any of the delicate flowers and exotic plants, lifted the fat Buddha off its stone base. The statue was light in his hands, and when he spun it upside down, he saw that the stained Buddha was hollow, an inexpensive replica.

Jack reached in with two fingers and pulled out a waterproof Ziploc freezer bag. Inside the clear plastic bag were three passports. He flipped open the passports and let out an excited breath. Three passports, three different pictures, three different names. All the same woman. All Mia.

God, she was good, he thought. This was the break he'd been waiting for. Jack had names, aliases, disguises, passport stamps, and travel dates. He could now start tracking the movements that had led to Mia's brutal death.

22

Arturo Delgado nursed an iced tea at a private table at the Hotel Casa del Mar, which had an expansive view of the colorful Ferris wheel on the Santa Monica pier. A young man slid into the chair next to him, placed an *L.A. Times* on the table, and ordered one of the same. As the waitress walked away, Arturo turned to face the newcomer.

"Nice suit, Paul."

"Understated, under the radar screen," Paul said. "Just the way I like it."

He was the picture of anonymity, with military-cut black hair and a face as nondescript as the suit of clothes he was wearing. But on closer inspection, his brown eyes were alive, intelligent, and dangerous.

"How is the family?" Delgado asked with a glimpse of warmth.

"Good, no complaints. Father is slowing down and my mother is ruling the roost."

"And the DEA?"

"Better than real estate. Uncle thinks that if I don't get greedy, I should do well."

"Wise counsel from a wise man," said Delgado with genuine respect. "This should help put some food on the table back home." He slid a thick envelope into the fold of the *Times*.

Paul picked up his newspaper, felt the heft of the package, and trusted the dollar amount without counting it. He snugged it down next to him on the seat.

"This will put a second story on the house I'm building in Medellin."

The young man discreetly pulled a nano flash drive out of his jacket pocket and handed it off to the old family friend under the guise of shaking his hand.

"It has all of her apps and downloads. There's a financial program, but it's protected and I couldn't find the password in the allotted time. We just got our hands on the iPad yesterday. LAPD was being tightfisted." His mouth turned down slightly. "To tell you the truth, I have many strengths, but computers are not one of them. The DEA has signed me up for classes."

"No worries, son. I have someone."

"This must be important to you," he said, tapping the newspaper.

"Let's just say that whatever is contained on the files could be very enriching."

Paul picked up his iced tea and clinked glasses with his benefactor.

"To your ongoing success, Mr. Delgado."

"Arturo," Delgado responded.

"Of course, sir."

In one week's time, the young naturalized citizen, and embedded U.S. federal agent, had signed the death warrant for a drug dealer in Ontario, and delivered information that could be worth a fortune to Arturo Delgado.

———

Jack and Tommy were sitting in a Norms restaurant in an Ontario neighborhood untouched by any economic tide. They had made good time down the I-10 in Tommy's rental car, and on the way they discussed the found passports. Each featured a different passport picture. Long blond hair, Mia's style when Jack first met her; short brunette, as she had looked now; and what appeared to be shoulder-length red hair with bangs. Jack thought the red hair looked like a wig and was probably collected with the rest of her belongings by the police in their initial sweep of the murder scene. Tools of the trade for someone on the run, an insurance policy that she wasn't able to collect on.

Detective Nick Aprea had suggested the location because of its proximity to the local gang scene. Jack had worked a drug task force case with Nick in the early 2000s. A no-nonsense cop, he was more than happy to oblige when Jack reached out. Because of his narcotics background, Nick had been involved in the task force takedown of the twenty-seven 18th Street Angels and promised to show Jack the lay of the land, which he said was bleak at best.

Norms was a classic California diner, and the interior hadn't been redecorated or dusted since the early sixties. The red Naugahyde booths were cracked, the yellow paint faded to a nicotine stain, the waitresses wrinkled, and the coffee bitter.

Nick had called ahead to say he was going to be twenty minutes late and to order without him. Jack had a reasonable expectation that Norms couldn't ruin a tuna on white toast and then worried that his detective abilities had atrophied when he took the first bite.

Tommy, unfazed by the concept of salmonella, ordered a blood-rare cheeseburger that he proceeded to oversalt. He then applied the perfect amount of ketchup, pickles, and raw onion, was admiring his handiwork for a beat—the burger two inches from his mouth—when a shouted "I can't cut my toenails anymore" made him pull up short.

A gent seated in the booth next to them—with wispy silver hair and severely challenged hearing—unwittingly shared his personal-hygiene dilemma with half of the diners in the room. He sat with two other wizened gentlemen who nodded like bobble-head dolls commiserating.

Tommy tore his eyes away from the men and, not missing a beat, said, "So, how's your back?"

"Fucking beautiful," Jack said while downing a Vicodin with lukewarm tap water.

Tommy choked and laughed at the same time, causing the octogenarians to interrupt their conversation and look up. Tommy winked at his elders and dug into his blood-rare cheeseburger and fries. Tommy was a man who was going to enjoy the ride.

Jack was glad when Nick Aprea finally showed. He was an ex-marine with the faded blue military tattoo on his thick forearm and the countenance to prove it. Strong, intelligent eyes, short brushed-back black hair with slashes of gray, and a smile that cut both ways. He wore the remnants of childhood acne, but the imperfection somehow made him more attractive to the opposite sex.

Divorced twice, remarried to a beautiful Filipino woman, Nick took life as it came. You made your own luck, he had told Jack, and life wasn't always fair. So fucking what. Herradura Silver tequila was his drink of choice, and he never short-poured.

He'd also protect you with his life, and from Jack's point of view, the man was a fighter pilot, not a passenger. A distinction bestowed on Jack by one of his own captains as he was moving up through the ranks of the NYPD.

Just as important for the present case, Nick was a man who could still take orders but didn't always respect the chain of command.

Jack and Tommy were standing out in front of Norms as Nick pulled to a hard stop in a huge black Ford Expedition and powered down the black-tinted windows.

"I'll drive," Nick said by way of hello and extended his hand to Jack and then to Tommy.

"You look like shit," Nick said as Jack slid into the passenger seat. "Your back?"

Tommy barked a laugh as he stepped up into the backseat. Nick gave him the eye, not knowing what had just transpired in the diner. He relaxed when he saw that Jack was smiling.

"Is it safe to leave my car parked here?" Tommy asked.

"Probably not," Nick said as he stepped on the gas pedal, peeled out, spitting gravel, and fishtailed onto the main drag. "I've got someone who'll fix you right up," he said, looking at Jack across the rearview mirror. "She's a Flip, twenty-three, and a masseuse. Totally legit, totally tight, and between boyfriends. She's not crazy about cops, but since you're *retired*," he said, hammering the word, "she'll probably make an exception."

"I'll take the offer under advisement," Jack said, enjoying the banter. "So I hear you corralled twenty-seven scumbags. I'm more interested in who was left behind."

"So's the LAPD, the DEA, and the FBI. Join the parade," Nick said. "But with budget cuts and the drug war spilling across the border and the two ICE agents who were ambushed and gunned down on Mexican soil, resources are thin to none. The powers that be pulled the plug on the operation. Chalked it up as a win for the good guys. You know how it plays, Bertolino. They get the stats, they're looking good."

Nick gave Jack and Tommy the nickel tour of Ontario, from the gigantic Ontario Mills mall to the Citizens Business Bank Arena to the Ontario Motor Speedway. The center of the city harked back in time; nowadays it was shabby and mean. They passed strip malls and liquor stores and clubs, where afternoon drug deals were conducted under blinking, buzzing neon lights. Auto-body shops where the 18th Street Angels tricked out their rides, like their brothers, and uncles, and grandfathers before them.

Jack took in the sights dispassionately but made note of locations. He'd seen it all on the streets of New York. Drugs fueled the scene, and with America's insatiable appetite, an unending supply was provided by men willing to kill and be killed to protect their profit margin.

Jack had never second-guessed his time spent in narcotics. Because every scumbag he locked up gave someone else a chance at life. It was either enforce the law or anarchy.

Nick pulled his SUV to the curb in front of John Burroughs High. It was late afternoon, and school had long been recessed for the day. The school was a series of single-level boxy structures with a chain-link fence surrounding it, giving off the vibe of a low-security prison. The only bright color on the otherwise tan buildings was the ornate spray-painted graffiti that covered the outbuildings and sidewalks and cinder-block walls.

Nick said, "This is where the farm team plays."

"Baseball?" Tommy asked.

"Nah, where they recruit new gang members," he stated as a point of fact.

"You know what I had when I went to school?" he asked rhetorically, not wanting an answer. "Baseball, and football, and hockey, and choir if you could hold a note. And gym class and recess. The works. All free. We were too tired to get into any real trouble. These kids here, they got squat."

"You developing a social conscience, Aprea?" Jack asked.

"I'm just sayin'. When they drop out and go bad—and there's a deep talent pool here—I'll be there to take them down. But I'm just sayin'."

Nick pulled a manila envelope out of a briefcase wedged between the console and passenger seat and handed it to Jack.

"Here's a list of all the Angels that got away. If you turn something up, call me. I'll have your back and try to provide resources. I'm up to my neck in alligators."

"Understood."

"There's a guidance counselor named Joan Sternhagen. She's either from Australia or New Zealand. I could never figure out the accent or why she'd choose to live in this dump, but she's plugged into the scene and could be a good resource. Use my name and she just might give you the time of day."

23

The flat winter sun blazed off the hood of the Impala sports sedan, turning the metallic blue a deep purple. The blinding reflection off the windshield obscured the occupants' faces until the driver of the car executed a left-hand turn and rumbled confidently down Main Street. Gut-thumping bass was a gift shared with anyone within a four-car radius.

Hector, in the occasional drug-induced moment of introspection, realized that his car, and everything that it stood for, was the only thing in his life that he had ever truly cared about. Love wasn't something that crossed his mind, that he could comprehend, that he could relate to even if it was sung in a song or was the theme of a movie. It was all white noise to Hector.

Johnny, mirrored sunglasses in place, turned the chrome knob on the radio until it clicked off and took the moment of silence to steel himself. Hector made an illegal turn across traffic, forcing the oncoming cars to a yanking halt, daring someone to honk.

The low-riding Impala bounced slightly as Hector pulled carefully into the ample parking lot of Royce Motor Coach Sales and Repair. Johnny reached into the backseat and pulled out what looked like dry cleaning and hiked it over his shoulder. Hector locked up, and they walked comfortably past two tricked-out luxury touring buses. These were the kinds of million-dollar vehicles that traveling rock bands used to move personnel and equipment from city to city. High-end custom paint jobs and nosebleed price tags.

Hector and Johnny made their way to the entrance of the oversize service bay with huge drive-on lifts that could accommodate four full-size buses. At fourteen thousand square feet, the building was the size of an aircraft hangar. In the back of the building was an obscured, fenced-in parking lot for spillover vehicles and surplus buses and motor homes that were stripped for spare parts.

Johnny made small talk with a man who appeared to be the station manager while Hector stood stone still, unblinking. The young men then disappeared into the recesses of the building while the manager made his way toward the showroom floor. The man straightened his navy blue utilitarian sports jacket, ROYCE MOTORS embroidered on the pocket. As his collar moved lower, just below the man's hairline, a faint ornate A could be read on the man's leathered neck. The 18th Street Angels tat had undergone some laser work, but the image, like a ghost of violence past, bled through.

The sound of air brakes discharged as one of the painted beauties lumbered into the work bay. When the bus had cleared the entrance, a black Crown Vic, driven by Johnny—Hector riding shotgun, methodically buttoning his police shirt—motored out of the building and blended into traffic like a reef shark.

Ricky Hernandez sat in front of his flat-screen television playing Six Days in Fallujah. He loved video games and how they could transport him from life on the street to the life of a hero. He was doing well, business was thriving.

Ricky had enjoyed a major windfall when he turned the dime on the Angels. His handler at the DEA kept him out of serving serious jail time after his own arrest, and allowed him to continue earning. It was a win-win. How could he know the feds were going to pick up twenty-seven of the mutts, but hell, it was all part of the game.

Fuck the Angels. Fuck 'em. They didn't give a fuck about Ricky or his homeboys. Got to look out for numero uno.

The sound of the video game's RPGs was so lifelike, he never heard Johnny expertly manipulate the kitchen door's lock open, or the faint sound of men moving quickly through the house into the living room. He was about to break his personal best. Ricky was captivated by the Iraqi body parts that exploded, blood flying, viscera exposed and scattered as his bomb hit the armored vehicle and blew the ragheaded fucks to hell.

The last thing he saw was a reflection in the fifty-two-inch Samsung LCD screen. Two figures. Police? He turned his head and then lost all control over his head, his body, and the sounds his body was making. A high-pitched whine, his white-light head, his heart beating through his throat as he bled out in convulsing, gushing waves of red.

24

Jack and Tommy were headed back to L.A., past the Ontario International Airport, and Jack made the turn toward the San Bernardino Freeway, a desolate stretch of four-lane blacktop. Used to the built-up East Coast, Jack enjoyed being able to go from urban sprawl to open country in a matter of minutes.

The sun was just dropping below the mountains behind them, taking the temperature with it. The empty acreage and fallow fields of scrub grass, weeds, and dry riverbeds on either side of the road took on a blue tint. The pale moon was still hugging the horizon, and a solid ribbon of white and red lights could be seen in the distance, a few miles away.

"Are you going to give Mia's passports to Gallina?" Tommy asked, breaking the silence.

"I've gotta get some food in my stomach," Jack growled, evading the question.

"It's a murder investigation."

"Masterful observation."

"I amaze myself."

"Hand me your phone."

Jack knew it was after hours, but he wanted to share the information he had with Kenny Ortega so he could get a head start in tracking Mia's money trail. He recited the three different names on her passports from memory, and where the passports had been stamped, re-creating the broad strokes of her itinerary. He signed off on Kenny's voice mail with, "We'll talk first thing in the a.m." Jack clicked off the phone.

"Satisfied?" Jack asked.

"You didn't call the cops."

"Do the feds count?" Jack said, enjoying the game.

"Where do you want to eat?"

Jack didn't answer. He was concentrating now on the rearview mirror, where he saw, to his alarm, four cars, moving as one, and rapidly closing the distance behind them, headlights out.

"I think we've got—"

"What?" Tommy interjected, reading Jack's tone of voice and not liking it.

"—company."

As the lead car of the four passed their Lexus on the right at eighty-five miles an hour, it jerked a left in front of Jack's vehicle and rhythmically pumped the brakes, red brake lights strobing.

The second car came alongside the driver's door and weaved dangerously close, forcing Jack to the right.

Jack eased his foot on the brakes when the third car filled his rearview mirror, threatening to crash into their car.

A fourth vehicle kicked up dust and gravel in its wake, driving on and off the shoulder, sliding in tight to Tommy's side of the Lexus.

They were all driving seventy miles an hour, and the passing landscape was a blur.

"They've got us fucking boxed in," Tommy hissed.

The cars were all late-model American, matte primer-gray junkyard specials, and from the tricked-out exhaust systems Jack knew that they had been modified for speed. Through the tinted windows he could just make out a man wearing a dark hoodie and a bandanna pulled high over his nose and mouth like a bandit from an old western.

The car off Jack's shoulder cranked the wheel hard, banging into the Lexus. Jack fought to keep the car under control. Tommy yelped.

Jack pulled his Glock nine millimeter from his shoulder rig, flicked off the safety, and handed it to Tommy. "I'm going to roll down your window, and I want you to shoot."

"I can't shoot the guy."

"I need you to shoot the car."

"I can't."

"We need a way out," Jack demanded. "As soon as I lower the window."

Jack powered down the passenger window.

"Now!"

Tommy paused.

"Kill the car, Tommy."

Tommy sighted and fired the gun. The sound inside their car was deafening.

"Again!"

Tommy fired, fired, fired into the hood of the aggressor's car.

The smell of cordite and smoke filled their nostrils. Jack pulled down hard on the steering wheel and banged the Lexus into the car that was veering dangerously close on his left. The sound of scraping metal and screeching, smoking tires was unnerving. But the Lexus didn't waver. Neither did the attacking vehicles.

Smoke and then flames inundated the car Tommy had fired on. The driver of the now impaired car was forced to drop off. He pulled onto the soft shoulder, but at seventy, the car went into a power skid and flipped, doing three full rolls until it came to a smoking, fiery stop.

"Fuck!" Tommy shouted.

Jack was in primal mode. He stomped on the gas pedal and

smashed into the rear bumper of the lead car. He was executing the PIT maneuver—precision intervention technique—he had learned twenty-five years ago as a rookie and never had to use.

The lead car looked like it was moving in slow-motion as it slip-sided into a 360-degree spin and then kept on spinning, finally coming to a bone-rattling, tire-burning stop in the middle of the four lanes.

"Hand me the gun," Jack said in a calm, measured voice.

As Tommy tried to put the gun in Jack's hand, the car on the left smashed into their rental car again, knocking the gun out of Tommy's hand and onto the car's floor mat. Tommy, breathing heavily, lurched for the weapon and slapped it firmly in Jack's hand.

Jack powered down his window and fired into the attacking car's windshield. At seventy miles an hour, the windshield shattered and imploded, raining razor-edged shards of glass into the driver's face. The driver swatted away stinging chunks of glass as if he was fighting a swarm of bees. He instinctively slammed on his brakes, and his car revolved in a precision 180 that forced the car on Jack's bumper to fall back or die.

The damaged Lexus shot forward into the night, clear of all pursuers. Jack watched in the rearview mirror as the three cars, in control again, moved like a pack of wolves back toward the destroyed vehicle, which was engulfed in flames now. They picked up their compadre, limping away from the conflagration, and raced off into the darkening night.

At long last Jack braked hard and pulled to the side of the road as the burning car, emitting a billowing cloud of thick black smoke, exploded in a fireball that reflected off Jack's and Tommy's tight faces.

Tommy tried to shoulder his door open, but it was too trashed. Jack, seeing that Tommy was in need of a wide berth, forced his door open and jumped out, eyes scanning the horizon, weapon ready. Tommy scrabbled over the center console, just cleared the open driver's-side door with his head, and hurled.

Jack looked at the train wreck of what was a brand-new fifty-five-thousand-dollar Lexus.

"I hope you signed the loss-damage waiver."

Tommy hurled a second time.

———————

At 6:30 A.M. Jack and Tommy pulled up in front of the loft building in the marina. They had spent most of the night at the Ontario police station giving statements and waiting for the powers that be to corroborate their status, their stories, and the legality of their paperwork.

As it turned out, the plates on the burnt-out hulk of metal were stolen. Plus, the VIN number on the chassis proved that the car had also been stolen. No surprises there.

If DDA Leslie Sager was upset by being awakened at two in the morning to verify Jack and Tommy's story, she didn't let on. She did sound droll when she told Jack that he was the gift that kept on giving. He heard something else behind the husky tone of her bedroom voice but was too spent to speculate.

Jack pulled the creaking, fender-scraping Lexus into the lot of the body shop, Prestige Body and Paint, that was located directly next door to his building. He'd let the rental car's insurance company and Visa's lawyers work out the details later.

Jack pushed open his door and exited as Tommy dragged himself over the console and almost fell out of the driver's-side door. They were met by a man named J.D., who was the owner of Bruffy's Tow and Police Impound across the street.

J.D. was in his midforties and had lived on the wild side for most of his teenage years. He wore the wisdom of coming out the other end alive in the lines on his face, his faded jailhouse tattoos, and his wind-burned skin.

He didn't say anything at first, just stared at the car.

"Tough night?" J.D. asked, master of understatement.

"Had better," Jack said, too tired to prolong the conversation.

Tommy announced to him, "I've got to hit the head, then I've got to hit the road."

J.D. wasn't going to be deterred. He had something under his arm that he handed over to Jack.

"Don't know if it's anything, but I eyeballed this car yesterday morning when I got called out on a pickup and again when I was making the drop-off. Got a bad feeling. They were staring at your building and nothing else. When I unloaded my tow and walked back to the front gate, they were in the wind."

"What time was that?" Jack asked.

"'Bout nine forty-five," J.D. stated. He looked at the car again and whistled, shaking his head. "What time did you leave?"

"About nine forty-five," Tommy said.

Jack scanned the sheet of paper that had been handed to him. It was a series of surveillance photos shot in thirty-second intervals. The license plate in the front of the Ford Focus could be read. The passenger was blurred, but the driver could probably be identified.

"We get more than our share of dirtbags," the repo man explained. "We're wired to the tits."

"Thanks, J.D."

"We've gotta look out for our neighbors."

"I'm glad to be sharing space with you," Jack said.

He stared at the sheet of pictures for a moment, trying to memorize the face. "I'm wondering if you know anyone who could hook me up with a ride. Something that blends, but has a few horses under the hood."

J.D. got thoughtful. "You lookin' to make some enemies?"

"Too late for that. I'm thinking more about retribution."

J.D. nodded his head as if he'd been there, done that, and sometimes it needed to be done. "I got a couple on the lot might fit the bill."

At that moment one of Bruffy's tow trucks rumbled up Glencoe.

The driver honked and waved at J.D. as he passed and made a left up to Bruffy's metal gate. J.D. followed the truck without uttering another word. Like you only get so many breaths in a lifetime, don't waste them talking shit.

Jack understood a little bit about that.

25

Arturo Delgado stood at the outermost point of the rock jetty that formed the entrance to Marina del Rey. A heavy concrete-and-stone seawall running perpendicular to the jetty, a hundred yards out, protected the man-made marina and its million-dollar yachts, high-rises, hotels, and condos from the capricious sea. These two man-made structures created the egress in and out of the waterway. The constant flow of boats painted a perfect moving picture, Delgado thought as a heavy formation of pelicans skimmed by, impossibly close to the choppy ocean on their way to points south.

It was seventy-six degrees, and the balmy wind was blowing and snapping his silver hair over his collar as he held a mobile phone tight to his ear.

Winter in Southern California.

He lowered his head and then turned back toward land, frustrated, as the wind made hearing almost impossible. He could see the broad white beach of the Marina del Rey strand curving on his left, all the way past the Santa Monica Pier, to the tip of Malibu. On his right, on the other side of the wide channel, was the beach at Playa del Rey. That vista stretched all the way past Manhattan Beach to Rancho Palos Verdes. The backdrop for the central channel, like a painted scrim, was the San Bernardino Mountains.

"Keep it down," Delgado said into the phone. "Keep your voice down, Manuel!"

"Where's my fucking money, Arturo!" Manuel Alvarez shouted into the phone from inside his eight-by-ten cell.

"Easy, Manuel, it won't do to have my partner die of a heart attack. Now keep your voice down. No amount of money in the bank is worth death row. Are you hearing me? Am I clear?" Delgado watched an eighteen-foot blue-and-white rental powerboat approach the open sea, think better of it, and wisely return to the safety of the channel, cutting dangerously close to a ketch that was struggling to unfurl its sails in the swirling breeze.

Alvarez was becoming a liability, he thought. If he was overheard incriminating himself, it could make things very difficult on the outside for Delgado to comport business, let alone stay out of prison himself.

"Did you find the iPad?" Alvarez asked, his volume corrected.

"I have a connection in the DEA. They will get their hands on her equipment after the LAPD is finished pissing on it. I should have something to report soon."

"The LAPD has it?"

"Because your men were too ignorant to get the device before they took her out. Now I'm sure she protected you with a password?"

Silence.

"Manuel?" Delgado growled.

"She did. But for security reasons she kept changing them. That's what she told me. If I could kill her again, I would."

"Think, Manuel."

"With my bare hands . . . We routed everything through the Caymans and then moved cash back to the States. But even with the password, without security numbers, codes, and clearances, I'm just another face on the outside looking in. She was the CEO and treasurer and I was the CFO of the corporations. It gave us both access to my funds."

"Not to worry. We'll find the money and make you whole."

At least half of the statement was the truth, Delgado thought.

"Is Bertolino still breathing the same stale air I am?" Alvarez challenged.

"Not for long. Bertolino will have many regrets before he dies. But die he will, my friend. On that you can bank."

Alvarez gave that some thought and Delgado pushed the phone tighter to his head, not sure if he had thankfully been disconnected.

"The bottom line should remain firm," Alvarez said, trying to regain control of the conversation. "Tell our friends down south that everything is moving forward. Now, how many shirts are being delivered?"

"Two hundred seventy-five. Enough shirts for everyone."

"It's a good start," Alvarez said. And then, "*Gracias,* Arturo," before he clicked off.

A heavyset woman, being pulled by a labradoodle, was threatening to enter Delgado's personal space. He pointed behind her, and when she turned her head, he tossed his cell phone. Over and over it flipped until it splashed into the churning surf.

26

It was five o'clock in the afternoon before Jack's eyes snapped open. The blue-gray January sky was already darkening. Heavy cloud cover was moving in off the Pacific, and by five thirty the sun would set and Jack's internal dinner alarm would start to activate.

Jack had gotten business squared away before an extended shower and . . . that was about all he remembered before passing out, on top of the bedcovers, the way he used to as a teenager after baseball practice, total exhaustion.

He woke with the same sour stomach he had endured for seventeen years living in his parents' home on Staten Island. Never secure, not knowing if his alcoholic father was on the prowl, looking for a wrong word, a wrong glance, tapping a razor too many times on the sink, anything that would set off a fight.

After the abuse his body had taken in the car the day before, Jack was positive an Excedrin was not going to cut it. He grabbed a Vicodin and swallowed it with some ice-cold orange juice that shocked his system awake.

DDA Leslie Sager had called to check up on Jack at first light while he was Skyping with Kenny Ortega in Miami. Ortega had agreed to run the aliases and follow the money.

Nick Aprea, duly notified, was already working on the trace of the license plate and ID of the men in the surveillance photo.

When Sager had suggested meeting for an early dinner, it sounded inviting, and he accepted. She offered to drive in his direction, which he also accepted. When Jack admitted that he was old school and dinner would be on him, *she* accepted, and Hal's would be fine.

Jack did a double take as the hostess, Rebecca, led Leslie through the crowded restaurant to his regular booth. She had an openness in her face, a sensual vulnerability that he hadn't seen when she was conducting her business. The deputy district attorney looked like a fox.

Jack understood that the workplace was a balancing act for any woman trying to rise through the ranks. Too strident, too forceful, playing in the old-boys' club and she'd be considered a bitch, although never to the woman's face. And prospects and good cases would dry up.

Too high strung, too emotional, and word would spread that she wasn't up to the job. And good cases would dry up along with her future.

"Mr. Bertolino," Rebecca said with a twinkle in her eye before turning on her heel and heading back to her station.

Jack had already leapt out of the booth when Leslie extended her hand.

"Mr. Bertolino," she said with the smile of a woman who held a secret. Women were a mystery to Jack.

"DDA Sager," Jack said, not wanting to overstep.

"Please, Jack, Leslie," she said matter-of-factly. They slid into opposite sides of the booth and Leslie gave him the once-over.

"You clean up just fine."

The last time she had seen Jack was when he had been released from the holding cell, not his finest moment.

"You sound surprised," Jack said easily.

"I'm not sure what I expected. But I'm glad you're in one piece."

Arsinio arrived and asked if they wanted cocktails. Jack looked the question to Leslie, who thought for a second.

"I'd like something red, dry, and full bodied tonight."

"Two Benzigers, Arsinio. Thanks."

"Good choice," Arsinio added, and he was gone.

"So," Leslie said. Her eyes took in the room, the art and the large pieces of sculpture. "This appears to be your usual haunt."

"I'm a creature of habit."

"I like it."

Jack wasn't sure if she was referring to him, or the art in the room, and didn't really care. It was all good in the moment.

"Are you okay?" she asked with genuine concern.

"Better than the Lexus."

Jack's eyes creased into a smile matched by hers. "You should have seen Tommy's face. And it was a rental car."

Leslie laughed, and it was free and easy. "He's a good advocate for you."

"He's a good friend to me. And last night he suffered a baptism by fire."

"I thought he might be joining us."

"Tommy's wife was understandably upset with the unexpected turn of events. Tommy had some splainin' to do," Jack said, doing his best Ricky Ricardo.

"And what's your professional opinion?" she asked.

Arsinio arrived with the wine and two menus, and Jack laid out the case as he thought it was coming together. He had a lot of holes to be filled in, but he felt certain that Mia's death wasn't a cartel hit. It might have been sanctioned, but with the addition of the found body part, and what had transpired in the past twenty-four hours, he was sure it was local muscle.

Dinner came and went, and Jack learned that DDA Sager had gotten her law degree from Northwestern, and after graduating second in her class, she was drafted by the Los Angeles District Attorney's Office. The snow had driven her west, and the job offer had cemented her decision to stay.

After four brutal years, where she had lived, breathed, and slept the job, she was ready to branch out and take some personal time, do some traveling. Leslie had staked out her territory and created an identity within the department. She was going to enjoy the fruits of her labor.

She wasn't fond of the politics but knew how to play the game. And she knew that ultimately it would be her conviction rate that would dictate her future. At present, she was satisfied. No, more than satisfied. Leslie Sager was fulfilled.

It was music to Jack's ears. A woman who didn't need saving.

The phone call came over double espressos. Nick Aprea reported that another body had been discovered under an overpass, same MO, different staging.

"Looks like our freaks," Nick said as he invited Jack to the party.

Jack excused himself and leaned down clumsily to say goodbye. Leslie brushed his cheek with her lips, missed, and kissed Jack's ear. It turned beet red and as the warmth spread, Jack knew he was blushing like a schoolboy.

All he could do was shake his head and say, "Okay, thanks."

Brilliant, he thought.

"You paid for dinner," she said softly, trying to let him off the hook but unable to conceal her smile.

"Okay . . . gotta run," he said, making a total mess of his exit.

Jack hurried past the bar patrons and felt the heat spread from his face down his back, where he hoped she was still looking but wouldn't dare turn around to check.

Life. Also a mystery to Jack.

27

Nick Aprea's personal invitation to the party was a figure of speech. Black humor, cop-style. When Jack pulled up to the crime scene, what was playing out was a spectacle—pure and simple.

A knot of cars blocked the way through the overpass in both directions, with more driving in. Colorful low-rider vehicles, souped-up Japanese racers, and high school starter cars. Gut-wrenching hip-hop was blaring from multiple sound systems like a battle of the bands. Idle spectators smoked and drank, talked and texted, and snapped pictures with their cell phones.

All extremely disturbing under the circumstances.

Jack was forced to park on the side of the road and control his fury as he walked toward the overpass, through the blind circus, to the scene of the crime. Nick waved to him over the heads of the throngs and met him halfway.

"Isn't this the shits?" he asked.

A second news helicopter entered the air space over their heads and started its circular pattern, shooting footage for late-night news on KABC Channel 7, its spotlight moving in patterns like an inverted klieg light. Nick couldn't hear Jack's reply, but he could read his intention.

"The killer was looking for publicity," Nick continued as he grabbed his cell phone and punched up Facebook. He pulled up the John Burroughs High School page. "And he hit it big."

On the miniature cell screen, in living color, for all to see, download, and share, was displayed a cruel picture of the murder victim. His body was roped to a concrete pillar, like a crucifixion. An explosion of garish color covered the graffiti-painted wall behind him like a death shroud.

"It's gone viral. A hundred thousand hits on YouTube in the first two hours. The kids were the first responders."

"How do these social media sites clear this kind of shit?" Jack said through a tight jaw.

"They thought it was performance art. How the fuck do I know? That ship's sailed."

A blue tarp had been erected to shield the body from prying eyes and media cameras. Two spotlights, the hum of a generator, the sound of the music, the smell of pot wafting in the air, and uniformed officers for crowd control gave the bizarre scene the feeling of a rock concert—or a medieval beheading.

Nick Aprea parted the crowd without saying a word. He and Jack walked up to the overpass, ducked under the police tape, and then edged up the slight incline, where they disappeared behind the canvas tarp.

The tortured tattooed body was naked from the waist up. The young man's throat was slit, his head hanging at an impossible angle, his face, a stark white death mask. His bare waist was bound so tightly to a thick concrete support beam that the rope had cut into his dead flesh. The young man's hands were outstretched, fastened with perfectly knotted ropes that hung from overhead beams. There were multiple stab wounds with no discernible pattern, just more punctures than seemed humanly possible. His abdomen was sliced just above the belt line, like a grinning happy face, entrails threatening to spill like a biology project gone very wrong.

What was conspicuously absent was any blood, other than some seepage from the stab wounds at the man's twisted feet. The murder had obviously occurred at another site and had been staged here for ultimate effect.

"Hell of a warning," Jack said to Nick.

Jack knew it was another message sent. He just didn't know the who or the why.

"The body has already been identified by a local cop working the gang unit," Nick said. He pulled out a pad and read, "Ricky Hernandez. Twenty-three. Not affiliated with the 18th Street Angels, but was arrested on two different occasions for selling dope. Looks good for Angels' dope. Location of his crib, unknown at this time."

"If he was selling Angels' product and skimming, this show would be quite a deterrent," Jack said, his voice flat.

"They'll be talking about it for generations," Nick added. "It's a clear message that thievery won't be tolerated."

Jack was thinking as he examined the damage. "Look at how neatly the knots are tied. Were you a Boy Scout?"

Nick gave him the you-must-be-fucking-kidding-me look, but acknowledged Jack's good work. "I'll have it checked out."

His cell phone chirped. He listened for an extended beat, nodded, and then covered the phone with his palm. "Okay, the locals found the house where Hernandez lives, or lived, whatever. They saw massive amounts of blood on the rug, thought someone might be in danger, and they *legally* entered the premises. That's definitely where the vic bled out. They said there was no forced entry and—"

Jack stopped him with, "Have the techs check the cylinders on all the locks into the house, look for any unusual scratch marks."

"Done." He picked back up on his talking to the detective at the other end of the line.

"Get him out of here!" Jack heard, and turned to see a red-faced Lieutenant Gallina and a stoic Detective Tompkins striding toward him.

Nick snapped off his phone and positioned himself between Jack and the detectives.

He spoke directly to Gallina, never breaking eye contact, never blinking, his voice so low the two detectives had to lean in to hear him speak:

"He's with me."

The tech crew had processed the scene, picking up cans and cigarette butts and wrappers. They had taken measurements and had video-documented the body and the overall crime scene and were, thankfully, in the process of lowering the body, the medical examiner at the ready. Jack, being careful not to contaminate the crime scene, or overstay his welcome, had used his cell phone to take his own pictures of the body and the graffitied wall. He'd look for matches on the tattooed thigh that had been found buried on the island in the L.A. River. He also inspected the wall of the overpass from an angle to see if any of the paint was wet, the markings recent. He came up empty.

Detective Tompkins stepped up behind him and said, "Let's take a walk."

Jack knew it was just a matter of time. He led the way around the blue tarp, down off the underpass rise, and started to walk through the crowd. Nick was talking to someone in the gang unit, and Gallina was working hard to look busy, pretending not to know what his partner was up to.

Tompkins caught up and started the conversation. "I had a couple of my guys bang on doors in the building where someone could have eyeballed the break-in of your loft, if it occurred."

So much for détente, Jack thought, his face tightening.

"Hey, I'm a doubting Thomas," Tompkins continued. "If I can't put my fingers in the bloody hole, it ain't dead."

But as far as Jack was concerned, the conversation was.

"Turned out these Southern California pot smokers couldn't tell one door from another in your building, let alone figure out if something hinky was going down."

"Where are you from?" Jack challenged.

"San Diego," he said, getting the irony. "Oh, we've got our share of airheads. But really, the movie industry attracts them like . . . everyone wants to be a star, nobody wants to do anything to earn it."

Tompkins walked by a kid who was passing a lit joint to his buddy. He snatched it out of the hapless kid's hand, flicked it to the ground, and crushed it with his polished black shoe. "A little respect, dickwad."

The kid was smart enough to dummy up.

There was still no love lost between the two men, but Tompkins dropped a couple of ticks on Jack's asshole meter. Jack never understood busting someone for three-guys-on-a-joint. It wasn't a narcotics bust at all in his book.

As they broke through the far end of the crowd, Tompkins continued. "C'mon, Bertolino. If you're all that, what do you got?"

"Are you going to let me see the murder book?" was Jack's answer.

"No can do. But I'll give to get."

In Jack's experience, sharing intel was the only way to make a big case. Everyone had their areas of expertise and the more you gave—if it was legitimate intelligence—the more you got. He'd taken his share of heat in the NYPD because of his relationships with the FBI and the DEA, but no one could argue with his stats.

Jack stopped to give Tompkins some hints. He told him about the scratches on his front-door lock. And then he offered up the aliases Mia was traveling under and her itinerary, as far as it could be traced by the stamps in the passports. Told him the information was generated by an old confidential informant who would remain confidential. Tompkins had no issue with that and added the information to his notepad.

"Was her phone found at the scene?" Jack asked, knowing the answer but not wanting to bust Molloy.

"No. But if the killers took it, that might be how they got your address."

"Makes sense. An iPad, anything like that?"

"No," Tompkins lied without blinking.

"How about the second earring?"

"Just the one on the body," he said. "It was a no-go locally for the rental on the black-and-white," Tompkins went on. "Although we did get a shot of the suspect's car on the San Diego Freeway around the time of the incident."

"The incident?" Jack repeated.

"Hey, I didn't know her. No disrespect meant. Oh yeah," he continued, unfazed, "no known family members living in Colombia. Mother died last year. We'll warehouse her belongings until we find some paperwork on relatives or whatever."

The notion that Mia had died alone in the world tugged at Bertolino's gut.

"Anyway, it was two guys, like you said," Tompkins continued. "Could've been black, white, Hispanic, a fucking Martian, for all the pictures were worth. Fuckin' technology. And we got your cell signal bouncing off towers that coincided with the time and location from where you reportedly made the call."

"So I'm off Gallina's radar?"

"He's not gonna invite you to his kid's confirmation." But his nod answered the question.

"Oh . . ." Tompkins added, and pulled a picture out of his pocket as if it was an afterthought.

It wasn't.

"This is a photo taken by the first responders on the scene."

It was a shot of Mia's Louis Vuitton luggage.

"And here's the photo we took the next day. Can you see how in this one there's a key in the uh, little webbed holder, and funny, but in this one, uh, you see anything in there?"

Jack shook his head and waited for the follow-up.

"Any ideas as to its whereabouts?"

"Not a clue."

Tompkins didn't press him. "Well, if anything else comes up, you'll keep us in the loop?" It wasn't a question. He handed Jack his card.

Jack thought about giving Tompkins a copy of the surveillance photo he had received from J.D. at Bruffy's Tow, but thought better of it. Nick wouldn't appreciate having Gallina, who wasn't familiar with the locals, bulldogging his way into his case.

Jack walked back in Nick's direction. He hadn't gotten any closer to the killer, but it had saved him a few steps.

28

"C'mere, Johnny, take off your sunglasses," Angelina said from the bed, squeezing her breasts until her nipples were as swollen and pouty as her lips.

Johnny hadn't slept in forty-eight hours, and he was being fueled by cocaine, fear, and adrenaline. He sucked down half of a monster line of pure Colombian cocaine with a rolled twenty, and hit Send on his computer. He then erased the execution, unplugged the phone, and pulled out the microSD card. He'd trash it, along with the Black-Berry, later in the day. His entire body was vibrating, and he feared he was having a heart attack.

Angelina slid out of bed, her naked tattooed body glistening in the reflected light from the nightstand. She had draped silk scarves over the sixty-watt bedside lamps earlier in the evening to create ambience in the shithole of an apartment Johnny called home. Angelina vamped over to Johnny with moves that she had seen runway strippers use. When he still didn't respond, she pulled one of the scarves off a lamp, and, like a sad version of Isadora Duncan, whipped it around her head like a lariat. She threw it over his shoulder from behind and then pulled it seductively toward her.

"C'mon, Johnny," she cooed. "Lemme see them pretty green eyes."

"Get the fuck away, I'm not gonna tell you again," he said with a staccato ferocity that startled them both.

"Fuckin' *maricón*!"

The words spilled out of her mouth before she could take them back. Her hand snaked out and she ripped the aviator glasses off his face, cutting the side of his nose with her painted fingernails.

"Fuckin' bitch!" Johnny swung from his heels with a closed backhanded fist. Angelina's head snapped to the side. Her eyes filled with tears, and she attacked, matching Johnny slap for violent slap.

Johnny was swinging because he had lost all control of his life, and he was spiraling to hell faster than he had ever imagined.

Angelina was striking back because fury came easily to her.

Both combatants stopped, sucking in air, crying, heaving, staring each other down. Angelina braced herself for the final assault that never came.

Johnny retreated, his eyes blazing with an intensity that Angelina had never seen before. He grabbed up his sunglasses that had gotten kicked under the bed and jammed them on. Blood was streaming down his cheek from under the mirrored lens. He pulled a baggy white T-shirt over his head, blood staining his collar. He snatched his stash bag out of his sock drawer, his computer, his phone, his wallet, and his keys, and tossed them all into a Nike sports bag.

Angelina tugged on his arm, whimpering, begging, and trying to stop the inevitable. Johnny yanked his arm away, snapping off one of her bloodred fingernails. He didn't look back as he stormed out, slamming the door behind him.

Angelina stood on the stained carpet, crying until her tears turned dark and cold. Finally, feeling miserable, she ripped off a matchbook cover and scraped together enough coke to form a perfect line. She rerolled the twenty-dollar bill Johnny had left behind into a tight straw and sucked up the crystal white powder in one heaving snort.

Angelina stood up, tall, naked, dangerous, and checked out her surroundings. She needed some ice for her face. There were no cuts, but there would be some swelling. She pulled a bottle of beer out of the minifridge and rolled it over her bruised cheek. Then she took a long pull of the cold brew.

Johnny would eventually come back. He always did after a fight. Her eyes searched the floor, trying to locate the fire engine red, six-inch fuck-me pumps she had tossed earlier in the night.

She spotted a rainbow reflection off a small object under the table. Maybe knocked off during the fight?

The microSD card. Angelina didn't know much about technology, but she picked it up and hid it in the change pocket of her purse along with the twenty. You never know, she thought. It might be insurance.

29

Jack had gotten his first full night's sleep in days. When he settled in, he thought about Mia some, and then his mind shifted to Leslie, and he wondered about love, and how it drifted in and out of his life, and what it all meant. He came up with nothing and passed out.

Sitting surveillance, on the other hand, was something that came easily to Jack. He'd sit for as many days as necessary to take down a cartel's money-laundering cell. Stay patient, keep his powder dry, and slowly unravel the cell until he had all the clients and cartel members under arrest.

The glory hounds would barge in as soon as they knew a location was active, take the money, and brag about the bust, put another notch on their belts. From Jack's point of view that was shortsighted law enforcement. The "office" in Colombia would simply shift some players from Chicago or Texas—or one of the other hubs in the drug trade—set up another money-laundering cell at another address, and be back in business in forty-eight hours. The money would then be used to enrich the cartels, assassinate politicians, and overthrow governments. Not to mention the devastation the drugs created in American society, the families destroyed, the innocent lives lost.

Jack was methodical. He made a database of all the licenses of the cars that frequented the suspect's house, stayed on top of the wiretaps, and traced the phone calls back to the source. Labor-intensive work. But when it was time to drop the hammer, he was able to cast a wide net.

When Colombia got word of Jack's arrests from their high-priced American lawyers who were kept on retainer, they knew the "sickness" was so great they were forced to rerack, rethink their strategy, and start again from scratch. That was how Jack liked to play the game. Let the kingpins know that someone had outsmarted them and their Harvard-educated lawyers and MBAs.

Today the surveillance would be different.

J.D. from Bruffy's Tow had been a man of his word and had made available the parked car Jack was now sitting in, sipping coffee he had purchased at a 7-Eleven before dawn.

The 1970 dark green Plymouth Sport Fury had patches of Bondo around the wheel wells and passenger door, but a gleaming 426 hemi engine under the hood. The windows were so dark, Jack had to take off his sunglasses in order to keep the car on the road. The black vinyl roof had rotted under the California sun, and all that was left was a smattering of old glue, flakes of vinyl, primer, and rust. The car, which looked like it should be up on cinder blocks in somebody's front yard, wasn't much to look at, but that was the point. It blended. And ate up the I-10 from L.A. to Ontario like a road rocket. The steering was a little loose, but that was to be expected in a car over forty years old.

Jack wished his body felt as loose as the car's steering, but the seats weren't built for comfort and his back was older than the car itself. Suck it up, he told himself.

Tommy Aronsohn had offered to stay in town, but Jack thought his friend looked relieved when he dropped him off at LAX. Couldn't blame him. Tommy promised to head back on a minute's notice, but what needed to be accomplished now was Jack's purview. He made a mental note to check the local hospitals for anyone who had checked in with broken bones or whiplash the night he and Tommy were attacked on the road.

He had exited his building at 5:00 A.M. through an opening in the garage, and he hurried down the concrete path that ran the length of the back of the property. Dressed totally in black, he'd done a quick run across Glencoe and entered Bruffy's Tow through a shadowed side gate. The precaution was too cloak-and-dagger for Jack's comfort level, but he still didn't know if someone was watching his building. Someone could have set up surveillance in plenty of structures in the surrounding neighborhood. He wouldn't have that answer until he was able to question the man in the photo.

Nick Aprea had done a DMV search on the car and gotten a name to match the face of the driver, David Reyes. Twenty-four, two arrests. One for methamphetamine, one for marijuana. The record he had accumulated as a minor was sealed. One of the local cops had shared a few leads as to the guy's potential whereabouts. And so here Jack sat.

He had done a drive-by of the apartment building listed on David's license, but when Jack got up close and personal, the unit was clearly empty.

He was now parked on a side street with a clear view of the Reyes family's home.

The neighborhood was lower middle class sliding toward poverty. Small, cookie-cutter California bungalows, faded pastel stucco, white gravel roofs, and dry patches of grass that couldn't be mistaken for lawn. So many electrical wires crisscrossed the dirt alleys running between the rows of houses, they took on the ominous appearance of spiderwebs. Despite how few possessions these Americans enjoyed, they were forced to live with metal bars on their windows.

It didn't seem right.

Jack pulled two Excedrin out of his pocket and swallowed them with a gulp of cold coffee. He thought about taking a Vicodin but was concerned about falling asleep. He booted up his laptop and checked out his loft in real time. Cruz Feinberg had installed two wireless microcameras, one lodged in an African mask that would capture anyone breaking and entering, the second secreted in a smoke alarm that covered the master bedroom and kitchen area. Cruz had the kind of genius and talent Jack would have drafted when he was running a team of narco-rangers in the NYPD. Independently thinking Cruz would have been a good fit.

From the computer screen Jack could see that all was quiet on the home front. When he looked out of the dark-tinted windshield, it was still quiet on the street.

He watched the occasional neighbor exit a house and walk up the road toward public transportation, or open one of their parked cars on the street. After a rough ignition, the vehicle would turn over, belch white smoke, and head off to some forgettable job. Jack did notice something conspicuously missing from this picture besides his suspect.

No paperboy. No rubber-banded papers being tossed from bicycles. Something that had been so important to Jack as a boy growing up on Staten Island was disappearing from modern life.

Jack's paper route had as many wise guys, for customers, as good guys. His neighborhood was full of Mafia soldiers, button men, you name it. He went to school with their kids. Just an everyday part of Jack's early education. When he joined the police force, he cut off all contact with childhood friends who went in the other direction, who chose to work for the Gambino crew. But his parents still lived on the same street, in the same neighborhood, and the "made men" kept a watchful eye. Dangerous men who protected their own.

Jack had failed to locate Reyes's car when he did his reconnaissance around the neighborhood before settling in between a group of other parked cars with a clear view of the house. He knew David's car might be garaged, or just used for the job, or he might just be wasting his time.

He had to take a leak but didn't want to jeopardize his cover. He'd force it out of his mind. Jack was never thrilled about having to piss in a bottle, although he'd done so many times in past stakeouts.

He decided that if he saw no movement in or out of the house by noon, he'd go get something to eat and try again in the late afternoon. He wanted to run by John Burroughs High and talk to the guidance counselor Nick had suggested. Aprea had promised to call her first thing this morning and grease the wheels.

Bertolino felt the approaching car before he saw it in his rear-view mirror and slid down low in his seat. The thudding bass rattled all the way through the Plymouth's chassis to Jack's stomach as a primer gray car ripped by, honked, and came to a chattering stop in front of the Reyes house.

The front door opened and Jack watched as his suspect appeared and took the front steps in one leap. He loped over to the waiting car with the grace of a wolf running in the wild. A good-looking middle-class kid. Dark hair, open face, full-blown macho attitude. Also a face full of cuts, as if he had run through a briar patch or had his front windshield explode in his face. Jack put his money on the latter.

He was wearing a navy blue industrial work shirt, and Jack could read ROYCE MOTORS embroidered in yellow thread on the back. The car peeled out and Jack let it move up the road as he jotted down the car's license number. When it made a left, he turned the key on the Plymouth and followed.

He one-hand dialed information. When the operator answered, Jack asked for the number and address of Royce Motors and scribbled that information onto his yellow pad as he made the top of the rise. He wasn't particularly worried about losing his man now because he would enter the address into his laptop at the next light and be at the location waiting when Reyes showed up for work.

But his blood pressure started spiking. He could feel his heart thudding in his chest. He was now sure that the primer gray car was one of the chase cars that had tried to force him and Tommy off the road. It was time to even the score.

The first stop was Royce Motor Coach Sales and Repairs. Jack drove around the joint to get a feel for the layout. It was an upscale organization. The massive building had the polished look of a Mercedes dealership.

He was securely positioned across from the entrance when, fifteen minutes after he had arrived, the primer gray car pulled into the lot and parked. There were now three men in the car.

David Reyes jumped out of the passenger side and pushed the front seat forward. He thrust his hand into the back, pulled out a pair of crutches, and then muscled out his buddy, who was dressed in the same work shirt.

The man's bruised forehead was almost as deep a blue as the shirt on his back. The plaster cast that encased his foot and extended up to his knee was covered with colorful graffiti and signatures. He grabbed the crutches and moved forward, swinging with the ease of a circus performer, his body battered but not his ego.

Jack snapped a few pictures and then stopped as a luxury bus pulled into the driveway and motored up to the entrance of the service bay.

An older man appeared from inside, wearing a navy blue sports jacket, and waved the vehicle in. Jack snapped a few close-ups of the man and then of the license plate on the bus.

Too much joy on the gangbangers' faces for a simple service call, Jack thought.

Maybe Beyoncé was onboard.

Jack downloaded the pictures onto his laptop and e-mailed them to Nick. Then he put in a call to the service department to find out the latest he could drop off a vehicle for repairs. Six o'clock, straight up. That's when Royce's service bay shut down for the night.

That gave him at least five hours. He called the high school and spoke with Joan Sternhagen. The guidance counselor *had* spoken with Nick Aprea, and agreed to meet with Jack after lunch. He'd hit the head, grab some food, go to the school, and be back in plenty of time to find out where the other two players in the primer gray car lived.

Not a bad morning, all in all. Jack was back in the hunt.

30

Jack was ushered into the guidance counselor's empty office by an officious secretary and told to wait. Like a penitent student, he was doing just that.

Except for baseball, Jack didn't have fond memories of high school. With the violence he had suffered at home, being a teenager was a rough time, with little joy. He was amazed by how just visiting a school—the sights, the sounds, the smells—could bring the feelings back. The office was Spartan, with pastel peach walls and dark brown wainscoting. A round clock on the wall reminded him that his life was passing every time the second hand jumped.

A buzzer sounded, classes were dismissed, and the hallways filled with the excited voices of liberated teenagers. Lockers banged, cell phones engaged, and the bleed from iPods created an ambient adolescent roar.

Joan Sternhagen walked into the room and smiled, thrusting her hand forward. It was a generous, engaging smile that imparted warmth and a feeling of well-being. She had bright, unblinking eyes, a narrow face, and a scooped chin that threatened to touch her thin, hooked nose. Jack couldn't miss the fact that she looked very much like a bird. Correct that, a peacock.

Jack stood politely and towered over the petite woman as he shook her hand.

"I pulled the files for the years you requested, Mr. Bertolino. Most everything is in the computer nowadays, but that only dates back the past few years or so. Now, let me get a good look at you."

She stood back and gave Jack the once-over. Jack wouldn't bet the house on it, but he decided that her accent was from New Zealand and not Australia. It was lilting and musical, and he couldn't help but smile.

"You have a strong smile that probably doesn't get used all that often. You are serious to a fault. The lines on your face read integrity, sincerity, and strength. I wouldn't want to be a badster going up against the likes of you. How am I doing so far?"

"A badster?" he said.

"Oh, you know, the criminal element."

"So far so good," Jack said while she walked around her desk, sat down demurely, and opened the files.

"I'm appalled by that horrible picture circulating on Facebook. Everyone in the school has seen it. That poor boy. Simply terrible. Nobody deserves to die like that."

Jack nodded in agreement. "Any rumors as to why he was killed?"

"None that were shared with me," she said wistfully. And then, "Let's get to work."

Jack eased down onto his straight-backed wooden chair and glanced at her threadbare padded swiveling office chair with envy. Joan swept her shoulder-length straight blond hair back behind her ears and pulled on a pair of tortoiseshell reading glasses that hung from a red braided cord around her neck.

"The kid I'm looking for was off," he said.

"Off how?"

"You know, different."

"You're not helping me, Mr. Bertolino."

"I know . . . sorry. I'm looking for someone with the potential to kill. The potential to slaughter the young man you saw on Facebook and be cold enough to post it to send a message."

"I think I understand."

"Let's just go down the list, and if anything comes up, anything jogs your memory, we'll talk about it."

"Fair enough."

She read the names of the teenagers Jack had provided and showed him the pictures that were on file.

Jack recognized Raymond Higueras as being the man on crutches. He looked at the file and took notes.

They were all teenagers-turned-men, sixteen-year-olds with the countenance of killers, and now all members of a notorious street gang. Joan went down the list and gave Jack her recollections or handwritten notes if the young men's case files had crossed her desk. He learned that most of the boys were latchkey kids, lower income. If there were two parents, they both worked. The 18th Street Angels provided these kids with emotional, personal, and financial security. Same story, different city. The common denominator was that the young boys had to kill to gain entrance to the promised land.

Joan's eyes softened when she reached Johnny Rodriguez's file.

"Good kid. No, great kid. Had all the potential in the world. Strong family, two sisters who graduated from John Burroughs with honors. It says here that he was enrolled in college prep classes, and then he dropped out of sight. I take that as a personal failure. These kids. When they fall, they fall very hard, Mr. Bertolino. I wrote a note in the margin."

She spun the file on her ink blotter to read her handwritten scrawl.

"His sister blamed a friend of his for . . . Oh."

Joan Sternhagen stopped at a particular name, looked up over the top of her reading glasses, and stared into the distance, trying to conjure up a memory.

"Hector Lopez."

"Who?" Jack asked. The name wasn't on his list.

"I don't remember too much. He was assigned to me, a habitual truant. A lot of kids, a lot of faces, a lot of problems," she explained.

"What do your notes say about Hector?"

Jack felt he was finally on to something and didn't want to stop the flow. Joan flipped through another folder until she located Hector's file.

"'Would rather be anywhere but sitting across from me,' is what I wrote at the time. He would say whatever was needed to end the interview. No college aspirations, tested in the lower seventy percentile."

"Was he in the gang?"

"Not as a matter of record . . ."

"But?"

"It seems likely. Hector's father abandoned the family in his junior year. It says he moved to Guadalajara. Hector dropped out his senior year." Sternhagen peered at Jack over her reading glasses. "I remember that he was big for his age. If there had been a football team at John Burroughs, he might have played." She added with regret, "I can't get through to them all. But I do what I can."

"Big, huh," Jack said to himself. And then, "Do you have a picture of Hector?"

"No, if it's not in my files, one didn't exist."

Jack wasn't sure he could accomplish anything more, and the loud ticks of the clock reminded him that he had to get a move on. He jotted down Hector Lopez's last known address, his father's work history, and then the current addresses of the various 18th Street Angels on the list, photocopied their pictures, and thanked Mrs. Sternhagen for her time.

He listened to the echo of his shoes as they reverberated on the scuffed linoleum floor and walked out of the school with increasing speed; he did not look back. He thought he'd hit a vein. He just had to see where it led him.

———————

Jack was driving with one hand, eating a bean, cheese, and rice burrito with the other. He had made a quick stop at a roadside taco stand; the Excedrin and caffeine were burning a hole in his gut, and he realized that the burrito might just create the perfect storm. But he kept on eating.

The late-afternoon crosstown traffic was bumper to bumper, and two blocks from Royce Motors the primer gray car raced past him, driving in the opposite direction.

Nobody worked a full day anymore, Jack thought.

He tried to execute a one-handed U-turn after their car had made a left onto the main thoroughfare. But he couldn't make the turning radius. He dropped the greasy burrito in his lap, banged the car into a tire-spinning reverse, and then nearly clipped the cars parked on the side of the street as the Plymouth lurched forward.

He picked up his food about the same time he caught sight of his quarry and then eased up on the gas, staying five cars behind. He finished off the burrito in two quick bites, wiping his hands onto his already stained black jeans. He'd worry about the salsa spill later.

Jack slowed as he watched the gray car pull off the road into a strip-mall parking lot. He drove past, keeping his eyes straight ahead, and in his rearview mirror watched the men exit their vehicle. Jack did a quick run around the block and pulled over to the curb a half block away. The man on crutches, Raymond Higueras, made his way into the Black Stallion Inn. The bar shared space in the low-rent mall with a Laundromat, a Mexican *panaderia,* and a store that sold wedding dresses.

The Black Stallion Inn had no windows, and the front facade was covered with rough-hewn planks. A blue neon horse with a wild mane reared up and down as if it were stomping a rattler to death. Jack enjoyed the symbolism, and as he watched the front door, another car pulled into the lot and parked. The two young men who walked into the bar had the dead eyes of gangbangers but were hardly street legal.

Nick had explained the tiered system of the 18th Street Angels while giving Jack and Tommy the tour of Ontario. It worked like the Mafia in Jack's old stomping grounds. There were the "made men," their lieutenants, and then the young sharks or soldiers who worked on their crews.

The 18th Street Angels, a Chicano street gang, also had three tiers: the Lil' Angels, the Angelitos, and at the top of the food chain, the 18th Street Angels. To make it into the top tier from one of the other two groups, a young gangster needed to prove himself by killing or assisting in the killing of a rival gang member, someone who had dissed the Angels in some way.

Jack checked his parking meter and saw that it was after six. The sun was about to shut down for the day. Staying close to the storefronts across the street, using their thrown shadows, he snapped off a series of pictures of the cars in the strip-mall lot, capturing as many license plate numbers as he could get from his vantage point.

He didn't want to make his presence known until he was ready.

Seeing the door to the Black Stallion Inn swing open, Bertolino dropped his camera, spun on his heel, and turned to face the window of a video store.

Raymond Higueras, finding a way to swagger on crutches, clomped across the lot with a young woman in tow. In the window's reflection he could see the couple walk over to a compact car. He braced the young girl against the car, and their good-bye kiss turned into a groping clinch.

Jack took the opportunity to walk back down the block to the Plymouth and get in. The woman was now in the driver's seat of a Toyota Corolla. She applied some lipstick in the vanity mirror, another thick layer of black eyeliner, and then drove out of the lot, waving good-bye to her bruised warrior. Jack snapped off a few shots of the old car as she drove past him. He could make a positive ID of the woman, but he wasn't sure if the pictures would read through the black tint of his windshield and the encroaching night sky.

Balancing on one crutch, Higueras pulled out a cigarette, lit it, and took a deep drag. The cigarette's tip glowed orange and his expression was smug as he glanced up and down the block on the exhale, not seeing anything that piqued his interest.

King of the world.

The door to the bar swung open again and his two coworkers spilled out, obviously feeling no pain, and sauntered over to their car. David Reyes helped Higueras into the backseat and they motored out. Jack fired up the Plymouth and waited until their car was a safe distance up the street before turning on his lights and carefully following.

———

All three men lived within a six-block radius of each other in south Ontario. Jack noted the two new addresses. Then he picked a point somewhere in the middle and parked. From here he would walk to his destination.

Raymond Higueras's house had a similar layout to the Reyes house. Every room in the small bungalow was lit as Jack, dressed in black, carefully made his way around the perimeter of the building, checking windows, his nine millimeter out of the shoulder holster and ready. He could hear a neighbor's television set, smell onions wafting from someone's kitchen exhaust, heard a few barking dogs, but thankfully the street remained empty. More important to Jack, none of the surrounding houses had a direct view of Higueras's front door.

Jack's target was alone in the house, lounging with his cast propped up on a scarred wooden coffee table, watching a rerun of *Two and a Half Men*. He'd taken his work shirt off and his cut, bare chest, from the neck down, was an inked shrine to the 18th Street Angels. Jack could see a small mirror next to his foot with a pile of cocaine big enough to satisfy an addict's itch for a week. A bottle of Dos Equis was sitting opened next to the mirror, and he realized that his own throat was bone dry.

Jack Bertolino had spent many years on the NYPD serving

warrants on drug cells and money-laundering cells with a team of trained men. Even with electronic battering rams, shields, automatic weapons, flash grenades, and a tactical plan firmly in place, each raid was a life-or-death experience. He never knew what was waiting on the other side of the door, whether he was going to get shot in the face as soon as he entered the premises.

Tonight Jack was going in alone, illegally, and without backup. There was no other way.

He checked the road for foot traffic one more time, and when he was sure it was all clear, he stepped silently up onto the small front porch and sucked in a breath.

Jack pounded his fist on the door and shouted, "Police—open the door! Open the fucking door!"

He heard a shuffling, the banging of crutches, something getting knocked over, a "shit" intoned from within. "What the fuck!" Higueras cried as he cracked open the door.

Jack's foot pistoned out, snapping the security chain and splintering the wooden door into the gangster's face, knocking him backward into the room. His broken nose gushed blood. His .38 skittered across the stained hardwood floor. His crutches toppled, his arms pinwheeled, and he crashed down hard on his back.

In a blur of motion Jack kicked the door shut behind him, straddled Higueras, and jammed the barrel of his Glock into the young man's throat.

Jack chambered a round. The precision metallic ratcheting sound a Glock nine millimeter makes when a bullet is forced out of the gun's clip and into the killing chamber is a universal sound that good guys and bad guys and wild animals alike all understand on a primal level. When he had Higueras's undivided attention, he flipped him onto his stomach, snapped a pair of plastic cuffs around his wrists, and shoved the gun into the base of his neck.

Jack fought to control his emotions as he prepared to conduct the interview. "Who ordered you to run the Lexus off the road?"

"*No habla,*" Higueras croaked.

"Bullshit. Your teacher's name was Gainey and she says you were mediocre, your rap sheet says you're a scumbag, so let's cut the crap. You tell me who paid you to run the Lexus off the road or I'll end this. Now."

Jack twisted the barrel of the Glock into Higueras's neck.

"Never got a name, just got more product. All over the phone," he lied.

"Who pulled the strings, scumbag? Set up the phone call?"

Raymond Higueras was in pain but not enough to spill. The coke and the beer were making him brave. Plus, time was running short. Jack didn't know if Higueras's squeeze was going to show up unexpectedly.

Jack lifted his gun and smashed it down onto the plaster cast, shattering it near the ankle. He shifted his weight and leaned his 180-pound frame onto the broken leg with his knee while he jammed Higueras's head into the floor. The gangster emitted a moan that set Jack's teeth on edge.

"Who pulled the strings?" he quietly demanded.

"My manager."

"At Royce?"

The boy's voice was sparked with pain. "He's an OG. He hires Angels on probation."

"Who runs him?"

"Fuck you. They'll kill me."

"Who killed the woman?" Jack said as the memory of Mia came flooding back. It took every ounce of his control not to pull the trigger.

"Fuck you, *pendejo.*"

Jack knew the clock was ticking. He dragged Higueras into the bathroom, opened the cabinet under the sink, and attached his bound hands to the drainpipe with another plastic cuff.

"You're a dead man," Higueras said, spitting as his broken nose streamed more blood into his open mouth.

"*No habla*, asshole," Jack said as he unleashed a backhanded snot shot that hit Higueras's jaw like a hammer. That would shut up his macho bullshit for a while, Jack thought as he wiped down the cabinet door with a rank towel, and moved into the living room.

Jack pulled up a sofa pillow that had been used to hide the cocaine and mirror. He kicked Higueras's gun into the center of the room so it could not be missed. The punk's prints were all over the .38, and he was headed back to prison for violating parole. New illegal drugs and weapons charges would dominate the next few years of his life.

Higueras's cell phone was lying on the wooden table and Jack pocketed it. He knew he was taking evidence, but nothing else he had done that night was by the book. Jack was traveling through new territory and needed all the help he could get.

Charlie Sheen was cavorting in bed with a voluptuous blonde as Jack turned up the volume on the television set, being careful not to leave prints. He then used the tail of his black T-shirt to close the front door behind him.

Jack walked silently through the empty streets toward the safety of the Plymouth. At night the neighborhood looked so suburban, almost pleasant. But behind the facade of normalcy, the area was controlled by stone-cold killers. Just like Jack's old neighborhood.

He took in deep breaths of the cold night air to slow his heart rate. When he slid into the car and locked the doors, he pulled out Higueras's cell phone, dialed 911, reported shots fired, and gave them Raymond Higueras's address. Jack was already motoring out of the area, heading in the direction of the I-10, before he heard the first approaching siren.

31

Jack wasn't much of a beer drinker, but he saw the bottom of the frosted mug before he came up for a breath. Nick Aprea was standing next to him at a quiet local bar in Manhattan Beach, and he signaled the bartender to pour another, like a man at a blackjack table requesting another card.

Then he bit into a lime wedge, licked some salt off his closed fist, threw back a shot of Herradura Silver, and tapped the bar again.

"It's a look," Nick said, referring to the salsa stain that had dried on Jack's black jeans. "Say, I got a call from Vince over in Ontario. Bad fuckin' luck for one of the Angels on the list you sent. His face doesn't match his picture anymore. Any idea how that happened?"

"Not a clue," Jack said as the bartender gracefully slid a second draft down the length of the bar. It came to rest directly in front of Jack's hand.

Jack lifted the mug and took a slow sip.

"Good to hear," Nick said. "They fielded an anonymous 911 call from Raymond Higueras's own phone. And yet *said* Higueras was sort of tied up at the time of the call. Contemplating some one-on-one with an orthopedic surgeon was how it was related to me."

"One of life's mysteries," Jack said, relaxing for the first time all day.

"Well, the phone should definitely disappear after it gives up its secrets, one would think."

"You should become a life coach, Nick, what with all your good advice."

Nick looked pleased with the idea. "I'm thinking of branching out. You're right. I'm full of untapped talent."

"You're full of something, that's for sure."

His smile grew broader. "That's what my wife tells me on a regular basis. I just nod and agree. Works out pretty well for the both of us."

Nick replayed the ritual with the lime, a pinch of salt, and then the tequila with the practiced skill of a priest blessing sacramental wine.

"I ran the manager's photo through ViCAP," Nick said after his face registered satisfaction with the Herradura. "Roman Ortiz is in fact an OG. Been a member of the 18th Street Angels since he was jumped in the late sixties, and he is purported to have deep ties to the Mexican Mafia."

Nick had just corroborated Higueras's story.

"Alvarez is paying protection money to the Mexican Mafia," Jack noted.

Nick rolled the implication of that around and continued.

"Roman did a twenty-year stint at Corcoran for first-degree murder. That was the only one he got nailed for, but his sheet woulda made Capone proud. He's a bad man who has been operating under the radar since his release in ninety-nine."

"Well, if he's an upstanding citizen, he shouldn't mind if we go up on his phones, work and home."

"In a perfect world," Nick said, meaning no fucking way, "I'd try reaching out to the feds when you have more than a hunch, something verifiable. Only way a wiretap will fly in this environment."

Jack understood and started thinking out loud. "I think we should check out the owner of the bus I saw roll into Royce Motors. If the coke's Dominican, it had to be hitching a ride west somehow."

"Good notion. I've got a friend at the DMV. Do you want me to drop the hammer on the other two players?"

"No. Let's keep our powder dry. They don't feel right for Mia. And the time line is wrong for the latest and greatest. They had their hands full trying to drive Tommy and me to an early grave when Ricky Hernandez was killed. I don't want to pull the alarm on Royce until I have a few more answers."

"Righteous."

Nick signaled for a third shot and threw a credit card onto the bar. Jack pushed it back and threw down his own. Drinks were on him.

"The tats on the severed thigh matched the gang ink on Hernandez," Nick said. "Ran with a group that operates next door to the Angels. They're taxed for the right to sell product in Angel territory. Someone was skimming or just looked at one of these crazy fucks sideways."

"What about the locks on Hernandez's door?" Jack asked. "Any scratches on the cylinder?"

"It looks like the killers entered through the back door. Yes, there were markings. The tech didn't think it was a clean enough match with yours for a conviction, but I'm thinking we're looking at the same guy or guys."

"There were two men in the car at Mia's," Jack said more forcefully than he intended. "And there's no way one man could have strung up Ricky Hernandez."

"We're on the same page."

"Anything on the knot used to hang our guy?" Jack asked.

"I'm gettin' to it . . ."

Nick pulled out his dog-eared pad and found the page where he had made the notation.

"Called a packing knot. First knot they teach Boy Scouts," he said, raising his eyebrows. "My guess, this is one kid that got booted out of the troop, if that's where he learned his technique."

"We weren't big on the Scouts on Staten Island," Jack said. "You could get smacked up the side of your head you walked around the neighborhood in that getup."

That elicited a snort from Nick, who continued, "Used for baling, parcels, oh, and uh, roasts. You know, as in meat."

"Meat, huh?"

"They also call it a butcher's knot."

Nick dropped that last detail, like a pebble in a still pond, and waited to see Jack's response.

Jack took a long pull on his beer, turned slowly, and his eyes locked on Nick's. "That makes an awful lot of sense."

"Sure as shit does."

———

Jack Bertolino was sitting in a small dark room. Soft music was being piped into his cubicle as he waited to receive a Swedish massage from a Thai masseuse.

Jack pulled off his T-shirt and stretched out in his underwear on a massage table. It was a little hot in the room and he decided to lie on top of the sheets. He wondered about the protocol as far as nudity went and thought staying in his skivvies was the right move.

He replayed the phone conversation he had enjoyed late the night before with DDA Leslie Sager. She had called to invite him to dinner, her treat, when their schedules permitted. Jack kicked himself for not making the call first, but was surprisingly happy to have received it. They decided that Saturday might work for them both and agreed to check in again on Friday.

Jack's back was knotted from last night's violence, and he knew that if he didn't get some work done on it he wouldn't be any good sitting surveillance. He also decided it would be better to keep some distance between himself and the 18th Street Angels for a few days, because after Raymond Higueras's story leaked, he was sure the gang would be on high alert and make his job that much more difficult.

He also had to stay cocked and locked at all times, because if they were going to exact retribution, they knew where he lived.

A lilting feminine voice from the other side of the door rang like a bell and asked if he was ready. Jack said yes. He looked forward to some relief, and then the door opened.

The woman screamed—ear piercing!

Jack twisted around, strained his back, and struggled not to fall off the table.

"Get under the sheet!" she hollered, way over the top.

"I've got my underwear on, for crying out loud. What's the problem here?" he said, startled. And Jack was not an easy man to startle.

The petite woman spat out a torrent of words. "I almost got shut down once, and I'm mildly autistic, and I have Asperger's syndrome, and I have a hard time editing myself, and I forgot my card."

Jack grabbed up the sheet and covered himself. They stared each other down for an extended beat.

"Are we all right here . . . because this was supposed to be relaxing," Jack said, knowing full well he had one foot out the door.

"I'm all right," she said. Her emotional state had turned on a dime.

"Good. At least one of us is."

The woman closed the door behind her and continued as if nothing had happened.

"Do you like it deep, medium, or light? Probably deep, right?" she asked, not waiting for an answer.

"No," Jack said, cutting her off, wanting to make sure they were on the same page. "No, I've had a few back operations. So medium."

Jack lay facedown on the table, under the sheet now, and found himself trying to clear his mind.

The young woman pulled out the oils, threw a new-age cassette into a small tape machine, checked the clock, and started working on his neck, moving slowly down his spine.

Better, Jack thought. His breathing soon turned deep and rhythmic.

He was starting to drift. Halfway down Jack's back the masseuse leaned in, pressing her thumbs deep into his muscle with an animal strength that belied her size. Bertolino saw a sudden bolt of white and almost elevated off of the table.

He emitted a growl, and the woman giggled.

"Sweet pain," she said and giggled some more. "Sometimes I can't monitor my own strength," she said in her most delicate voice.

Jack didn't respond, but he wanted to wring this little woman's neck. He forced himself to start thinking about baseball, and taxes, and the bills that were sitting on his desk. He suffered through a half hour of sometime torture before his cell phone rang. He gratefully reached for it.

"No cell phones are allowed," she barked, agitated again.

Jack jumped off of the table, opened the door, and gestured her out. He put the phone to his ear once the door was closed.

The call was from Gene McLennan, the Los Angeles DEA agent who had been the first one to tell him about the 18th Street Angels over lunch at Phillipe's.

"What the hell are you up to, Bertolino?" he said with a smile in his voice.

"I was getting some physical therapy."

"Is that what they call it these days?"

Everyone's a comedian, Jack thought.

"I'm glad you got cleared of those charges," he went on. "I was certain you were getting the bum's rush."

"Thanks, Gene. What's up?"

"Right," he said. "All business with you. Good. Got a call from an old CI, and he shared something that I thought might be of interest."

Jack wanted to tell him to get on with it. He was sitting in a dark room in his underwear but chose to let his silence move the conversation forward.

"Some foreign product has filtered into the local system in the past twenty-four hours."

That caught Jack's attention. "Foreign?"

"As in, it could be more Dominican. Word on the street is the Los Zetas aren't happy, and there could be blowback. Thought you'd want to know."

"Thanks."

"Any traction between Alvarez and the Angels?" McLennan asked.

"It's a solid maybe. I'll keep you in the loop."

"Do that, Jack. Let's talk soon."

"Question," Jack said before McLennan could hang up. "Was Ricky Hernandez under contract?"

The silence said it all.

"You still there, Gene?"

"Why do you ask?" he said in an even tone.

"Just looking to motive. His death was quite a statement."

"Stay in touch." And the line went dead.

Jack clicked off the phone, surprised by the call. He couldn't help but question the timing.

––––––––––

Arturo Delgado was pacing in a tight windowless room filled with every form of electronic gear imaginable: large computer servers, multiple keyboards, five twenty-seven-inch screens set up in a semicircle on a long workstation occupied by a fifty-year-old woman. She had downloaded the information off the nano flash drive Arturo had provided, and was presently concentrating on the central monitor, which was scrolling numbers and letters in various configurations at mind-numbing speed. The room was meat-locker cold to keep the servers from overheating.

Arturo didn't feel the cold; he was on the hunt. He remembered exactly how old he'd been and what it had felt like the first time he had a five-thousand-dollar balance in his bank account in Colombia. When his drug dealings created a twenty-thousand-dollar windfall, he took his mother out to a fancy dinner and bought her a thick gold chain. And when he hit the hundred-thousand-dollar mark, he was living in the city and thought there would be no end to his good fortune.

He was a drug dealer on a grand scale and a killer when needed. But not a thief. Arturo thought about all the wealth he had amassed in his lifetime and all that he had lost and decided that for twenty-four million, he could add thief to his résumé.

He looked over at the woman, who was now writing in tight script on a legal-size yellow pad.

Ex-IRS agent Margaret Monahan had lost her faith in the federal government at one point in her life, but not her talent. She started freelancing in the underground economy and traded her major medical and dental coverage for a Mercedes, travel, and personal freedom.

She pushed away from the workstation in her Herman Miller desk chair and swiveled toward Delgado. Her expression could only be described as admiring.

"She was good, I'll give her that," she said with raised eyebrows.

"If she was that good, she would still be alive," Delgado added impatiently.

"But she had some poetry in her. Divine retribution. You wouldn't understand, Arturo, you're not a woman."

"Tell me."

"Her password," Margaret said, spelling out h-a-i-r-a-n-d-m-a-k-e-u-p.

"What does it mean?"

"What does a woman need when she's going to travel? When she's on the run? Hair and makeup. To change her look, Arturo."

Delgado didn't appreciate the intended message. He wasn't amused.

"I'll need an hour or so to go over the records. Why don't you get some lunch? There's a passable Peruvian restaurant on the corner and Chinese a few doors past. I'll text you when I'm ready."

Delgado's stomach started to growl, and not from hunger.

Kenny Ortega's face lit up the computer screen, and his enthusiasm was infectious. "I'm thinking of taking two weeks' vacation and flying out. It's killing me that you're having all the fun," he said, Skyping from his fifth-floor office in the Miami Federal Building. He could see a foursome teeing off on the seventeenth hole of the public golf course across the causeway. For the first time in a long time, he was happy to be plugged in and gainfully employed.

"Yeah, it's a fucking laugh riot, Ortega," Jack said from inside his loft, eliciting another bout of laughter from his friend.

"C'mon, you're out there trying to keep all those starlets to yourself. You used to be a giving man."

"Busted, but it's hard work having to beat them off with a stick."

"Now you're talking, brother."

With the pleasantries out of the way, Kenny got down to business.

"Nothing on Arturo Delgado. He's entirely off the grid if he's still alive, and that's up for debate. Word from the 'office' was that he was called back to Colombia after his failure with operation Green Door. Faced a tribunal—that shredded his leg with an AK while he was hanging over an interrogation pit—and disappeared."

Jack kept mum, but after spotting Delgado in person, he seriously doubted he was out of the game. It did explain the slight limp.

"I spoke with your old buddy Mateo. He sent his best. He's a real estate mogul now. Can you believe it? Found a way to flip foreclosed properties. He's making a killing right here in Miami while everybody else is still losing their shirts. But he'd do anything for *el jefe*. Said he'd put in a few calls and get back to me."

Jack didn't doubt it for a second. Mateo was the best CI he had ever worked with. Brilliant, sharp looking, and fearless. Photographic memory. If he hadn't been sucked into the cartel's lure of easy money, with his quick wits and MBA he could have ended up the CEO of General Electric. He was that good. As it was, Mateo had worked off a twenty-five-year prison sentence and owed his personal freedom to Jack Bertolino.

"Delgado's still alive," Jack said with dead certainty.

"Then we'll find him," Kenny said with equal conviction. "The bus you tagged at Royce Motors is owned by Travel Associates," he went on. "They have a fleet of eight to ten at any given time. Our particular bus was leased to Outlaws Incorporated. They're an L.A.–based hip-hop label and management company that handles all the tours for their recording artists."

"Just for curiosity's sake, I'd like to take a look at Travel Associates," Jack said, "see if there's any connection to Royce Motors or maybe a dummy corp for Outlaws Inc."

Bertolino had e-mailed Kenny the information obtained from Nick Aprea's DMV search, and true to form, Ortega had gotten the job done.

"Are we thinking money laundering?"

"Just thinking."

"Don't hurt yourself."

"And?" Jack knew there was more. With Ortega, there was always more.

"The bus had two outstanding parking tickets—no great whoops on that score, right?—but are you ready for this? The bus was illegally parking in front of the Fountainebleau."

"Miami."

"Yes, sir . . . the hip-hop group Gold Nickel was playing at Mansion, over on Washington, in South Beach, and our bus was their chariot. The group checked out of the hotel Monday morning and should have rolled into L.A. on Wednesday, couple hours before you eyeballed it."

"About the same time foreign product started hitting the street, according to McLennan. Foreign as in Dominican," Jack said.

"A thousand keys were brought in on a go-fast boat the week before the concert. We tracked it from Colombia to the Dominican Republic; it evaded radar offshore. A piece of that could be what showed up on your coast."

"The time line works."

Jack liked the progression. Coke picked up and delivered to Miami. Bus arrived in town. Drives back to L.A. with the drugs in the cargo bay or in a trap, a secret compartment. Dominican coke floods the streets of Ontario.

"The driver of record was arrested last year on weapons charges," Ortega said, on a roll now. "Carrying a concealed nine mil. He moonlights as security for Outlaw's talent. Charges were dropped when his lawyer delivered his permit to carry. He's connected, but no known gang affiliations.

"But here's the kicker. Three other men hired as roadie-slash-bodyguards, also doing concert security, all clean, except for one"—Kenny rifled through a stack of papers—"Thomas Vegas. He came up clean, but his brother was one of the twenty-seven picked up in the 18th Street Angels raid. Coincidence?" Ortega said with a flourish. "I think not."

"Great work, Kenny. Really."

"That's why they pay me the big bucks," he said, deflecting the praise. Attaboys were a rare commodity in the DEA.

"I'm gonna have to spend some quality time at Royce Motors," Jack said, moving it up on his priority list.

"Tread lightly. After last night, you're a walking bull's-eye."

"Speaking of targets, was Ricky Hernandez under contract?"

"A card-carrying G-man, working off time. Gave up the Angels' farm. He wasn't loved, but he'll be missed. Messy business, that. Why do you ask?"

"McLennan was tight-lipped when I ran it by him. Just looking for motive. Same MO as Mia."

"Gene has one foot out the door and doesn't want to jeopardize his pension. Cut him some slack."

Jack could live with that explanation. "Anything on Vista Haven?"

"I put in for a flight to Mykonos. Can you believe that the suits up here denied my request?" he said. "But Michael Kingman, the owner of Vista Haven, is a nonstarter. I'll interview his buddy Greg Stavos again when they're back in port the end of next week. Anything more at your end?"

"Still nothing with the P.O. box key. There are hundreds of potentials," Jack said, letting the irritation he felt enter his voice.

"I have Mia flying out of Miami," said Kenny, "but she'd become Sylvia Kole by the time she checked into the Ritz-Carlton Grand Cayman. She was styling, and money was not an issue. The concierge remembered her. Couldn't forget her tip, or her natural red hair."

"That woman had sand," Jack said with pure admiration.

"More than I can say for the banks. They're being less than forthcoming. I'll need more to go on before I can expect any cooperation."

"I'll work it at my end. Signing off."

"Till later, *mi hermano*."

32

Too much information, too little time, Jack thought as he worked his way through Pro's Ranch Market, back to the manager's office, dodging shopping carts, wailing toddlers, and employees stocking shelves.

The market had the feel of an outdoor festival with the colorful banners and a mariachi band that played near the La Cocina, where the staff served up fresh Mexican dishes. With the volume of the music and the crowd of shoppers trying to compete, the decibel level in the store was earsplitting but festive.

Their La Tortilleria cranked out homemade corn tortillas. Su Panaderia offered fresh-baked bread, empanadas, cakes, and doughnuts. Then there was house-made cheese, fresh produce, and meats of all kinds. Jack was getting an appetite but chose to stay on mission.

The manager was averting a crisis in the seafood department, Jack learned after he had knocked on the office door. The assistant manager promised he was due back in five. That gave Jack time to sample the tortillas and some fresh salsa from one of the many demo stations.

He stopped at the meat department and watched as one man, a knife, and an upright band saw took apart a side of beef, cutting and slicing the meat into steaks, ribs, and chops with skill and finesse, his once white butcher's apron splattered with blood. Piling the scraps and fat onto one side of the large cutting table, he neatly stacked the finished product on the other. It left Jack feeling uneasy.

Big man, big smile, and a big hand greeted him as the door to the manager's office opened and Jack was ushered inside. The silence was welcome as the door was closed, and Manager Joseph Cardonas—a man who looked like he had visited the demo stations once too often—offered Jack a seat.

"I can see you've got your hands full, so I'll make this short," Jack said as he flipped open a pad and checked the notes he'd taken in Sternhagen's office. "I'm looking for information on an employee who worked here from the late nineties until two thousand three. Name's Hector Lopez."

Joseph's eyes creased into a smile, which Jack didn't understand. The manager read Jack's confusion. "I'm happy to look, but Lopez is a very common name. I wasn't here in the nineties, took over in two thousand seven. James Alfaro ran the shop back then. He's been retired three years now in August. That's when I was transferred up from Phoenix."

"Anything you can do to help would be appreciated."

"Why the interest?"

"Just trying to close the door on an ongoing case," he lied, par for the course now that he was a PI.

Jack had chosen to dress like a cop that morning, but was still surprised when Cardonas didn't ask for his ID. But Jack wasn't about to question his good fortune.

The manager clicked some keys on his computer and then a few more. And then a few more. And then he cursed politely. And then he scrolled down another list and thankfully stopped.

"It's telling me that eight Lopezes worked here from ninety-five to two thousand three. Five of them were female, one Ramon Lopez is deceased, Miguel Lopez was fired in two thousand for dipping into the till, and Freddy Lopez is in his early thirties now and left Pro's Market to open his own organic produce store. No Hector Lopezes on file. Not to say he wasn't here. It's not a complete list. The supermarket strike in 2006 got nasty and someone hacked into corporate and many of the files were wiped clean. Nobody won in that strike. I can give you a printout if you like."

Jack was disappointed but let the man print out a sheet.

He walked out of the store with a bag of fresh corn tortillas and the address of the retired manager, James Alfaro.

Ex-IRS agent Margaret Monahan was all business, trying to keep any trace of emotion out of her voice. Arturo Delgado was not a man she liked to disappoint. She had pulled up another chair for Delgado, who sat stiffly at her side.

"The records only go back for a five-year period," Margaret explained.

Delgado knew that was when Alvarez first went away and Mia took control of the books.

"So, for that five-year period, regular payments were made into three different offshore corporations that had been set up in the Grand Caymans, Panama, and the Dominican Republic."

She laid out the entire convoluted process. A year ago Mia had merged the three corporations, and all of the monies, close to the twenty-four-million mark, were transferred to the Cayman IBC and a new corporate entity.

Over the course of the past year she'd slowly acquired the shares of the consolidated companies until she controlled 98 percent of the bottom line. Two months ago, she'd liquidated her shares and wire-transferred the entire sum of twenty-four million dollars to the HSBC Bank Canada in Vancouver. And then two weeks ago she'd zero-balanced that account and wired the money to God knows where.

"It could have gone into a Swiss bank account, or any of the offshore banking centers that protect these sorts of transactions," she concluded. "Without account numbers, passwords, and verified signatures, there's no way to get to the money even if we could trace it."

Margaret sat perfectly still. She worried that if she reached out and touched Arturo Delgado's face, her hands would blister.

———

The Alfaro house was painted a bright pastel blue with a black slate roof, an upper-middle-class California ranch. The garden had so many flowering annuals in bloom that it looked like a commercial for a garden center.

Jack sat uncomfortably on a blue Adirondack chair that matched the color of the house, with James Alfaro seated next to him. He had brought the tortillas as a gift, and the man gratefully received them.

"It's not my shop anymore, so I don't go back all that often. A man can do only so many victory laps."

"I know what you mean," Jack said, hoping to expedite the interview but not wanting to offend.

"I liked golf, but it didn't like me back, so the garden won." Alfaro's face broke into a deep craggy smile that showed off straight teeth the color of aged ivory. His hair was astonishingly white and offset his dark brown skin, which had seen more that its share of sun.

"Looks like a piece of heaven," Jack commented. "Now, what I'm interested in," he said, trying to steer the conversation, "is anything you can tell me about an employee who worked for you back in the late nineties till about two thousand three. Name's Hector Lopez."

Jack knew that he was on to something as soon as the name passed his lips. Alfaro's expression darkened.

"Funny thing about that," he said.

"How so?"

"I remember Lopez very well. He was a good man. Hard worker. Loved America. He was a citizen and proud of it. Never missed a day of work and then one day he picked up and left without a word. No thank you, no good-bye, no nothing. Wasn't right."

"What do you think happened?"

"A man doesn't leave a wife, a son, and a high-paying job to move back to Mexico. People are dropping dead crossing the desert to come in illegally."

Obviously, the man had spent some time worrying over this.

"Any ideas?"

"I went over to the Lopez home after a couple of days of not hearing word one. Thought there might have been a family emergency or something. Maybe he had a heart attack. Something."

"Who did you speak to?"

"I spoke with Hector Junior. Or tried to."

Alfaro looked like he was struggling with the memory, and Jack didn't want him to get lost and lose his train of thought.

"What was the problem with the boy?"

James's brow furrowed, and then he made a mental decision and continued. "He was off somehow."

Jack had used the same description when he'd met with Joan Sternhagen, the guidance counselor. He sat up a little straighter.

"Off how, Mr. Alfaro?"

"It was something about his eyes. Like he was challenging me. Said his father was homesick and went back to Mexico to visit his family. But I remembered very clearly that both of Lopez's parents had passed away the previous year, within a month of each other. Father first, mother died of a broken heart soon after. We had discussed it, you see. And I approved a two-week paid vacation so he could go back to—"

"Guadalajara," Jack interjected.

"That sounds about right, to handle the arrangements," the older man said in almost a musing tone. "I asked the boy if I could speak with his mother and was told she wasn't at home. Again, it was more a challenge than a statement. You know," he went on, "I had the strangest feeling that she was in the living room, listening to our conversation, but I didn't push it. I asked the kid to have his father give me a call when he spoke with him, and I left. What could I do?"

Jack hiked up his shoulders by way of an answer, not wanting to stop the flow.

"I looked back at their house as soon as I got into my car and watched the boy close the door. Big kid, built like a bull. He had the strangest smile on his face. It was . . . unnatural somehow. Made me feel bad, you know, in my stomach."

"And you never spoke with Mr. Lopez again?" Jack asked.

"Never. Not a word. I spoke with my wife about it and then filed a police report the following week. But, well, you know how it is. Cops—oh, excuse me, the police—couldn't spare the time. A wetback gone home. End of story."

Jack had butted heads with racism in his career. Hell, the old Irish guard had never been fond of the Italians. Some things never changed.

"I'll look into it," Jack said, "let you know if I discover anything of interest."

"I'd appreciate that," Alfaro said before he turned thoughtful again. "Didn't seem right . . . good pay . . . benefits . . . great butcher . . ."

"Lopez was a butcher?"

Jack got that familiar itch on the back of his neck—like an electric current—when a case was about to break, or when a piece of a puzzle fit snugly onto the game board.

"Talented man. Up for a promotion to run the entire department."

Jack and Mr. Alfaro stood at the same time. Both men grunted in unison. Jack stretched his back. There was a storm front moving in, and the clouds blowing over the San Bernardino Mountains were taking on an ominous gray hue.

A butcher. A butcher's knot. Jack didn't believe in coincidences.

33

The sky opened up, and the Mustang's windshield wipers struggled to keep up with the rain.

Jack wondered why Hector's name hadn't come up on any of the gang lists. He wasn't even sure he was an 18th Street Angel but decided to find out before moving forward with the investigation.

He also wanted to talk with Hector's mother before confronting her son. If he was his man, Jack didn't want to spook him. If his father was in Guadalajara, that's where Hector would jackrabbit to if pressed.

The physical description, the father's occupation, the connection to the knot used to hang up the last victim made Hector Junior a compelling lead. But that was all he was at this point. He knew better than anyone to never jump to conclusions.

It was getting late, and Jack didn't want to get caught sitting in the parking lot called the I-10 in rush-hour traffic, but he was on a roll. He cross-referenced the GPS map with his list, and saw that the last known address for Johnny Rodriguez was his mother's house. It was only two miles away and closer than the Lopez house.

When Jack arrived, an attractive twenty-something woman stood on the other side of the open doorway holding a chubby baby boy on her dungaree-clad hip. The baby, who couldn't have been more than six months old, held on to her white peasant blouse with bunched-up, dimpled fists.

The woman tossed back her shoulder-length brown hair, and her clear brown eyes eyed Jack suspiciously and then with fear.

"Is Johnny dead?" she asked. The first words out of her mouth.

She tightened her grip on the boy, who picked up on his mother's emotions and erupted, from serene to wailing in an instant.

Jack stood on the covered porch and wiped the rain that was dripping off his nose with the back of his hand. The brown-shingled house was welcoming, even in the rain, with green fabric-covered patio furniture and flower boxes filled with purple pansies. The woman shifted the boy onto her shoulder and rocked him.

"Why would he be dead?" Jack asked gently.

It didn't work.

"Who are you?" she asked accusingly. She glanced beyond Jack and could see the silver Mustang parked in front of the house. "You're not a cop."

"My name's Jack Bertolino. I came to ask about one of Johnny's friends in the 18th Street Angels. Hector Lopez. Do you know him?"

"Johnny's all right?"

"As far as I know. Is he in any trouble?"

"He's nothing but trouble," she said bitterly.

Jack would delve into Johnny's story later.

"What can you tell me about Hector?"

"Who are you?" she repeated.

The baby turned on a dime again and started cooing. One fist in his mouth, the other gripping his mother's neck.

"I'm a private investigator," Jack said and pulled out his license, flipping it open for her to read.

There's a first time for everything, Jack thought.

"Why are you looking for Hector?"

"His father and Hector are estranged. Hector Senior hired me to make sure his son was all right. I'm just doing research for the preliminary report."

Jack didn't particularly like lying, but sometimes it was the only way to get information. Especially when he wasn't standing behind the power of a shield.

"I thought his father was dead," she said, puzzled.

"What makes you say that?" Jack asked, pretending to be amused by the notion.

"Just something I heard back in high school. So you're a private investigator?"

"Guilty."

"I'm Diane."

Jack extended his hand; Diane held the baby with one arm and gave Jack a firm handshake.

"I was a production assistant at Sony Studios. I got downsized as soon as I ballooned two dress sizes and they discovered I was pregnant."

"Doesn't seem right," Jack said, feeling a slight thaw in the ice flow.

"Johnny," she said wistfully. "He could have been anything he wanted to be. My brother had it all. Looks, brains, personality—and then he met Hector."

"What can you tell me about him?"

"I don't know a thing about him except that he ruined my brother's life. He got Johnny involved in the gang."

"Hector's a member of the Angels?"

"For sure. Nobody would even talk about Hector at John Burroughs, and he had dropped out by the time I moved over from middle school. Kids were afraid of him. I mean really terrified."

"Why?"

Master of interrogation, he mused.

"Just teenage stuff mostly. Rumors, you know?"

"Humor me," Jack smiled, laying on the charm.

"They said he killed someone."

She let that hang in the air for a moment and stroked her baby's fine blond hair. "Doesn't sound like much now with everything that's going on, but they were only fifteen."

"Any ideas?" Jack asked, prompting.

"It doesn't make any sense now, I mean, after what you've told me, but at the time his father had walked out on the family ... or he hadn't."

Interesting, Jack thought, hoping there was more.

"That's all I know. Johnny's breaking Mom's heart, but at this point there's nothing we can do. We talked about an intervention, but he won't listen to reason."

"What does your brother do for a living, if you don't mind my asking?"

"Gang business, whatever that entails, and cars. My mother calls him a grease monkey. It's killing her. He could have been a lawyer, or whatever, now he works on cars," she said like a question. "The Angels used to be a car club is what I hear."

"Does he live here?"

Diane shook her head and shifted the boy to her other hip.

"Johnny moves around a lot. We don't even have an address for him. He calls us when he feels like it or needs his laundry done or wants a hot meal."

"Would you be willing to give me his phone number?"

That got an instant shutdown. "No. He's still my brother."

Jack liked this young woman. He even respected her misplaced loyalty.

"Listen, Diane. If you hear from Johnny or hear anything regarding Hector, you can call me day or night at this number. It's my cell. If Johnny needs help in any way, you can give him *my* number. I have some friends. I'll do what I can."

"Why would you help?"

Jack looked beyond her into the living room and saw the pride Diane's mother took in the house. He observed the loving way Diane held her son, the pain she felt for her brother.

"He comes from solid people. He might be looking for a way out of a bad situation. Sometimes we make decisions early on in our lives that we'd change if given the opportunity."

Jack handed Diane his card, another first.

"I still don't understand," she said.

"Payback," he informed her. "I had people in my life who lent a hand to help me. Simple as that."

Diane remained skeptical, but Jack had given her something to think about.

"Let me give you my number in case you hear anything," she offered.

She ripped off a piece of a junk mail envelope from the front table and scribbled a number with one hand while expertly juggling the baby on her hip with the other.

"Do you know if Hector still lives at his mother's address?" Jack asked.

"I wouldn't know. I wouldn't think so. He's a little old for that. It'd be queer. I don't even know where the house is. Other side of the tracks, if you know what I mean. I only know that he exists because he turned my brother's life to shit."

That set the baby off again. Jack hadn't heard a set of lungs like that on a kid since his son, Chris, was born.

The rain didn't bother Hector. Nothing bothered him when he was behind the wheel of his blue Impala. He liked the thundering sound the heavy car produced under the floorboards as it powered through the flooded intersections, and the rooster tails his tires created that splashed oncoming cars and the occasional unlucky pedestrian.

Johnny was more moody than normal, Hector thought, and getting on his nerves. He should just make up with that cunt of a girlfriend of his and get on with it. They were building something large. No time for the weak.

The men had made a drop-off in Colton and now in Fontana, the last of the night.

Hector put on his right-turn signal and appreciated the click, click, rhythmic clicking sound it made as he pulled into the Speedway Garage on Eighteenth Street. He turned off the windshield wipers, shut the car down, and he and Johnny climbed out. "Yo, Hector, Johnny, *como está*, bros?"

The three men did sharp fist pops, and Frankie stood back and admired Hector's ride.

"You ever sell, you sell to me."

"Right, I'll keep that in mind, *ese*," Hector said, meaning over his dead body.

Frankie's wiry frame was tattooed from the neck down. His thin bare arms were two solid sleeves of colored ink. He was one of the best mechanics in this part of the state. He worked on the dragsters that frequented the NHRA-sanctioned Fontana Auto Club Speedway, a NASCAR track, and a drag racer's paradise.

There were two hydraulic lifts in the shop, which was designed like a man-cave garage. Spotless red enamel floors, every tool on the planet in custom-made shelving, surround sound stereo, three wide-screen televisions, a wet bar, rolled-and-tucked black leather couches, and large framed posters of drag-racing heroes of the past.

Hector loved to get loaded and watch the nitro funny cars spew flames out of their exhaust systems, like medieval dragons, hitting speeds of up to three hundred miles an hour. The smell of the spinning, smoking, burning rubber tires mixed with the nitrous oxide fumes, and then the launch of the twin rear-end parachutes—as the insane cars rocketed across the finish line at the end of the eighth-mile race—was like being in church. Not that Hector had many memories of church.

"Hey, they finally got that crazy Bin Laden fuck," Frankie said, overly animated. He'd been dipping into his own product.

"Someone killed your father?" Johnny joked.

"Not funny." Frankie was a vet and had done two tours of duty, one in Iraq, and then in Afghanistan, running the motor pool, and was no one to fuck with. He had come back to the States a full-blown drug addict. "Asshole wasn't waiting for any twenty-seven virgins. He was hooked into the same shit we were banging in Kabul." He pronounced Kabul like "Kabool."

Johnny laughed, knowing Frankie was referencing the pornography the Seals reportedly had found in the upper-floor room where Bin Laden had been killed.

Hector did a complete recon of the shop, making sure it was empty, and that the bathroom was clear, before he opened up the driver's-side door of the Impala. He turned over the engine and then inserted a special key under the dashboard.

The metal grille of the radio speaker rose up from the dash like a periscope, exposing the trap, and he pulled out a kilo brick of cocaine wrapped in green cellophane.

Frankie grabbed a brown paper bag from one of his red-enameled Craftsman toolboxes on wheels, and handed over sixteen thousand dollars in rubber-banded hundreds. No need to taste the drugs or count the money. The rules were clearly delineated. Death would follow a fuckup.

Hector added the bag to the rest of the cash in the trap, turned the key in the opposite direction, and watched with pride as it disappeared back down into the dash. Even if the cops stopped them—unless they knew the compartment was there—nobody would find the drugs or the money.

"I need quantity," Frankie said, the businessman now. "I can triple sales. I'm controlling four colleges, and they've got the hunger and the means. I'm glad you're moving out of the crystal."

"We've got something big in the works. Give us a few days, we'll change your life," Johnny said.

Hector nodded to Johnny: enough said, let's fuckin' book.

And then a cell phone chirped and all three men reached down.

It was Johnny's. He pulled it off his belt, checked the incoming number, walked to the far end of the shop, and answered.

He talked in hushed tones, longer than was comfortable in the present circumstance, and then clicked off. He could feel the two men burning holes in his back before he turned abruptly and caught them staring and wondering who was on the other end of the line. Fuck 'em. They couldn't read the growing panic he felt behind his mirrored sunglasses.

Johnny sauntered over to the Impala, slapped palms with Frankie, and got into the car. He stared straight ahead.

Hector gave Frankie a final nod, slid behind the wheel, and backed out of the custom shop.

The sound of the rain banging on the white hardtop almost drowned out the voices wreaking havoc in Johnny's head.

Frankie watched the blue Impala disappear into the stormy night before he pulled out his cell phone and punched in a number.

34

"What else did she fucking say?" Hector demanded as he drove the Impala dangerously fast on the rain-slicked road. The wipers had given up the fight, and Johnny wasn't sure how Hector could see, let alone navigate through the pelting rain.

"That's it. That your father hired a private investigator because he was worried about you."

"That would be one fucking great trick, wouldn't it?" Hector spoke with raw menace. "Be very careful now. What did she say about me?"

"First of all, don't tell me to fucking be careful. Second, she doesn't know shit about you, because nobody knows shit about you. There's nothing she could have said. He wanted to know where you lived. She doesn't have that answer. She doesn't even know where I fucking live."

"What was this cop's name?"

"He wasn't a cop," Johnny said, with a level of sarcasm he regretted. Johnny always tried to keep in mind who he was dealing with.

"What the fuck was his name?"

"He didn't give a name, he just asked a few questions and left."

"Could it have been that guy we fucked with?"

"What guy?"

"Don't mess with me, Johnny. That place in the marina. The guy that braced Higueras."

Johnny was still reacting to the terrifying news that someone had tracked down his mother's house. "I don't know."

"Why is it you're always so smart, the expert in all things, and now you sound dim? Why is that, *ese?*"

Johnny didn't take the bait.

"If it was the marina guy, we'll have to kill him," Hector went on matter-of-factly. "Mando has no say in it. When I told Mando we probably scared him off with the arrest, he said—oh . . . fuckin' Bertolino's the prick's name—Mando said he don't scare. He gets even."

"If you had left the knife we used on the girl," Johnny said, "he'd still be in jail."

Hector's silence was chilling. Johnny's hand slid down to his gun, though it gave him no comfort.

Johnny wasn't about to give up any more information than was needed to keep Hector in line. This Bertolino guy knew where he grew up and his association with Hector. He was on their trail. It was only a matter of time before it all came slamming down on their heads. The man had also told his sister that he would help if help was needed.

Johnny had been doing some serious thinking. He had researched immunity and the FBI's Witness Protection Program. Nothing was off the table at this point. Hector was spinning out of control, and Johnny wasn't going down the drain with him. He hadn't lost all his common sense.

Hector pulled out his phone and hit the speed dial as he roared through a yellow light, sending thick plumes of water cascading onto opposing traffic.

———

Jack Bertolino decided to do a drive-by of the Lopez residence on his way back to the I-10. When he pulled up in front of the house, he decided that it gave the term "residence" a bad name. There was something bankrupt at the core of the California ranch. He couldn't put his finger on it, but it looked dry and neglected even in the wet storm.

It also looked deserted. He depressed the parking brake and stepped out of his Mustang into a hidden pothole full of muddy rainwater. He cursed as he ran up onto the stoop with an overhang so small, rain still slanted in on his back, drenching him. He knocked three times, hard, and was surprised when the front door swung open.

He could hear a phone ringing in the background and had to look down into the face of a slight woman with thinning home-permed hair, who he guessed was Hector Lopez's mother.

Being the king of improv, Jack came up with a snappy gambit. "Are you Mrs. Lopez?"

The woman nodded her head. Her intense brown, owlish eyes were unblinking. She didn't seem surprised by the intrusion.

"*No habla ingles,*" she said, and Jack half-believed her.

"*Hector Lopez, tu hijo,* your son, does he live here?"

"No. Hector no lives here."

Jack made a mental note to learn how to speak Spanish. His mental notepad was so full, he couldn't read his mental writing anymore.

But he could smell a hot dinner cooking on the stove. His stomach churned, he was drenched to the bone, and he was really pissed off. Jack wanted his life back, pre-Mia.

"Do you want to get the phone, and then we'll talk?"

He mimed the telephone with a hand-to-his-ear bit, and raised his eyebrows. Marcel Marceau was rolling over in his French grave, Jack thought.

"Hector no lives here," she repeated.

Mrs. Lopez started to slowly close the door. Jack hated to do it, but he wedged his foot into the doorjamb, like a traveling salesman, before the door was shut entirely.

"Do you know where I can find him?" he said through the five-inch opening.

"Hector no lives here."

Jack pulled his foot out, feeling slightly embarrassed as the woman slammed it shut. He heard the bolt being thrown.

He understood the honest fear of cops felt by the immigrant population. He just wasn't sure if that's what was motivating this woman.

As long as Jack was here and already wet to the bone, he decided to do a little snooping. He walked a ways up the driveway on the side of the house and could see an unattached ramshackle garage that looked derelict. Off to the left was a large overgrown backyard that was separated from open county property by a barren fruit tree situated next to a rusted chain-link fence. Nice piece of land, he thought, if it wasn't for the high-tension electrical towers that loomed overhead.

A light in the house snapped on, and he caught a glimpse of Mrs. Lopez staring out of the kitchen window with those crazy eyes. That woman needed to get some sleep, Jack thought as he waved in a friendly way and jogged back to his car before she called the police. He'd pick up a quarter-pounder and a hot cup of coffee on the road, and pay his dues on the I-10.

———

"Answer the phone, you dried-out old bitch," Hector shouted, his voice filled with so much hatred for his mother it made Johnny want to puke.

Hector disconnected, hit Redial, and again pressed the cell phone to his ear. Then he checked the printout to make sure there was a connection, one hand on the steering wheel, not concentrating on the road. Johnny could see that the yellow light they were approaching was about to turn red. There was no way they were going to make it.

"We're gonna miss the light," he said in measured tones.

"Answer the phone, bitch."

Hector accelerated.

"Light's turning red, Hector. Slow down," he said, sharper now.

"Shut the fuck up, Johnny."

"It's a red fucking light!"

"Let them stop for me."

Hector slammed his foot down, pedal to metal; the 315-horsepower V8 engine kicked in and rocketed toward the intersection.

Johnny tensed his body, prepared to die.

The pictures turned to slow motion. The hapless man in a Toyota Camry to Johnny's right realized he was about to T-bone Hector's car. His eyes went wide; his mouth contorted into a silent scream as he slammed on his brakes and went into a hydroplaning spin.

The sound of wrenching steel, breaking glass, and horns blasting was frightening and then receded into the background as the Impala sped safely through the intersection, leaving a three-car collision behind it.

The rain drummed onto the hardtop, keeping time with Johnny's beating heart.

"Answer the phone, *putana*!" Hector raged, red faced.

Hector and Johnny circled around the back of Royce Motors and blinked the Impala's lights at the entrance to the fenced-in lot. The chain-link fence was eight feet high with a green canvas liner to keep out prying eyes.

The large double gates swung open, and a pair of 180-pound brindle English mastiffs bared their teeth, drool flying as they swung their black-masked faces back and forth and glared at the new intruders with their devilish green eyes.

The rain had slowed to a drizzle, but the large puddles throughout the vast dirt lot reflected the overhead amber security lights and gave the entire scene the look of a science fiction movie.

Roman Ortiz snapped his fingers, and the two massive guard dogs were stilled.

Hector motored in, being careful to avoid the muddy puddles. The doors swung shut behind him and were locked by a pair of Lil' Angels with AK-47s strung over their chests like bandoliers. He pulled up to a double-wide tan aluminum trailer, like one you might see at a construction site, and parked next to a row of tricked-out cars and gray primer specials.

Hector and Johnny exited the Impala and were greeted by Roman, who walked up and clapped them both on the back. He was in good spirits.

"What's up, boss?" Johnny asked Roman. "Looks like we're going to war."

There were more Angels than normal, everyone was armed to the teeth, and the tension in the air was palpable.

"Just protecting what is ours and guaranteeing our future," Roman said, exuding an aura of calm. And then as a subtle warning, "Arturo Delgado is here. Overseeing his investment."

Their conversation was cut short as the door to the office swung open and Mando walked out of the trailer, his dead eyes probing, his palms raised skyward, demanding to see his team's results.

Hector just nodded his head. He knew the little man was putting on an act for Delgado. All was good.

Johnny wasn't thrilled to see Mexican Mafia Mando but nodded deferentially. He now understood the tension. It wasn't the stormy weather; it was the disruption in the energy field created by Arturo Delgado.

The half-acre lot was filled with the carcasses of rusting buses, cars, mobile homes, and trucks, all in different stages of disrepair, all cannibalized as needed for parts.

In one corner Johnny could see the police car that he had driven to kill the woman up on the hill in Sherman Oaks. A young man worked under a canvas tarp as he stripped off the last of the white 3M Controltac. The plastic wrap had been applied to make the car look like an authentic black-and-white. The Ford was almost entirely black now, and once the light bar was removed, it would never be identified and tied to the crime, a small favor.

At the far end of the lot were four extra-large orange roll-up steel doors that provided entrance to the rear of the Royce Motors building and two heavy-duty metal ramps to accommodate the buses.

Hector knew the drill; he walked back to the Impala and engaged the trap. He pulled out his bags of cash and followed Mando, Roman, and Johnny into the office.

Arturo Delgado was seated comfortably behind the wooden desk. It was the first time he had made a physical appearance at Royce Motors. There could be no mistakes now.

Hector nodded to the alpha male in a room filled with alphas before he dumped thirty-two thousand dollars onto the top of the desk, next to another neatly stacked group of banded bills, and moved away. He knew better than to speak unless he was spoken to.

The extra munitions now made sense to Johnny.

The bundles of hundreds never disappointed.

Johnny's friend David Reyes was manning the industrial vacuum sealer. He gave them a nervous glance but kept an eye on the task at hand. His face was still a mass of small red welts from when Jack Bertolino had shot out his windshield at seventy miles an hour.

Roman set up three shot glasses next to the money, like a poker dealer, and poured shots of Patrón. Arturo Delgado, Mando, and Roman clinked glasses while their soldiers looked away, not wanting to interfere with their leaders' ritual.

"To continued success," Roman said, and then deferred to Delgado, a move not lost on Mando.

"The future is ours," Delgado proclaimed.

The men slammed back their tequila.

The money disappeared as quickly as the liquor. It was vacuum-sealed and weighed on digital scales. A pound of hundreds, forty-eight thousand dollars. Two hundred seventy-five keys of coke equaled 4.4 million dollars.

A quarter million would go to the Angels; two hundred thousand would go into Manuel Alvarez's new account; Delgado would dip his beak, amount unspecified; and the rest would make its way, after being laundered, to the Dominican Republic and then back to Colombia.

The plastic-wrapped bags of money were loaded into military rucksacks. The 18th Street Angels each grabbed two apiece, and with Delgado and Mando leading the way, the men filed out of the office and made their way to the Royce Motors rear entrance.

The large dogs came up to Roman's waist and loped along, shadowing Roman and the new stranger step for step. They heeled dutifully, occasionally nuzzling Roman's hand, a silent warning to anyone foolish enough to challenge their master.

David Reyes leaned toward Johnny. "Raymond got fucked up good, man."

"I heard."

"His leg, it's bad, man. We gotta kill the fucker that done him. I think it was that dude from the car. I'm gonna personally make him pay for my face, bro. I used to be pretty. Now I'm all fucked up."

It always amused Johnny when David started talking street. He had graduated from John Burroughs with a 3.5 grade average and did all of the Angels' accounting. College had been in both of their futures until they met up with Hector.

"Right."

"That *pendejo*'s gonna pay. That's all I'm sayin'.'"

Roman used a key and one of the orange metal doors rolled up and open. He and Delgado were the first men up the ramp.

Mando waved Hector forward, and the two gangsters conferred

in hushed tones as they walked through the cavernous structure, down a long passageway created by new million-dollar buses waiting to be sold. The painted beauties were parked at angles, their custom artwork spotlit like runway models to entice rock groups, corporations, movie companies, and sports teams to pull out their checkbooks. Anyone who spent time on the road and could afford a luxury ride.

"They're layin' out Ricky on Sunday. Should I make an appearance, you think?" Hector asked Mando, deferentially.

"No, man, didn't you ever see *The Godfather, ese*? Marlon Brando at the wedding, man? There were feds crawling up their asses, taking pictures of all the gangsters' cars. Nobody knows you exist. That's some scary shit we've got goin' on. Understand?"

"Yeah, I do," Hector said and liked the concept.

Welding sparks fountained like a supernova in the distance as the men reached the service bay and stared with admiration.

The bus that had been used to transport the hip-hop group Gold Nickel, and the drugs from Miami, was elevated onto one of the lifts near the front of the shop. Large metal panels on either side of the exhaust system had been removed, and men were strapping the rucksacks of cash already weighed and installing them like insulation. One side of the bus was fully packed.

All eyes in the shop turned to Arturo Delgado, who gave a slight nod of approval.

The team of men wearing protective headgear stepped back under the bus, sparks flying as they seamlessly welded the metal panel back into place.

Whatever else was happening, Johnny thought, business was expanding. He'd have a big payday. And then his gaze drifted to the dead eyes of his partner and he decided then and there that he was not going to follow Hector into hell.

35

Jack felt like he had squeezed two days into one as he merged from the I-10 onto the San Diego Freeway. The rain had stopped, and he was only fifteen minutes from home. He was still wet to the core and looking forward to a hot shower and bed. He thought about giving Leslie Sager a call, but if he remembered correctly, they had agreed to talk on Friday for a Saturday-night date. He could sorely use the company of a woman, though, just to change his mental state if for nothing else.

Being married had its advantages. When his marriage was good, it was very good, and Jeannine had a way of bringing Jack out of his immersion in a case. She helped him compartmentalize so he could enjoy some semblance of a home life.

Sometimes just the scent of a woman could do the trick. Oh yeah, Jack Bertolino was definitely ready for a date.

Jack pulled his Mustang into the driveway of his building, hit the remote, and drove through as the gate swung open. He parked, reached over to close his laptop, and stopped. He decided, on second thought, that he should check out Cruz's handiwork.

Jack clicked the loft icon on his desktop, and when the picture pixelized and became clear, Jack felt a pounding erupt in his temples and the pit of his stomach drop. Someone in a dark hoodie was in his loft, walking past the first hidden surveillance camera toward the bedroom area.

Jack jumped out of the car, pulled his Glock out of his shoulder holster, and ran for the door. He banged into the building, keyed the stairwell door, and started running up the flights of stairs.

When he got to the fourth floor, he stopped for a moment to catch his breath. He loaded his nine millimeter and silently slipped out of the stairwell, being careful not to let the heavy door slam shut behind him.

Jack crept along the open walkway and saw that the blinds were still drawn in his unit. He was mindful of shadows as he crouched down and moved past his front window.

Jack did a silent three count to still his breathing. His hand depressed the door handle, and he pushed the metal door open.

He followed his gun in and found the front of his loft empty. He eased the door closed behind him and took a few silent steps deeper inside. He stopped, froze in place, and tried to listen for movement over the pounding in his ears.

His eyes scanned the loft, and he caught a reflection in the glass windows in the rear of the loft.

The intruder was exiting the bathroom.

Jack took three rapid steps forward. Gun raised. Finger on the hairpin trigger.

"Down on the floor!" he roared. As he cleared the edge of the wall, his gun was trained on the intruder's heart.

"What the hell!"

Chris screamed and dropped to his knees. The color drained from his face.

"Chris!" Jack shouted as he lowered his weapon. He slid it back into his shoulder holster, wanting to hide it. "What the hell are you doing here?"

"Dad, are you out of your effing mind?"

Jack hurried to his son and wrapped his arms around him. Chris was clearly in shock and Jack all but lifted him onto the edge of his bed.

"I am so sorry, so sorry. This is really, really not a good time."

"Why couldn't you just tell me that, like a normal person? Words would have worked a hell of a lot better than a gun."

"All I could see on the surveillance video was a man in a hoodie." Jack sighed. "I had the camera installed after the break-in. I should have given you a heads-up."

His son was becoming outraged. "You shoulda given me something . . . instead of a heart attack!"

"What the hell are you doing walking around in a hoodie?" Jack yelled back.

"What are you, the fashion police? Christ, Dad, you scared the shit out of me!" Chris shouted.

The emotional intensity behind his words slowed them both down a click.

"Back at you, Son," Jack said, almost panting now, trying to keep his eyes from tearing up.

"Don't 'Son' me," Chris said, still angry at being frightened. "I'm trading you in for a better effing model."

"I wouldn't blame you, I really wouldn't blame you."

They sat still, side by side on the bed, the only sound the muted traffic passing on Glencoe.

"You want a beer?"

Jack didn't wait for an answer. He needed one. Rising from the bed and moving to the kitchen, he slid the leather holster off his shoulder and firmly stowed the entire rig in a drawer.

He pulled two Pacificos that Tommy had left behind out of the fridge. He had to fight to stop his hands from shaking as he popped the tops and handed one to his son.

Jack would have eaten the barrel of his own gun if he had shot his son. His life would not have been worth living.

He sat back down on the edge of his bed and draped an arm around Chris's shoulder and pulled him close. They sat there in silence until their world stopped spinning.

Hector turned the key and stepped into the dark house. He closed the door behind him, walked through the kitchen, and silently pushed open his mother's bedroom door.

The fragile woman was propped up in bed, eyes wide open, unwavering, with a shotgun across her lap, pointed directly at Hector's face. A grouping of glass-enclosed holy candles provided the only illumination. The room was a shrine to the Virgin Mary.

"What did you say, Mom? To the man who stopped by," Hector asked in a whisper.

"Hector no lives here."

Hector had his answer. He nodded his head, satisfied, and put a large roll of twenties onto his mother's scarred wooden bureau, next to one of the many porcelain religious objects.

He looked back at his mother, his face carved of stone, and closed the door behind him.

"Hector no lives here," she said to herself. Or to the Virgin Mary.

At two thirty A.M., Felix, the owner of the Black Stallion Inn, exited his establishment followed by Angelina, who tended bar, and Izel, who worked as the waitress-barback. Felix, who owned the entire strip mall, was an original 18th Street Angel.

With the help of David Reyes he had turned the bar, the Laundromat, the *panaderia,* and the wedding store—which had displayed the same wedding dresses since the late '80s—into a successful money-laundering operation. He took 7 percent off the top of any transaction, and he was getting fat without too much stress.

While Izel lit a cigarette, Felix used three different keys in three different locks and checked twice to make sure the red wooden door was securely fastened. It paid to be careful, and that was good for the gang.

As soon as he was satisfied, a black Town Car appeared as if on cue and drove Felix off into the night.

Angelina exchanged a few last words with Izel, who painted a new layer of red onto her lips before she headed to her Toyota Corolla. She spotted Johnny and threw him a wave and a you-fucked-up-good look before getting into her car and driving off.

Angelina pulled out a cigarette and lit it with a Bic lighter. Then she walked slowly toward Johnny's 2011 silver Toyota Prius, parked at the far end of the lot.

Johnny was also careful. He knew that driving the boring car would escape the eye of local law enforcement.

He leaned across the console and opened the passenger-side door. "Get in, Angelina," he said with a mixture of bravado and tenderness.

She stood in place as if still trying to make up her mind. Johnny didn't push. They were both bad actors who had played this scene before, too many times to count.

She handed the lit cigarette to Johnny, who took a long drag, and she slid into the seat and closed the door.

Gato Barbieri was playing on Johnny's iPod because it always made Angelina pliant and wet.

Johnny pulled out of the lot and headed up into the hills instead of home. It was where the fiery couple would usually go to talk, make up, and make out. She pulled out a Baggie of high-grade marijuana and rolled a perfect joint. Angelina was good with her hands. Just the thought of her touch could get Johnny hard.

He threw out the cigarette, and she moved in with the joint. She put the lit end into her mouth and blew out a stream of smoke that filled Johnny's lungs and gave him an instant high.

They drove in silence, anticipating the sexual release to come.

————————

It was too late to be up and still too early for Jack to sleep. He would suffer in the morning, but adrenaline was the only clock his body was listening to. He'd set Chris up on the pullout couch in the office and moved his laptop computer over to the kitchen island.

The first thing he did was download the recent phone calls made on Raymond Higueras's phone. Then he downloaded all received calls and the address book. The last download was all of the pictures.

One phone number had gotten the most play in the previous week, and when Jack looked it up on the national phone database, it was assigned to Royce Motors—more specifically, to the general manager, Roman Ortiz. A call was placed before and directly after the gang tried to run Jack and Tommy off the road.

As he scrolled through the pictures, he stopped on a series of eight pictures of Jack walking up the block for coffee the day after Mia was killed.

The photos brought the pain flooding back. And anger to the surface.

Pictures of him pulling out of the driveway in the Mustang and pictures of him returning home.

That was enough. Jack pulled out a yellow pad, and in longhand he laid out the case and everything he knew up to this point. All the pieces were still rough, but certain elements were coming together.

Delgado, Alvarez, the Mexican Mafia, the 18th Street Angels, Royce Motors, Dominican coke, the way the drugs came into the country, how they were distributed, and how the investigation should move forward.

The ringleader, the puppet master, was Arturo Delgado. Jack felt it in his gut. The operation had his stink all over it.

Delgado provided the drugs and Alvarez was the conduit. Colombia was supplying Alvarez because he hadn't named names. He was paying protection money to the Mexican Mafia, and with their connections to the 18th Street Angels, that was how the deal was struck.

With all of the turmoil between Los Zetas and the Sinaloa cartel at the U.S.-Mexican border—and with the stepped-up law enforcement—it was a perfect time for Delgado to infiltrate the southwest territory from the East Coast, rebuild his reputation, and build up the Angels' power base.

Alvarez had a reason to kill Mia and twenty-five years' worth of reasons to go after Jack Bertolino.

Mia had either been followed into Los Angeles from Canada, or gotten caught in the web because Jack was under Delgado's microscope. A crime of opportunity.

Royce Motors seemed to be the nexus of the action, with Roman acting as facilitator.

Jack wanted to find out when the next Outlaws Inc. group was traveling to Miami. He'd bet the house that the bus would return to L.A. with another load of cocaine.

With Roman's connection to the transportation and one of the security men the brother of an 18th Street Angel, the musical groups using the buses might be totally unaware of the scam, unaware that they were being used. But ripe for the fall if anything went wrong.

Jack googled the Mansion, the club in Miami where Gold Nickel had its booking, and checked their upcoming schedule of performers.

Then he pulled up the Outlaws Inc. Web site, clicked on their talent page, and compared lists.

Ricci Jay and Wisteria, a progressive hip-hop, jazz-fusion group, and one of the Outlaws' up-and-comers, was scheduled to play the following weekend. The concert was already sold out.

He still wanted someone to look at the books of Travel Associates. It had the feel of a money-laundering operation, and he wouldn't be surprised if it was a dummy corporation tied to the Angels. And with Roman the general manager at Royce Motors, it was a good fit. It would be easy to pad salaries, fake work orders that were requisitioned but never completed, and also pad the bottom line for new buses sold.

Jack was dead sure of one thing. He would have to get Chris to hit the road until things calmed down. This was the wrong time for his son to be visiting.

He copied Kenny Ortega and Nick Aprea on all of the data and turned off his computer. But he couldn't turn off his brain. He had kept the new information about Hector to himself.

Any way you cut it, with three bodies and a similar MO, he was dealing with a serial killer. Jack wasn't kidding himself. If it was Hector, he wanted the first shot at the man.

———

The windows of the Prius were just starting to defog. The view was framed in the remaining condensation. The sky was star filled, the streetlights on the valley floor sparkled, and the dark blue sky was edged in a faint salmon pink.

Johnny and Angelina were sitting in the back of the Prius with the front seats moved all the way forward. Johnny's tattooed chest glistened with sweat, and Angelina's pierced nipples were rock hard from the cold mountain air.

No one in the car was feeling any pain.

"I don't like it, you know, when we fight," Johnny said.

"You don't fight," she said breathily. "You gore. You're my bull, Johnny."

Better than being called a *maricón*, Johnny thought, but remained silent.

"How's Felix?" he asked instead.

She threw him a look. "Getting rich while my arches drop. That guy won't let me wear flats cause he likes to see my ass in high heals."

"Can hardly blame him. As long as all the old man does is look."

Angelina didn't like that response.

"That's all he does, right? Look?" Johnny asked with attitude.

She just smiled and leaned over and bit Johnny's nipple a little too hard. He resisted the urge to slap her and pretended it didn't hurt. Angelina knew better.

"I'm a one-man girl. Don't trouble yourself."

Angelina put her tongue in his mouth and gently worked the bulge in his pants. Then she put her mouth up to his ear.

"I love my Johnny," she said in a whispered tone that made him hard again.

He pulled off his sunglasses and stared into her eyes. "You feel like taking a trip?"

She stirred, disturbed by the change in direction their conversation was taking. "Where you gonna take me that I haven't already taken you?"

"Pick a spot. Someplace you've seen in a magazine."

"Mexico?" she said.

"Shit, we live in Mexico."

Angelina looked mystified. "Why are you talking about a trip now?"

"I'm thinking somewhere we've only read about. France, Italy, Spain. At least we could communicate in Spain," he pointed out. "And the food's supposed to be good."

"What's going on?" Angelina asked, cutting to the chase.

"Why the fuck are you always so negative?" Johnny said defensively. This was not going to be easy. "I'm talking about taking you the fuck out of Ontario, and the fuckin' Stallion, and you're giving me the fifth degree?"

"Because you've been acting weird for a while now. No fooling, Johnny. I mean strange even for your pretty self. I don't know what to expect anymore. No offense."

"Fuck you."

Johnny grabbed his shirt off the front seat, opened the door, and jumped out, slamming it behind him. He put on his mirrored sunglasses and let the cold night air dry his sweat and clear his head.

He heard the car door open but didn't turn around. He felt Angelina put her arms around his waist and her fingers move down the front of his pants.

"I'm sorry, *mi amor*. You're right. I'll think about it. Somewhere special."

Johnny wanted to say more but kept his own council. He turned and picked up Angelina, who instantly wrapped her legs around him. He pushed her up against the car and could feel the heat of her sex boring into his bare waist. He put his tongue into the golden ring that pierced her right nipple, Angelina tugged on the back of his long black hair, and Johnny became aroused for the third time that night.

36

Jack worked the stove while Chris sipped black coffee from a mug. He had scrambled some eggs and cooked turkey bacon, his only concession to being health conscious. When the toast popped, Chris jumped off the stool. He burned his hand while he grabbed the slices and threw them onto his plate, where he proceeded to drench them in butter.

"What time is Macklin showing up?" Jack asked as he scooped the eggs onto two plates and pushed one in front of his son.

"He should be here in fifteen," Chris said, grabbing a strip of bacon and polishing it off in a swallow before it reached his plate. "He said I could crash with his friends from UCLA. They play ball, so we can get a little work-playtime in."

"And when are you driving back?"

"Early Sunday. I've still got some homework and a seven thirty practice on Monday." He gave his father a sideways glance. "And trust me, I'm gonna call you before I show up next time."

"That would probably be wise," Jack said, thankful that his son had recovered. He still hadn't been able to forgive himself for what had almost happened the night before.

Jack waited for him to go on. He didn't want to push his son but was anxious to hear how he was feeling about the team and the coach and just playing in general. Jack watched, amazed, as his son shoveled down the eggs. Did he eat like that as a kid? Yeah, he thought, he probably did.

"I decided to double my hustle and see if that would work," Chris finally said.

"And how's that going?"

"Coach Fredricks didn't stare directly at *me* when he lectured the team about commitment. I still don't think he's gonna put me in the starting lineup this year, but you never know. A lot of things can happen in a season."

"That's true," Jack said, happy with the direction the conversation was taking. "How's your mother?"

Chris smiled. Jack was always trying to do the right thing, keeping the divorce on an even keel to protect his boy.

"She worries too much, calls too often, complains about Jeremy"—he looked to check out his father's reaction when he spoke the Jeremy word—"too often, and other than that, she's still mad I didn't pick a school closer to home."

"So everything's normal," Jack said, eliciting a snorting laugh from his son.

"You're giving yourself too much credit if you think life at home was ever normal."

"And nobody appreciates a wiseass," Jack said, smiling.

Both of their cell phones chirped at the same time. Chris was already in motion, picking up his knapsack and heading for the door.

"I'll be right down," he said into the phone.

"Jack Bertolino here," he said, heading toward the door to walk Chris to the street. "Hello?"

The voice on the other end of the line was tentative.

"My sister, she told me I could, uh, call, ya know. If I wanted to talk."

"Hold on." Jack hugged his son, trying to keep the urgency out of his voice. "I've got to take this. Call me as soon as you're settled."

"Love you, Dad." Chris burst out the door, running toward the elevator.

"Are you still there?" Jack asked cautiously, trying to keep his voice uninterested.

"Yeah, still here," Johnny Rodriguez answered. "Don't know if I'm gonna stay on long. Depends."

"Well, I'm in the dark here, and you've got to fill in the blanks. Who am I speaking with?"

"Don't fuck with me, bro, you know who I am, all right."

"Okay, Johnny, what can I do for you?"

"Well, better. I think that will be a two-way street. It's up to you."

Jack walked to the rear of the loft, slid open the glass doors, and walked out onto the balcony. His eyes scanned Glencoe and settled on a Volkswagen Jetta, parked in a red zone next to Bruffy's Tow. That was probably his son's friend Macklin. The window was rolled down, and the scrubbed young driver looked like a jock.

"You tell me how you want to start the conversation."

"I've been involved in some things that I witnessed, some things, but I didn't do them."

Dead silence.

"Depends on how involved."

"I think you know."

"I'm not that smart."

Jack's eye caught Chris start across the busy traffic on Glencoe. In his mind he thought, Oh, he's got it.

Then a car abruptly sped up and Jack's heart stopped.

"I've been breakin' the law," Johnny confessed.

Chris was struck by a seven-thousand-pound Escalade. He was thrown through the air with such force, his young body disappeared from Jack's line of vision, obstructed by the corner of his building.

Hot tears seared Jack's eyes, blinding him to everything except the pain. "Chris!" he shouted, already in motion as he pounded out the door, down the hallway, and banged into the stairwell, bypassing the elevator.

"Are you hearing me?" Johnny asked, confused.

Jack would never remember running down the four flights of stairs.

He blasted out of the stairwell and slammed the front door open.

"Fuck you, man, *fuck* you!" Johnny hung up, hearing muffled sounds, but not quite sure what had just transpired.

J.D. from Bruffy's was in front of his tow yard, stopping the flow of traffic.

Chris's broken body had been thrown under a parked white Econoline van with a bicycle strapped to its front bumper.

Jack ran around the other side of the van and lay down on the sidewalk by the curb, trying to view his son's face. He reached under the van with his hands and stroked his cheek. "I'm here, Chris. Lay still, we'll get you out," Jack cried to his son's motionless body.

Chris was unconscious, and his arm was twisted at an unnatural angle. Jack could see something white jutting out just below Chris's elbow. Horrified, Jack realized it was a piece of bone that had broken through Chris's perfect skin.

The van shifted and a scruffy man who called the van home stepped out over Jack, disoriented, and stumbled away as if he had awakened from a bad dream. Jack was praying feverishly to God and he never noticed.

The waiting room at St. John's in Santa Monica was the same as hospitals the world over. Only the modern art on the pastel walls was of a higher quality than most. The air was thick with worry and grief and anger. Jack had lost count of how many times he had looked up at the Seiko wall clock. Was it really six o'clock? How could time be passing if it felt like it was standing still?

The fire department had responded within minutes and used a

large hydraulic jack to lift the van while the paramedics extricated Chris. With precision and compassion they had strapped him to a backboard to immobilize him against spinal injury, slammed fluids into his system to prevent shock, and secured him in the ambulance.

Jack didn't remember much about the frenetic drive to St. John's. Sirens wailed, and he was tossed about in the back of the LAFD ambulance. His eyes never wavered from his son's still form. The only picture that remained with him, one that would haunt him for the rest of his life, was how fragile and otherworldly white his son's face looked.

Two hours had passed since the surgeon's last report. They were going to keep Chris sedated, and wait for the swelling in his brain to go down, before conducting further neurological tests. They couldn't determine yet if he had suffered any permanent brain damage. The MRI had been inconclusive. The doctor said the next twenty-four hours would tell.

An orthopedic specialist had been called in to operate on his arm, and the good news, the doctor said, was that the surgeon was a genius, and the break was clean; there was no gross muscle or nerve damage. They would be setting the bone and inserting titanium pins. Because of his age, theoretically the bone should heal stronger than before the accident.

The big unknown was the acute nature of the head trauma. Chris had been thrown headfirst into the concrete curb.

Brain damage—theoretically—should heal—head trauma— titanium pins—inconclusive—sedation. Jack wanted to shut down. His heart was broken. He was awash with guilt.

Jack had called New York and spoken with Jeannine, who understandably fell apart when she heard the news and the circumstances that had led up to the attack. She and Jeremy were already on a flight out of LaGuardia, and Jack had arranged for a car to meet them at LAX.

Tommy had been ready to drop everything and fly out if needed. Jack asked him to stay put, but he appreciated the heartfelt offer.

Macklin was sprawled across three seats, red eyed and emotionally spent. Chris's friend had chased after the Escalade and was able to write down the first four numbers of the license plate before losing the big car in traffic and barely avoiding a collision himself.

He and Jack had both given statements to the LAPD.

Yes, Jack had seen the car purposely veer into his son. No, it was not an accident, but attempted murder.

Macklin had corroborated his story, and the cops immediately put out an APB, an all-points-bulletin, to search for the hit-and-run driver of a black Cadillac Escalade with front-end damage.

Jack's cell phone chirped just as a registered nurse walked by. She threw him a dirty look and pointed to a sign prohibiting their use. Jack pulled out the phone and walked it toward the exit doors.

"Bertolino."

"What the fuck are you up to, man? You told me to call."

Jack was in no mood for a punk's attitude. "I'm going to ask you something, Johnny. If you answer honestly, we can talk about your problem. If you lie to me, I'll hunt you down and kill you."

"Stop with the macho shit, *ese*. You don't scare me. I've faced the devil, you see. Ask away."

"Who ordered the hit on my son?"

"What?"

"Who ran my son down?"

The voice sounded genuinely flustered. "Don't know anything about a hit on anybody's son. And *you* are strictly off-limits. Orders. So it wasn't Angels' business or I'd know about it."

Jack thought about the implications if Johnny was telling the truth.

"Who gives the orders?"

Johnny said more reluctantly, "A chain-of-command thing. Never really know where it originates."

Delgado was all Jack could come up with. He would never deal directly with the soldiers, but would still control the play.

"You still there, man? Don't go doing another disappearing act on me, or we're done."

"No, I'm here. I've got to get back inside. Let's talk tomorrow and we'll set something up. Give me a number where you can be reached."

"I'll call you. And don't waste your time; I've got more phones than you've got dollar bills. Later."

———————

"So, are you ready to go?" Johnny asked Angelina as she stepped out of the bathroom dressed in skintight black jeans and a lacy black bra that pushed her breasts together, accentuating her cleavage.

It was good for tips, she'd said.

She had an eyeliner pencil in her hand and Johnny could see that only one of her strong, unblinking brown eyes had been lined. The bruise on her cheek from their fight had faded, and now, with the foundation she wore, had disappeared altogether.

"Yeah, I've been giving it some thought," she said. "I got a few ideas. I'll run it by Felix tonight if it's not too busy. I can get Izel to cover the bar. You think she can handle it? Yeah, she can. When do you want to go?"

Angelina stepped back into the bathroom and started to carefully apply the black liner to her other eye. Johnny thought it made her look hard but not enough to mention it.

"Don't ask Felix. Don't talk to Izel or anyone else."

She finished up and walked back into the room, opened the closet, and pulled out three blouses and held them up for Johnny to make the decision.

"The blue number," he said.

She hung the other blouses back in the closet. "I'm not getting fired, Johnny," she said, buttoning the blouse and checking herself out in the bathroom mirror. Satisfied, she walked back into the bedroom and stood facing him.

Johnny was sitting on the edge of the bed. He took off his sunglasses and put his hands around her waist and pulled her a little closer.

"I'm not talking about a vacation. I'm talking about making a change, starting over somewhere. Somewhere new. Haven't you ever thought about that?"

"You're not making any sense," she said, checking her watch.

"How much do you love me?"

"Enough to put up with your crap." She stared into his hazel eyes and could see something was off. "Are you in trouble?"

Johnny didn't answer right away. He knew he was taking a big risk confiding in Angelina.

"Big-time. And if I don't make big-time changes, I'm going to end up taking a bullet, or locked up forever. Either way I'm a dead man. It's just a fact of my life right now."

Angelina put her arms around his neck and pulled him close. He could smell the perfume he loved, especially when it mixed with their sweat.

She suddenly pushed him back. "What happened, Johnny?"

"It didn't just happen, but it's going to hell and taking me with it."

"Make some sense!"

"We have a big deal coming up, and I've been saving and investing. It's time."

Angelina was no-nonsense now. "It's crazy is what it is. I can't just leave. My family, my home, my job. And they'd find us. I'm not gonna spend my life hiding out. That's crazy."

No compassion or empathy now. Dark, powerful, and cold emotions. Her eyes bored into his.

Johnny stayed aloof, not letting her read his thoughts. He did realize, though, that it was time for him to change his tune. "You're right, just crazy talk, between you and me. Only. Right?" Johnny wasn't asking. "I've just gotta be careful is all."

"That's right, baby, I don't want anything to happen to my

pretty boy. So what's coming up?" she asked as if she wasn't really interested.

"Just some good business opportunities. You know, I can't say. It's better if you don't know."

She nodded her head in agreement even though her pursed lips showed what crap she thought it was. "You watch who you talk to, Johnny. Stop the crazy talk. They're not going to let you leave. It don't work like that. And if you run, they'll find you."

"Not necessarily."

"Johnny!"

"I'm just saying . . . hey, forget it. It's just talk is all."

But Angelina could read Johnny like a book and she didn't like where the story was heading.

"Who were you talking to?" She nodded outside the apartment door.

"What?"

"Why'd you take the call outside?" she asked, not pulling any punches.

"You fucking spying on me?" Johnny asked. His eyes turned cold.

"No, Johnny. I stepped out of the bathroom is all, and I saw you were outside on the phone."

An easy lie came to him. "Hector, I was talking to Hector, and you were steaming up the room. I needed some air. We're gonna connect later."

Johnny stood up from the bed, wanting to end this conversation.

"C'mon, I'll drop you off at the Stallion. Everything's cool."

"Doesn't feel cool, Johnny."

"Everything's cool, I've got it under control."

"You better."

"I do."

He gave her his best tough look, and her face softened some.

"That's better," she said. "We gotta enjoy what we got. Will you still take me somewhere new, like you said? Someplace I've seen in a magazine?" Angelina sounded young and vulnerable now, and Johnny was hooked.

"Anywhere you want."

"That's my strong bull. I'll start looking for someplace sexy." Angelina checked her cell phone for the time. "Shit, I'm late. Damn you, Johnny, Felix is gonna dock my pay." And she was out the door.

Johnny slid on his mirrored sunglasses, ready to face the night. He was worried he had said too much, but Angelina would be cool, he decided. Christ, she couldn't keep her hands off him.

———————

Angelina banged through the red door and all but ran into the Black Stallion. It was still early and only about fifteen patrons were scattered around the room. It would be full to the rafters by nine.

Felix glared at her from his regular booth as she smiled and mouthed "sorry." He shook his head to say what else is new, and went back to his paper.

Angelina put on an apron, scooted under the bar, and spelled Izel, who was prepping lime wedges.

"Glad you could make it."

"Johnny's all mouth, all the time. I lost track."

"Everything's under control. Except the prick is over in the corner. Fat fuck gives me the creeps. Why don't you get Johnny to make him disappear?"

Angelina could see Hector, sitting by himself, nursing a Dos Equis. She walked to the end of the bar and got his attention.

"You ready for another?"

"I'm good."

"Johnny's outside."

"Okay."

But Hector didn't move.

"I thought you were hanging tonight?"

"News to me."

Angelina turned away, pulled some lemons out of the fridge, and started peeling off the skins to make lemon strips. She went on as if it was business as usual. As if she wasn't chilled to the bone. Johnny had talked about running away. So if he wasn't talking to Hector, who the hell was it?

37

The lights were dimmed in the ICU. Jack had been camped out in the room for hours, watching his son lying in a state somewhere between life and death. His right arm, his pitching arm, was encased in a full plaster cast, braced away from his rib cage with a piece of padded aluminum and now elevated slightly off his body by a metal rope-and-pulley system.

The nurses were monitoring his brain activity for any signs of internal bleeding or increased swelling. Four other beds were occupied, human beings kept alive by modern technology, separated only by the thin veil of white hospital curtains.

The doctor reported that he would keep Chris sedated for at least another twelve hours. He was resting comfortably and Jack should think about doing the same thing. Jack wasn't sure how the doctor knew what his son was feeling but didn't argue the point. He didn't have the strength. He also refused to leave.

The orthopedic specialist had been pleased with the results of his operation, and Jack was grateful. It went without a hitch, the surgeon's words. A few months of physical therapy and Chris should be able to throw a ball again. Hopefully, by next season. Should. Hopefully. Jack was trying to stay optimistic.

Jeannine was due to arrive any minute, and Jack wished he

could teleport himself to any other place on earth. The sound of the monitors and the constant green blip of lights that moved across the multiple screens became mind numbing. The adrenaline that had fueled the first fourteen hours of the ordeal had dissipated and left him feeling drained. Jack's eyelids started fluttering, his head started nodding like a heroin addict's, and he fell into a deep and disturbed slumber.

He was back on Staten Island, just a kid. Eight or nine. Playing with a friend of his at Miller Field, an old army base. They were throwing at Pigeon Tower.

Pigeons used to lay their eggs in the rafters and the kids would toss the eggs off the edge of the tower, amazed at the popping sound they made on impact and the yolk art created on the weed-strewn lot below.

A couple of guys drinking down at the beach were on the prowl. When they saw Jack and his buddy, Sal Traina, exiting the tower, they beat the shit out of them. Just for fun.

Franky Risucci, a sanitation guy who lived next door to the Bertolinos, asked Jack what had happened. Franky's brother was connected to organized crime. They all used to fish off the rocks and eat veal parmigiana sandwiches together. Lou Terracino, another neighborhood tough, was there and itching for retribution.

Jack and Sal stood by the curb, all lumped up, and watched as Franky and Lou took off in a bright orange Camaro. The air was thick with the smell of burning rubber and testosterone heading down the road toward Pigeon Tower.

Those two guys were beaten to within an inch of their lives. You never fucked with anybody from the neighborhood. Violence was met with violence, a simple formula. And Jack, even in his dream state, was gearing up.

His eyes blinked open and dread enveloped him when he realized where he was sitting and who was standing in front of him.

Jeannine was leaning over Chris, and her boyfriend, Jeremy, was standing in the doorway to the ICU, looking extremely uncomfortable.

Chris had always said that Jeremy looked like a thinner version of Jack, and although he was loath to admit it, he could see the resemblance, a second cousin maybe.

An RN pushed past Jeremy into the room and said in a hushed but firm tone, "We can only have one family member in the ICU at a time."

Jeannine looked fiercely down at Jack, and his heart sank. He could read her pain and knew he was the cause. He stood up, stroked his son's face, and walked out past Jeremy into the hallway.

Jeannine was right on his heels, and he turned to face her, his arms at his sides. Jeremy had the good grace to move down the hallway and let this family emergency play out.

"What are you doing, Jack?" she asked, so cold and so intense it threw him.

Jack wanted her to scream and slap him and carry on. He was prepared for that. He was caught totally off guard by his ex-wife's control.

"Why?" she continued. "You're not a cop anymore. It ruined the family, and now . . . you just ruined our son's life. Are you proud of yourself, Jack? Can you look yourself in the mirror? What? What do you see? Everything you touch—"

And Jeannine crumbled like a sand castle. Jack reached out, and she collapsed into his arms and continued, between sobs, talking, leaning into his shoulder. Jack could feel the terrified heat radiating off her body and the ragged tears bleeding through his shirt.

"Everything you touch turns to . . . turns to . . . just shit, Jack. Everything you touch turns to shit."

Jack held her fast; there was nothing he could say and no argument to be made.

————————

Jack walked out of St. John's to wait for his cab. A marine layer had settled in, bringing with it a damp fog. Jack was numb, and needed a shower and some food. He was thinking about the metal rope-and-pulley system supporting his son's broken arm, and then his mind drifted to the rope and the butcher's knot that had supported the mutilated gang member and the belt used to hang Mia.

Hector. Hector Lopez was his strongest lead. Jack wasn't an FBI profiler, but Hector had the capability and the psychological history to support Jack's theory.

Gallina and Tompkins had stopped by on the heels of the LAPD uniforms, and showed Jack the surveillance photos from Bruffy's Tow. The blurry images of a Cadillac Escalade, seconds before it smashed into his son, breaking his body and leaving him for dead. The driver was out of focus, obscured by the speed he was traveling, and a wide-brimmed hat that he wore raked to the right side masked his face from the camera.

Arturo Delgado.

Jack had given them all of the information to date he had on Delgado. He wasn't optimistic that they would be successful in apprehending the man, but it never hurt to try. Jack was pleased that they were at least on his son's case, that they realized there was a connection.

Jack checked his watch and grabbed his wrist. His hand was shaking. Pure rage. He was about to call the cab company again when a black Town Car emerged from the fog and pulled to a stop by the curb.

The back door swung open and a large, well-dressed man in an Armani suit, who was built like a defensive tackle, stepped out. He glanced up and down the empty street before saying, "Jack, friends from the old neighborhood heard about your troubles and reached out to me. If there is anything I can do, help in any way, all you have to do is call, twenty-four/seven. We take care of our own, Jack, no strings." He handed Jack an embossed card.

"Thank you," Jack said, making a mental note to talk to his mother about neighborhood gossip and wondering if he was now in debt for his simple words of gratitude.

"Does your son need security?"

"The LAPD left a man."

"Can I offer you a lift?"

By way of an answer, Jack's yellow cab pulled to the curb behind the Town Car.

"I'm good."

"You have friends. We're here for you."

The man slid back into the backseat and closed the door. The car dipped slightly from the man's weight and then silently pulled away from the curb.

Jack looked down at the card—no name, only a phone number—and pocketed it. He'd put a name with the face when the dust settled.

———

As Jack stepped off the elevator, he noticed that a single rose and a card lay neatly on his doormat. He picked up the gift and then pulled out his Glock nine millimeter after he inserted his key and discovered the front door was unlocked. It took him a second or two before he realized that, in a panic, he had run out of the loft without locking the door behind him.

He still entered cautiously and cleared the loft. Holstering his weapon, he unstrapped his rig and put it down on the kitchen island. He grabbed a coffee mug, filled it with tap water, and placed the rose in it. It was long stemmed and he had to balance it against a kitchen cabinet. Then he opened the envelope.

A short but sweet note from DDA Leslie Sager, an offer to help in any way she could, personally or professionally. And if Jack felt the need for company, he could call or stop by at any time over the weekend.

Jack wasn't sure he'd be fit company.

He started doing the breakfast dishes from the day before. As he wiped the dried scrambled eggs off the plates, he found that his vision was blurred. When he wiped his eyes with the back of his sleeve, he realized that he was crying.

38

The Holy Cross section of Bellevue Memorial was a large expanse of grass, scattered conifers and evergreens, brass name plaques, and no headstones. It had more of a park feel—except for the dead.

Bouquets of colorful flowers were placed haphazardly at different gravesites and seemed to spring up from the vast green lawn like tufts of wildflowers.

The Holy Cross area was designated for Catholic burials. It didn't matter that you were a drug-dealing gangster, Jack thought. Jesus forgave, and the Catholic church did his work for a fee.

"So, is junior going to be living with you when he starts physical therapy?" Nick Aprea asked.

He and Jack were sitting in Nick's behemoth Ford Expedition. They had passed the funeral procession on the road and were the first to arrive. Nick positioned them with a straight-on view of the burial site.

His SUV blended in perfectly with the other SUVs, low riders, and after-market Japanese performance cars.

Nick nursed a venti Starbucks coffee—black, no sugar—with one hand, and snapped pictures of the gangbangers' license plates as they passed in perfect order and slow, respectful motion. They'd been sitting in the SUV for about an hour before the casket was thankfully lowered into the freshly dug hole and the first of the mourners split off and headed back toward their rides.

"I haven't thought it out that far. But I'm hoping he won't have to miss the entire semester of class work."

"Well, if he does," Nick said with raised eyebrows, "he should try some Eastern medicine along with the Western."

"Yeah?" Jack answered.

"Hey, is that Gallina and Tompkins in the Crown Vic?"

Both men glanced to the left as an unmarked Ford drove by with as much stealth as a circus bear in a swimming pool.

"Yeah," Nick went on. "I had some work done on my shoulder after the gunshot wound a few years back. A through and through. Muscle damage. It was okay. The guy healed me."

"Oh yeah? What's his area of expertise?"

"Area of expertise? You sound like a fucking cop," Nick joked.

"What the fuck does he do?"

"Better. He's a Korean acupuncturist. And get this. He's blind. A *blind* acupuncturist."

Jack glanced sideways to see if Nick was pulling his chain. "You putting me on?"

"That'd be hopeless."

"Because it's too soon, you know, for humor."

"No kidding."

"Then? Then . . . ?"

"He's a fucking blind man. What can I say," Nick said defensively. "His other senses are heightened, you know, more acute. Guy's a genius." Jack wasn't buying it, and Nick added, "He healed me, for chrissakes. Only left one needle in my shoulder, one time."

Jack couldn't help himself and laughed. It felt good.

"I could never go back to the neighborhood, you know?" Jack said. "Hey, you hear about Bertolino, he sent his kid to a blind acupuncturist and this Korean guy played pin the tail on the fucking donkey with his boy. *Not* gonna happen."

"Eh, your call."

"See that broad?" Jack asked.

"That broad?" Nick said, feigning shock.

"Excuse me, Mr. Enlightened."

"I'm just saying."

"Okay, do you see that refined woman with gang tats on her neck and tits leading with her attitude and wearing so much eyeliner I can make a positive ID from here?"

"Really?"

"Yeah. Outside the Black Stallion, trading spit with one of the pricks who tried to run me and Tommy off the road."

"Oh, you mean the guy who's threatening a lawsuit?"

"Really?" Jack sounded unconcerned.

"No, but he could. Your license doesn't read 007. There are consequences."

"I'll remember that, Obi-Wan. Don't lose her."

Nick started the SUV and struggled to do a three-point turn in his beast, finally following the Toyota Corolla down the hill.

Jack had called the nurses' station twice on the drive into town and twice been told that the doctor had decided to wait another few hours to wean his son off the drugs. They would call him in plenty of time to be at the bedside when he woke.

Johnny had promised to call, but Jack wasn't holding out too much hope. And he didn't expect to run into him at the funeral. If he was a party to the murder, everyone would expect him to be there, to make a statement. He'd sounded scared, not stupid. Jack would track him down if need be.

Nick followed the old Corolla as it pulled into the Black Stallion's minimall lot and chose to park across the street. Izel switched off the key and waited as the old Corolla's engine turned over and bucked until it finally died with a belch of black smoke.

Izel pulled down the vanity mirror, whose light had burned out years earlier, and applied another thick swatch of eyeliner.

Jack and Nick were standing at her door when she exited her car.

"Afternoon, ma'am," Nick said with a Cheshire cat–eating grin on his face.

"What the fuck you want?" Izel said, no niceties intended.

Nick flicked open his gold shield.

"I'm Detective Nicholas Aprea and this is Inspector Jacques Clouseau. We're looking for a Hector Lopez. We were informed that you knew his whereabouts."

"You don't wanna find him," she said, with all the grace of a rattler.

"Let us be the judge of that," Jack said harshly.

"I never heard of him. Never heard of no Hector nobody."

"You heard enough to be afraid," Jack said, reading her body language. "We're not here to jam you up. Just tell us where we can find the guy."

"I'm smart enough not to know him."

It was a standoff.

"Give us something and we won't have to take you down for questioning," Nick said.

Izel looked behind her at the empty lot and the closed red door before she answered.

"You find Johnny Rodriguez, you'll find Hector. They're attached at the hip."

Izel walked past them and then stopped in the center of the broken macadam lot. "You find Hector, make sure he doesn't take you all to hell with him."

"Explain," Jack demanded.

"You didn't hear nothin' from me."

Jack nodded his head, signaling it was agreed.

Izel's eyes scanned the lot for a second time. Her hand raked the bruise on her forehead from the backhand punch and then she blurted out with fury, "Fuck Hector. *Fuck him to hell.* Ask him where he buried his father."

Izel turned on her heel, pulled open the heavy wooden door, and disappeared into the Black Stallion.

Jack filled Nick in on the details of his developing case against Johnny and Hector. The interviews with the retired manager of the market, Hector's mother, his conversation with Johnny's sister, and the details of the call with Johnny that had come in yesterday at the hospital. And how all the pieces might fit together. Nick didn't seem too surprised.

"Yeah, I already knew about Hector. No, I wasn't snooping. I got a call from Mrs. Sternhagen—hey, is she from New Zealand or Australia?—and she gave you a gold star on her report for being very polite. And I knew you'd get around to telling me when the time was right."

"New Zealand."

"I don't know what kind of deal you could offer if it's a capital murder case. Multiple, at that. Have you run it by the feds?"

"You're the first."

"I thought so. I meant about Sternhagen being from New Zealand. I'll nose around with a DA friend of mine about the other. Keep it vague."

"If I can't set something up, I'll tell him anything he wants to hear to get him talking."

"You'd lie to a killer? You'll have the ACLU all over your ass. Trampling on his civil liberties and so on." Nick mock-slapped himself on the forehead. "But, oh yeah. I forgot. You're not a cop. You're a PI. You get paid to lie."

"Did I ask for this grief?"

"No, and it's free of charge." Nick paused, thinking, then added on a much more sober note, "One other thought. If Hector's our man, he's a death machine, he likes his work. If you get a drop on him, I don't want you getting close unless I'm riding shotgun."

Jack Bertolino all but ran down the waxed linoleum floor of the hospital ward. He was trying to keep his temper in check while he scanned the hallway for room 2-C. Chris had been weaned from the drug cocktail two hours ago and moved to a private room—information he'd only discovered when he arrived at the front desk.

That had to be a good sign, he thought—he prayed—as he rushed past nurses' stations and empty hospital beds.

Jack stopped at 14-C and averted his eyes from an elderly woman who appeared to be in serious pain, and then saw the young LAPD uniform sitting in a folding chair up the hallway on the right. The door to 2-C was open. He nodded to the officer, his heart beating out of his chest. He stepped in, and almost lost it again.

Chris was sitting up in bed, a goofy drug-induced grin on his face. His braced arm jutted forward as if he was offering to shake hands. Jeannine was sitting in a chair at the foot of his bed looking relieved. An uneaten rolling food tray was hovering over his son's lap. The room was filled with flowers, and the sun that spilled into the room created an aura of light around his boy.

Jack couldn't talk. He stared at his son, memorizing every detail of his alert face.

"Hey, Dad, you look like shit."

"You wanna play a little one-on-one for money?" Jack shot back.

Chris's face twisted with mirth, then pain. "Don't make me laugh. It hurts my head."

Jack walked over and kissed his son on the forehead, just under the gauze bandage that was wrapped like a turban around his head.

Jeannine started talking as if she was in midthought, obviously still in a state of shock. "Dr. Stein was, well, surprised to say the least. He stopped the medication, said it should take a few hours for Chris to regain consciousness. Sure enough, his eyes popped open, just like that. Chris looked at the doctor and recited his full name, the president's name, the year he was born, and today's date."

"You watch too much television," Jack said, smiling.

"Stein said he'd never seen anything like it. And then things started moving so quickly I forgot to call. Sorry."

"I'm here."

"That's good, good. I'm so . . ."

Jeannine started crying again, and Chris's eyes filled, and Jack joined the party.

"What a scare," he said quietly.

"The doctor told me I was out for the season, but good to go for the next. So I'll make dean's list this year, and then wow them on the field next year."

"Sounds like a plan."

Jack felt humbled, and unworthy of having this miracle of a young man.

"Where's Jeremy?" Jack asked.

"Back at the hotel. Nice accommodations. Very nice view of the boats, thank you. Although they slow-cook the eggs in the restaurant and you know I don't like runny eggs."

Jack was so happy, her critical eye didn't bother him.

"I told him to stay put," she went on. "This was for family, however it turned out."

"God, Mom, did you think I was going to end up selling comic books at Schotzy's?"

"Only if you were the author."

"Okay, that's better." Chris's eyes flickered and closed, and he was out.

Jack looked into Jeannine's blue eyes and remembered the woman he'd once loved more than life itself.

"Oh, no, don't look at me like that. You're still not off the hook with me, mister."

The truce was over. Everything was back to exactly the same: undeclared warfare.

Jack said, a little roughly, "So, you want me to take over?"

39

The lights in the ultramodern bedroom were dimmed. Miles Davis was playing *Kind of Blue* in hidden surround sound speakers. On a flat screen, the sound muted, Woody Allen was sitting with Diane Keaton in a rowboat on the lake in Central Park. The black-and-white images shifted the light on an open pizza box, with a few scraps of crust left, an open bottle of cabernet, and two glasses. One had lipstick markings on the rim. Articles of clothing were draped haphazardly over a red Barcelona chair next to the bed. A slight, crisp breeze was blowing in through the open French doors.

DDA Leslie Sager stood on the balcony of her twenty-third-floor condo on the Wilshire Corridor. She wore a thick white cotton bathrobe she had picked up at Ventana's during her last visit to the spa in Big Sur. She was feeling relaxed.

Jack Bertolino was under the covers of Leslie's bed, taking stock of the positive turn his life had taken in the past twelve hours.

Chris was on the mend. He'd have to remain in the hospital for at least a week until Stein was sure there was no neurological damage or cranial bleeding. But he thought his son's recovery was nothing short of miraculous and wasn't really worried at this point, just being careful. Jack was pleased with the doctor's care. You can't keep a Bertolino down, Jack thought proudly.

Jack had left the hospital when his son fell asleep for the night.

He dropped Jeannine off at the Jamaica Bay Inn and called Leslie on the off chance it wasn't too late for a visit.

Jack slipped on his jeans and walked barefoot and bare chested onto the balcony. He put his arms around her waist and stood staring out at the view.

Leslie's condo had a clear shot all the way to the Pacific Ocean. To the left he could see the three light green towers that hovered over the marina. The sky was cloudless, and even with the light pollution, the stars were plentiful. The crescent moon was bright enough to reflect off the dark sea.

Leslie turned into Jack and they kissed. It was thoughtful and sweet.

"I'm a sucker for a good pizza," she said.

Jack tried to conjure up a witty comeback but came up dry. He smiled and kissed her again. "Thanks for the flowers," he finally ventured. "It was very thoughtful."

"I don't know how you did it. If it had been my child, I would have been a total basket case."

"It wouldn't have served Chris. And it wouldn't have served me."

"And I don't know how you do it every day."

"Yeah." He took a moment before answering. Everything was moving so rapidly, he hadn't had much time for introspection. Finally, he said, "I was trying to simplify my life when I moved out here."

"I can see that worked out well."

That elicited a crooked grin from Jack.

"I'm starting to think you can't ever escape your past."

"My father used to say that men make plans, God laughs."

"He's got one hell of a sense of humor."

Leslie touched Jack's chest and felt the chill. She took him by the hand and led him back into the warmth of her bedroom, closing the French doors behind them.

Jack poured some more wine into their glasses. They sat propped up on her down pillows and watched Woody Allen running down a Manhattan street.

"Were you in love with her?"

Jack knew she was talking about Mia.

"No . . . but I don't fall into bed, and I don't fall in love . . . easily."

They turned back to the screen and watched Woody chase a dream that was already gone.

————

Johnny was in the shower trying to scrub away his demons. Angelina had worked the early shift and was sitting on the bed in one of Johnny's wife-beater T-shirts. Her tattoos were bleeding color from under the thin shoulder straps like lightning bolts. She peered into the bathroom and then walked over to Johnny's desk. She opened his wallet, rifled through the contents, and saw a number written in ballpoint on a slip of paper, wedged behind his driver's license. She picked up his new phone and punched in the number.

"Bertolino here . . . Johnny?"

Angelina apologized for the wrong number, in Spanish, and clicked off. She recognized the name from a story her brother had been telling at the bar.

"Did you say something?" Johnny shouted from the bathroom as he turned off the shower.

"No, why? You got a guilty conscience?" She put the phone back on his desk and returned quickly to the bed, her heart sinking.

Johnny wasn't sure what she meant and didn't really give a shit. He had enough on his plate. He'd decided to blow off Bertolino. They didn't have any proof. If they did, it would be the police dogging his ass and not some fucking private investigator. He'd have Hector kill the guy if he got too close. Angelina was right. Better to enjoy what they had. He didn't want to move to Ohio or some-fucking-where, anyway.

———————

"Who was that?" Leslie asked after Jack had hung up the phone.

"Sorry, I was expecting an important call, and it was just a wrong number, I think."

"Huh." She watched as he rose to his feet, on the move once again. "Go ahead. I won't take offense."

"Thank you," Jack said as he pulled on his shirt, buttoning as he talked. "Things are getting to that point. I have to get an early start or the train will leave without me."

"Stay safe."

Jack kissed her on the lips and then leaned down for an extended hug. She was warm and inviting through her nightgown, and he broke off the embrace before he lost his will.

"I'll do my best."

Jack didn't say he'd call, because they both knew he would.

———————

Johnny didn't remember falling asleep, but he was awakened with a blazing hard-on. Angelina was naked, the blinds were drawn against the early morning sun, and she blew a shotgun of sweet pot into his smiling mouth.

He decided to play along as she pulled the handcuffs out of their sex drawer, and before he could jump up to take a piss, his hands were secured to the bedposts with the cuffs. His feet were spread and tied with the silk scarves she had used to cover the lamp shades, and a pair of green silk panties was draped over his eyes.

It was such a hot scene that Johnny was afraid he'd come before Angelina worked some magic with her well-trained muscles.

Through the pot haze he suddenly realized something was wrong. He shook his head and saw through a gauzy veil of green that Angelina had a bottle of Windex in her hand and was wiping down the surface of his desk.

"What's going on? Get over here," he demanded.

He thrashed his head back and forth, and the panties slid off his face.

Angelina grabbed Johnny's Nike sports bag and filled it with his stash, his phone, and his laptop. She left his wallet, minus the cash, and his keys. She wouldn't be caught dead driving a Prius.

"What the fuck are you doing?" Johnny asked, trying to keep the alarm out of his voice. Was she ripping him off? Angelina started throwing on clothes with the speed of a quick-change artist.

"So you thought I would turn my back on my brother?" she finally said in a voice Johnny didn't recognize. "My father? My family? You ain't pretty enough for that, homeboy. You're twenty-three. Let's see how long that works for you."

"Gimme the fucking keys, Angelina. Unlock the fucking cuffs," Johnny said with as much menace as a spread-eagled, manacled man could muster. It didn't work.

When she turned, Johnny could see that she was wearing a single pendant pearl earring. If Johnny could get any more freaked, that image cemented it. Angelina had found his jewelry stash. He had planned to break the earring down and turn it into another piece that couldn't be traced back to that woman they had killed up on the hill. This could tie Johnny directly to the murder.

"I was talking crazy, but it was just talk," he pleaded. "You were right. We'll go away for a few weeks until everything settles down, and then things'll go back to normal."

"I know you talked to that cop, Johnny."

Ice.

Johnny swallowed down a rush of bile and fought the impulse to vomit. The panic he felt was overwhelming. He started to hyperventilate; his breaths came in short pulsing spurts. He bucked on the bed and tried in vain to rip free. Johnny Rodriguez was not going to die.

"Please, Angelina. Don't make me beg here. Give me the fucking keys, and let's talk this out."

"You want me to give you something, pretty boy?"

Angelina turned on her heel and opened the apartment door.

Hector was standing there. His eyes were blazing from cocaine, tequila, and fury.

As she started past, he grabbed her by the throat with one meaty fist, lifted her off the ground, and pushed her up against the stucco wall.

"Are you sure?" he hissed.

Angelina's eyes turned red and bugged out of her skull as she fought to breathe and jerk her head up and down. The pendant earring swung wildly.

Yes, she mouthed.

Hector let her down, and in one motion ripped the pearl earring out of her lobe. She screamed as hot blood streamed down her neck. She cupped her ear, picked up Johnny's sports bag, and tried to run, but her legs had turned to stone. She couldn't move.

Hector stepped into the apartment, turned sharply, and glared at Angelina. His eyes were damned. Hector quickly closed the door.

She could hear some of Johnny's muffled pleas, but it was all one-sided. Angelina knew that she'd be haunted for the rest of her life when she heard him scream, "Bless me, Father, for I have—"

40

"Jimmy Smits, I think he's the one," Kenny Ortega said, opening his arms expansively and then snugging his tie, looking very self-satisfied on the Skype screen. The blue Miami sky was dazzling and painted with bold white cumulus clouds outside his fifth-floor window.

Jack took the bait, enjoying his friend's exuberance. "For what?"

"To play me in the movie, Bertolino. I've got the accent, the Latino swagger. You want to know why I'm in full-blown swagger mode?"

Jack could hear a knock on Kenny's door and watched as his secretary, Claire, dropped a Subway sub onto her boss's desk and started out of the room.

"Thanks, Claire. See that? I'm taking lunch at my desk," Kenny said as if he was imparting some great wisdom. "That's how busy I am."

"So what's up?"

"I'm in swagger mode because my boss thinks I'm brilliant. When's the last time anybody called you brilliant, my friend?"

"I'll get back to you on that."

"Last night! Your ears must have been ablaze because yours truly gave it up for the man. And you are the man. How's your boy?"

"On the mend."

"That's what I wanted to hear. My day is going from good to great."

"The flowers were appreciated."

Ortega steamrolled over the compliment. "Brilliant. Oh yeah. The division chief said it before he could take back the word. I think it pained him to throw out a compliment."

"Is there a point?"

"I made your case against the 18th Street Angels, Royce Motors, Outlaws Inc., and Travel Associates. You were sniffing up the money tree and hit the jackpot."

Jack raised his eyebrows in expectation.

"A limited-liability corporation was formed for Travel Associates. Take a guess as to who's the president of the LLC? Marie Ortiz. And who is the treasurer? Her husband, R. E. Cortez Junior. Roman Enrique Ortiz!" he shouted, not waiting for an answer. "Fucking Roman!

"Now, let's take a look at Outlaws Inc. and the one member of the band's crew who wouldn't have raised a red flag if you hadn't started the inquiry. Thomas Vegas—whose brother is an OG in the Angels—is listed as security for the bands. But when we dug a little deeper, we discovered that Travel Associates had placed him in that position. It was a clause they wrote into their lease agreement with Outlaws Inc., purportedly to protect their property, namely, their bus, once it arrived in Miami. The same was true on the bus's return to California."

"So, on his watch, it's drugs in and money off," Jack said. "It feels like Outlaws Inc. could be the patsy in all of this. The groups change, but the bus remains the constant."

"That's our thinking," Ortega agreed. "Now it gets even better. Eight to ten buses were listed on Travel Associates books at any one time, but when we did a DMV search, only six buses were on record. Two other buses had been sold a year ago, and two six months ago, respectively, at Royce Motors, under the watchful eye of one Roman Ortiz."

"The buses were bought with dirty money," Jack said. "And then resold for clean. Very smart. They made a double profit and laundered up to a million a pop."

"Correct," Kenny said. "I spoke with our friend who shall remain nameless, in the 'office,' and a big load of Dominican is due to arrive in the Miami area the day before the Outlaws bus comes into town for the Ricci Jay and Wisteria concert at Mansion."

"And the DEA's letting the drugs slide through?" Jack asked, amazed, but getting caught up in the buzz.

"They bought your argument. The big picture, I kept saying. Not only that, but once the fully loaded bus leaves the Sunshine State, I'll be winging my way to California in a DEA jet to head up the organized crime drug enforcement task force that will shut down the Angels, confiscate their coke, tie off a money-laundering cell, and put a real crimp in Manuel Alvarez's lifestyle behind bars. Well, that's the plan anyway."

"Damn, Kenny, that's good."

"So, let's take down some scumbags, Jack, and have some fun. Gene McLennan is briefing Nick Aprea as we speak. Now, there are still some hurdles to clear, and our manpower and technical reach won't be all encompassing, but a task force it will be."

Jack smelled a rat. "What hurdles?"

"Whether I can get you an invite into the room, into the play."

"It's my play."

"No confusion there, my friend. Let me work my magic."

Jack wasn't surprised. On an occasion like this, not having a shield was a detriment.

"I know you'll get it done," Jack said. Then he remembered something else he needed. "On another note, could you run the cell tower coordinates on a phone number? It might be nothing . . ."

"I trust your gut. Give me a few minutes, and I'll get back to you, *mi hermano.*"

Jack pulled out his cell and read off the wrong-number call he had received in Leslie Sager's bed the night before. Ortega signed off.

Jack put his computer to sleep and smiled all the way over to the coffeemaker in his kitchen and refilled his mug.

———————

Diane Rodriguez, Johnny's sister, was trying to spoon-feed some Gerber carrots and peas into her son's mouth when her cell phone rang. The baby responded by screaming in brain-tingling tones, which proved that his lungs were functional.

In one motion she plucked him out of his high chair and answered the phone.

"Hello, this is Diane."

"Diane, Jack Bertolino here. We met the other day at your house."

"It's my mother's house," she said, guarded.

"Ah, sorry," was all Jack could think of to say. "Listen, I'm having a little problem, and I'm hoping you can help."

Jack was in his Mustang, driving up Lincoln Boulevard toward Santa Monica and St. Johns to visit his son. He was speaking on his Bluetooth device.

"I'm kind of tied up, with the baby and all."

"I understand. I'll just take a minute of your time," Jack said, powering on. "I received a call from your brother two days ago."

"Really?" She sounded pleased.

"We started a dialogue. He was going to call me back yesterday, and I haven't heard from him. If I'm going to be able to help, we really have to get the ball rolling." He let her absorb that, then made his pitch. "I know you're not comfortable giving me his number, but wondered if you'd give him a call and tell him now's the time."

The baby was drooling peas and carrots down Diane's blouse, but she didn't seem aware of it.

"Are you still there?" Jack asked.

"Uh, yeah. Uh, okay. Okay. Let me get Logan fed and changed, and I'll get back to you, one way or the other."

"Thank you, Diane. I'll wait for your call."

Chris was propped up in his bed with a quarter-pounder inches from his mouth when Jack entered the hospital room. His son visibly relaxed and took an ungodly large bite. His appetite was obviously back.

"Don't tell Nurse Ratched," he said with a full mouth.

His friend Macklin had a large order of fries in his lap, along with the empty wrapper of a quarter-pounder. The young man cleaned up well, and was in far better shape than the night of the attempted murder. Jeannine looked guilty as she ate her Filet-O-Fish and her Diet Coke, her imaginary concession to health-conscious fast food.

Jeremy, who Jack knew was a health food nut, stood in the corner. He washed down a bite from a power bar with a sip from his ever present bottle of whatever spring water was in vogue.

"Well, he had to eat something," Jeannine said. "You should have seen the color of the turkey."

"It's all good," Jack said, and it was heartfelt. "Has Dr. Stein been in?"

"First thing this morning," Jeremy supplied, even though Jack had directed the question to Jeannine. "If there are no changes in Chris's condition, he's pushing to have him released tomorrow afternoon. I've rented a car, and if it's all right with you, we'll drive him back to Stanford and get him set up with the local doctors."

"Damn insurance companies," Jeannine added.

Jack decided not to start a debate. He was confident that Stein had his son's best interests at heart and let it go.

"That would be appreciated, Jeremy. Thank you."

Jack wasn't sure how he felt about sharing a position of power with Jeremy, but knew he wanted Chris back up north sooner rather than later. He didn't want anyone more afraid than they already were.

"Coach Fredricks has access to the best doctors in the business," Chris said. "He was very cool about the whole thing and said he and the team would stand by one of their best new prospects."

"How about that?" Jeannine said, beaming. "One of their best new prospects. I had a very nice conversation with the man, and he assured me the accident wouldn't have any bearing on Chris's scholarship."

"Well, terrific. That's good news, Son."

Jack had mixed feelings about not being there to field the phone call, but he had no one to blame but himself.

Adding insult to injury, his cell phone vibrated, and the tone alerted Jack and everyone else in the room to the fact that he'd received a text.

Jack gave an apologetic nod to the group, walked out into the hallway, and fielded the text. It was from Diane Rodriguez:

I CALLED JOHNNY AND LEFT A 911. HE ALWAYS RESPONDED B 4. I AM
SCARED AND CAN'T LEAVE THE HOUSE. IF U PROMISE ME NO POLICE,
I'LL GIVE YOU HIS ADDRESS. PROMISE ME.

Jack texted back PROMISE and felt a pang of guilt.

———————

He thanked the young officer guarding his son, and didn't have long to wait for a response and Johnny's address. His phone rang while he was transcribing the information, and he took a call from Kenny Ortega. The coordinates of the cell phone wrong number he had inquired about earlier had bounced off cell towers that placed the female caller in the middle of the 18th Street Angels' territory. Jack loved redundancy in this business. He knew Diane was telling the truth, and that he wouldn't be wasting the trip.

Jack walked back into room 2-C, and everyone in the room knew from his demeanor that he had to leave.

"Dad and I got to spend some quality time together," Chris said, trying to smooth his exit. "He's working a case," he directed to Macklin.

What a kid, Jack thought.

"I thought you retired," Macklin felt compelled to say.

"So did I," Jack answered lamely. "Love you, Son. I'll try and get back before lights-out."

Jeannine was the very stiff model of composure, and Jeremy gave Jack a friendly nod, happy, no doubt, to see him go. Jack couldn't abide the man.

Taking a French fry from Macklin, he held it up and pointed it at Jeremy. "You ever hear about that issue with plastic and bottled water? You save your own health, but trash everybody's else's."

Jack popped the fry into his mouth, turned on his heel, and walked out of the door.

41

The peeling paint on the green door vibrated as the door slammed in a mindless way in the hot winter wind howling down off the San Bernardino Mountains.

Jack knew that a murder had been committed inside the low-rent apartment, but he'd found no visible blood and no body. He had alerted Nick, Gallina, and Tompkins, and wasn't looking forward to their scrutiny.

From the color of the splintered wood it appeared that the bed-posts had recently been ripped off the frame. Two cut silk handkerchiefs skirted the bottom legs. The bed had been stripped and from the stains on the mattress it appeared that sex had occurred, but not necessarily a crime.

Not necessarily a murder, but the apartment smelled of fear and death. Jack wasn't confused about the energy in the room.

Nick was the first one to exit the apartment and step up to Jack. "It smells like a French whorehouse or my dorm room at college. Did you notice that as dirty as the place was—"

"The desk had been wiped clean," Jack said, finishing Nick's sentence. "And the shower knobs, and that little fucking fridge. Who uses a fridge like that anymore?"

"College students living in dorms. For beer and huh, beer. I could get a tech unit in, but I don't see probable cause. And the sister's *feelings* won't play at the department."

Jack pulled out a small envelope and handed it to Nick. "I found it in the carpet under the desk. I think there's blood on the tear."

Curious, Nick opened the envelope and shook it out onto his notebook to avoid contamination.

A red-painted fingernail.

"So I'll call in the tech squad."

Lieutenant Gallina walked out of the apartment, followed by Tompkins.

"Smells like sex in there," Gallina said, scrunching up his face. "Funky. Why is this the first we're hearing about Johnny Rodriguez?"

Jack was cool about his oversight. "It was all preliminary until I got the call from his sister. Hector Lopez was just another potential on my list. I can't prove he's relevant yet. The two of them are supposed to be attached at the hip, though. And I think they're good for Mia."

Gallina gave him a dark look. "I'm gonna call in a crew and have them do their thing. Too many bodies showing up," he muttered.

Nick handed them the evidence envelope.

"Whose is this, and where the fuck did it come from?" Gallina asked, losing his patience.

Nick threw a glance at Jack.

"I found it under the desk," Jack answered. "Don't know who it belongs to, but when I know, you'll know."

"Christ, this is no way to run an investigation," Gallina said. "Okay, keep me in the loop."

"Lieutenant, can we keep his sister out of this for the time being? If she thinks I called in the cavalry, I'll lose her as a contact. She may be valuable."

Gallina looked like he was going to blow his top. "Okay, Bertolino," he growled. "But if her brother turns up dead, she's ours."

Jack nodded his thanks.

"But don't hold out on me. I want this put to bed as much as you two do. You two do," he repeated, mocking himself. "Christ, I can't talk anymore."

He stormed off toward his car as two black-and-whites rolled onto the scene. A fresh-faced uniform exited his vehicle with a roll of yellow crime scene tape, and went to work cordoning off the entrance to the apartment.

Tompkins stepped in close. "They found the Escalade at the Long Beach Airport, long-term parking. Front-end damage, no prints. Stolen. We looked at the security camera at the lot and—"

"All it showed was a guy in a wide-brimmed hat," Jack said.

"You got it. I googled it. It's called a Panama."

"Arturo Delgado. You find him, you're a hero," Jack said evenly. "I find him, he's dead."

That seemed reasonable to Tompkins.

Hector drove up into the mountains and hung a left off the paved road. He jumped out of the car to pull back a metal gate, then closed the gate behind him when he had driven through. His car disappeared around a bend in a rutted dirt fire road.

Mando had been furious when he heard about Johnny turning rat. It was a personal affront. He liked the kid, but he sanctioned the kill. They could have no weak links. No question. He offered to have someone else do the job, but Hector felt personally responsible and wanted it done right. He wanted his friend to disappear off the face of the earth.

Johnny was Hector's last tie to anything that could be construed as a personal relationship. Hector wasn't really sad. He didn't really feel anything. Strange. He was concerned about Angelina. She was a loose end, and that didn't sit well with Hector. She did have bigger balls than Johnny, and she was the one who had made the call. She would implicate herself if she went to the authorities. And she had Angel blood running through and through.

Hector would have a conversation with her brother and make sure he kept her in line. He nodded to himself as he bumped along. That was the right decision.

He soon pulled the car over to the side of the fire road and carefully backed up under a canopy of evergreen tree branches. His car would be hidden from police helicopters and prying eyes. Hector had work to do.

Johnny had been wrapped in his own sheets. Less potential DNA evidence left behind, Hector thought as he humped the dead body over one shoulder and carted it deep into the pine forest. Johnny's lifeless head banged roughly against a tree trunk as Hector made an abrupt turn while he scouted out the perfect burial site.

"You ain't so pretty now, huh, Johnny?"

Hector wasn't sure if he had said it out loud, or just thought it, but it made him laugh nonetheless. After scanning the area, he settled on a slight ridge, and threw the body down onto the pine straw.

Upon impact the sheet pulled off Johnny's naked upper body. One of his arms was pinned at an impossible angle behind his back. The other flopped over his head, revealing the handcuff still attached to his wrist. His hazel eyes were partly shut, dulled, covered in an opaque film. His neck was a solid mass of purple and blue bruises. Some of his tattoos were obscured by the blood that had settled in his chest while lying in the Impala's trunk. His tongue protruded from his mouth and was dark and distended.

Johnny Rodriguez had been strangled to death.

Change the pattern of the kill, slow down the search, leave no blood evidence behind, Hector mused, proud of his God-given talent.

He walked back to the Impala to retrieve his tools. His knives, a folding spade with a serrated blade, two rolls of three-millimeter plastic drop cloths, duct tape, a joint, matches, and a twelve-pack of Dos Equis. Might as well take some time and enjoy nature.

Hector locked up his beauty, started back up the trail, and sucked in full breaths of the fresh, chilled, pine-scented air.

———————

No one looked up when Jack Bertolino entered the Black Stallion, but everyone knew that he wasn't a regular. Jack knew he'd worn out his welcome before he stepped over the threshold. He felt the frigid silence as he walked up to the bar and grabbed a stool.

He'd experienced a similar feeling as a young undercover detective when he found himself in a mob-owned private club on Mulberry Street. It was the wrong address, and the guys let him know before they'd wiped the espresso off their lips that he was on their turf, and if he wanted to enjoy the rest of his afternoon, he'd move on.

Jack could see the back of a woman, who he thought was Angelina, giving him the evil eye in the expanse of mirror that backed the bottles of booze, creating the illusion of a double row and a grander space. The mirror worked for them both.

Jack picked out Izel at the far end of the bar as she wiped glasses and held them up to the light to check for lipstick marks before placing them in an overhead rack for the evening rush. She pretended not to notice his existence. He hadn't come to hang her out to dry.

An older gentleman who had the feel of a gangster sat in the power booth, reading the newspaper and looking like he owned the place. The man never glanced up from his article.

Must be damn good reading, Jack thought.

Johnny's sister, Diane, had been extremely upset on the phone when Jack gave her the update. He promised to call again as soon as he heard anything related to Johnny's whereabouts, making sure to leave out the detail about the cops being involved. She in turn had provided him with Angelina's name, where she worked, and the extent of her relationship with Johnny as she understood it. Jack thought the time was ripe to rattle a cage or two.

Angelina grabbed a bar napkin and slapped it down in front of Jack. One of her fingernails was a different color and thickness from the rest. It was artificial, and the polish was a lighter shade of red.

"What can I get you?" she said, all business.

"I want a draft, and I want to talk to your boyfriend."

"You and me both. This dating thing is crazy," she deadpanned.

"Johnny Rodriguez," he said so that the entire room could hear. Jack felt the OG's eyes snap up before he caught him in the mirror.

Unruffled, Angelina pulled a draft and set it down in front of Jack.

"Old news. He broke up with me a month ago. Said I wasn't in the same socioeconomic class or some shit like that. Can you believe it? Who the fuck drives a Prius anyway?"

"When's the last time you saw him?"

"You a cop?"

"Is that a problem?"

Angelina looked at him like he was something she had stepped in and couldn't get off her shoe.

"I haven't seen him, like, socially. I mean, he comes around and I serve him like any other customer, you know?"

"That must hurt."

"What the hell are you talking about?"

"Your ear. Looks painful."

Angelina's hand went reflexively to the bandage on the lobe of her torn ear, and her eyes flickered for a second and then went cold.

The older gentleman was out of his booth and moving toward the bar.

"I'm looking for Hector," Jack said to Angelina.

"We get a lot of Hectors. Don't you know where you are, fool?" Angelina marched off to the far end of the bar, ducked under, and disappeared into a back room.

Felix was now standing at Jack's side, violating his personal space, staring into the mirror. No eye contact. Two young soldiers had taken flanking positions. Everyone was armed. Izel finished with a tray of limes and then followed Angelina's path under the bar.

"Drink's on me. Time to vamoose."

Jack turned slowly, stared at Felix, and memorized his face.

"I'm looking for Johnny Rodriguez and Hector Lopez," he said, quietly this time.

"Be careful what you wish for. Your time is up."

Two more young thugs entered the bar and stood off to one side, poised for whatever was needed, ready to do gang business.

The numbers weren't adding up in Jack's favor, and he had already gotten what he came for. He threw a ten on the bar, turned, and walked out.

———

Jack rapidly crossed the street and headed down the sidewalk. He could see in the reflection of the retail stores that the two young thugs had followed him out as far as the parking lot and then turned back, confident that they had kept their machismo intact.

He made a left at the corner, jumped in the old Plymouth Fury, and waited a few more moments before turning the key. He was pleased with the sound the 426 hemi engine produced. After a few blocks he pulled to the curb on a side street that afforded him an unobstructed view of an alleyway and the delivery entrance to the Black Stallion.

Jack was about to dial his son's number at the hospital when the back door to the Stallion flew open, and Angelina pounded up the alley, away from Jack's position. She had her car keys dangling from one hand, and what appeared to be an overnight bag filled to the max in the other. He calmly put his phone away.

As soon as Angelina had reached the cross street, Nick Aprea in his Expedition, and Gallina and Tompkins in their government-issue, skidded to a stop and blocked her way.

Nick was the first out of his car and grabbed Angelina in a heartbeat. She went to slap him, and in a move he had perfected in hand-to-hand combat training in the marines, he spun her around and cuffed her before she had time to call him a *maricón*.

Tompkins took it from there. He grabbed Angelina by her cuffed wrists, shoved her into the rear of their undercover ride, jumped in beside her, and slammed the door. Gallina hit the gas and made a tire-spinning exit. Grabbing her overnight bag, Nick stepped up into his SUV and followed smoothly in their wake. In less than fifteen seconds, Angelina ceased to exist.

The plan was for Nick to lead the interview since he was up to speed on Jack's case and Johnny and Hector's history. Gallina and Tompkins agreed to take second position after much heated debate.

With Johnny's wallet and the keys to his new Prius left behind on top of his spotless desktop, no one was optimistic that he was still alive.

The wrong-number phone call—corroborated by Ortega in Miami—had been generated from Johnny's apartment and from Johnny's clean phone. And the woman's voice sounded a lot like Angelina's. If she knew he was talking to Bertolino and the cops, Johnny Rodriguez was as good as dead.

Jack was going to sit surveillance on the Lopez house. He was confident someone in the Angels would contact Hector and let him know he was in the crosshairs. If Hector had anything of value hidden at the family home, Jack felt certain he'd clear it out before he hit the road. It's what he would do before taking an extended trip, and he had the feeling that it was Hector who was going to vamoose for a long time.

———

"I told Jeremy that he had to take Mom back to the hotel or I'd start banging my head against the wall. She was driving me nuts," Chris said.

"She's just worried about you," Jack said from his parked location. He was two blocks from the Lopez residence, but no one could come or go without being made.

"You don't have to worry about me—'cause I know you are—Macklin is hanging. I really made a mess of his weekend."

"You get special dispensation from the church for butting heads with a Cadillac. And if the report from the police is correct, you made out better than the car's grille."

Chris laughed. "My father thinks I have rocks in my head," he directed at Macklin.

"I'm cool," he said. "Tell your dad not to worry."

"I heard him," Jack said. "He's a good friend."

"Dad said you were a mook."

"What's a mook?" Macklin asked.

"Is the cop still there?" Jack interjected.

"Yeah, not much of a job. It would bore me to death."

"Just don't give him a hard time."

"Yeah, yeah, yeah. Oh, Uncle Tommy called to check up and said he's going to sue. I told him we didn't even know who did it yet, but he's going to sue anyway on general principles."

"Gotta love him. What are you doing for dinner?"

"There's a pizza place down the block; Mack'll pick one up. Doesn't taste like home, but it's better than green Jell-O."

"Okay, I'm signing off. I will definitely see you before they release you."

"If you pass a Krispy Kreme on the way in, grab me a few doughnuts for the drive. Please."

"I'll see what I can do. Love ya, Son."

"Okay, Dad."

And Chris hung up.

Jack returned to his patrol. Where were all the people? he wondered as the streetlights snapped on. A stray dog meandered down the center of the road, not concerned about getting hit because road traffic was nonexistent. And then, as if he'd willed some kind of activity, a battle-scarred produce truck rattled up the block, parked in front of the Lopez house, and honked the horn, three long blasts.

The front door opened, and Mrs. Lopez walked out and around to the back of the truck. The owner of the truck greeted her with a smile and a few words and opened the rear doors. Jack could see crates of fruits and vegetables. One of her neighbors walked across the street and joined her as they picked over, squeezed, prodded, and smelled the fruit before choosing a basketful.

The women paid the bill out of ancient change purses and disappeared behind locked doors. The truck rumbled down the road, and made a left where it dead-ended. Jack enjoyed the silence, and the smattering of stars that appeared in this rural neighborhood. He heard three extended blasts of the horn. The traveling grocer was selling his wares on the next block over. The sliver of moon gave off no light in the darkening winter sky. Jack's back had seized up, and the Excedrin was having no effect other than giving him a case of heartburn.

Jack decided to get proactive. He grabbed his small Maglite from the glove box and slipped out of the car, keeping in the shadows. The pools of light created by the streetlamps guided him to a fallow field at the end of the dead-end block. But now that he was walking on the county land that ran along the back of Hector's property, he was on his own. The gigantic electrical towers loomed overhead, and served as markers for Jack as he slowly made his way back toward his destination. The electric current running through the high-voltage lines snapped and buzzed like summer insects.

Jack stopped to get his bearings, and pulled some brambles off his socks that were cutting into his ankles. He moved forward until he was standing directly behind the chain-link fence that bordered the Lopez house. He could make out the occasional shadow crossing what he thought must be the kitchen window.

Jack used the overhanging branch of an old neglected orange tree that was on the corner of the property to help him jump the chain-link fence. He landed heavier than planned and stopped short to make sure no one had heard.

He could see the outline of a lean-to that was attached to the back of the garage with what appeared to be a thick cutting block and bench inside. A rusted grill had been discarded next to the shed, and a few rakes and shovels were propped against the building.

Jack carefully edged closer, using the garage to shield himself from the rear windows of the house. He moved past the lean-to and stopped short at the window on the side of the garage.

It was too dark to make out anything on the inside, and the window's thick layer of dirt made it impossible to see even with light. But Jack hadn't come this far not to try.

He cupped the Maglite with his hand to stop any light from bleeding in the direction of the house. At first he couldn't make out a thing. Then he found a small opening where a condensation drip had cleaned a narrow channel on the dirt-caked glass.

Jack raked the light in a compact arc and found himself looking in at a furnished space. Low rent, but livable.

It looked like a derelict building from the outside, but someone— and Jack felt certain it was Hector—called the garage home. Jack extinguished the light and quickly returned to the protection of the lean-to. This time he discovered an old wooden door that provided access into the rear of the garage. It was locked.

Of course, he thought.

He turned on the light again, found a wooden milk crate that held some rusty tools, pulled out a small screwdriver, and went to work on the door. He placed the Maglite in his mouth, used the tail of his T-shirt to dampen the sound, and tried to pry the lock open.

The screwdriver slipped, grazed the palm of his hand, and the Maglite fell out of his mouth and onto the dirt. He silently cursed and bent to pick up the rusted tool. He then reached for the light.

Jack saw the shadow of a boot in the Maglite before he sensed Hector's presence. He tried to stand up but was stopped by the sound of his skull being cracked. An explosion of color skyrocketed behind his eyes, and then Jack Bertolino's world turned black.

42

Jack's eyes blinked open to excruciating pain. His hands and feet were bound together with duct tape, and he was hanging from a rafter in Hector's little slice of heaven. His feet dangled about two feet off the garage floor, and he wasn't sure if his shoulders were dislocated. His mouth had been taped shut. The garage door was closed, but the track lighting that was attached to the same wooden beam as Jack provided nightmarish pools of light.

Jack's vision was blurred, and when it came into focus he saw double. Now he knew how his son must have felt, and it made him angry. He quickly contained that rush, however. Jack knew he had to control his emotions if he was going to come out of this alive.

But seeing two Hectors was a terrifying image. His tormentor was brutish, bare chested, cut, and deadly. His body was covered in tortured ink and gang graffiti. His eyebrows were so thick he appeared simian.

Hector sat in his Barcalounger nursing a beer, lost in thought. When he saw that Jack was awake, he swiveled the chair around to sit facing him fully. His eyes were heavy lidded and demonic.

In one motion he jumped out of the chair and slammed a punch into Jack's abdomen that sent him spinning. Jack feared that if he puked, he might choke to death on his own vomit. He fought for control.

Hector, like a boxer controlling a heavy bag, stopped Jack's body from spinning. Jack's eyes watered and snot ran out of his nose. As soon as his body stilled, Hector nailed him in the kidneys with a series of roundhouse punches. The pain in his back howled so hard that Jack passed out.

Jack's eyes flickered open, and he was overpowered by the smell of beer. Hector stood in front of him, shaking a bottle of Dos Equis. He sprayed Jack's face, eyes, and hair with the foamy brew until he was revived. The salty sweat and beer that ran into his eyes stung like fire ants.

"Did the cops know about Johnny?" Hector asked, his voice hollow yet taunting.

Jack shook his head no. Let him think that killing Johnny was a mistake. Maybe piss him off.

"Do the cops know you're here?"

Jack nodded while he tried to make sense out of his situation and discover a way out. Hector had been busy during the time Jack was unconscious.

A large military duffel bag had been packed with personal belongings. Jack could see his Glock, his leather rig, and his phone sitting on top of Hector's clothes. A mirror was set next to his chair with the remnants of cocaine. Hector liked to mix business with pleasure.

Jack's ears began to roar, as if he was caught in a wind tunnel, when he looked down and saw that two five-gallon metal jerry cans had been placed directly under his feet. The smell of gas permeated the ripe scent of beer and sweat and angry testosterone.

He tried to swing free, but the muscles in his arms and shoulders were numb and useless. His wrists were bound tight with butcher knots.

Hector disappeared behind Jack and then reappeared holding a third full can of gasoline. He gave the room what appeared to be a final look of appraisal mixed with nostalgia. Then he unscrewed the top of the jerry can and splashed gasoline over every surface in the garage.

He filled the empty bottle of Dos Equis with gas and cast the metal can to the side. He walked up to Jack and pulled out one of his razor-sharp knives.

Hector's eyes had a crazed glint. He put the knife to Jack's neck, and then in one fluid motion sliced the black T-shirt off his body and yanked it free, causing him to rock and sway and spin in a dizzying pattern.

Hector shoved the torn cloth into the neck of the beer bottle and created a wick.

Jack couldn't talk, he couldn't scream. He couldn't slow his crazy death spin.

Hector placed the Molotov cocktail on the seat of his prized Barcalounger, lit a match dispassionately, and set fire to the wick.

Picking up his duffel bag, he sauntered past Jack and out the back door.

Seeing the flames move up the T-shirt wick toward the bottle, Jack bucked his legs wildly, trying to escape.

He didn't see the explosion but heard the ignition, the whump, and the blast. Glass shards knifed into his back as Jack spun toward the front again, where he could see Hector's possessions being inundated with fire.

Flames curled, shot up the wall, and melted the flat-screen television like a Dali painting. The recliner had become a deadly torch. The bed and sheets created unbearable heat. Jack prepared for a painful death, because as soon as the fire hit the two jerry cans filled with gas, Jack's flesh would melt like the television, and he would cease to be.

He spun toward the back door, which had been left open by Hector's exit. It created a draft that forced the flames toward the front of the garage.

As Jack's body twisted back around, the garage door jerked up and open.

Hector's mother stood in the opening with her shotgun butted against her thin shoulder, pointed directly at Jack's face. Through the flames Jack could see that she wore a nightgown and a haunted expression.

The resolute woman fired.

Jack didn't blink. He refused to face death with his eyes shut.

Rather than feeling a burst of pain, however, he fell painfully onto the jerry cans of gasoline, knocking them over and spilling their contents, yet he hardly noticed. He was free. He desperately rolled over the broken gasoline-soaked garage floor toward the back door. With a violent wrench he forced himself up onto his knees. Jack scrabbled through the door, out into the field of weeds, putting as much distance between his body and the garage as possible.

The concussive explosion sent debris, flames, and smoke shooting into the air in a spectacular fireball. Burning embers singed Jack's bare back and arms as the force of the blast threw him face-first to the ground. A length of rope was still attached to one wrist, bound tight with a butcher's knot.

Gotcha, motherfucker.

Through the smoke, Jack could see the slight old woman use the shotgun as a makeshift crutch, and hobble into the safety of her house. He made a mental note to thank Hector's mother for saving his life—and passed out.

43

Nick Aprea stared at Jack's tortured back with eyes that could chisel granite. An EMT was plucking out shards of glass, applying topical disinfectant and bandages. His lower back was black and purple from the beating Hector had administered with his bare knuckles. His shoulders and arms would be sore for weeks, but other than muscular strain, nothing was torn or broken. The crushing blow he had taken to the back of his head had swollen to the size of a walnut, but didn't require stitches. He had clearly suffered a concussion, but it wasn't his first. It didn't worry Jack as much as it did the paramedics. Jack had refused to be admitted to a hospital against recommendations to do so.

The last thing he wanted was to be lying in a hospital bed next to his son's. He wanted to get patched up; say good-bye to Chris, Jeannine, and Jeremy without worrying anybody; and get on with the business of running Hector to ground.

Nick Aprea gave a mixed review on the Angelina front. She wasn't talking, but after procuring a warrant—that DDA Sager had helped expedite—they had discovered an 8GB microSD card in her billfold, Johnny's phone, and what appeared to be his computer. The LAPD tech specialists were in the process of downloading the information from his devices and scanning the computer's hard drive to reconstruct data that had been erased.

Local news helicopters flew in a circular pattern overhead, creating the feel of a war zone. Red, blue, and white lights flashed on fire trucks, emergency vehicles, police units, and news vans.

Hector's garage had burned to the ground. All that was left was a smoldering blot on the rural landscape.

The strobe's colored lights from the emergency vehicles played on Nick's face as he searched for words.

"You know, I can't honestly say anything, because I would've done the same," he finally stated. "You know, going in without calling me. Like I asked you to."

"Small favors," said Jack.

"But you should've fuckin' called me."

"Funny way of keeping your own counsel."

Both men grunted at the shared camaraderie.

The main house was unscathed. A local Hispanic detective was interviewing Hector's mother, but no one held out much hope that she could provide anything of interest. She was high on Jack's list for sainthood. He had made a mental note to pitch the idea the next time he talked to the pope.

On Jack's suggestion, the LAPD had agreed to foot the bill for a crew with a cadaver dog and ultrasound equipment to search for the remains of Hector Lopez Senior. That was the least he could do for the old woman. She'd endured the pain of not knowing for long enough.

———————

The clock was ticking on the drug scene. The Outlaws' bus had arrived in Miami. Kenny Ortega and his crew over at DEA had tracked the shipment of cocaine from the Dominican Republic to one hundred miles off Miami's shores. They followed three go-fast boats in a Coast Guard AWACS helicopter as the boats swooped in, picked up the floating parcels, and raced back to Miami cloaked in darkness.

As soon as Ricci Jay and Wisteria finished their gig, and the tour bus was loaded and on the road, Kenny would fly to the West Coast where the DEA, LAPD, and Ontario police would have twenty-four-hours' lead time to gather for a TAC meeting and strategize how to proceed. Jack hadn't been invited to the party yet, but he wanted in bad.

Nick had more than enough ammunition to call in the cavalry, close down the Black Stallion, round up the usual suspects, and bring them in for questioning. But Jack argued to whoever would listen to keep their powder dry and take the 18th Street Angels down right. Take them down so that they wouldn't be back out on the street in three months selling their poison, taking lives, and destroying families, like they'd done in the city of Ontario for the past fifty years.

Jack was singing to Nick's choir, and he called off the hunt until after DC-day, delivery of the cocaine.

Gallina and Tompkins had rolled onto the scene after Nick, grumbling about the distance and the time of night. They looked almost happy to see Jack alive and well, and they were positively elated when they signed off on the evidence bag that contained the rope and butcher's knot. That tied Hector to the last murder and the attempted murder of Jack Bertolino.

"There are better ways to gather evidence," Gallina said, "but there isn't better evidence."

Jack, in a conciliatory mood, nodded his thanks.

"Hey, I talked to Aprea earlier, and he agreed," Gallina went on. "I called in a few favors to keep your name out of the papers until the drug deal goes down. Let them think that you fried."

"Nice," Jack said.

"There's a good chance Hector Lopez will be there for the action. Let him think he got away with it."

"Makes sense."

"Let's give him enough rope . . ." And Gallina swung the evidence bag and almost cracked a smile.

Tompkins added, "After that Angelina broad spends a night in county, with the added evidence she isn't aware we have in our possession, my guess is she'll be a little more forthcoming."

Nick offered to drive Jack home, and he gratefully accepted, while Tompkins agreed to drive Jack's undercover ride back.

Jack Bertolino downed two Vicodin, courtesy of the EMTs, and a cold beer. Fuck red wine, Jack thought, a simple joy, beer. In fact, this specific beer was the best beer he had ever tasted.

Jack was running late again. He had stopped downtown to meet with a computer sketch artist, where they came up with a passable rendering of Arturo Delgado and a startling likeness of Hector Lopez. Jack gave a second statement about what had transpired the night before, hit the Santa Monica Freeway, and enjoyed a clear shot to St. John's.

The bag of Krispy Kremes tempted Jack all the way to the hospital. He denied the urge, although if he'd been fishing for a date, the bag of fried, sugared dough would have made great bait. The nurses' smiles were sweeter than the doughnuts.

All he wanted to do was get his family on the road and out of harm's way.

In the hallway he ran into Dr. Stein, who gave his son a clean bill of health. The swelling in his brain had diminished, and he should experience no lasting effects from the head injury. His arm would take time, but with proper care, should be healed in three months, and then with a regimen of physical therapy, back to normal in six months or so.

Noticing the massive bump on Jack's head, the doctor asked if he was feeling all right. Jack faked his way out of a prolonged discussion and Dr. Stein's generous offer to inspect his wound.

Jack let the bag of doughnuts lead him into the hospital room, hoping it would provide camouflage. The attempt failed.

"You look like shit," Chris said, worried.

"It's nothing, and you have to find a new way of greeting your old man. Hi, Dad, would work just fine."

Chris ignored Jack's banter. "It *looks* like something. I tell you, Dad, you have to find a new line of work. This one doesn't seem to be working out too well."

"Thanks for the vote of confidence. What time's checkout?" he asked, thinking evade, evade, evade.

Jeannine couldn't hold back any longer. "We're just waiting for a wheelchair," she said in clipped tones. "I was worried you weren't going to make it in time. Jeremy's already downstairs in the minivan he rented."

"That was thoughtful of him," Jack said, trying to cut off her attitude at the pass.

"I'm going to caravan up with them," Macklin said, attempting to ease the tension in the room. Smart kid, Jack thought.

"Good idea," he said. And then, "Say good-bye to Jeremy for me."

Big mistake, Jack realized.

"Well, you can say good-bye to him yourself. I mean, you can hang around long enough to see us down to the car, can't you? That is, if you can find the time."

"Oh, yeah, sure," Jack said as he tried to control his baser impulses.

A young candy striper entered the room pushing a wheelchair. Chris and Macklin both sat up a little taller, shy smiles plastered on their young faces, and both Jack and Jeannine softened some when they witnessed the boys' reactions.

Chris acted like he was in terrible pain as she helped him into the chair. Off they went, down the hall and into the elevator. When they emerged in the hospital lobby, Jeannine hung back a little.

"Were you trying to outdo your son?" Jeannine asked, sotto voce, referring to the bandage on the back of Jack's head. "Should you be walking around? Are you all right?" she said with genuine concern.

"I'm fine. Dr. Stein looked me over," he said, not entirely a lie.

"Well, please be careful. Are you going to be able to come up north after we leave?"

"I'm planning on it. After this business is taken care of," Jack said sincerely.

She gave him a flat look of disbelief. "Well, from the mouths of babes to the warrior's ears. You should listen to your son. This new business venture doesn't seem to be your cup of tea. You don't seem to be very good at it."

With the state his body was in, Jack couldn't really argue the point.

"It's temporary. I have a few things to clean up," Jack said, just trying to end the conversation.

Macklin drove up in his Jetta and pulled behind the minivan. Jack opened the door for Jeannine and gave her a quick buss on the cheek. He shook Jeremy's hand and winked at his son, who already had his hand buried in the doughnut bag. He closed the door, knocked good-bye on the top of the car, and walked back toward the parking structure.

———

The elevator door on the third floor of the parking garage dinged open. Jack took one step out, spun on his heel, and grabbed for the gun that wasn't there.

"Whoa, whoa, Mr. Bertolino, friend, not foe."

A thirty-something dark-haired man with a thick New York accent, dark circles under his eyes, and long sideburns that were shaved to a point stepped out of the shadows with his hands held high. He had a scrap of paper that he slowly proffered to Jack.

"I was told to keep an eye out on your boy," he explained, "and something came up you should know about. After hours there's only one way in and one way out," he said, referring to the hospital hours, "and so I was having a smoke. About two in the mornin', an older gent cruised around the hospital twice, and then parked on the other side of the boulevard, facing the entrance. When he saw that I was interested, he pulled out. I got his license number. Could be nothing, but, I mean, it was your boy up there."

"What did he look like?"

The man scratched the back of his head. "Couldn't get a fix on him, Mr. Bertolino. He was wearing some . . ."

"Hat with a wide brim?" Jack said, wanting to be wrong.

"Guy drives a Bentley and dresses like it's Halloween."

"Thank you, uh?" Jack said, asking for a name.

"Peter."

"Peter," Jack said.

Anticipating Jack's question, Peter said, "Vincent Cardona wants you to know you've got friends, Mr. Bertolino."

One mystery solved, Jack thought.

Peter started walking away and then stopped short. When he turned around, he had a .38 Colt in his hand. He carefully offered the weapon to Jack, electric-taped grip first.

"Looks like you're short. It's clean."

"I'm good."

"I'm just saying, if it was my kid." Peter holstered the gun, and took the stairs down.

Jack walked over to his Mustang. At last he allowed himself to give in to an overwhelming sense of fatigue. He did not discard the slip of paper. He placed it securely in his wallet. He would deal with favors owed at a later date.

44

Mando rocked intently on an office chair in the beige double-wide trailer on the back lot of Royce Motors. He was talking on the phone with his feet up on the utilitarian desk where twelve hundred kilos of pure Colombian cocaine would be sitting in less than thirty-six hours.

Hector stood at the window, looking out through the dusty miniblinds.

A few of his gang members were working on their rides, but none had the class of his Impala. He had watched the late-night news, and he felt little to nothing when he saw what was left of his garage from moving pictures taken from the news choppers. Again on the morning news, no big story, just a fire, no mention of a body discovered in the debris. Maybe there was nothing left of Bertolino. Maybe he got cremated and blew away like dust in the dry San Bernardino wind.

Hector turned when Mando jumped up from the desk, voice raised. "He's dead, *ese*. Barbecued."

Arturo Delgado sat in the front seat of the navy blue Bentley Continental Supersports he had parked outside Venice Exotic Rentals, holding a cell phone to his ear.

"Don't *ese* me, Mando. You're not that good," Delgado said, enjoying the fact that he had gotten a rise out of the little man. "Bertolino is planting tomato plants on his balcony, for chrissakes. If the drugs weren't on their way, I would call off the deal entirely."

Delgado was actually unimpressed with the Bentley's ride. It was well appointed, he thought, looking at the burled wood and hand-stitched leather, but for the $280,000 price tag, he thought it fell short.

"You don't call nothing off, *ese*. You need me as much as I need you. Show some respect," Mando ordered.

"Your boy is turning into a weak sister," Delgado taunted. "Can't take orders and then can't get the job done."

"Words have power, Arturo." Mando's voice got deathly quiet again. "Watch what you say. You're too old for regrets."

Delgado clicked off. He didn't take threats from anyone. He had the power of the Colombian cartels behind him. It didn't matter on what side of the border you found yourself. Colombia was still king in the cocaine trade. He turned off the car's ignition, stepped out, and walked into the small showroom.

A clean-cut man with blond surfer hair and a Tommy Bahama shirt worn over khaki pants had jumped out of his black leather seat before the door had closed behind Delgado.

"How did you enjoy the ride, Mr. Franklin?"

"I'm leaning more toward the Maybach," Delgado answered matter-of-factly. "It's more understated."

"Well, you know I'm also a broker, Mr. Franklin. I can get you the best deal on the best cars." He flashed a bright, big-toothed California smile.

A well-worn catchphrase, Delgado thought. "You've given me something to think about, Larry," he said as he handed over the keys. "And I reward loyalty."

Larry wasn't sure what that meant, but he went back to his desk and placed the contract for the rental and Delgado's fake passport on top of the leather-clad desktop. Delgado checked the numbers and paid with cash.

―――――――

Jack washed the potting soil off his hands. He had stopped by Home Depot on his way back from the hospital. As tired as he was, he knew he couldn't sleep. He gave Nick the license plate number and description of the car provided by his "friends," and then bought two healthy tomato plants, a second pot, and two small cages to support the plants as they grew heavy with fruit. No reason not to be optimistic.

It always amazed Jack what a brush with death could do to alter your outlook on life.

And it wasn't just working in the soil with his bare hands that brought him peace, but Leslie was going to stop by after work for an early dinner at Hal's.

The phone rang as he was drying off his hands. He finished up and grabbed the phone on the fourth ring, a second before it would have gone to voice mail.

"Bertolino here."

"Hey, it's Gene," McLennan said, as if the call was a regular occurrence. "How are you feeling?"

"Dead on my feet, but not dead."

"I hear you had a hell of a time. Everyone's talking about it in the office. Talk about being hung out to dry. Sorry. That was in bad taste."

It was, but it didn't bother Jack a bit. He did want Gene to get on with the reason for the call. "What's up, Gene?"

"Okay, it's highly irregular, but because of the extenuating circumstances, and the fact that you built the case at great personal risk, the powers that be—"

"Am I invited in?"

"Shit, yeah. But let a man have some fun with it. Christ, Bertolino, it's all business with you. But anyway, listen, don't take offense at this, but you are to be seen and not heard unless directly asked for your input. And most important, you check your weapon at the door. The federal government will not accept the liability for you getting your ass shot off."

That would be easy, Jack thought. Hector had already obliged by taking his Glock. He wondered if Gene himself wanted his hands tied behind his back, but he was not going to rock the boat. He'd be a team player to get in.

"Did I lose you?" McLennan asked.

"No, I'm here. Good."

"So we're on the same page?"

"We're good."

"We meet at fourteen hundred hours downtown. Gives Ortega plenty of time to acclimate," he said, as if Ortega was flying in from the Middle East. "If you come to my office ten minutes early, we can walk into the conference room together, and I can do the intros."

"Thanks, Gene," Jack said, greatly relieved that the bust wouldn't go down without him. But if he ID'd Hector Lopez, or Arturo Delgado, he thought, feeling a deep burn start at the back of his neck, all bets were off.

———————

Delgado nursed a grande iced coffee in a Starbucks a block south, across Lincoln Boulevard from Venice Exotic Rentals. He watched the young, pierced, and tattooed baristas happily working, buzzed on their own product. He had always been careful never to fall into that trap. It had destroyed many strong men. He took a sip of his cold black brew, which provided as much stimulant as he required, and stood stiffly when his cab pulled up to the curb.

As he slid into the backseat, he could see a patrol car through the windshield roll up in front of Venice Exotic Rentals, lights flashing, and two uniformed officers all but run inside.

Delgado changed his destination in case the cops eventually located his driver. The Third Street Promenade to do a little shopping, he told the cabbie. It was a good spot for people watching. He could grab a late lunch and pick up another cab from there.

Arturo Delgado pulled the brim of his hat to one side as they drove past the patrol car and took a deep sip of his coffee, although he didn't need the caffeine pick-me-up anymore. He was already wired.

Angelina sat in her jail cell, waiting for the next round of interrogation to begin. Her court-appointed attorney had dropped by first thing in the morning to say the detectives had uncovered some new evidence and would get to her later on in the day. She had been advised to say nothing, and Angelina didn't have to be told twice. The cops would never be able to use her own words against her in a court of law. She had the support of the 18th Street Angels. She could hang tough.

She stirred restlessly. She sure could use a fat line of cocaine or some weed. This cold-turkey shit was for the birds.

A trustee delivered a sandwich and a carton of milk on a tray. At the sight of it she couldn't believe how hungry she was.

When Angelina picked up the Saran-wrapped bologna and American cheese, she discovered that a small clipped piece of newspaper had been placed under her sandwich.

It looked like random newsprint when she first picked it up, although it was cut to the exact size of her sandwich and left her a bit confused. But when Angelina turned it over, her hand started to tremble.

There was a cartoon figure of a mean rodent. The print ad was for an exterminating company located in Ontario.

The ad read: WE KILL RATS DEAD. GUARANTEED SATISFACTION.

Angelina's hand constricted into a fist and crumpled the warning. Stricken, she dropped her sandwich onto the tray. Lying down on the bunk, she pulled her knees up to her chest into the fetal position. She started rocking and she couldn't stop.

———

Leslie Sager walked into the loft, giving the place a brief glance, said, "Nice digs," and stepped into Jack's arms. Their lips locked before their arms, and when she wrapped herself around him and squeezed his back, "Ugh," Jack grunted through the kiss.

They continued, and she lowered her hands some.

"Oww," he groaned with a little less subtlety.

She moved her hands to the safety of his lower back.

"Owww."

Leslie disengaged. "Turn around," she ordered.

Jack complied.

When she pulled up his T-shirt, she tried not to gasp. The bruises on his lower back were a yellow-tinged purple-black. The cuts, from the exploding glass, were dressed, but there were far too many of them, and they looked painful.

"I know you're the man, Mr. Bertolino," she said gently, "and if you weren't so good at your job, I'd tell you that this might be the right time to start thinking about a new life choice."

Jack smiled at the recurring theme. Turning around, he kissed her again. Leslie stood with her arms outstretched, not wanting to touch him, and finally settled for draping her arms on his shoulders and clasping her hands around the back of his head.

"Yeowww!"

Nervous laughter broke off the kiss. Breaking free, she pulled a bottle of cabernet out of her oversize bag and handed it to Jack. It was a bottle of Benziger.

"We're done," she said and smiled. "For now."

The choice of wine wasn't lost on Jack. He pulled two wine-glasses out of the cupboard, the opener out of the drawer, and made short work of pulling the cork.

"Do you want to talk business?"

"Is Angelina talking?"

"She'll talk, all right, but she jumped up from the interrogation table, got in Gallina's face, and screamed that she wouldn't say word one until she got the same deal Bertolino promised Johnny. She had to be restrained." Leslie added with a smile, "The good lieutenant went through the roof."

Jack poured two glasses of wine and handed one to Leslie. He was starting to enjoy giving Gallina a heart attack.

"Who the ef is Jack Bertolino to be making deals with anyone, and what the ef did he promise?" She took a sip of the red and gave it a purr of approval. "He calmed down some when she couldn't be specific, because she didn't know."

"I never got that far with Johnny," Jack said. "I didn't think we'd get anything from Angelina. She looked to be made of stone."

"We found a chip in her purse. A microSD card. I don't think she knew what it was, but it had a partial of her thumbprint on the front, and Johnny's print on the back." She scowled and looked away. "When we downloaded the video content, we were treated to one sick scene. I'll have nightmares for a month."

"And?"

"It clearly showed Hector butchering Ricky Hernandez, the young gangster who was found hanging from the overpass. Johnny was in charge of documenting the brutality with a BlackBerry. The video had no sound, but a few jerky shots of the cameraman's shoes matched a pair found in his apartment. Plus, we got one very clear reflection of Johnny's face on the television screen. Ricky must have been playing a video game when he died, because when Johnny's face was reflected on the screen, I saw an RPG hit that looked like it exploded behind his head."

"Movie magic. I wonder who the tape was made for?"

"I'll ask Angelina when she decides to talk. We put the home movie on ice. If it leaked to the public, we could have a panic until Hector's brought down. Very hard images to watch, Jack, less than human. It's the worst of us."

Jack thought about Mia again and put down his wineglass.

"Ask her what happened to her ear. What kind of earring was she wearing?"

Leslie had a pretty good idea of where he was headed with the line of questioning.

"I'll mention it to Gallina. The broken fingernail you found in Johnny's apartment, and now the phone card, threw a wrench in Angelina's time line as far as her breakup with Johnny. It looks like she might have been complicit in her boyfriend's disappearance. Her attorney said that she'd deliver Johnny and Hector if we guaranteed her the witness protection program."

"Sounds like it makes sense to deal. She's only good for accessory, any way you cut it," Jack pointed out.

"We don't need her for Hector at this point, but she might have answers to Johnny's whereabouts and the infrastructure of the 18th Street Angels. Speaking of which, the Angels reached out to her in county. A note threatened death if she talked."

It was Jack's turn to frown. "Fucking perfect, pardon my French. We can lock them up, but we can't protect them. What a system."

Leslie picked up her bag and her glass of wine, and started toward the bathroom.

"Why don't you relax for ten minutes or so while I freshen up, and we can hit the road."

"Sounds like a plan."

But finding the right position was easier said than done. Jack tried to lie on his back and it was a no-go. He rolled onto his stomach, but his face dive into the weeds had taken its toll. He rolled onto his side—no, that didn't hurt—and finally found some comfort.

"I'm starved. I know exactly what I'm going to order," Leslie said from inside the bathroom. She opened the door and walked out looking fabulous.

Jack was passed out on the bed, dead to the world. Leslie smiled—lying down had been her idea—and sat in his leather chair.

She swiveled it around and watched the rise and fall of his chest while she enjoyed her glass of cabernet.

DDA Sager wasn't sure where their relationship was headed, but Jack Bertolino was the first man she had sparked to in a long time. She was a big believer in trusting chemistry. She liked his candor. She liked his line about not falling into bed or love easily. She thought he was engaging; she liked him. Leslie decided to give it a go.

45

Manuel Alvarez paced in his cell like a feral cat. He had pulled his noise-reduction headset off one ear and replaced it with the cell phone.

"No call, no word, no fucking nothing?" he said to Delgado in a threatening tone. "I'm the boss and you decided not to keep me up to speed? I'm not on all yours' radar fucking screens 'cause I'm locked up like a dog in this shit hole? Is that it, Arturo?"

Delgado's voice was calm and serene. "The deal is proceeding as planned. But the news is all good, Manuel. I met with my contact and we have the information that was stolen from you. In fact, I've located your money."

Alvarez sat down on the edge of his bed. "Are you fucking with me, Arturo?" But the anger in his voice had been replaced by a guarded excitement. "Is it true?"

"You are once again a rich man, Manuel. The trustee has all of the paperwork, the trail of your fortune and everything you need to retrieve it."

Alvarez turned to face trustee 776325, who was standing guard.

"You have something of mine?" Alvarez asked as he got up from the bunk and moved close to the bars. He was having a hard time controlling the joy that welled up in his chest.

The trustee nodded his head, picking up a Walter Mosley book.

As he handed it through the opening of the cell door, the man pulled a jailhouse shank from under the hardcover book, and jammed it into Alvarez's windpipe, twisting as he buried it to the hilt of the makeshift handle.

The cell phone clattered against the hard cell floor.

Alvarez moved his lips, but nothing but blood dripped out. He was not going to die like a chump. In a shocking blur of motion, Manuel ripped the knife out of his throat, and shoved it into the trustee's chest.

Alvarez then fell to his knees, choking on his own blood.

Trustee 776325 called for help, but his heart had stopped beating before the alarm could be sounded. His cries were drowned out by the shouting, banging, and wailing that provided the business-as-usual audio backdrop in the penitentiary.

The sun had just dropped below the horizon, leaving behind a dark blue sky, a light powdering of stars, and a thin crescent moon. The sound of the generator buzzed as the spotlights snapped on, flooding the overgrown quarter-acre behind the Lopez house with harsh light.

A damp chill had descended on the technical crew that had nearly finished walking the grid on the property with their ground-penetrating radar device. The GPR used high-frequency radio waves to locate potential burial sites and human remains.

A cadaver dog and his handler had made several alerts over the past hour. The first two had turned up a cache of pig bones. The final alert had occurred on the back of the property near an old orange tree.

Jack and Tompkins watched as the yellow Lab walked around the tree a few times and then sat down, making eye contact with his handler. A strong signal that a body had once been buried at that location.

Most buried bodies give off a rectangular signature pattern below the surface that has been repeated in burial ceremonies since the beginning of time. Jack wasn't sure Hector had performed a ceremony as such, but the signal from the GPR did show reflectors beneath the surface that could be associated with human remains. The printout showed a round pit rather than a coffin shape, but the crew was optimistic.

Jack stood looking over the ruins of Hector's garage. Gallina walked up and handed Tompkins a Starbucks provided by the Ontario PD, and the pair shifted from foot to foot nervously as the retrieval crew continued their painstaking work.

"It's human," one of the men working with a small trowel next to the orange tree shouted back to the group. He dug a little deeper, and then, using a brush, moved away some loose dirt and pulled out a football-size plastic parcel that looked like it had been chewed open in sections.

"The rats got to it."

Jack and company walked the length of the field, and in the spotlight they could plainly see what was a moldering human skull, minus the jawbone, with frightening brown hair and holes where eyes used to see. It had been expertly wrapped in a piece of plastic drop cloth and bound with duct tape.

Hector's signature, Jack thought.

Before anybody could comment, the man who had made the discovery brought up a second package from the makeshift grave. Larger, with more weight. "There's more down here," he said.

"Guy's an animal. Killed his own father, cut him up," Gallina said with disgust.

"They all start somewhere," Tompkins added. And then, "Could've been you," he said without judgment and threw a look to Jack.

Jack was done here. He started to walk back toward his Mustang. He'd seen enough of death to last a lifetime.

"Hey, Bertolino." Jack stopped and waited for Gallina to catch up. "I ran the description of Mia's earring past our beauty queen. Said I found it in Johnny's apartment with her prints all over it and her blood DNA on the clasp. She freaked, said she didn't know where Johnny got it. Her lawyer gave her the eye, and she dummied up again. I got what I needed, though, thanks."

Jack nodded his head.

"And for the record. I have no issue if the feds offer a deal. I just want the butcher."

Gallina returned to the burial site, and Jack continued on to his Mustang. As he turned the corner of the house, Mrs. Lopez appeared at the front door and handed him a bag of fresh oranges.

"*Gracias,*" the old woman said.

Jack returned the thank-you with feeling.

"*Muchas gracias* to you, Mrs. Lopez."

46

Jack liked to run his TAC meetings first thing in the morning, when his men and women were sharp. This was going to be a dangerous mission, and in the old days he would have told his subordinates to be extra careful. The problem was, it wasn't his meeting to run. He was an invited guest.

He knew basically what would be said. The purpose of this tactics and tactical meeting was to lay out the ground rules for the raid on Royce Motors, the arrests of the 18th Street Angels, and the confiscation of the cocaine. Who was responsible for what? What departments, what vehicles, what communication devices, what frequencies, what weapons, where the emergency vehicles would be located, the helicopters, the armored vehicles. Who would lead the initial assault on Royce Motors. Who was backup, who was coordinating. Crowd control, traffic control. The last thing they wanted was to lose any civilians in the crossfire. It had to be specific to the most finite detail or lives could be lost.

The Angels had already given ample proof that they had no respect for human life. And Jack didn't want anyone risking their lives any more than was humanly necessary to take them down.

Kenny Ortega was the government liaison, but since Gene McLennan knew the local players, he would be running the show on the ground. Kenny had called Jack before his plane touched down.

Kenny always had the ability to get him pumped for the job at hand. They planned to meet in the conference room and then get caught up after the meeting.

Gene's polished black shoes clicked smartly on the waxed floor of the Federal Building. He stayed a half step in front of Jack, moving with purpose, in an attempt to set the parameters of Jack's participation.

Gene had been dubious when he tried to confiscate Jack's weapon and learned that Hector Lopez was the gun's proud new owner, but he wisely didn't push the point.

McLennan made a sharp left and banged through the double glass doors of the conference room. Two dozen men and women all looked up in unison at the abrupt entrance.

McLennan took his place at the head of a large rectangular table. To his left was a large Lucite screen set up for a PowerPoint presentation. He nodded to the tech in the back of the room. She gave him a thumbs-up, tapped a few keys, and a pyramid of the digital photos Jack had taken on surveillance appeared on one side of the high-tech screen. Jack's computer-generated portrait of Arturo Delgado topped the pyramid and Hector Lopez was two rows down, front and center. On the other side of the screen was a satellite photo of Royce Motors, the lot behind the Royce building, and the surrounding neighborhood.

Jack walked to the back of the room and took a place with the latecomers who had missed getting seats and stood drinking coffee. He nodded to Nick and Kenny, and shifted his focus to McLennan.

"I want to thank the San Bernardino Sheriff's Department, the Riverside Sheriff's Department, and the Riverside Police Department for making the drive into town," McLennan said, like a college professor. "I'm Gene McLennan, DEA."

The detectives were an irreverent group who weren't overly impressed by the feds. They wore jeans and T-shirts, a few suits, and some pantsuits on the women, as well as shoulder holsters, thigh holsters, belt holsters, and ankle rigs. Jack felt right at home.

"I'll make a few introductions, and then you can all reach out and handle the rest when we're broken into groups. Kenny Ortega, Miami DEA and the man who sold the government on our case. Nick Aprea, LAPD Narcotics. Some of you remember Aprea from the drug task force and the arrest of the twenty-seven 18th Street Angels on RICO charges back in April. And retired inspector Jack Bertolino, who is the major reason we're here today, and who will be doing a ride-along by invitation of the federal government."

Nick couldn't help himself and audibly groaned on the ride-along comment. Ortega bit his tongue, while Jack remained nonchalant. He was an observer. The crew, who had already been brought up to speed by Ortega about the origins of the case, hadn't missed the slight.

"I'll give the overview, and then, Kenny, you can bring us up to speed regarding the origins of the drugs and the possibility of a turf war spilling over the border if we don't shut down the 18th Street Angels operation."

"He earned his place," Nick finally said. He just couldn't help himself.

"What, Detective Aprea?" McLennan asked tightly.

"Where'd you get the pictures on your wall of shame?"

"Jack Bertolino provided them."

"Sitting surveillance on his own nickel. Who turned us on to Royce Motors and the entire scheme?" Nick said.

"I'm not questioning the retired inspector's bona fides."

"Bertolino earned his invitation to the party, is all I'm saying."

"Point well taken, Nick," Gene said, and then turned back to the room. "Oh, and Craig Millhouse, IRS Criminal Investigations, will speak to the Angels' laundering operations."

Gene McLennan was seasoned and smooth and continued without missing a beat.

"We put a GPS on the bus after it landed in Miami and have been tracking it back across the country. Thomas Vegas, whose brother is a member of the Angels, has put in a total of twelve calls to Roman. We're up on Roman's phone, and Royce Motors, thanks to DDA Mike Apke, who expedited our request. Their ETA is fourteen hundred hours, and after they unload the band and luggage at Outlaws Inc., Thomas promised to deliver the suits—as he referred to the drugs—by sixteen hundred hours. Civilian traffic should be thin at that hour, and that's in our favor. I'm estimating their time frame is twenty minutes total, in and out. A minimum of ten cars, the dope gets broken into ten, twelve parcels, and is gone. If we're late, we're lost. We may be light on manpower, but not on talent. If we all stay sharp, we will prevail."

––––––––––

"His TAC plan is sound. My only issue with McLennan," Jack said, "is in the split of manpower. He's light on the back lot. If it all goes to hell, the rats'll be jumping ship. And they won't be driving out the way they came in."

Jack sat next to Kenny Ortega and across from Nick Aprea in his favorite booth at Hal's.

"The satellite photo showed a loading dock. What looked to be a five-foot clearance," Kenny said.

"The damn Google map I pulled off my Mac indicated ramps. There's got to be some other way to move those buses and equipment in and out," Jack maintained.

"How many warrants have you served?" Nick asked Jack, changing the subject.

"Hundreds."

"How many have gone without a hitch?"

"We were always careful, to a fault. I'm still here to tell the story."

"And God willing, we'll be here tomorrow night toasting our good fortune."

All three men clinked glasses—Nick, his Herradura; Jack, his red wine; and Kenny, his rum and Coke.

Jack felt something hard bang into his knee, and when he reached down he felt cold steel being placed into his hand. Nick didn't blink his eyes; he casually signaled Arsinio for another shot.

Jack slipped the automatic weapon into his side jacket pocket and took a sip of wine. He felt another sharp prod on his right leg. He reached down and felt the carved wooden handle of what felt like a classic Colt .38. Kenny stared off to the right, admiring the art on the wall or the blond woman at the bar standing next to it. Jack leaned forward and snugged the Detective Special in the small of his back.

47

At three thirty the first Angels car drove past the surveillance step van and command center, pulled into the lot at Royce Motors, and disappeared into the recesses of the building. The traffic was thinning, but McLennan had stationed cars in a two-block radius surrounding the complex to stop traffic once the order was given to deploy. The plan was to keep the operation confined on-site, but for contingency's sake the cars had been dispatched.

An invitation had been extended to Jack to watch the bust on the multiple screens in the DEA truck with McLennan, Ortega, and a three-man tech crew. With cameras covering the front of Royce Motors and the back lot, this would be the eyes and ears of the operation. All of the feds, cops, and vehicles were linked by a special radio frequency, and the players would be updated as the offensive dictated.

Jack had begged off, however, and was situated down the block in the dark green Plymouth, tucked safely away from incoming eyes. He had a list of the players, his assigned radio, his binoculars, his weapons, three extra-speed loaders for the .38, and extra clips for the nine-millimeter automatic. Jack was hunting big game: Hector Lopez and Arturo Delgado. He had a strong feeling that Hector would be a part of the drug crew, and Delgado would be standing tall at a distance somewhere, high on a ridge, like ancient nobility, watching the action and protecting his investment.

Nick Aprea had been assigned to lead the assault on the back lot with an armored battering truck to break through the fence, three unmarked cars, and ten heavily armed warriors.

Kenny Ortega would exit the DEA step van, and lead the frontal assault. Eight vehicles were secreted in a warehouse a block from Royce Motors and would power through the front entrance, blocking all egress after the arrival of the bus.

McLennan wanted to give the 18th Street Angels a full five minutes to start off-loading the drugs before dropping the hammer. Let the scumbags feel like their deal was going down without a hitch, and then make them feel some pain.

The clock was ticking.

Jack counted a total of nine cars drive onto the lot and into the service bay, but from his angle couldn't make a single positive ID.

McLennan's voice crackled and announced that the ETA of the bus was fifteen and counting. Thomas Vegas had put in a call to Roman, giving him the update.

A cherried-out blue Impala with a white roof drove by, and the hair on the back of Jack's neck stood at attention. He couldn't see a face, but the thickness of the driver screamed Hector.

Instead of making the left onto the lot, the car continued on past Royce Motors, and made the left on the next side street.

McLennan's voice came over the speaker warning Nick and the men covering the back that one of the Angels was doing reconnaissance, headed their way, and to stay low.

Thirty seconds later, the Impala—having circumnavigated the block—swung around the corner, drove past Jack, and made the turn into the building. It was Hector Lopez. Jack forced some deep breaths to slow his heart rate and remain focused.

It was game time.

A large tricked-out bus with colorful graphics on the wide side panels drove slowly up the street. Turn signals flashed, air brakes squealed, and the bus pulled into the Royce Motors parking lot. Roman walked out of the service bay dressed in his sports jacket as if it was business as usual. The dutiful general manager guided the bus inside like a signalman at an airport.

"Five minutes and counting, folks. Let's keep our minds clear and our weapons ready. And let's be safe," McLennan said.

They would remain under a prearranged radio silence until the call to deploy.

Jack checked his loads.

Nick Aprea hand-signaled his men.

Ortega checked out the images on the twelve video screens, and then glanced at his Remington tactical shotgun with a four-round extension. His hand strayed reflexively to his tactical thigh holster, where he patted the butt of his Beretta M9.

The tour bus was hoisted up on the hydraulic lift with the speed of a NASCAR racer during a pit stop. Two men in protective helmets had their welding torches lit. Sparks flew as they made short work of cutting into the bottom panels.

Arturo Delgado stood shoulder to shoulder with Mando and Roman. He looked grimly satisfied with the proceedings.

The men had parked five cars facing the front of Royce Motors for a fast exit, and five cars, including Hector's Impala, faced the expansive showroom with the long row of dazzling buses. They would exit past the buses, down the ramps, and out through the back, per Delgado's game plan.

Each of the Angels' trunks stood open, waiting for their share of the cocaine.

Roman had assigned another fifteen heavily armed gangsters and Lil' Angels for on-site security.

Mando checked his watch, got the go-ahead from Delgado, and

addressed the men. "Ten minutes max and you're on the road. No speeding. No tricks. Don't bring down no heat. I want calls from every one of you when you land, and then that number turns to dust."

Murmurs from the gangsters and proud fist pumps. This was a big payday, the beginning of a new era for the 18th Street Angels.

The first panel came off, and a cadre of Angels started pulling down kilos of cocaine wrapped in dirty tan cellophane. The first 120 keys went to Hector, who stashed them in his trunk, threw a tarp over the bricks, and carefully lowered the lid.

"Yo, Hector, man, where's Johnny?" David Reyes asked, filled with nervous energy as he sidled up behind Hector.

Hector did a slow turn and just stared. No words. Dead eyes. Reyes quickly moved away, picked at a scab on his face, and waited for his allocation.

Hector got behind the wheel of his Impala, turned over the engine, and waited for the go signal.

The drugs were methodically handed off in a bucket brigade and secured in car trunks. The drivers started their engines, ready to exit as planned.

Arturo Delgado watched as the 18th Street Angels worked with military precision and felt optimistic about the future.

Three minutes to go.

Jack pulled up his binoculars and scanned the rooftops surrounding Royce Motors. It was all quiet. And all clear.

Two minutes to deployment.

Jack could feel the ground vibrate before he could see what caused the disturbance.

Two eighteen-wheel tractor-trailer trucks rumbled down the street in his direction. In a surprise move, when they were twenty-five yards from Royce Motors, the rear truck pulled alongside the lead truck, and they drove side by side, filling both lanes of traffic.

The big rigs pulled to a squealing stop, totally blocking the road in both directions plus the entrance to Royce Motors.

The truck driver blocking oncoming traffic powered down his passenger window and waved a manifest, as if asking the other driver for directions.

"What the hell's going on?" Gene McLennan's voice crackled, breaking the radio silence.

Jack watched with growing alarm as McLennan jumped out of the surveillance van and marched toward the big rigs, red faced. When he had covered half the distance, he waved his arms and signaled for the drivers to move on.

The back hatches of the eighteen-wheelers dropped down, creating ramps.

A commando dressed in full military cammo gear stepped out from behind one of the trucks and open fired with a MAC-10 machine gun.

The back of Gene McLennan's head vaporized. His body pulsed as the force of the bullets slammed through him. Red sprayed from his back in a downward pattern, and he fell to the ground, dead before anybody could react.

Los Zetas, Jack thought. The drug cartel was retaliating against the Angels on American soil. The operation was turning into a full-blown cluster fuck.

Two armor-plated narco tanks powered out of the bowels of the trucks and smashed through the wall of Royce Motors with their folding battering rams.

The black steel-plated beasts with gun turrets looked like something out of a *Mad Max* movie.

"What the fuck was that?" Mando shouted. To the men whose cocaine was already loaded, he cried, "Go! Go! Go!" He swung around the AK that was strapped to his neck and prepared for the assault.

The second bus panel fell to the service-bay floor.

"It's a fuckin' tank, man," shouted the Lil' Angels spotter who had run into the service bay white faced. He slapped his AK-47 nervously, fighting to maintain.

The first of the Angels cars sped out of the service bay and was promptly rammed by the lead monster, which pushed it up against the wall of the building, crushing the driver-side door and instantly killing the driver.

"Fuck!" Mando said as he let loose with a deafening chatter of firepower. He was forced to find cover when four guns snaked out of the side portholes of the tank and returned fire. High-velocity bullets ricocheted off the concrete floor and cut down the fifteen-year-old Lil' Angels spotter.

Arturo Delgado picked up the fallen gangster's automatic weapon and squeezed off a few tight bursts. The last time Delgado was this close to an AK, he was staring at the wrong end of the barrel. He was happy to return the favor but didn't plan on staying long enough to see how this shitstorm played out. There would be time for retribution later.

"Go! Go! Go!" Kenny Ortega shouted over the radio deploying the team. "Man down! Use extreme caution, there are two Zetas narco tanks heading into Royce Motors. I repeat, there are two monsters headed into the front of Royce."

The second tank stopped as Ortega speed-dialed for reinforcements. The top-mounted gun turret rotated in his direction, and Kenny could see, on the video screen, something glint in the afternoon sun.

"The fucking thing's going to fire on us! Out! Out! Out!"

Ortega pushed the three-man crew out of the step van and followed in their wake.

An RPG was launched.

A flash of light and the explosives whistled across the distance, leaving a contrail of death, and slammed into the side of their command center. It exploded on impact, sending debris flying, blacking out all communications. Ortega and his men dove for cover.

Jack Bertolino's jaw tightened. He threw his car into gear. His foot hit the gas pedal, unleashing 426 horses. His tires spun, smoked, engaged, and roared away toward the back lot of Royce Motors. Nick Aprea would need his support, and it was the only way out for Hector and the Angels.

The lead narco tank's turret turned in the direction of the bus.

Mando and the 18th Street Angels unleashed a barrage of automatic-weapons fire. Their bullets pinged off the inch-thick steel plates that protected the men inside.

The Zetas commando stepped from behind the monster and unleashed his own firepower.

Armando "Mando" Barajas's body pulsated in place and then dropped down hard with full-metal-jacket bullets shredding his throat. His Angels gangsters backpedaled.

The men with the welding torches had just completed their job, but stood frozen in place as one of the men's welding helmets was hit by incoming from the interior of the monster, knocking him to the ground and out.

Bullets rained into the cocaine that was left unpacked in the undercarriage of the bus, creating a massive crystal white cloud of dust. Bullets tore into the second welder's shoulder. He spun with the impact, staggered backward, and raised his torch.

The high-intensity flame ignited the cloud of cocaine powder into a flash bomb that enveloped his body. He went running out of the service bay, a human torch. The commando killed him with one short burst of his weapon.

A rocket-propelled grenade was launched from the turret.

It impacted the bus's gas tank and exploded. Instantly the large metal vehicle flung out a wide spray of shrapnel. The ensuing secondary explosion blew out the front of Royce Motors and knocked Roman to the ground.

Delgado reached down a hand, and raised his comrade to his feet. The two warriors backed deeper into the cavernous recesses of Royce Motors, and rapidly made their way past the long line of million-dollar buses. Blood dripped from Roman's ear.

The Zetas commando silently stalked his targets, waiting for a clear shot.

Roman stopped, listened. All he could hear was ringing in his ears. But he detected movement. He leveled his AK and gave a whistle and a hand gesture.

The commando raised up, getting a bead on Delgado. His finger depressed the trigger.

One of Roman's dogs leaped. One hundred and eighty pounds of English mastiff clamped its jaws on the Zetas warrior's neck. The man's MAC-10 fired multiple wild rounds that shattered mirrored bus windows and punctured painted metal, until the weight of the dog pulled them both to the ground. The second dog appeared on the instant, teeth bared, drool flying. His razor-sharp teeth tore into the man's thigh. The commando's screams were overwhelmed by deep guttural growls as the two dogs, in full blood frenzy, ripped the man to shreds.

An Angels driver saw the dogs and panicked. Swerving to avoid them, he lost control and crashed his car into the front of one of the showroom buses. His body was thrown headfirst through the windshield, where he lay slumped on the hood.

Jack skidded to a stop just outside the rear gate, which was flapping open and closed. He could hear automatic weapons' fire and peered carefully inside the lot, staying low to the ground.

Nick Aprea was hunkered down behind his assault vehicle, being fired upon by men positioned next to the double-wide, and another crew of 18th Street Angels who used junked cars and buses for cover.

"Lay down some suppressing fire, I'm coming in," Jack shouted.

Nick got up and raked automatic bullets in an explosive arc.

Jack scrabbled low and slid to safety next to Nick.

"Somebody tipped the Zetas," he said. "They've got two narco tanks pushing through the front. We've gotta hold down the fort."

The first of the Angels cars drove out of the back entrance, down the ramp, and powered toward the gate.

Then a second car.

Jack fired into the first one. The windshield spidered and caved in on the driver. It was David Reyes. The thug managed to juke his car around Nick's vehicle, smash the gate off its hinges, and skid sideways onto the road, where Ontario PD blew out his tires.

Nick stood up, took dead aim, and fired an assault rifle as the second car passed. The driver was dead before he hit the street. His car drove straight into one of the unmarked police cars and ramped up the hood.

The trunk of the Angels car snapped open.

One hundred twenty kilos of cocaine were flung out in a cascade. They smashed as they hit the concrete road. Billowing clouds of crystal white powder scattered in the wind. The car flipped, rolled, and came to rest, spinning on its roof.

The ten armed men who were part of Nick's assault team fanned out and slowly exerted pressure on the gangsters.

One of the Angels showered the team with AK cop-killer bullets.

"Ahhhhhh! My leg. I'm hit. I'm hit . . . !" came the primal scream of a wounded detective.

Nick ran out without any hesitation. Automatic-weapons fire sizzled by his ears and sent up plumes of dirt at his feet. Nick grabbed the wounded man by the collar and dragged him to the safety of his vehicle. He tightened his belt around the cop's leg and returned to the battle.

The Angels shooter let out another short burst and ran up the metal ramp. He turned and aimed his AK at a pursuing agent.

Hector's speeding car exited the building and hit his own man squarely in the back, breaking his body. The impact sent the gangster flying, his arms flailing, his rifle spinning, off the platform to the ground below.

Hector's blue Impala missed the ramp and went airborne, out and over the broken dirt surface.

Jack saw his chance and ran from cover. He held pistols in both hands and fired into the engine block. The car landed hard, the chrome bumper ate dirt. The tires bounced, fought for purchase, and Jack emptied his clip into Hector's car, being careful not to hit his prey. He wanted Hector Lopez alive.

Jack holstered the Colt and slammed a full clip into the automatic.

Hector floored the vehicle, but the steering column locked. He lost control and smashed into the front of the double-wide trailer, splitting it open like an aluminum can.

The Impala's engine dripped fuel and caught fire. Hector shouldered the twisted car door open and fell to the ground seconds before flames inundated the front seat.

He dropped his gun and scrabbled for it as the blaze spread to the wood-paneled walls of the trailer.

Hector desperately extended his fingers, reaching for the Glock nine millimeter, but Jack's boot savagely kicked it away. "You!" Hector roared. He grabbed Jack's leg and dragged him down. He raised a bloody fist to smash his face. Jack saw the blood, saw red, and exploded a left into Hector's neck. The big man grabbed for his throat, gulping for air. Jack flashed on Mia and hammered a right into Hector's face, knocking him back.

Kenny Ortega and the eight government cars were now fully deployed in front of Royce Motors. One of the DEA agents, in a heroic move, ran up to the second tank, pulled the pin on a flash grenade, and dropped it down the turret. It clattered, men shouted, and it blew. Smoke poured out of the turret and all of the gun portals. Seconds ticked down. Kenny and the men had weapons trained on the monster. The side door was flung open, and four Zetas gunmen stumbled out of the armored vehicle, where they were met with overwhelming force. "Drop your weapons! Now! Drop your weapons now!" They assumed the position and were led away in handcuffs.

The men in the lead narco tank were firing from the gun portals on both sides of the armored vehicle. The four Angels cars that were supposed to exit the front of Royce Motors had been disabled, the drivers dead or on the run.

Kenny Ortega and his team responded to the attack by shooting out the tires of the monster, crippling the behemoth but not shutting it down. Reinforcements were on their way, but Kenny had to stop the killers inside the tank before there was any more loss of life. He slammed a four-shot magazine extension into his TAC 4 and started cautiously forward.

Arturo Delgado and Roman shook hands and split up. Delgado headed toward the back entrance, where he thought he had the best chance of escape. He slapped another clip into his assault rifle and hugged the shadows.

Roman climbed into one of the million-dollar buses and fired up the engine. He shifted the vehicle into gear and slowly pulled out of the row and into the center aisle. He opened the door and whistled. Roman was joined by his dogs.

The bus gained speed as it drove through the spotlit pools, past the crashed Angels car and the downed Zetas commando. Roman was doing twenty by the time he got to the end of the long line of buses.

Roman pulled hard on the wheel, and the bus jerked to the left, barely making the opening that led past the service bay to freedom.

He clipped the back of the lead narco tank, stunning the occupants, and shearing off the bus's mirror. He was doing thirty now. The Zetas gunmen shattered the bus's rear windows as it powered past, gaining more speed.

Roman was doing a Hail Mary play with his life on the line. He'd had a good run, he thought. Time to pay for some sins. He drove straight toward the feds, cops, and sheriffs.

———

Kenny Ortega thought the mission couldn't get any worse until he saw the bus clip the back of the tank and power toward his men. He stepped front and center and fired his Remington TAC 4 shotgun, once, and again and again into the bus's windshield. Red blood sprayed from Roman's mouth as he choked and stomped with his full weight onto the gas pedal. Ortega dove out of harm's way as the bus hit the retaining wall that surrounded Royce Motors, ramped sideways onto its left eight tires, and continued to barrel-roll over onto its side. The bus's forward momentum wiped out four government vehicles before coming to a spark-flying, metal-screeching halt beyond the big rigs that were beached in front of Royce's blown-out front entrance.

The door to the bus wheezed open and the two English mastiffs jumped out, green eyes ablaze. Ortega's men were about to fire on the beasts, but without Roman to give the kill order, the dogs were docile, in shock, and walked in aimless circles. Blood still dripped from their muzzles as they waited faithfully for their master.

It would be a long fucking wait, Kenny Ortega thought as he slapped a fresh magazine into his shotgun and ran toward the lead tank with the blown-out tires.

The turret turned toward the cops and Kenny could see that a rocket-propelled grenade was about to be launched. He leveled his TAC 4, fired, and missed. The concrete around Kenny pinged with bullets. He chambered another round and fired.

His second shot found its mark.

Buckshot filled the turret like angry wasps, and the grenade launcher dropped out of sight.

There was a muted explosion. Kenny could hear screams from inside the armored tank. The door opened, smoke poured out, and three Zetas gunmen dismounted with their hands held high. The man who was going to fire from the turret was dead, and the driver fell out of the vehicle, dazed. He assumed the position where he landed.

———

Hector Lopez spit blood, wrapped Jack in a bear hug, and rolled him farther inside the burning double-wide. Grunting fiercely, he grabbed him by the throat and muscled him down with all of his might. Pieces of the insulation and tar roof were raining down like flaming pieces of napalm. The smoke was thick and noxious. But the men were oblivious.

Jack was not going to tempt death again. He let a roundhouse fly that found its mark on the side of Hector's head. The bear of a man flinched and Jack let loose with a blistering combination of punishing blows to Hector's head and face and neck that knocked him onto his back. Jack rolled to his knees and threw a punch from his core. He felt Hector's cheekbone shatter, and he hit him again and again. For Mia, for himself, for Hector's father, and for all of the people Hector would have killed in the future if he wasn't taken down at this very moment. Jack unleashed so much fury that his knuckles bled, sweat stung his eyes, and when he pulled himself back from his blinding rage, Hector was out cold.

Jack saw his stolen weapon on the floor of the flaming double-wide. He reached over and pulled his old Glock from underneath a smoldering ember.

He thought about leaving Hector behind. There would be a certain poetic justice. Instead, growling at his own conscience, he grabbed the killer by his hair and dragged him from the burning office structure, down the steps, to the hard-packed dirt. Hector's eyes blinked open and he was about to put up more of a fight when Jack yanked back his head and shoved his Glock into the killer's mouth.

Hector Lopez closed his eyes and tried to calculate a way out. Nothing.

Jack was breathing hard, and his finger was itching on the trigger.

Nick Aprea stepped up next to his friend and calmly said, "The building's gonna blow. Here." And threw down a pair of handcuffs.

Bertolino uncocked his weapon, but before he could slap on the cuffs, Hector's head exploded, sending clots of blood and gray matter spraying Jack's shirt.

Jack looked toward the rear entrance and saw the wide brim of a black hat, then a muzzle flash as a series of bullets struck wide of their intended mark.

Arturo Delgado.

Jack took off running at him. He power-loaded his backup weapon, ran a zigzag pattern, and returned fire as he forced Delgado into the building in search of cover. Then Jack sprinted up the ramp and disappeared into the inner recesses of Royce Motors.

Nick Aprea said a silent prayer for his friend as he dragged Hector's lifeless body clear. In another few seconds the double-wide and Hector's 1960 blue Impala sports sedan with the white roof and white side scoops were enveloped in flames and black acrid smoke.

Pools of lights alternated with areas of total darkness in the cavernous hangar that housed the rows of million-dollar buses. Jack heard movement deeper inside the warehouse and followed his ears, trusting his senses as he stalked Arturo Delgado.

Delgado was dressed in black and with his black hat all but disappeared in the dark shadows.

Bertolino moved closer as he dodged from the safety of one bus to the next. When he thought he was close, he stood stone still, trying to get a bead on his prey. He wanted to take Arturo alive but would be happy to put a bullet into his forehead.

———————

Delgado moved through the pitch black as he neared the center aisle and muted shadows that separated the two long rows of buses. He had already spent half of his AK rounds. Still, he had enough left to destroy his quarry. He decided he would start with Bertolino's knees and move north from there.

He felt Jack more than he saw him, but knew he was a heartbeat away. Jack took a step into a shallow pool of light to get his bearings. Delgado stilled his breath and slowly turned to fire.

From out of nowhere, a bloody hand snaked up and grabbed Arturo Delgado by the metal brace on his leg and started to drag him down. Delgado roared. He lowered his AK and fired wildly. One-handed, the weapon arced up, spraying bullets in a crazy pattern of death. Delgado kicked and struggled to stay on his feet, finally planting two hands on the weapon and firing a head shot that killed the Los Zetas commando who had been mauled by the English mastiffs and left for dead.

Silence.

Delgado fought to control his panicked breath and ascertain Jack's position. He hoped Bertolino couldn't hear the pounding of his heart.

Jack's fist exploded out of the darkness, knocking Arturo's head into the side of the bus. His hat went flying as he spun into the center of the aisle. He tried to fire again, but Jack punched him hard, snapping the cartilage in his nose, and blinding him for a second. The AK-47 went sliding across the concrete floor, under a bus, and out of Delgado's frantic reach.

The man who had faced the cartel's tribunal took off running into darkness while Jack pursued.

"Why'd you come back?" Jack shouted, hoping his words would slow the man down.

"I could ask the same question, but we both know the answer," Delgado said as he spit blood from his mouth. Bending down, he yanked a nine-millimeter pistol from one of the dead Angels' hands. He let four rounds fly toward Jack's voice.

––––––––

Jack could have shot him dead, but they'd been down too many roads for such an easy end. Delgado was going to pay.

"You can't get out," Jack said in calm, measured tones.

"How well do you know me?"

"I know things about you that would shame your mother."

"She'd tell me to pull out the white flag."

"Better than being carried out."

"Not if you've been where I have."

"You're breaking my heart, Delgado."

"I got close."

Jack started having second thoughts about not shooting Delgado in the head when he had the chance, as he moved silently toward the sound of Arturo's voice. He stopped, and then turned ninety degrees. He looked upward and noticed a catwalk running around the circumference of the great room.

The sound of metal tapping metal caught Jack's attention. Delgado was climbing the metal ladder to the catwalk, fifty feet above the showroom floor, used to service the air-conditioning units. A faint red light at the far end of the narrow walkway signified an emergency exit. The man's metal brace had given him away.

Jack ran toward the sound and started up the ladder, taking two rungs at a time.

Delgado sighted and shot the nine millimeter twice. Jack jerked his body out of the line of fire. One of his hands slipped and he swung sideways. He dangled thirty feet above the floor before he managed to regain his footing and continue his pursuit.

Delgado dry-fired twice and in frustration threw the empty pistol down at Jack, grazing his shoulder before it clattered to the floor below.

Jack kept climbing. He reached Delgado a few rungs before the top and grabbed for his leg. Delgado mule-kicked and connected with the side of Jack's head. The blow blinded him in a flash of pain, then fueled his rage. Nothing was going to stop him from taking down the man who'd tried to murder his son. Jack shook it off and grabbed again and again as Delgado tried to smash his hands. Fighting, kicking, and scrabbling.

Delgado was one step away from the floor of the catwalk and dove up onto the metal surface as Jack reached for the brace on his leg and missed. Delgado scrambled to his knees and then got to his feet as Jack pulled himself up.

Both men fought to fill their lungs with air, and they came to the same realization. The exit door was behind Jack, and Delgado would have to go through him to get there.

Delgado charged and swung a roundhouse fist that connected with the side of Jack's face. Jack parried and snapped Delgado's head back with a solid shot to the jaw. The desperate man would not go down.

Delgado charged again and bellowed like a wounded bull engaged in a primal fight for his life.

Jack leaned to the left, and using Delgado's momentum grabbed him by the wrist and pulled him forward.

Delgado stumbled past Jack. He tried to regain his footing. He overcompensated. Arturo Delgado's arms flailed as he slid over the side of the catwalk. His hands fought for a grip on the slick metal railing and held for an instant. His manic eyes found Jack's and pleaded for help. His hands slipped and his fingers betrayed him.

Time froze.

Delgado swan-dived backward, arms and legs spread wide. His body smashed onto the roof of a spotlit bus. The force shattered the side windows. The sound of his skull being impaled by the GPS antenna sticking out of the custom paint job made Jack's stomach roil. He stared over the side of the catwalk at the scene below.

Arturo Delgado, with his long silver hair, patrician face, black suit, and broken body looked like a demon making a snow angel on the crushed metal. A large pool of blood began to halo around his head. The impact engaged the bus's security system. The shrill pulsing alarm was a perfect match for the harsh tableau.

Overhead lights snapped on in the huge room and armed men deployed from both directions.

Jack remembered that he wasn't fond of dizzying heights as he held on tight and climbed cautiously down the metal ladder. Nick Aprea was standing at the bottom, ready to run interference with the other cops if needed.

"Where's Delgado?" he asked.

Jack pointed to the roof of the bus.

"Hitching a ride?" Nick asked.

"His last."

———

Outside, news choppers were circling the late-afternoon sky like buzzards, filming the aftermath with long-lens cameras. Emergency vehicles rolled up and exited the scene. Sirens wailed as the body count and cleanup began. Local media vans with their dishes pointed skyward were being kept at bay until the task force had completed processing the arrests. The local Ontario hospitals had been notified, and triage units were set up to handle the wounded. The order was to bandage them up and ship them to jail.

The drivers of the eighteen-wheelers had been handcuffed and taken into custody without incident. They pled ignorance.

ICE and the ATF had been called in to process the Zetas soldiers, the narco tanks, and the semi-rigs, all part of the Zetas cartel's criminal enterprise.

The police were doing a thorough search of the remaining buses, and rooms, and crawl spaces in and around Royce Motors to make sure no one had escaped law enforcement's net.

The fire department was on-site, throwing thick bands of water onto the flames shooting out of the double-wide. They wanted to make sure the fire didn't spread to the rusted piles of junked cars and buses and tires that littered the back lot. Hector's Impala had melted down to its frame.

Jack and Nick drove the Plymouth to the front of Royce Motors and caught up with Kenny Ortega. The men stood side by side and surveyed the carnage.

"He only had a month left," Kenny said with the distant eyes of a combat soldier as the silent EMT ambulance drove away with Gene McLennan's body.

"He went out in the saddle," Nick said. "*Semper fi.*"

Jack couldn't talk. He wiped some blood off his face from one of the grazing punches Delgado had landed, and surveyed the battlefield with the eye that hadn't swollen shut. He'd have to endure hours of debriefing and depositions before he made it home. He was in shock, but knew his back pain had a long memory and would return with a vengeance.

Still, right at this moment, he was satisfied. It was over.

48

Kenny Ortega immediately boarded a plane to Washington, D.C., to be debriefed by the head of the DEA. The chairman wanted a full report regarding the 18th Street Angels and the Zetas cartel's incursion onto American soil. Then he'd head off to a Senate subcommittee hearing, where he had been called upon to testify about the war on drugs.

Nick was going to take a few personal days. Spend some quality time with his young wife and little girl.

The loss of life in the line of duty had that effect on the men and women in law enforcement. It hit hard.

Jack Bertolino spent an hour on Skype with his son, who was healing nicely. He made plans to drive up over the weekend.

Then he started prepping a sauce and invited Leslie over for a meatball dinner. Somewhere between the cutting of the garlic, sweet onion, and fresh oregano, Jack found some peace.

He answered the knock on his door and stood aside as Leslie Sager walked in, looking terrific. She put down a bottle of wine on the center island and did a slow turn back.

"Why are you standing sideways?" she asked.

A reasonable question, he thought.

"I look like shit," Jack said as he exposed his swollen eye, which had turned the color of an eggplant. "Thought I'd be the one to deliver the news."

Leslie didn't blink, didn't laugh, but her eyes narrowed and crinkled at the corners, threatening to turn into a smile.

"Go ahead," Jack said, "say it."

Leslie pursed her lips, nodded her head a few times, and then, "Well, Mr. Bertolino, you most definitely look like shit today."

Then she turned to face the stove. "Smells great." She picked up a spoon and tasted the sauce. "Fantastic."

"Thank you." He spun her around and planted a kiss on her perfect lips.

"Were your ears ringing today?" she asked.

"They were, but it's still from the Impala blowing up."

"The governor talked to the mayor, who talked to the chief of police, who talked to the DA."

"Lotta talking."

"And this talk's not cheap. There might be a job offer in your future. Keep it on the Q.T., but it's something to think about. I didn't want you caught by surprise."

It was too late for that, Jack thought. "How and why?"

"As it turns out, Gene McLennan had given you full credit for the operation in all of his preliminary reports. Then Kenny Ortega corroborated, and Nick Aprea sang your praises to the LAPD brass. They've decided you're a wasted resource."

"What do you think?"

She kept a lawyer's neutral face. "It's your life. I'm good however you play it."

Leslie handed Jack the bottle of Benziger to open and continued. "Good work, Jack. They said to take a few days, a few weeks, whatever's comfortable, and then they'd like to have a sit-down."

Jack popped the cork, poured, and raised his glass. "To Gene McLennan." They clinked, shared a drink, and took a moment for a fallen comrade.

"What's the word on Angelina?"

"The DA said he'd deal."

"What's she offering?"

"She set up Johnny. He wanted to run, but she made sure he didn't get very far. She doesn't know where Hector buried him, but she's sure that he's dead."

"So?"

"She's offering Hector for the murder, the entire command structure of the Angels, their ties to the Mexican Mafia, and Felix's money-laundering operation."

Jack was impressed. "That's worth a trade. She'd be dead if she stayed in Ontario." He stirred the sauce and carefully moved the meatballs around in the pot. "They float," he said with a burst of youthful pride.

Leslie moved over and made the requisite oohs and aahs, but Jack didn't mind. It was one of his aunt's secret recipes and still impressed the hell out of him.

"What are the suits thinking about?" he asked, moving the conversation back in his direction.

"Maybe a paid consultancy. You get the power of the badge without having to wear a uniform."

"Hmmm."

"Sleep on it."

"I'd rather sleep with you."

"That's nonnegotiable. Let's eat."

Jack poured the rigatoni into the colander and the steam stung his bad eye. It was well worth the sacrifice, he thought.

It was high noon before Jack put in a call to Cruz Feinberg from his Mustang, but he wasn't surprised when he heard that the talented young man had come up empty. There were thousands of P.O. boxes in L.A., and Cruz had a full-time job.

Jack drove past Vista Haven and slowed to a stop. Mayor wasn't out front watering his ivy. Michael Kingman had returned from his vacation, but was presently at his real estate office, getting caught up on paperwork. He had nothing to add to the case, but he expressed his heartfelt regrets.

The house sat silent, empty and austere.

Jack thought about Mia and her last few hours on earth. He wished her peace, put the car in gear, and headed down to the valley.

He had forgotten to eat breakfast and decided to stop at a little place called the Pita Kitchen on Van Nuys Boulevard near Ventura. The place made falafels, gyros, souvlakis, and Greek salads. The neighborhood newsstand was situated next door.

Bertolino picked up a *New York Times* and dug into his gyros on pita, a classic New York City taste treat. Jack used to grab one, wrapped in foil, in the Village before heading down to the Staten Island ferry.

He always made a mental promise to wait and eat when he got home, but the smell prevailed. Jack was weak willed but happy. There were worse sins.

Jack wiped some tzaziki sauce off his fingers before he picked up the sports section and glanced across Van Nuys Boulevard.

Michael Kingman's face was plastered across a bus bench. The sign read: MICHAEL KINGMAN, PLATINUM SALES AND PLATINUM SERVICE. NUMBER ONE REAL ESTATE AGENT IN THE VALLEY.

Suddenly, Jack got a feeling that startled him. He belted down the rest of the sandwich, cleaned off his area, and jaywalked across Van Nuys Boulevard dodging traffic. He sat down on the bench and looked back at the row of small retail establishments across the street.

And there it was. In bold, painted letters.

DICKENS BOX.

The storefront could've been anything. But then in very small print it read, POSTAL SHIPPING CENTER. And then, almost as an after-thought, 24-HOUR MAILBOX RENTALS.

Dickens Box was located on the corner, next to Lou's Shoe Repair, and down from the Pita Kitchen and the Sherman Oaks Newsstand.

Jack thought about Mia's state of mind when she'd arrived in Los Angeles. About Mia's passports and the way she hid them close at hand for a quick escape. This was it. He felt it in his bones.

When he walked through the doors of Dickens Box he saw two walls of brass P.O. boxes. Two middle-aged Asians who had the comfortable feel of husband and wife were servicing the counter beyond. The woman looked up, smiled, and told Jack she'd be right with him.

Jack moved to the front, pulled out Mia's key, and without too much effort, located the corresponding box.

The gentleman was busy fingerprinting a young woman who needed a document notarized. His wife had her back turned and was filling a box with green plastic popcorn, readying it for shipping.

Jack inserted the key, opened the box, and pulled out two thick manila envelopes. He slid them under his arm, quickly closed up, and waved to the shop owners, who smiled and waved back as he left. Not entirely legal, Jack thought, but Mia would have approved.

If Jack had still been in the police department, he could have used their resources to track down the offshore accounts he'd discovered in Mia's paperwork.

Something to think about, he mused.

After some quick talking and tap-dancing on the phone, Jack learned from the owners of Dickens Box that Mia had opened the account for her P.O. box online, while in Canada, and mailed the contents of the two envelopes from there. The name confused them at first. The box wasn't registered in Mia's name, but to a Sylvia Kole, an attractive woman with "natural" red hair they had met when she came to pick up her key.

In one manila envelope were copies of Manuel Alvarez's financial history, from his original offshore corporation on the Caymans that Mia had split into three separate corporate entities when she took control of his books, to the merger she orchestrated, that allowed her to steal his fortune.

Also included in the file was a list of contact numbers in Colombia, which, if worked with a proper regression analysis, could lead the feds to the source of the drugs, do some serious damage to the cartel, and get an indictment handed down against the kingpin.

That's some damn fine work, Jack thought.

The second envelope held Mia's personal financial records, and the name of a law firm she held on retainer to dispose of her estate, should she ever come to harm. Mia had been reasonably afraid for her life. You don't try to take down a Colombian cartel on a whim.

This money appeared to be separate from the drug proceeds, wealth Mia had earned risking her life as a confidential informant for the DEA, the NYPD, and the federal government.

Jack copied Kenny Ortega, who had been stymied when he first approached the offshore banks about Mia's financial dealings. This new information should help him pry open a few doors, and maybe get Kenny a bump in pay.

49

One million seven hundred thousand.

The number made him feel uncomfortable, but that was the amount of money Mia had left to Jack Bertolino in the event of her death.

Kenny Ortega had followed the money trail, chased down the accounts, and then run the entire equation past the DEA and the United States District Attorney's Office.

Mia had cleaned Manuel Alvarez out of twenty-four million dollars. The total sum of that drug money—to the penny—she had bequeathed to the United States government.

So the feds, pleased with their unexpected windfall, had no issues with Jack Bertolino. He was no longer working for the state, so from their point of view regarding his inheritance, no harm, no foul.

Tommy Aronsohn had been brought in to handle the paperwork, and in rare bureaucratic form, Mia's will, and the disposition of her estate, had been signed off on and the money wired to Jack's personal account in a matter of days.

Jeannine got wind of Jack's good fortune and tried dipping her beak. But with the divorce finalized, her move was a nonstarter.

Jack wasn't at ease with the gift, but he could now well afford to splurge on a third tomato plant. He decided on purple heirlooms to go along with his beefsteaks and plums.

He scored the root ball with a kitchen knife, and then, as he leaned over the pot and lowered the plant into the hole he had prepared in the soil, a flash of light or a bright reflection caught his eye.

Jack kept working, backfilling the roots, tamping down the rich soil so that there were no air bubbles, but not tight enough to stop water from nourishing the plant.

And he saw it again, like the sun reflecting off a mirror. He felt that electric charge on the back of his neck.

Jack placed the plant next to the other tomatoes, picked up his watering can, and homed in on where the light was emanating from.

He started counting windows in the high-rise condo building with the light green glass exterior, never looking directly at the light source, and being careful not to overwater.

Eighteen floors up, the south-facing corner unit. He poured water around the edges of the pots, wiped his hands on his jeans, and walked back into the loft.

He speed-dialed Nick Aprea as he moved toward the elevator. Nick was in his car, heading downtown on the 10, but would be able to meet Jack in the condo's lobby in fifteen minutes.

Jack was in the lobby of the Azzura del Rey in less than four minutes.

Jack, Nick, and the building manager soon walked down a wide hallway filled with Jasper Johns original modern art, hung and lit like a museum exhibit.

A Mr. Jay Ricardo had leased out the unit two months ago. He signed a six-month lease-option agreement and paid in full. If all went well with a business deal he was involved in, his plan was to purchase the unit. His credentials were impeccable. The unit was a steal, down 30 percent from just two years earlier.

Through the window at the far end of the hallway Jack could see a breathtaking southern view of the marina, and down the Pacific coastline. Lumbering jets appeared from out of thick cumulus clouds and made their first banking turns over the ocean.

"Delgado always had good taste," Jack said to Nick.

"There must be a mistake then, because as I said, Jay Ricardo lives in this unit." The manager's patience was ebbing.

An iconic painting of an American flag by Jasper Johns was hung directly across from Delgado's unit.

"Thanks for the heads-up," Nick said, failing to keep the attitude out of his voice.

The manager looked like someone out of central casting. Impeccably coiffed and groomed, dressed in a fine Hugo Boss suit, he would have been right at home in a Fortune 500 boardroom.

Jack in his jeans and black T-shirt pulled out his Glock and chambered a round.

Nick in his unkempt sports jacket pulled out his Beretta from his shoulder rig as they neared the door.

"Don't you think that's a little much?" the manager asked nervously.

"We'll take it from here," Jack said as he snatched the key from the man's manicured fingers.

Nick ushered the manager back to the service elevator and hit Lobby. "Thank you. We'll return the keys before we leave," he said as the elevator doors whooshed closed.

Jack and Nick stood on either side of Delgado's door, and Jack knocked.

The only sound was the muted classical music piped into the hallway.

He knocked harder this time, waited a beat, and inserted the key.

Jack was the first man in, leading with his weapon. Nick fanned out as they entered and walked from room to room clearing the condo apartment, just in case Delgado had been working with a partner.

"All clear," Nick said from the bedroom.

"All clear," Jack said.

He walked through the kitchen and up to the telescope. He

peered into the eyepiece, turned the focus knob, and when his eyes adjusted was treated to a bird's-eye view of his own balcony, with his bench, his Weber grill, and his three tomato plants.

Because of the reflective surface on the windows, he couldn't see much inside his loft, but when he panned down he could see the front bumper of his sterling gray Mustang in the parking garage below.

Jack moved away and let Nick take a look at the invasion of his privacy. Nick peered through the lens of the telescope, and it pissed him off royally.

Jack thought about the progression of events and the time line of the past few weeks. It hurt however he replayed it in his mind.

"Mia flew into my play," Jack said quietly. "Alvarez, through Delgado, got lucky, almost a twofer. If Mia hadn't reached out to me, she'd still be alive."

Nick thought about that and then spoke with the certainty of friendship. "Don't beat yourself up," Nick said. "I know. Fuck me. Easier said than done, right, partner?"

The wisdom of the pure at heart, Jack thought.

"*El jefe.*"

"Mateo," Jack said, recognizing the caller's voice through the haze of sleep. "What's up, brother?"

"Sorry if my timing's off."

"I'm up."

It was actually four o'clock in the morning, and Leslie was asleep next to him in the bunk.

"You're a good man, and a bad liar, my friend. But I have some information that you might find interesting."

Jack let him talk.

"Manuel Alvarez ordered Mia's death, and his man on the outside was our old friend Arturo Delgado."

"And the reason you woke me?"

"The kill was sanctioned by the Colombians."

"And?"

"The Ordinola family runs the cartel."

Jack sat up in bed on that piece of information.

"Jose Ordinola?" he asked.

"At some point Mia discovered that the animal who had committed sacrilege on her body, who ordered the blessed life cut out of her womb, who tossed her like garbage on the side of the road—that Jose Ordinola—was supplying Manuel Alvarez's cocaine," Mateo said with tears in his voice.

"You're sure?"

Mateo knew this was the news Jack had been waiting for and was happy to deliver.

"She got him, Jack. She got him good. When Mia was sticking it to Manuel Alvarez, she was sucking Jose Ordinola dry. That is why she took the risk."

"Thank you, Mateo."

"Sleep well, *el jefe*."

And Mateo clicked off.

"Is everything okay?" Leslie murmured after Jack had set down the phone. She rolled up against him, and he could feel the warmth of her breasts through the T-shirt she had borrowed to sleep in.

"Everything's perfect."

She fell back asleep, buzzing lightly, or maybe it was more of a purr.

Jack listened to the waves lapping on the fiberglass hull of the used Cutwater 28 cabin cruiser he had recently purchased. The snapping of the lines on the aluminum masts of the harbored sailboats and yachts, and the slight roll of his able craft, helped him relax.

When he had written out the check to the previous owner, the man confided that selling the boat was the best day of his life. Jack was happy to oblige.

He thought about Mia, and Leslie, and Gene McLennan, and how they had come into his life, and how they were all interconnected in some way, and wondered what the hell it all meant.

Then his mind drifted to his son. Jack didn't know if he was dreaming or praying, but Chris was standing on the pitcher's mound at Sunken Diamond, playing to a sold-out Stanford crowd. Chris shook his head twice before settling on a pitch. He wound up and let the fastball fly, high on the inside. The batter swung from the heels and missed. On the sound of the hardball smacking the catcher's mitt, the umpire shouting ste-e-e-rike three and the roar of the crowd, Jack Bertolino fell into a deep and peaceful slumber.

Acknowledgments

First and foremost, I would like to thank Karen Hunter for her unyielding faith, judgment, and loyalty; John Paine for his editing magic; Brigitte Smith and the crew at Simon & Schuster for keeping the ball rolling; Victoria Mathews for her meticulous copyediting; and my attorney, Les Abell, with gratitude and deep appreciation for standing by me.

Thanks to Bruce Cervi, Gordon Dawson, Deb Schwab, Kathryn Solorzano, Annie George, Diane Lansing, Deborah Lansing, Molly Miles, and John Wright for reading rough first drafts and lending their time, friendship, and support.

Special thanks to Bob Marinaccio, an amazing friend, who read every rewrite, permutation, and new idea, with a critical yet positive eye. And especially to Vida Spears, for reading, listening, advising, and loving.

About the Author

John Lansing started his career as an actor in New York City. He spent a year at the Royale Theatre playing the lead in the Broadway production of *Grease*. He then landed a costarring role in George Lucas's *More American Graffiti*, and guest-starred on numerous television shows. During his fifteen-year writing career, Lansing wrote and produced *Walker Texas Ranger*, cowrote two CBS Movies of the Week, and he also co-executive produced the ABC series *Scoundrels*. John's first book was *Good Cop, Bad Money*, a true crime tome with former NYPD Inspector Glen Morisano. *The Devil's Necktie* is his first novel. A native of Long Island, John now resides in Los Angeles.

31901063044384

Printed in the United States
By Bookmasters